Enid Blyton's

SCHOOL STORIES

COMPILED BY
Mary Cadogan
&
Norman Wright

WITH A FOREWORD BY
Anne Fine
Children's Laureate

*Hodder
Children's
Books*

Enid Blyton's

SCHOOL STORIES

COMPILED BY
MARY CADOGAN
&
NORMAN WRIGHT

Hodder
Children's
Books

First published in Great Britain in 2002
by Hodder Children's Books

10 9 8 7 6 5 4 3 2 1

A Catalogue record for this book is available from the British Library

ISBN 0 340 84145 1

Printed and bound in China

Hodder Children's Books
a division of Hodder Headline Limited
338 Euston Road
London NW1 3BH

CONTENTS

Foreword

Introduction

FOREWORD

≈ BY ≈

ANNE FINE

Most of us adored Enid Blyton. Effortlessly, her books taught whole generations of us to read as easily as we breathe. From having Noddy read to us in bed, we moved on to reading for ourselves: Amelia Jane, the Sunshine Story Books, up the Magic Faraway Tree and away with the Famous Five and Secret Seven.

On to her school stories. What is it about boarding schools that so enchants even the child who walks fifty yards down the road for lessons, and is back home by tea-time? The closed world? The fact that, seen only in one context, each character – pupil or teacher or caretaker – can become a most satisfyingly vivid simplification?

There's more to Blyton's school stories than some people care to admit – just as her vocabulary is wider and, as with the nature of Whyteleafe School, for example, the educational issues she raises are those we still think about today. But that's not why we rushed through the library doors and over to the BL shelf, desperately hoping to find another book bearing that distinctive signature with the two little dashes.

No, what drew us was her sheer and unmatched readability. Sweeping us away from tiresome families and drab routines, she made so many of us readers for life. No wonder we're prepared to admit how much we loved the worlds she created for us. Worlds like these.

INTRODUCTION
ENID BLYTON'S SCHOOLDAYS

Enid Blyton was born in Lordship Lane, East Dulwich, London, on August 11th 1897. When she was only a few months old her family moved to Beckenham, Kent, an area where Enid and her brothers, Hanly and Carey, spent their childhood. Although Beckenham is now a very busy place, when Enid was a child it was still almost a country village and she and her father, Thomas, would often go for long nature walks across the fields, through the woods and along the winding lanes close to their home. Here he would teach her about all the plants, birds and animals that they saw. At the age of five Enid's father gave her a small garden area of her own, where she grew seeds bought with her pocket money. Enid read every book she could find on natural history. Years later Enid wrote that she found some of these books written for children very boring and determined that some day she would write her own nature study books for children which would be far more exciting!

Enid's first school was almost opposite her home and she loved every minute of her time there. Many years later, when she came to write her autobiography for children, she still remembered every detail of that first small school: "I remember everything about it – the room, the garden, the pictures on the wall, the little chairs, the dog there, and the lovely smells that used to creep out from the kitchen into our classroom . . . I remember how we used to take biscuits for our mid-morning lunch and 'swap' them with one another – and how we used to dislike one small boy who was clever at swapping a small biscuit for a big one . . ."

She enjoyed music, nature, games and listening to stories, but best of all she liked writing stories and poems. When she was very young she would make up stories to tell her brothers but as she got older she began to write them down in exercise books. The one thing Enid was not very good at was mathematics and she found even fairly simple sums difficult.

Another of Enid's great joys was reading. Her father encouraged this and she was soon busily dipping into the hundreds of books in his bookcase. Enid seems to have read everything she could find including the *Children's Encyclopaedia*, which she says she read and re-read! She loved *Alice in Wonderland*, *The Water-Babies*, *Black Beauty* and *Little Women*, but her favourite book was *The Princess and the Goblin* by George MacDonald, which she read a dozen times or more. It wasn't just the story she enjoyed, but the wonderful atmosphere the book had. She also read myths and legends and Hans Andersen's fairy stories, although she found the fairy stories by Grimm too frightening.

Her father not only helped her with her reading but also taught her to play draughts and chess, and encouraged her to learn to play the piano. He enjoyed music and played the piano and the banjo. His sister was a concert pianist and Thomas Blyton hoped that his daughter too had a gift for music.

Enid's mother, Theresa, was far more down to earth than her husband and believed that Enid should spend more of her time helping round the house and looking after her two brothers. This often led to rows between the headstrong Enid and her mother.

When she was ten years old Enid went to St Christopher's, a larger school in Beckenham, where she was to spend the rest of her schooldays, eventually at the early age of sixteen becoming its Head Girl and holding this position for two years. Enid loved St Christopher's and it is interesting that, although she did not use its name for any of the main schools in her stories, she sometimes mentioned it (for example, when the St Clare's girls play matches against St Christopher's teams). Although hockey and netball were the most popular winter games for girls during Enid's schooldays, at St Christopher's the regular game was lacrosse, and of course Enid often featured this in her stories of Whyteleafe, St Clare's and Malory Towers. She did well at sports, becoming tennis champion and captaining the lacrosse team.

St Christopher's lacrosse team.
Enid Blyton is standing second from the right, top row.

She also worked hard at her studies, partly perhaps to take her mind off a sad event that took place when she was a young teenager. Her parents were not getting on very well and often had fierce rows. When she was thirteen her much-loved father walked out of their home and left the family. Enid, with whom he had shared his love of nature, books and music, was devastated by his leaving and even though he kept in touch with her and still took her for walks and on theatre visits, she never really recovered from this family break-up. Because of his insistence that she should work hard at her music she continued her piano practice for an hour every day for several years after he had left home, even though she eventually decided against the musical career which he had planned for her.

Enid threw herself into games, lessons and other activities at St Christopher's with an enthusiasm similar to that shown by the heroines of her stories, and she was popular with both staff and pupils. It seems that she based some of her fictional characters and happenings on actual girls, teachers and events that took place there.

During her schooldays she kept a detailed diary which, sadly, she destroyed after her mother discovered and read it. Although we shall never know what thoughts and feelings Enid recorded when she was a schoolgirl, we can find clues about her real-life dreams, aspirations and friendships in the stories which she was to write later on.

St Christopher's school photo.
Enid Blyton is sitting third from the right, third row down.

One aspect of her time at St Christopher's which is certainly reflected in the books is her flair for practical jokes: apparently she devised and played many lively tricks on her teachers and class-mates, using rubber- and tin-pointed pencils, artificial blots and so on, which she bought from local shops. Other activities were the production of a small magazine by herself and her two close friends who also created their own secret code and, during holiday times, communicated with each other by coded postcards.

Throughout her schooldays, Enid continued to write stories and poems and, in her mid-teens, she had the satisfaction of winning a national poetry competition and having some verses professionally published.

A high spot of her years at St Christopher's was a visit to Annecy in France as the guest of Mademoiselle Louise Bertraine, the school's French teacher. Enid was then sixteen and, in this first trip abroad, she revelled in the excitements of the journey, and the colour and light of the lakes and mountains that she saw in France. Her friendship with Mademoiselle Louise Bertraine continued for several years, and it seems that this mistress was the direct inspiration for the teacher whom the St Clare's girls both respected and loved, and nicknamed "Mam'zelle Abominable".

After doing some Sunday School teaching when she was nineteen, Enid realised that she wanted to make teaching and writing for children her career. Her father still had ambitions for her to study music, but she persuaded him instead to help her to train as a teacher. Her own schooldays were over, but through her wonderfully vivid school stories she was later able to share the essence of them with her many readers from all over the world.

In preparing this Treasury of Enid's school stories, we have, of course, chosen lots of adventures set in her most famous boarding schools. However, Enid also wrote day school stories for younger children, and a few about schools that catered exclusively for boys. We have included some of these, as well as stories about co-educational and girls' schools which are not so well known as Whyteleafe, St Clare's and Malory Towers.

We hope you will enjoy reading them all, and also looking at how so many different artists have depicted Enid's school heroes and heroines.

Mary Cadogan and Norman Wright

THE NAUGHTIEST GIRL IN THE SCHOOL

AN EXTRACT

≈ ILLUSTRATED BY ≈

Max Schindler and W. Lindsay Cable

*Elizabeth Allen is a spoilt child who has only ever been taught by a governess
and has never been to school. When she learns that her parents are sending her to
Whyteleafe, a boarding school out in the country, she decides to be so naughty that
she will be sent home by half-term. She makes a start by being rude to almost everyone
when she joins the group of children and teachers travelling to the school by train.
When they arrive at Whyteleafe she continues to be The Naughtiest Girl.*

CHAPTER III
ELIZABETH MAKES A BAD BEGINNING

It was half-past one by the time the children arrived, and they were all hungry for
their dinner. They were told to wash their hands quickly, and tidy themselves and
then go to the dining-hall for their dinner.

"Eileen, please look after the three new girls," said Miss Thomas. A big girl, with
a kindly face and a mass of fair curls, came up to Belinda, Elizabeth, and another
girl called Helen. She gave them a push in the direction of the cloakrooms.

"Hurry!" she said. So they hurried, and Elizabeth soon found herself in a big
cloakroom, tiled in gleaming white, with basins down one side, and mirrors here
and there.

She washed quickly, feeling rather lost in such a crowd of chattering girls. Helen
and Belinda had made friends, and Elizabeth wished they would say something to
her instead of chattering to one another. But they said nothing to Elizabeth,
thinking her rude and odd.

Then to the dining-hall went all the girls and took their places. The boys clattered
in too.

"Sit anywhere you like today," said a tall mistress, whose name, Elizabeth found, was Miss Belle. So the children sat down and began to eat their dinner hungrily. There was hot soup first, then beef, carrots, dumplings, onions and potatoes, and then rice pudding and golden syrup. Elizabeth was so hungry that she ate everything put before her, though at home she would certainly have pushed away the rice pudding.

As it was the first day the children were allowed to talk as they pleased, and there was such a noise as they told one another what they had done in the holidays.

"I had a puppy for Easter," said one girl with a laughing face. "Do you know, my father bought a simply enormous Easter egg, and put the puppy inside, and tied up the egg with a red ribbon? Goodness, didn't I laugh when I undid it!"

Everybody else laughed too.

"I had a new bicycle for my Easter present," said a round-faced boy. "But it wasn't put into an egg!"

"What did you have for Easter?" said Eileen to Elizabeth in a kindly tone. She was sitting opposite, and felt sorry for the silent new girl. Belinda and Helen were sitting together, telling each other about the last school they had been to. Only Elizabeth had no one to talk to her.

"I had a guinea-pig," said Elizabeth, in a clear voice, "and it had a face just like Miss Thomas."

There was a shocked silence. Somebody giggled. Miss Thomas looked rather surprised, but she said nothing.

"If you weren't a new girl, you'd be jolly well sat on for that!" said a girl nearby, glaring at Elizabeth. "Rude creature!"

Elizabeth couldn't help going red. She had made up her mind to be naughty and rude, and she was going to be really bad, but it was rather dreadful to have somebody speaking like that to her, in front of everyone. She went on with her rice pudding. Soon the children began to talk to one another again, and Elizabeth was forgotten.

After dinner the boys went to unpack their things in their own bedrooms, and the girls went to theirs.

"Whose room are the new girls in, please, Miss Thomas?" asked Eileen. Miss Thomas looked at her list.

"Let me see," she said, "yes – here we are – Elizabeth Allen, Belinda Green, Helen Marsden – they are all in Room Six, Eileen, and with them are Ruth James, Joan Townsend and Nora O'Sullivan. Ask Nora to take the new girls there and show them what to do. She's head of that room."

"Nora! Hi, Nora!" called Eileen, as a tall, dark-haired girl with deep blue eyes went by. "Take these kids to Room Six, will you? They're yours! You're head of that room."

"I know," said Nora, looking at the three new girls. "Hallo, is this the girl who was rude to Miss Thomas? You just mind what you say, whatever-your-name-is, I'm not having any cheek from *you!*"

"I shall say exactly what I like," said Elizabeth boldly. "*You* can't stop me!"

"Oho, can't I?" said Nora, her blue Irish eyes glaring at Elizabeth. "That's all *you* know! Get along to the bedroom now, and I'll show you all what to do."

They all went up a winding oak staircase and came to a wide landing. All around it were doors, marked with numbers. Nora opened the door of Number Six and went in.

The bedroom was long, high and airy. There were wide windows, all open to the school gardens outside. The sun poured in and made the room look very pleasant indeed.

The room was divided into six by blue curtains, which were now drawn back to the walls, so that six low white beds could be seen, each with a blue eiderdown. Beside each bed stood a wide chest-of-drawers, with a small mirror on top. The chests were painted white with blue wooden handles, and looked very pretty.

There were three wash-basins in the room, with hot and cold water taps, to be shared by the six girls. There was also a tall white cupboard for each girl, and in these they hung their coats and dresses.

Each bed had a blue rug beside it on the polished brown boards. Elizabeth couldn't help thinking that it all looked rather exciting. She had only shared with Miss Scott before – now she was to share with five other girls!

"Your trunks and tuck-boxes are beside your beds," said Nora. "You must each unpack now, and put your things away tidily. And when I say tidily I *mean* tidily. I shall look at your drawers once a week. On the top of the chest you are allowed to have six things, not more. Choose what you like – hairbrushes, or photographs, or ornaments – it doesn't matter."

"How silly!" thought Elizabeth scornfully, thinking of her own untidy dressing-table at home. "I shall put as many things out as I like!"

They all began unpacking. Elizabeth had never packed or unpacked anything in

her life, and she found it
rather exciting. She put her
things neatly away in her
chest-of-drawers – the piles
of stockings, vests, blouses,
everything she had brought
with her. She hung up her
school coat and her dresses.

The others were busy
unpacking too. Whilst they
were doing this two more
girls danced into the room.

"Hallo, Nora!" said one, a
red-haired girl with freckles
all over her face. "I'm in your
room this term. Good!"

"Hallo, Joan," said Nora.
"Get on with your unpacking,
there's a lamb. Hallo, Ruth –
I've got you here again, have
I? Well, just see you're a bit
tidier than last term!"

Ruth laughed. She was the
girl who had handed round
her sweets in the train, and
she was plump and clever.
She ran to her trunk and
began to undo it.

Nora began to tell the new girls a little about the school. They listened as they
busily put away their things in their drawers.

"Whyteleafe School isn't a very large school," began Nora, "but it's a jolly fine one.
The boys have their lessons with us, and we play tennis and cricket with them and we
have our own teams of girls only, too.
Last year we beat the boys at tennis. We'll beat them this year, too, if only we can get
some good players. Any of you new girls play tennis?"

Belinda did but the others didn't. Nora went on talking, as she hung up her dresses.

"We all have the same amount of pocket-money to spend," she said. "And it's plenty
too. Two pounds a week."

"I shall have a lot more than that," said Belinda in surprise.

"Oh no, you won't," said Nora. "All the money we have is put into a big box, and we each draw two pounds a week from it, unless we've been fined for something."

"What do you mean – fined?" asked Helen. "Who fines us? Miss Belle and Miss Best?"

"Oh no," said Nora. "We hold a big meeting once a week – oftener, if necessary – and we hear complaints and grumbles, and if anyone has been behaving badly we fine them. Miss Belle or Miss Best come to the meeting too, of course, but they don't decide anything much. They trust us to decide for ourselves."

Elizabeth thought this was very strange. She had always thought that the teachers punished the children – but at Whyteleafe it seemed as if the children did it! She listened in astonishment to all that Nora was saying.

"If there's any money over, it is given to anyone who particularly wants to buy something that the meeting approves of," went on Nora. "For instance, suppose you broke your tennis racket, Belinda, and needed a new one, the meeting might allow you to take the money from the box to buy one – especially if they thought you were a very good player."

"I see," said Belinda. "It sounds a good idea. Look, Nora – here are the things out of my tuck-box. What do I do with them? I want to share them with everybody."

"Thanks," said Nora. "Well, we keep all our cakes and sweets and things in the playroom downstairs. There's a big cupboard there, and tins to put cakes into. I'll show you where. Elizabeth, are your tuck-box things ready? If so, bring them along, and we'll put them into the cupboard to share at tea-time."

"I'm not going to share," said Elizabeth, remembering that she hadn't been naughty or horrid for some time. "I shall eat them all myself."

There was a horrified silence. The five girls stared at Elizabeth as if they couldn't believe their ears. Not share her cakes and sweets? Whatever sort of a girl was this?

"Well," said Nora, at last, her merry face suddenly very disgusted. "You can do what you like, of course, with your own things. If they're as horrid as you seem to be, nobody would want to eat them!"

CHAPTER V
ELIZABETH IS NAUGHTY

Later that day, Elizabeth goes to meet the headmistresses, who are not at all as she imagined.

Elizabeth pushed open the door and went into the big drawing-room. It was a lovely room, with a few beautiful pictures on the walls, and glowing cushions on the chairs and the couches. The two mistresses were sitting on chairs near the window. They looked up as Elizabeth came in.

"Well, Elizabeth! We are very glad to see you at Whyteleafe School," said Miss Belle. She was young and pretty, but Miss Best was older, and, except when she smiled, she had rather a stern face.

"Sit down, Elizabeth," said Miss Best, smiling her lovely smile. "I hope you have made a few friends already."

"No, I haven't," said Elizabeth. She sat down on a chair. Miss Best looked at her in surprise, when she answered so shortly.

"Well, I expect you will soon make plenty," said the headmistress. "I hope you

will be very happy with us, Elizabeth."

"I shan't be," said Elizabeth in a rude voice.

"What a funny little girl!" said Miss Belle, and she laughed. "Cheer up, dear – you'll soon find things are very jolly here, and I am sure you will do your best to work hard, and make us proud of you."

"I'm not going to," said Elizabeth, going red. "I'm going to be as bad and naughty and horrid as I can possibly be, so there! I don't want to go to school. I hate Whyteleafe School! I'll be so bad that you'll send me home next week!"

The little girl glared at the two mistresses as she said all this, expecting them to jump up in anger. Instead they both threw back their heads and laughed and laughed!

"Oh, Elizabeth, what an extraordinary child you are!" said Miss Belle, wiping away the tears of laughter that had come into her eyes. "You look such a good, pretty little girl too – no one would think you wanted to be so bad and naughty and horrid!"

"I don't care how you punish me," said Elizabeth, tears coming into her own eyes – but tears of anger, not of laughter. "You can do all you like – I just shan't care!"

"We never punish anyone, Elizabeth," said Miss Best, suddenly looking stern again. "Didn't you know that?"

"No, I didn't," said Elizabeth in astonishment. "What do you do when people are naughty, then?"

"Oh, we leave any naughty person to the rest of the children to deal with," said Miss Best. "Every week the school holds a meeting, you know, and the children themselves decide what is to be done with boys and girls who don't behave themselves. It won't bother *us* if you are naughty – but you may perhaps find that you make the children angry."

"That seems funny to me," said Elizabeth. "I thought it was always the teachers that did the punishing."

"Not at Whyteleafe School," said Miss Belle. "Well, Elizabeth, my dear, perhaps you'd go now and tell the next child to come in, will you? Maybe one day Whyteleafe School will be proud of you, even though you are quite sure it won't!"

Elizabeth went out without another word. She couldn't help liking the two headmistresses, though she didn't want to at all. She wished she had been ruder to them. What a funny school this was!

She spoke to Helen outside the door. "You're to go in now," she said. "The Beauty and the Beast are waiting for you!"

"Oh, you naughty girl!" said Helen, with a giggle. "Miss Belle and Miss Best — the Beauty and the Beast! That's rather clever of you to think of that, Elizabeth!"

Elizabeth had meant it to be very rude. She did not know enough of other children to know that they always loved nicknames for their masters and mistresses. She was surprised that Helen thought her clever — and secretly she was pleased.

But she stuck her nose in the air and marched off. She wasn't going to be pleased with anything or anybody at Whyteleafe School!

She wandered round by herself until the supper-bell went at seven o'clock. She felt hungry and went into the dining-hall. The children were once more opening their tins of cakes, and a lively chatter was going on. It all looked very jolly.

There were big mugs on the table and big jugs of steaming hot cocoa here and there. There were piles of bread again, butter, cheese, and dishes of stewed fruit. The children sat down and helped themselves.

Nobody took any notice of Elizabeth at all, till suddenly Helen remembered what she had called Miss Belle and Miss Best. With a giggle she repeated it to her neighbour, and soon there was laughter all round the table.

"The Beauty and the Beast," went the whisper, and chuckles echoed round. Elizabeth heard the whispers and went red. Nora O'Sullivan laughed loudly.

"It's a jolly good nickname!" she said. "Belle means Beauty, and Best is very like Beast — and certainly Miss Belle is lovely, and Miss Best isn't! That was pretty smart of you, Elizabeth."

Elizabeth smiled! She really couldn't help it. She didn't want to — she wanted to be as horrid as possible — but it was really very pleasant to have everyone laughing at her joke.

"It's strange, though," she thought. "I meant to be horrid and rude, and the others just think it's funny. I guess Miss Belle and Miss Best wouldn't think it was funny, though!"

Nobody offered Elizabeth any of their goodies, and she did not like to offer hers, for she felt sure everyone would say no. The meal went on until half-past seven, and then after grace was said the children all got up and went to the playroom.

"When's your bedtime?" said Nora to Elizabeth. "I expect it's eight o'clock. You'd better see. The times are on the notice-board over there. My bedtime is at half-past eight, and when I come to bed I expect all the rest of you to be safe in bed."

"I don't want to go to bed at eight o'clock," said Elizabeth indignantly. "I go to bed much later than that at home."

"Well, you shouldn't, then," said Nora. "No wonder you're such a crosspatch! My mother says that late hours make children stupid, bad-tempered, and slow."

Elizabeth went to see the times for going to bed. Hers was, as Nora had said, at eight o'clock. Well, she wouldn't go! She'd be naughty!

So she slipped out into the garden and went to where she had seen two or three big swings. She got on to a swing and began to push herself to and fro. It was lovely there in the evening sunshine. Elizabeth quite forgot that she was at school, and she sang a little song to herself.

A boy came into the place where the swings were, and stared at Elizabeth. "What are you doing here?" he said. "I bet it's your bedtime!"

"Mind your own business!" said Elizabeth at once.

"Well, what about you going off to bed, and minding *yours!*" said the boy. "I'm a monitor, and it's my job to see that people do what they're told!"

"I don't know what a monitor is, and I don't care," said Elizabeth rudely.

"Well, let *me* tell you what a monitor is," said the boy, who was just about Elizabeth's size. "It's somebody put in charge of other silly kids at Whyteleafe, to see they don't get *too* silly! If you don't behave yourself I shall have to report you at the Meeting! Then you'll be punished."

"Pooh!" said Elizabeth, and she swung herself very hard indeed, put out her foot and kicked the boy so vigorously that he fell right over. Elizabeth squealed with laughter – but not for long! The boy jumped up, ran to the swing and shook Elizabeth off. He caught hold of her dark curls and pulled them so hard that the little girl yelled with pain.

The boy grinned at her and said, "Serve you right! You be careful how you treat me next time, or I'll pull your nose as well as your hair! Now – are you going in or not?"

Elizabeth ran away from him and went indoors. She looked at the clock – quarter-past eight! Perhaps she would have time to go to bed before that horrid Nora came up at half-past.

So she ran up the stairs and went to Bedroom Number Six. Ruth, Joan, Belinda, and Helen were already there half undressed. Their curtains were pulled around their cubicles, but they were talking hard all the same. Elizabeth slipped into her own cubicle.

"You're late, Elizabeth," said Ruth. "You'll get into trouble if you're caught by a monitor."

"I have been," said Elizabeth. "But *I* didn't care! I was on the swing and I put out my foot and kicked him over!"

"Well, you're very silly," said Ruth. "You will get into trouble at the Meeting if you don't look out. And that's not pleasant."

"I don't care for any silly Meeting," said Elizabeth, jumping into bed. She remembered that Nora had put her three photographs into the locked box, and she jumped out again. She went to the box and tried to open it – but it was still locked. Nora came in at that moment and saw Elizabeth there.

"Hallo, kid," she said. "Do you want your things back? Well, apologise and you can have them."

But Elizabeth was not going to say she was sorry. She made a rude face at Nora, and flung herself into bed.

"Well, you *are* a sweet child, aren't you!" said Nora mockingly. "I hope you get out of the right side of your bed tomorrow!"

Then there was a creak as Nora sat on her bed to take off her stockings. A clock struck half-past eight downstairs. "No more talking now," said Nora. "Sleep tight, all of you!"

THE NAUGHTIEST GIRL AGAIN

AN EXTRACT

≈ ILLUSTRATED BY ≈

Max Schindler and W. Lindsay Cable

Elizabeth Allen has settled down at Whyteleafe School and is no longer the Naughtiest Girl there. In the new term she has many adventures, but one of the most exciting events is an important lacrosse match against Uphill School. Elizabeth has been chosen for the team, but gives up her place to Robert — who has been prevented from playing in a previous match after she wrongly accused him of playing mean tricks on her.

CHAPTER XX
THE GREAT LACROSSE MATCH

Saturday came, marvellously bright and sunny. There was a frost in the morning, and the grass glittered white. But it disappeared in the sun, and everyone agreed that it was a perfect day for the match. Elizabeth tried her very hardest to be glad that it was such a fine day. It was lucky for Robert; but she couldn't help feeling disappointed that she wasn't playing. She had missed playing the Saturday before because it rained and now that it was so fine, she couldn't play!

"Well," she said to herself, "it's your own fault, Elizabeth Allen; you shouldn't have been so foolish – then you would have been playing today!"

She went up to Robert when she saw him. "I'm glad it's fine for you, Robert," she said. Robert looked at her and knew what she was feeling.

"I wish you were playing too," he said. "Never mind – it will be your turn next time!"

The day kept fine. All the team who were going to play were in a great state of excitement. Nora was playing, and she told the others that Uphill School had never been beaten by Whyteleafe yet.

"If only we could beat them just this once!" she said. "But I hear they've got an awfully good team. Eileen says they haven't lost a match yet this term. They really are frightfully good. All I hope is they let us get *one* goal!"

"Oh, Nora! We must get more than that!" cried Peter, a strong, wiry boy who was in the team. He was a marvellous runner and catcher. "For goodness' sake let's put up a good show!"

"We'll do our best," said Robert.

The morning went slowly by. Dinner-time came and the team could not eat very much, for they were all so excited. Elizabeth knew how she had felt the Saturday before. Oh, how she *did* wish she was going too! It was so terribly disappointing – but she was glad that she had been big enough to give up her place to Robert.

The sun shone in through the window. It was going to be a wonderful afternoon for a match. Elizabeth swallowed a lump in her throat. It was all very well to be big and brave and give up something because you thought it was right – but it didn't make the disappointment any less. Joan saw her face and squeezed her hand.

"Cheer up!" she said. So Elizabeth tried to cheer up and smile. And then she noticed something going on at the next table. People were getting up and talking – what was happening?

"It's Peter! He doesn't feel well," said Joan. "Isn't he white? I believe he's going to be sick. I didn't think he looked very well at breakfast this morning."

Peter went out of the room, with Harry helping him. He did look very green. Mr Johns went out too. Mr Warlow looked at his watch. He hoped Peter would soon recover – because the coach was coming to fetch the team in twenty minutes.

Mr Johns came back in five minutes' time. He spoke to Mr Warlow, who looked disappointed. "What's happened to Peter?" asked John, who was at the same table. "Is he better?"

"He's got one of his tummy upsets," said Mr Johns. "Very bad luck. Matron is putting him to bed in the Sanatorium."

"Golly!" said John. "Won't he be able to play in the match then?"

"No," said Mr Warlow. "It's bad luck for our team. Peter was one of the best. We must choose someone else."

The news spread round the tables, and everyone was sorry about Peter. He really was such a good player. And then one by one the children called out something:

"Let Elizabeth play!"

"What about Elizabeth?"

"Can't Elizabeth play? She gave up her place to Robert!"

"Well," said Mr Warlow, looking at his notebook, "I had planned to get

someone else next time — but as Elizabeth really deserves a trial, she shall play!"

Elizabeth's heart jumped for joy. She could hardly believe the good news. Her face went bright red and her eyes danced. She was sorry for Peter — but after all Peter had played in dozens of matches, and would again. Oh, she was really, really going to play after all!

"Good for you, Elizabeth!" called her friends, all pleased to see her shining face. The whole School knew, of course, that Elizabeth had given up her place in the match to Robert, and now they were really glad that she had her reward so unexpectedly.

Elizabeth sat happily in her place. Joan clapped her on the back, and Jenny grinned at her. "Things always happen to you, don't they, Elizabeth?" said Jenny. "Well, you deserve this piece of luck!"

"Elizabeth! I'm so glad!" called Robert from the end of the table. "We shall be playing in our first match together! That'll be fun!"

Elizabeth couldn't eat anything more. She pushed her pudding-plate away. "I shall feel sick, like Peter, if I eat any more," she said.

"Well, for goodness' sake, don't then!" cried Nora. "We can't have another player going sick at the very last moment!"

Elizabeth rushed off to change with the others into her gym things. She found time to peep into the San with a book for Peter. "I'm sorry, Peter, old thing," she said. "I hope you'll soon be all right. I'll come and tell you about the match when it's over."

"Play up!" said Peter, who still looked rather green. "Shoot a few goals! Goodbye and good luck!"

Elizabeth shot off, her heart singing. It was too marvellous for words. Everyone laughed at her face and everyone was glad for her. She found Robert and took his arm.

"Sit next to me in the coach," she said. "We are the only ones who have never played in a match before — and oh, Robert, though I'm awfully happy, I feel a bit nervous!"

"*You* nervous!" said Robert, with a laugh. "I can't believe it. A fierce person like you can't be nervous!"

But Elizabeth was! She was very anxious to do her best in the match, to do her best for Whyteleafe School. Suppose she played badly! Suppose she didn't catch the ball but kept dropping it! It would be dreadful.

"Still, there won't be anyone from Whyteleafe watching to see if I play badly," she comforted herself. She looked at Robert as he sat beside her in the coach, looking burly and stolid and not a bit nervous. It was nice to be playing with him after all.

"I simply can't imagine how I hated him so much," thought Elizabeth. "It seems to me that if we dislike people, we see all the worst side of them because we make them show that to us — but if we like them, then they smile at us and show their best side. I really must try to give people a chance and begin by liking them, so that they show their best side at once."

The coach soon arrived at Uphill School, which, as its name showed, was at the top of a steep hill. It was a much bigger school than Whyteleafe, and had the choice of far more children for its lacrosse team than Whyteleafe had. The Whyteleafe children looked at the opposing team and thought that they seemed very big and strong.

The teams lined up in their places. The whistle blew, and the game began. The Uphill team were certainly strong, but there were some fine runners in the Whyteleafe team. They missed Peter, who was the finest runner of all – but both Robert and Elizabeth seemed to have wings on their feet that afternoon. They had never run so fast in their lives before!

Both children felt honoured to play in the match, and were determined to do their very best. Elizabeth's nervousness went as soon as the game began. She forgot all about herself and thought only of the match.

She and Robert often threw the ball to one another. Both children had practised their catching every day for some weeks, and were very good at it. Neither of them dropped the ball, but passed it beautifully.

"Good, Robert! Good, Elizabeth!" cried Mr Warlow, who was with the team. "Keep it up! Shoot, Elizabeth!"

Elizabeth saw the goal not far off. She shot the ball at it with all her might. It flew straight at the goal – but the goalkeeper was on guard and shot the ball out again at once.

"Well tried, Elizabeth!" cried Mr Warlow.

Then the Uphill team got the ball and sped off towards the other goal, passing gracefully to one another – and then the captain shot hard. The ball rolled right into the goal, though Eileen, who was goalkeeper, did her best to stop it.

"One goal to Uphill!" said the umpire, and the whistle blew. The game began again, and both Robert and Elizabeth were determined not to let the Uphill team get the ball if they could help it.

Elizabeth got the ball in her lacrosse net and sped away with it. She was about to pass it to Robert, who was keeping near her, when another player ran straight at her. Elizabeth tripped over and fell. She was up again in a trice – but the ball had been taken by the Uphill girl. Down to the goal sped the girl, and passed the ball to someone else.

"Shoot!" yelled all the watching Uphill girls, and the ball was shot towards the goal. It rolled inside before Eileen could throw it out.

"Two goals to Uphill!" called the umpire. He blew the whistle for half-time, and the girls and boys greedily sucked the half-lemons that were brought out to them. Oh, how lovely and sour they tasted!

"Now play up, Whyteleafe," said Mr Warlow, coming out on to the field to talk to his team. "Robert, keep near Elizabeth – and, Elizabeth, pass more quickly to Robert when you are attacked. You two are running like the wind today. Shoot at goal whenever there's a chance. Nora, feed Elizabeth with the ball when you can – she may perhaps be quick enough to outpace the Uphill girl marking her."

The children listened eagerly. The Whyteleafe team were feeling a little down-hearted. Two goals to none!

The whistle blew. The match began again. Nora got the ball and passed it at once to Elizabeth, remembering what Mr Warlow had said. Robert kept near to her and caught it when she passed it to him. He passed it back again, and the girl sped towards the goal.

She flung the ball with all her might. The goalkeeper put out her lacrosse net quickly – but the ball bounced off it and rolled into the goal.

"One goal to Whyteleafe!" said the umpire. "Two to one."

Elizabeth was thrilled. She couldn't keep still but danced up and down even when the ball was nowhere near her. Nora got the ball. She passed to Robert, Robert passed back, and Nora ran for goal. She shot – and once more the ball rolled right in! It was too good to be true!

"Two goals to Whyteleafe!" said the umpire. "Two all, and ten minutes to play!"

The Uphill children, who were all watching the match eagerly, began to shout: "Play up, Uphill! Shoot, Uphill! Go on, Uphill!"

And the Uphill team heard and played harder than ever. They got the ball – they raced for goal. They shot – and Eileen caught the ball neatly and threw it out again! Thank goodness for that!

Two goals all, and three minutes to play. Play up, Uphill! Play up, Whyteleafe! Three minutes left – only three minutes!

CHAPTER XXI
THE END OF THE MATCH

"Three minutes, Robert!" panted Elizabeth. "For goodness' sake, let's play up. Oh, how I hope that Uphill School don't shoot another goal!"

The ball flew from one player to another. Elizabeth ran to tackle one of the Uphill girls, who was a very fast runner. She hit the girl's lacrosse stick and made the ball leap up into the air. Elizabeth tried to catch it but the ball fell to the ground. She picked it up in her lacrosse net, and tore off with it.

But another girl tackled her, and although Elizabeth tried to dodge, it was no use at all. She fell over and the ball flew into the air. The Uphill girl caught it neatly and raced off with it. She passed it to another Uphill girl who threw it vigorously down the field to the girl by the goal.

The girl caught it, and shot straight for goal. It looked as if the ball was flying straight for the goal-net – but Eileen saved it by flinging herself right out of goal! She fell over as she caught the ball, but somehow she managed to fling it to a waiting Whyteleafe boy. He caught it and was off up the field like the wind.

"Pass the ball, pass it!" yelled Elizabeth, dancing about. "Look out! There's a girl behind you! PASS!"

The boy passed the ball just as the Uphill girl behind him tried to strike at his stick to get the ball. It flew straight through the air to Elizabeth. She caught it, and sped off, followed by a swift-running Uphill girl.

Elizabeth passed to Robert who was nearby. An Uphill girl ran at him – and he passed the ball back to Elizabeth, who ran for goal. Should she shoot from where she was? She might get a goal – and she would win the match for Whyteleafe!

But Robert had run down the field and was nearer the goal now – she ought really to pass to him! Without another moment's delay Elizabeth threw the ball straight to Robert.

He caught it – and flung it at the goal. It was a beautiful shot. The girl in goal tried her best to save the goal, but the ball flew past her stick and landed right in the corner of the net. Goal to Whyteleafe!

And almost at once the whistle blew for Time! The match was over!

"Three goals to Whyteleafe!" shouted the umpire. "Three goals to two! Whyteleafe wins! Well played!"

Then all the watching Uphill girls cheered too, and clapped their hardest. It had been an excellent match and everyone had played well.

"Another second and the whistle would have blown for Time!" panted Elizabeth. "Oh, Robert! You were marvellous to shoot the winning goal just in time!"

"Well, I couldn't have if you hadn't passed me the ball exactly when you did," said Robert, his breath coming fast as he leaned on his lacrosse stick, his face flushed and wet. "Well, Elizabeth – we've won! Think of that! We've never beaten Uphill before! Oh, I'm glad you shot a goal too!"

The two teams trooped off the field and went in to wash. It was nice to feel cold water, for they were all so hot! The two captains shook hands, and the Uphill girl clapped Eileen on the back.

"A jolly good match!" she said. "It's the first we've lost this term. Good for you!"

Elizabeth hadn't been able to eat much dinner, but she made up for it at tea-time. There was brown bread-and-butter and blackberry jam, currant buns and an enormous chocolate cake. The children ate hungrily, and the big plates of bread-and-butter and buns were soon emptied.

"I'm longing to get back to Whyteleafe to tell the good news," said Robert to Elizabeth. "Aren't you? Oh, Elizabeth, I *am* glad you played after all – and I can't tell you how glad I am that I was able to play! I hope we play in heaps more matches together. It was marvellous being able to pass the ball so well to one another!"

"You shot that winning goal well," said Elizabeth happily. "Oh, I'm so tired, but so happy. I feel as if I can't get up from this form! My legs won't work any more!"

They all got back into the coach. They waved goodbye to the cheering Uphill girls, and the coach rumbled off. The children sank back into their seats, their faces still red with all their running about, and their legs tired out.

But as soon as they got near Whyteleafe School they all sat up straight and looked eagerly to see the first glimpse of the Whyteleafe children, who would all be waiting to hear the result of the match.

Joan and Jenny and Kathleen had been looking out for the coach for the last half-hour. When they heard it coming they tore to the big school door. Dozens of other children ran with them. It was always the custom at Whyteleafe to welcome home the children who had been to an Away Match.

The lacrosse team waved their hands wildly as the coach rumbled up to the big school door.

"We won! We won! Three goals to two!"

"We've won the match. It was marvellous!"

"It's the first time Uphill have been beaten!"

"Three goals to two! Three to two!"

The Whyteleafe children cheered madly when they heard the news. They swarmed out round the coach and helped down the team, whose legs were still very wobbly from all the rushing about they had done.

"Jolly good! Oh, jolly good!" cried everyone. "Come along in and tell us all about it!"

So into the gym went the team, and Miss Belle and Miss Best, and Mr Johns too, had to come along and hear all the excitements of the afternoon. Mr Warlow spoke for a while and told how well everyone had played. Then John shouted out: "Who shot the goals?"

"Elizabeth, Nora – and Robert," said Mr Warlow. "Good goals all three. Robert's was the most exciting because he shot his almost as the whistle went for Time. Another second and it would have been too late!"

"Three cheers for Nora, Elizabeth, and Robert!" cried everyone, and they clapped them on the back. How pleased and proud those three children were! Elizabeth almost cried for joy. To think she had actually shot a goal for Whyteleafe in her very first match. It was too good to be true.

Nora had played in many matches and shot many goals, so she just grinned and said nothing. But Robert was as pleased and proud as Elizabeth, though he did not show it quite so much.

Elizabeth slipped her arm in his. "I'm *so* glad we both had the chance to play together," she said. "And oh, Robert, you don't know how pleased I am that I've done something for Whyteleafe, even if it's only to shoot a goal! I hated Whyteleafe when I first came here – but now I love it. Wait till you have been here a term or two and you'll love it too."

"I love it already, thank you," said Robert. "And what's more, I mean to do a whole lot more for it than just shoot a goal!"

There was a special supper that night for the winning team! Hot sausages appeared on the table, two for each one of the team. How delighted they were! And not only that, but anyone who had sweets or chocolates made a point of offering them to the team, so that by the time the bed-bell went, both Robert and Elizabeth felt that they couldn't eat anything more at all!

THE NAUGHTIEST GIRL IS A MONITOR

AN EXTRACT

≈ ILLUSTRATED BY ≈

Max Schindler and Kenneth Lovell

It is Elizabeth Allen's third term at Whyteleafe and she is proud to have been made a monitor. Julian Holland, an attractive, dare-devil new boy, becomes her special friend, but when Elizabeth suspects and accuses him of stealing they have a dreadful quarrel. He then plays several tricks on her, which get her into trouble in class. Elizabeth, still convinced that he is stealing, feels forced to bring this up at a School Meeting.

CHAPTER XV
A STORMY MEETING

The children filed into the big hall for the usual School Meeting that night. Elizabeth was excited and strung-up. She longed to get the Meeting over, and have everything settled.

"Any money for the Box?" said William, as usual. Ten pounds came in from a boy who had had a postal order from an uncle. Arabella put in two pounds – her birthday money. She had learnt her lesson about that! She was not going to be reported for keeping back money again.

Two pounds was given to everyone. Then William and Rita dealt with requests for more money. Elizabeth could hardly keep still. She felt nervous. She glanced at Julian. He sat as usual on the bench, a lock of hair falling into his eyes. He brushed it back impatiently.

"Any complaints?" The familiar question came from William, and a small boy sprang up before Elizabeth could speak.

"Please, William! The other children in my class are always calling me a dunce because I'm bottom. It isn't fair."

"Have you spoken to your monitor about it?" asked William.

"Yes," said the small boy.

"Who is your monitor?" asked William.

A bigger boy stood up. "I am," he said. "Yes — the others do tease James. He has missed a lot of school through illness, so he doesn't know as much as the others. But I spoke to his teacher, and she says he could really try harder than he does, because he has good brains. He doesn't need to be bottom very long."

"Thank you," said William. The monitor sat down.

"Well, James, you heard what your monitor said. You yourself can soon stop the others teasing you, by using your good brains and not being bottom! You may have got so used always to being at the bottom that it didn't occur to you you could be anything else. But it seems that you can!"

"Oh," said James, looking pleased and rather surprised. He sat down with a bump. His form looked at him, not quite knowing whether to be cross with him or amused. They suddenly nudged one another and grinned. James looked round, smiling too.

"Any more complaints?" asked Rita.

"Yes, Rita!" said Elizabeth, and jumped up so suddenly that she almost upset her chair. "I have a very serious complaint to make."

A ripple of whispering ran through the school. Everyone sat up straight. What was Elizabeth going to say? Arabella went rather pale. She hoped Elizabeth was not going to complain about *her* again. Julian glanced sharply at Elizabeth. Surely — surely she wasn't going to speak about him!

But she was, of course. She began to make her complaint, her words almost falling over one another.

"Rita, William! It's about Julian," she began. "I have thought for some time that he was taking things that didn't belong to him — and yesterday I caught him at it! I caught him with the things in his hand! He was taking them out of the old games locker in the passage."

"Elizabeth, you must explain better," said Rita, looking grave and serious. "This is a terrible charge you are making. We shall have to go deeply into it, and unless you really have proof you had better say no more, but come to me and William afterwards."

"I *have* got proof!" said Elizabeth. "I saw Julian take the biscuits out of the locker. I don't know who they belonged to — Miss Ranger, I suppose. Anyway, Julian must have found them there, and when he thought we were all asleep at night he went to take them. And I heard him and saw him."

The whole school was quite silent. The first formers looked at one another, their hearts beating fast. Now their midnight feast would have to be found out! Julian would have to give away their secret.

William looked at Julian. He was sitting with his hands in his pockets, looking amused.

"Stand up, Julian, and tell us your side of the story," said William.

Julian stood up, his hands still in his pockets. "Take your hands out of your pockets," ordered William. Julian did so. He looked untidy and careless as he stood there, his green eyes twinkling like a gnome's.

"I'm sorry, William," he said, "but I can't give any explanation, because I should give away a secret belonging to others. All I can say is – I was not stealing the biscuits. I was certainly *taking* them – but not stealing them!"

He sat down. Elizabeth jumped up, like a jack-in-the-box. "You see, William!" she said, "he can't give you a proper explanation!"

"Sit down, Elizabeth," said William sternly. He looked at the first formers, who all sat silent and uncomfortable, not daring to glance at one another. How good of Julian not to give them away! How awful all this was!

"First formers," said William gravely, "I hope that if any one of you can help to clear Julian of this very serious charge, you will do so, whether it means giving away some secret or not. If Julian, out of loyalty to one or more of you, cannot stick up for himself, then you must be loyal to him, and tell what you know."

There was a silence after this. Rosemary sat trembling, not daring to move. Belinda half got up then sat down again. Martin looked straight ahead, rather pale.

It was Arabella who gave the first form a great surprise. She suddenly stood up, and spoke in a low voice.

"William, I'd better say something, I think. We *did* have a secret, and it's decent of Julian not to give it away. You see – it was my birthday yesterday – and we thought we'd have a – a – a midnight feast."

She stopped, so nervous that she could hardly go on. The whole school was listening with the greatest interest.

"Go on," said Rita gently.

"Well – well, you see, we had to hide the things here and there," said Arabella. "It was all such fun. We didn't tell Elizabeth – because she's a monitor and might have tried to stop us. Well, Julian hid my biscuits in the old games locker – and he went to get them after midnight, when the feast had begun. I suppose that's when Elizabeth means. But they were *my* biscuits, and I asked him to get them, and he brought them back to the common-room where we were. And I think it's unfair of Elizabeth to accuse Julian of stealing them. She's done that before. The whole form knows she's been saying that he takes money and sweets that don't belong to him."

This was a very long speech. Arabella finished it suddenly, and sat down, almost panting. Julian looked at her gratefully. He knew that she would not at all like telling the secret of the midnight party – but she had done it to save him. His opinion of the vain little girl went up sky-high – and so did everyone else's.

William and Rita had listened closely to all that Arabella had said. So had

Elizabeth. When she had heard the explanation of Julian's midnight wanderings she went very white, and her knees shook. She knew in a moment that in that one thing, at any rate, she had made a terrible mistake. William turned to Elizabeth, and his eyes were very sharp and stern.

"Elizabeth, it seems that you have done a most unforgivable thing – you have accused Julian publicly of something he hasn't done. I suppose you did not even ask him to explain his action to you, but just took it for granted that he was doing wrong."

Elizabeth sat glued to her seat. She could not say a word.

"Arabella says that this is not the only time you have accused Julian. There have been other times too. As this last accusation of yours has been proved to be wrong, it is likely that the other complaints you have made to the first form are wrong too. So we will not hear them in public. But Rita and I will want you to come to us privately and explain everything."

"Yes, William," said Elizabeth in a low voice. "I'm – I'm very, very sorry about what I said just now. I didn't know."

"That isn't any excuse," said William sternly. "I can't think what has happened to you this term, Elizabeth. We made you a monitor at the end of last term because we all thought you should be – but this term you have let us all down. I am afraid that already many of us are thinking that you should no longer be a monitor."

Several boys and girls agreed. They stamped on the floor with their feet.

"Twice you have been sent out of your classroom," said William. "And for the same reason – disturbing the class by playing foolish tricks. That is not the behaviour of a monitor, Elizabeth. I am afraid that we can no longer ask you to help us as a monitor. You must step down and leave us to choose someone else in your place."

This was too much for Elizabeth. She gave an enormous sob, jumped down from the platform and rushed out of the room. She was a failure. She was no good as a monitor. And oh, she had been *so* proud of it too!

William did not attempt to stop her rushing from the room. He looked gravely round

the well-filled benches. "We must now choose another monitor," he said. "Will you please begin thinking who will best take Elizabeth's place?"

The children sat still, thinking. The Meeting had been rather dreadful in some ways – but to every child there had come a great lesson. They must never, never accuse anyone of wrong-doing unless they were absolutely certain. Every child had clearly seen the misery that might have been caused, and they knew that Elizabeth's punishment was just.

Poor Elizabeth! Always rushing into trouble. What would she do now?

CHAPTER XVI
ELIZABETH SEES WILLIAM AND RITA

A new monitor was chosen in place of Elizabeth. It was a girl in the second form, called Susan. Not one child outside the first form had chosen a first former. It was clear that most people felt that the first form would do better to have an older girl or boy for a monitor.

"Arabella, it *was* brave of you to own up about the midnight feast," said Rosemary admiringly. All the others thought so too. Arabella felt pleased with herself. She really had done it unselfishly, and she was rather surprised at herself for doing such a thing. It was nice to feel that the rest of the form admired her for something.

One person was feeling rather uncomfortable. It was Julian. He felt very angry with Elizabeth for making such an untruthful and horrible complaint about him – but he did know that it was because of his tricks she had been sent out of the room twice, and not because of her own foolishness. Partly because of his tricks and their results, Elizabeth had lost the honour of being a monitor.

"Of course, William and Rita might have said she couldn't be because she complained wrongly about me," said Julian to himself. "But it sounded as if it was because of her being sent out of the room. Well, she doesn't deserve to be a monitor anyway – so why should I worry?"

But he did worry a little, because, like Elizabeth, he was really very fair-minded, and although he did not like the little girl, he knew that dislike was no excuse at all for being unfair. He had come very well out of the whole affair, thanks to Arabella. But Elizabeth had not. Even Harry, Robert, and Kathleen, her own good friends, had nothing nice to say of her at the moment.

The meeting broke up after choosing the new monitor. The children went out, talking over what had happened. You never knew what would come out at a School Meeting.

"Nothing can be hidden at Whyteleafe School!" said Eileen, one of the older girls. "Sooner or later everyone's faults come to light, and are put right. Sooner or later our good points are seen and rewarded. And we do it all ourselves. It's very good for us, I think."

Miss Belle and Miss Best had been present at the Meeting, and had listened with great interest to all that had happened. William and Rita stayed behind to have a word with them.

"Did we do right, Miss Belle?" asked William.

"I think so," said Miss Belle, and Miss Best nodded too. "But, William, have Elizabeth along as soon as ever you can, and let her get off her chest all that she has been thinking about Julian – there is clearly something puzzling there. Elizabeth does not get such fixed ideas into her head without *some* reason. There is still something we don't know."

"Yes. We'll send for Elizabeth now," said Rita. "I wonder where she is."

She was out in the stables in the dark, sobbing against the horse she rode each morning. The horse nuzzled up to her, wondering what was upsetting his little mistress. Soon she dried her eyes, and sat down on an upturned pail in a corner.

She was puzzled, deeply sorry for what she had said about Julian, very much ashamed of herself, and horrified at losing the honour of being a monitor. She felt that she could never face the others again. But she knew she would have to.

"What is the matter with me?" she wondered. "I make up my mind to be so good and helpful and everything and then I go and do just the opposite! I lose my temper. I say dreadful things – and now everyone hates me. Especially Julian. It's funny about Julian. I did see that he had my marked pound. I did see that one of my sweets fell out of his pocket. So that's why I thought he was stealing the biscuits, and he wasn't. But did he take the other things?"

Someone came by calling loudly. "Elizabeth! Where are you?"

Messengers had been sent to find her, to tell her to go to Rita and William. She could not be found in the school, so Nora had come outside to look for her with a torch.

At first Elizabeth thought she would not answer. She simply could not go in and face the others just yet. Then a little courage came to her, and she stood up.

"I'm not a coward," she thought. "William and Rita have punished me partly for

something I *haven't* done – because I really *didn't* play about in class – but the other thing I *did* do – I did make an untruthful complaint about Julian, though I thought at the time it was true. So I must just face up to it and not be silly."

"Elizabeth, are you out here?" came Nora's voice again.

This time the little girl answered. "Yes. I'm coming."

She came out of the stables, rubbing her eyes. Nora flashed her torch at her. "I've been looking everywhere for you, idiot," she said. "William and Rita want you. Hurry up."

"All right," said Elizabeth, feeling her heart sink. Was she going to be scolded again? Wasn't it enough that she should have been disgraced in public without being scolded in private?

She rubbed her hanky over her face and ran to the school. She made her way to William's study. She knocked at the door.

"Come in!" said William's voice. She went in and saw the head-boy and girl sitting in arm-chairs. They both looked up gravely as she came in.

"Sit there," said Rita in a kindly voice. She felt sorry for the headstrong little girl who was so often in trouble. Elizabeth felt glad to hear the kindness in Rita's voice. She sat down.

"Rita," she said, "I'm terribly sorry for being wrong about Julian. I did think I was right. I honestly did."

"That's what we want to see you about," said Rita. "We couldn't allow you to say any more about Julian in public, in case you were wrong again. But we want you to tell us now all that has happened to make you feel so strongly against Julian."

Elizabeth told the head-boy and girl everything – all about Rosemary's money going and Arabella's; how her own marked pound had gone – and had appeared in Julian's hand, when he was spinning coins; and how her own sweet had fallen from his pocket.

"You are quite, quite sure about these things?" asked William, looking worried. It was quite clear to him that there *was* a thief about – somebody in the first form – but he was not so sure as Elizabeth that it was Julian! He and Rita both thought that whatever the boy's faults were, however careless and don't-careish he was, dishonesty was not one of his failings.

"So you see, William and Rita," finished Elizabeth earnestly, "because of all these things I jumped to the conclusion that Julian was stealing the biscuits last night. It was terribly wrong of me – but it was the other things that made me think it."

"Elizabeth, why did you think you could put matters right yourself, when the money first began to disappear?" asked Rita. "It was not your business. You should not have laid a trap. You should have come straight to us, and let us deal with it. You, as a monitor, should report these things to us, and let us think out the right way of dealing with them."

"Oh," said Elizabeth, surprised. "Oh. I somehow thought that as I was a monitor I could settle things myself – and I thought it would be nice to put things right without worrying you or the Meeting."

"Elizabeth, you must learn to see the difference between big things and little things," said Rita. "Monitors can settle such matters as seeing that no one talks after lights out, giving advice in silly little quarrels, and things like that. But when a big thing crops up we expect our monitors to come to us and report it. See what you have done by trying to settle the matter yourself. You have brought a terrible complaint against Julian, you have made Arabella give away the secret she wanted to keep, and you have lost the honour of being made a monitor."

"I felt so grand and important, being a monitor," said Elizabeth, wiping away two tears that ran down her cheek.

"Yes – you felt *too* grand and important," said Rita. "So grand that you thought you could settle a matter that even Miss Belle and Miss Best might find difficult! Well, there is a lot you have to learn, Elizabeth – but you do make things as hard for yourself as possible, don't you!"

"Yes, I do," said Elizabeth. "I don't think enough. I just go rushing along, losing my temper – and my friends – and everything!" She gave a heavy sigh.

"Well," said William, "there is one thing about you, Elizabeth – you *have* got the courage to see your own faults, and that is the first step to curing them. Don't worry too much. You may get back all you have lost if only you are sensible."

"I think we had better get Julian here and tell him all that Elizabeth has said," said

Rita. "Perhaps he can throw some light on that marked pound – and the sweet. I feel certain he didn't take them."

"Oh – let me go before he comes," begged Elizabeth, who felt that Julian was the very last person she wanted to meet just then. She pictured his green eyes looking scornfully at her. No – she couldn't bear to meet him just then.

"No – you must stay and hear what he has to say," said Rita firmly. "If Julian didn't take these things, there is something peculiar about the matter. We must find out what it is."

So Elizabeth had to sit in William's study, waiting for Julian to come. Oh dear, what a perfectly horrid day this was!

CHAPTER XVII
GOOD AT HEART!

Julian came at once. He was surprised to see Elizabeth in the study too. He gave her a look, and then turned politely to William and Rita.

"Julian, we have heard a lot of puzzling things from Elizabeth," said William. "We are sure you have an explanation of them. Will you listen to me, whilst I tell you them – and then you can tell us what you think."

Julian listened whilst William told all that Elizabeth had poured out to him and Rita. Julian looked surprised and puzzled.

"I see now why Elizabeth thought I was the thief," he said. "It did look very odd, I must say. Did I really have the marked pound? And did a sweet of Elizabeth's really fall out of my pocket? I heard something fall, but as the sweet wasn't mine, I didn't pick it up. I saw it on the floor, but I didn't even know it had fallen from my pocket. I certainly never put it there."

"How did it get there then?" said Rita, puzzled.

"I believe I've got that pound now," said Julian suddenly. He felt in his pockets and took out a brand-new coin. He looked at it closely. In one place a tiny black cross could still be seen. "It's the same pound," said Julian.

"That's the cross I marked," said Elizabeth, pointing to it. Julian stared at it thoughtfully.

"You know, I'm sure, now I come to think of it, that I didn't have a bright new pound like this out of the Box that week," he said. "I'd have noticed it. I'm sure I got two old pounds. So someone must have put this new coin into my pocket – and taken out an old one. Why?"

"And someone must have put one of Elizabeth's sweets into your pocket too," said William. "Does any boy or girl dislike you very much, Julian?"

Julian thought hard. "Well, no – except, of course, Elizabeth," he said.

Elizabeth suddenly felt dreadfully upset when she heard this. All her dislike for Julian had gone, now that she felt, with Rita and William, that Julian hadn't taken the money or sweets, but that someone had played a horrible trick on him.

"Elizabeth just hates me," said Julian, "but I'm sure she wouldn't do a thing like that!"

"Oh, Julian – of course I wouldn't," said poor Elizabeth, almost in tears again. "Julian, I don't hate you. I'm more sorry than I can say about everything that has happened. I feel so ashamed of myself. I'm always doing things like this. You'll never forgive me, I know."

Julian looked gravely at her out of his curious green eyes. "I have forgiven you," he said unexpectedly. "I never bear malice. But I don't like you very much and I can't be good friends with you any more, Elizabeth. But there is something I'd like to own up to now."

He turned to William and Rita. "You said, at the Meeting, that Elizabeth had twice been sent out of the room for misbehaving herself," he said. "Well, it wasn't her fault." He turned to Elizabeth. "Elizabeth, I played a trick on you over those books. I put springs under the bottom ones and they fell over when the springs had untwisted themselves. And I stuck pellets on the ceiling just above your chair, so that drops fell on your head when the chemicals in them changed to water. And I put sneezing powder in the pages of your French book."

William and Rita listened to all this in the greatest astonishment. They hardly knew what Julian was talking about. But Elizabeth, of course, knew very well indeed. She gaped at Julian in the greatest surprise.

Springs under her books! Pellets on the ceiling that turned to water! Sneezing powder in her books! The little girl could hardly believe her ears. She stared at Julian in amazement, quite forgetting her tears.

And then, very suddenly, she laughed. She couldn't help it. She thought of her books jumping off her desk in that peculiar manner. She thought of those puzzling drops of water splashing down – and that fit of sneezing. It all seemed to her very funny, even though it had brought her scoldings and punishments.

How she laughed. She threw back her head and roared. William, Rita, and Julian could not have been more surprised. They stared at the laughing girl, and then they began to laugh too. Elizabeth had a very infectious laugh that always made everyone else want to join in.

At last Elizabeth wiped her eyes and stopped. "Oh, dear," she said, "I can't imagine how I could laugh like that when I felt so unhappy. But I couldn't help it, it all seemed so funny when I looked back and remembered what happened and how puzzled I was."

Julian suddenly put out his hand and took Elizabeth's. "You're a little sport," he said. "I never for one moment thought you'd laugh when I told you what I'd done to pay you out. I thought you might cry – or fly into a temper – or sulk – but I never thought you'd laugh. You're a real little sport, Elizabeth, and I like you all over again!"

"Oh," said Elizabeth, hardly believing her ears. "Oh, Julian! You *are* nice. But oh, what a funny thing to like me again just because I laughed."

"It isn't really funny," said William. "People who can laugh like that, when the joke has been against them, are, as Julian says, good sports, and very lovable. That laugh of yours has made things a lot better, Elizabeth. Now we understand one another a good deal more."

Julian squeezed Elizabeth's hand. "I don't mind the silly things you said about me, and you don't mind the silly things I did against you," he said. "So we're quits and we can begin all over again. Will you be my friend?"

"Oh *yes*, Julian!" said Elizabeth happily. "Yes, I'd love to. And I don't care if you make hail or snow fall on my head, or put any powder you like into my books now. Oh, I do feel happy again."

William and Rita looked at one another and smiled. Elizabeth seemed to fall in and out of trouble as easily as a duck splashed in and out of water. She could be very foolish and do silly, hot-tempered, wrong things – but she was all right at heart.

"Well," said William, "we have cleared up a lot of things – but we still don't know who the real thief was – or is, for he or she may still be taking other things. We can only hope to find out soon, before any other trouble is made. By the way, Elizabeth, if your first accusation of Julian was made privately and secretly, as you said, how was it that all the first form knew? Surely you did not tell them yourself?"

"No, I didn't say a word," said Elizabeth at once. "I said I wouldn't, and I didn't."

"Well, I didn't say anything," said Julian. "And yet the whole form knew and came to tell me about it."

"Only one other person knew," said Elizabeth, looking troubled. "And that was Martin Follett. He was in the stables, Julian, whilst we were outside. He came out when you had walked off, and he offered me a pound in place of mine that had gone. I thought it was very nice of him. He promised not to say a word of what he had heard."

"Well, he must have told pretty well everyone, the little sneak," said Julian, who, for some reason, had never liked Martin as much as the others had. "Anyway, it doesn't matter. Well – thanks, William and Rita, for having us along and making us see sense."

He gave his sudden, goblin-like grin, and his green eyes shone. Elizabeth looked at him with a warm liking. How could she *ever* have thought that Julian would do a really mean thing? How awful she was! She never gave anyone a chance.

"He's always saying he does as he likes, and he's not going to bother to work if he doesn't want to, and he doesn't care what trouble he gets into, and he plays the most awful tricks – but I'm certain as certain could be that he's good at heart," said Elizabeth to herself.

And Julian grinned at her and thought: "She flies into the most awful tempers, and says the silliest things, and makes enemies right and left – but I'm certain as certain can be that she's good at heart!"

"Well, goodnight, you two troublemakers," said William, and he gave them a friendly push. "Elizabeth, I'm sorry about you not being a monitor any more, but I think you see yourself that you want to get a bit more common sense before the children will trust you again. You do fly off the handle so when you get an idea into your head."

"Yes, I know," said Elizabeth. "I've failed this time but I'll have another shot and do it properly, you see if I don't!"

The two went out, and William and Rita looked at one another.

"Good stuff in both those kids," said William. "Let's make some cocoa, Rita. It's getting late. Golly, I wonder who's the nasty little thief in the first form. It must be somebody there. He's not only a nasty little thief, but somebody very double-faced, trying to make someone else bear the blame for his own misdeeds by putting the marked pound into Julian's pocket!"

"Yes, it must be someone really bad at heart," said Rita. "Someone it will be very difficult to deal with. It might be a girl or a boy – I wonder which."

Julian and Elizabeth went down the passage to their own common-room. It was almost time for bed. There was about a quarter of an hour left.

"I'm coming into the common-room with you," said Julian, and Elizabeth squeezed his arm gratefully. He had sensed that she did not want to appear alone in front of all the first form. It was going to be hard to face everyone, now that she had been disgraced, and was no longer a monitor.

"Thank you, Julian," she said, and opened the door to go in.

MISCHIEF AT ST ROLLO'S

≈ ILLUSTRATED BY ≈

C. Holland

*Michael and Janet are a brother and sister who don't want to go away
to boarding school, even though it is a co-educational one where they will
not be separated. This story describes how they settle in at their new school,
and with friendships and rivalries, tricks and a midnight feast,
have an adventurous time there.*

CHAPTER I
A NEW SCHOOL

"I don't want to go to boarding school," said Michael.

"Neither do I," said Janet. "I don't see why we have to, Mother!"

"You are very lucky to be able to go," said Mother. "Especially together! Daddy and I have chosen a mixed school for you — one with boys and girls together, so that both you and Mike can go together, and not be parted. We know how fond you are of one another. It's quite time you went too. I run after you too much. You must learn to stand on your own feet."

Mother went out of the room. The two children stared at one another. "Well, that's that," said Janet, flipping a pellet of paper at Michael. "We've got to go. But I vote we make our new school sit up a bit!"

"I've heard that you have to work rather hard at St Rollo's," said Mike. "Well, I'm not going to! I'm going to have a good time. I hope we're in the same class."

There was only a year between the two of them, and as Janet was a clever child, she had so far always been in the same form as her brother, who was a year older. They had been to a mixed school ever since they had first started, and although they now had to go away to boarding school, they both felt glad that they were not to be parted, as most brothers and sisters had to be.

"Only one week more of the hols," Mike said gloomily, going to the window. "And look at this sickening rain! If it keeps on like this I shall be quite glad to go to school. Anyway, the Christmas term is always rather fun."

The last week of the holidays flew past. Mother took the children to the shops to get them fitted for new clothes.

"We do seem to have to have a lot for our new school," said Janet, with interest. "And are we going to have tuck-boxes, Mother, to take back with us? You know — with cakes and sweets in."

"If you're good!" said Mother, with a laugh. "Now just let me check this list — three pairs of grey shorts for Mike — one pair for you and two short grey skirts — six pairs of school socks . . ."

But the children were not listening. They wanted to hear about tuck-boxes, not shorts and skirts and socks!

Mother did get them their tuck-boxes — one each for them. She put exactly the same in each box — one big currant cake, one big ginger cake, twelve chocolate buns, a tin of toffee and a large bar of chocolate. The children were delighted.

The day came for them to go to their new school. They couldn't help feeling a bit excited, though they felt rather nervous too. Still, they were going to go together, and that would be fun. They caught a train to London, and Mother took them to the station from which the school train was to start.

"St Rollo's School," said the big blue label on the train. "Reserved for St Rollo's School." A great crowd of boys and girls were on the platform, talking and laughing, calling to each other. Some were new, and they looked rather lonely and shy. Janet and Mike kept together, looking eagerly at everyone.

"They look rather nice," said Mike to Janet. "I wonder which will be in our form."

Both boys and girls were in grey, and looked neat and smart. One or two masters and mistresses bustled up and down, talking to parents, and warning the children to take their places. Janet and Mike got into a carriage with several other boys and girls.

"Hallo!" said one, a cheeky-looking boy of about eleven. "You're new, aren't you?"

"Yes," said Mike.

"What's your name?" said the boy, his blue eyes twinkling at Mike and Janet.

"I'm Michael Fairley and this is my sister Janet," said Mike. "What's your name?"

"I'm Tom Young," said the boy. "I should think you'll be in my form. We have fun. Can you make darts?"

"Paper darts," said Mike. "Of course! Everyone can!"

"Ah, but you should see my new kind," said the boy, and he took out a notebook with stiff paper leaves. But just as he was tearing out a sheet the guard blew his whistle, and the train gave a jerk.

"Goodbye, Mother!" yelled Mike and Janet. "Goodbye. We'll write tomorrow!"

"Goodbye, my dears!" called Mother. "Enjoy yourselves and work hard."

The train chuffed out of the station. Now that it was really gone the two children felt a bit lonely. It wasn't going to be very nice not to see Mother and Daddy for some time. Thank goodness they had each other!

Tom looked at them. "Cheer up!" he said. "I felt like that, too, the first time. But you soon get over it. Now just see how I make my new paper darts."

Tom was certainly very clever with his fingers. In a minute or two he had produced a marvellous pointed dart out of paper, which, when it was thrown, flew straight to its mark.

"Better than most darts, don't you think?" said Tom proudly. "I thought that one out last term. The first time I threw one it shot straight at Miss Thomas and landed underneath her collar. I got sent out of the room for that."

Janet and Mike looked at Tom with much respect. All the other children in the carriage laughed.

"Tom's the worst boy in the school," said a rosy-cheeked, fat girl.

"Don't take lessons from him – he just doesn't care about anything."

"Is Miss Thomas a mistress?" asked Mike. "Do we have masters *and* mistresses at St Rollo's?"

"Of course," said Tom. "If you're in my form you'll have Miss Thomas for class-teacher, but a whole lot of other teachers for special subjects. I can tell you whose classes it's safe to play about in, and whose classes it's best to behave in."

"Well, seeing that you don't behave well in *anybody's* classes, I shouldn't have thought you could have told anyone the difference," said the fat girl.

"Be quiet, Marian," said Tom. "I'm doing the talking in this carriage!"

That was too much for the other children. They fell on Tom and began to pummel him. But he took it all good-humouredly, and pummelled back hard. Mike and Janet watched, laughing. They didn't quite like to join in.

Everyone had sandwiches to eat. They could eat them any time after half-past twelve, but not before. Tom produced a watch after a while and looked at it.

"Good!" he said. "It's half-past twelve." He undid his packet of sandwiches. Marian looked astonished.

"Tom! It simply *can't* be half-past twelve yet," she said. She looked at her wrist-watch. "It's only a quarter-to."

"Well, your watch must be wrong then," said Tom, and he began to eat his sandwiches. Janet looked at her watch. It certainly was only a quarter-to-twelve. She felt sure that Tom had put his watch wrong on purpose.

It made the other children feel very hungry to watch Tom eating his ham sandwiches. They began to think it would be a good idea to put their watches fast, too! But just then a master came down the corridor that ran the length of the train. Tom tried to put away his packet of sandwiches, but he was too late.

"Well, Tom," said the master, stopping at the door and looking in. "Can't you wait to get to school before you begin to break the rules?"

"Mr Wills, sir, my watch says five-and-twenty-to-one," said Tom, holding out his watch, with an innocent look on his face. "Isn't it five-and-twenty-to-one?"

"You know quite well it isn't," said Mr Wills. He took the watch and twisted the hands back. "Put away your lunch and have it when your watch says half-past twelve," he said. Tom gave a look at his watch, then he looked up with an expression of horror.

"Sir! You've made my watch half an hour slow! That would mean I couldn't start my lunch till one o'clock!"

"Well, well, fancy that!" said Mr Wills. "I wonder which is the more annoying – to have a watch that is fast, or one that is slow, Tom? What a pity! You'll have to eat your lunch half an hour after the others have finished!"

He went out. Tom stared after him gloomily. " I suppose he thinks that's funny," he said.

Marian laughed. "Well, it is!" she said. "It just serves you right! You're always trying to be so smart."

Tom put away his lunch, for he knew quite well that Mr Wills might be along again at any moment. At half-past twelve all the other children took down their lunch packets and undid them eagerly, for they were hungry. Poor Tom had to sit and watch them eat. His watch only said twelve o'clock!

At one, when all the others had finished, he opened his lunch packet again. "Now, of course," he said, "I'm so terribly hungry that ham sandwiches, egg sandwiches, buttered scones with jam, ginger cake, an apple and some chocolate won't nearly do for me!"

The train sped on. It was due to arrive at half-past two. When the time came near, Janet and Mike looked out of the windows eagerly. "Can we see St Rollo's from the train?" asked Janet.

"Yes. It's built on a hill," said Marian. "You'll see it out of that window. It's of grey stone and it has towers at each end. In the middle of the building is a big archway. Watch out for it now – you'll soon see it."

The children looked out, and, as Marian had said, they caught sight of their new school. It looked grand!

There it stood on the hill with big towers at each end, built of grey stone. Creeper climbed over most of the walls, and here and there a touch of red showed that when autumn came the walls would glow red with the crimson leaves.

The train slowed down at a little station. Everyone got out. Some big coaches were waiting in the little station-yard. Laughing and shouting, the children piled into them. Their luggage was to follow in a van. The masters and mistresses climbed in last of all, and the coaches set off to St Rollo's.

They rumbled up the hill and came to a stop before the big archway. The school looked enormous, now that the children were so close to it. All the boys and girls clambered down from the coaches and went in at a big door.

"Well – welcome to St Rollo's!" said Tom Young, with a grin. "I like the look of you two. We'll have some fun and mischief this term, shall we? I bet you know a few tricks, don't you?"

"Yes," said Mike, grinning back. He liked Tom very much. "What do we do now? Go up to our rooms and unpack?"

"Yes," said Tom. "I'll take you to see Matron first. She'll tell you where your dormitory is – that's the place we sleep in, you know. You don't have bedrooms at boarding school – you have dormitories – sounds much grander!"

The two children followed Tom up the stairs to a large and cheerful room, into which the afternoon sun poured. A plump, smooth-cheeked woman was sitting there.

"Hallo, Matron," said Tom, going in. "I've brought two new ones to see you. Are they in my dormitory? I hope they are."

"Well, I'm sorry for them if they are!" said Matron, getting out a big exercise book and turning the pages. "What are their names?"

"Michael and Janet Fairley," said Mike. Matron found their names and ticked them off.

"Yes — Michael is in your dormitory, Tom," she said. "Janet is across the passage with Marian and the girls. I hope they will help you to behave better, not worse. And just remember what I told you last term — if you play any tricks on me this term I'll send you to the Headmaster!"

Tom grinned. He took Mike's arm and led him away with Janet. "You'll soon begin to think I'm a bad lot!" he said. "Come on — I'll show you everything."

CHAPTER II
SETTLING DOWN

There was plenty to see at St Rollo's. The dormitories were fine big rooms. Each child had a separate cubicle with white curtains to pull around their bed, their dressing table, and small cupboard. The children's luggage was already in the dormitory when they got there.

"We'll unpack later," said Tom. "Look, that will be my bed. And yours can be next to mine, Mike, if I can arrange it. Look — let's pull your trunk into this cubicle, then no one else will take it."

They pulled the trunk across. Then Tom showed Janet her dormitory, across the passage. It was exactly the same as the boys', except that the beds had pink eiderdowns instead of blue. After that, Tom showed them the classrooms, which were fine

rooms, all with great windows looking out on the sunny playgrounds.

"This is our classroom, if you're in my form," said Tom. Janet and Mike liked the look of it very much.

"I had that desk there at the front, last term," said Tom, pointing to one. "I always try to choose one right at the back — but sooner or later I'm always made to sit at the front. People seem to think they have to keep an eye on me. Awfully tiresome!"

"I wonder where our desks will be," said Mike.

"Bag two, if you like," said Tom. "Just dump a few books in. Where do you want to sit?"

"I like being near the window, where I can look out," said Mike. "But I'd like to be where I can see you too, Tom!"

"Well, I shall try and bag a desk at the back as usual," said Tom. He took a few books from a bookshelf and dumped them into a desk in the back row by the window. "That can be your desk. That can be Janet's. And this can be mine! All in a row together!"

Tom showed them the playgrounds and the hockey fields. He showed them the marvellous gym and the assembly hall where the school met every morning for prayers. He showed them the changing rooms, where they changed for games, and the common-rooms where each class met out of school to read, write or play games. Janet and Mike began to feel they would lose their way if they had to find any place by themselves!

"We'll go and unpack now," said Tom. "And then it'll be tea-time. Good! We can all have things out of our tuck-boxes today."

They went to their dormitories to unpack. Janet parted from the two boys and went into hers. Marian was there, and she smiled at Janet.

"Hallo," she said. "I saw Tom taking you round. He's a kind soul, but he'll lead you into trouble, if he can! Come and unpack. I'll show you where to put your things. I'm head of this dormitory."

Janet unpacked and stowed away her things into the drawers of the dressing table, and hung her coats in the cupboard. All the other girls were doing the same. Marian called to Janet.

"I say! Do you know any of the others here? That's Audrey near to you. And this is Bertha. And that shrimp is Connie. And here's Doris, who just simply can't help being top of the form, whether she tries or not!"

Doris laughed. She was a clever-looking girl, with large glasses on her nose. "We're all in the same form," she told Janet. "Is your brother in Tom Young's dormitory?"

"Yes," said Janet. "Will he be in my form too?"

"Yes, he will," said Doris. "All the four dormitories on this floor belong to the same form. Miss Thomas is our form-mistress. She's nice but pretty strict. Only one person ever gets the better of her — and that's Tom Young. He just simply doesn't care what he does — and he's always bottom. But he's nice."

Meanwhile Mike was also getting to know the boys in his dormitory. Tom was telling him about them.

"See that fellow with the cross-eyes and hooked nose? Well, that's Eric."

Mike looked round for somebody with cross-eyes and a hooked nose, but the boy that Tom pointed to had the straightest brown eyes and nose that Mike had ever seen! The boy grinned.

"I'm Eric," he said. "Don't take any notice of Tom. He thinks he's terribly funny."

Tom took no notice. "See that chap over there in the corner? The one with spots all over his face? That's Fred. He gets spots because he eats too many sweets."

"Shut up!" said Fred. He had one small spot on his chin. He was a big, healthy-looking boy, with bright eyes and red cheeks.

"And this great giant of a chap is George," said Tom, pointing to an under-grown boy with small shoulders. The boy grinned.

"You must have your joke, mustn't you?" he said amiably. "And now Mike whatever-your-name-is, let me introduce you to the world's greatest clown, the world's biggest idiot, Master Thomas Henry William Young, biggest duffer and dunce, and, by a great effort, the bottom of the form!"

Mike roared with laughter. Tom took it all in good part. He gave George a punch which the boy dodged cleverly.

There was one other boy in the room, but Tom said nothing about him. He was not a pleasant-looking boy. Mike wondered why Tom didn't tell him his name. So he asked for it.

"Who's he?" he said, nodding his head towards the boy, who was unpacking his things with rather a sullen face.

"That's Hugh," said Tom, but he said no more.

Hugh looked up. "Go on, say what you like about me," he said. "The new boy will soon know it, anyway! Be funny at my expense if you want to!"

"I don't want to," said Tom.

"Well, *I'll* tell him then," said the boy. "I'm a cheat! I cheated in the exams last term, and everyone knows it because Tom found it out and gave me away!"

"I didn't give you away," said Tom. "I've told you that before. I saw that you were cheating, and said nothing. But Miss Thomas found it out herself. Anyway, let's drop the subject of cheating this term. Cheat all you like. I don't care!"

Tom turned his back on Hugh. Mike felt very awkward. He wished he hadn't asked for the boy's name. Eric began to talk about the summer holidays and all he had done. Soon the others joined in, and when Hugh slipped out of the room no one saw him go.

"It should be about tea-time now," said Tom, pulling out his watch. "Golly, no it isn't! Half an hour to go still! My word, what a swizz!"

Just then the tea-bell rang loudly, and Tom looked astonished. Mike laughed. "Don't you remember?" he said. "Mr Wills put your watch back half an hour?"

"So he did!" said Tom, looking relieved. He altered his watch again. "Well, come on," he said. " I could eat a mountain if only it was made of cake! Bring your tuck-box. What have you got in it? I'll share mine with you if you'll share yours with me. I've got a simply GORGEOUS chocolate cake."

It was fun, that first meal. All the children had brought goodies back in their tuck-boxes. They shared with one another, and the most enormous teas were eaten that day! Janet went to sit with Mike, and the two of them gave away part of all their cakes. In exchange they got slices of all kinds of other cakes. By the time they got up from the tea-table they couldn't eat another crumb!

"I hope we don't have to have supper!" said Mike. "I feel as if I don't want to eat again for a fortnight. But wasn't it scrumptious!"

The children had to go and see the headmaster and headmistress after tea. Both were grey-haired, and had kindly but rather stern faces. Mike and Janet felt very nervous and could hardly answer the questions they were asked.

"You will both be in the same form at first," said the headmaster, Mr Quentin. "Janet is a year younger, but I hear that she is advanced for her age. You will be in the second form."

"Yes, sir," said the children.

"We work hard at St Rollo's," said Miss Lesley, the headmistress. "But we play hard too. So you should have a good time and enjoy every day of the term. Remember our motto always, won't you: 'Not the least that we dare, but the most that we can!'"

"Yes, we will," said the two children.

"St Rollo's does all it can for its children," said Miss Lesley, "so it's up to you to do all you can for your school, too. You may go."

The children went. "I like the heads, don't you, Mike?" said Janet. "But I'm a bit afraid of them too. I shouldn't like to be sent to them for punishment."

"I bet Tom has!" said Mike. "Now we've got to go and see Miss Thomas. Come on."

Miss Thomas was in their classroom, making out lists. She looked up as the two children came in.

"Well, Michael; well, Janet," she said, with a smile. "Finding your way round a bit? It's difficult at first, isn't it? I've got your last reports here, and they are quite good. I hope you will do as well for me as you seem to have done for your last form-mistress!"

"We'll try," said the children, liking Miss Thomas's broad smile and brown eyes.

"I'm bad at maths," said Janet.

"And my handwriting is pretty awful," said Michael.

"Well, we'll see what we can do about it," said Miss Thomas. "Now you can go back to the common-room with the others. You'll know it by the perfectly terrible noise that comes out of the door!"

The children laughed and went out of the room.

"I think I'm going to like St Rollo's very much," said Janet happily. "Everybody is so nice. The girls in my dorm are fine, Mike. Do you like the boys in yours?"

"Yes, all except a boy called Hugh," said Mike, and he told Janet about the sulky boy. "I say – is this our common-room, do you think?"

They had come to an open door, out of which came a medley of noises. A record player was going, and someone was singing loudly to it, rather out of tune. Two or three others were shouting about something and another boy was hammering on the floor, though why, Janet and Mike couldn't imagine. They put their heads in at the door.

"This can't be our common-room," said Mike. "The children all look too big."

"Get out of here, tiddlers!" yelled the boy who was hammering on the floor. "You don't belong here! Find the kindergarten!"

"What cheek!" said Janet indignantly, as they withdrew their heads and walked off down the passage. "Tiddlers, indeed!"

Round the next passage was a noise that was positively deafening. It came from a big room on the left. A radio was going full-tilt, and a record player, too, so that neither of them could be heard properly. Four or five children seemed to be having a fight on the floor, and a few others were yelling to them, telling them to "Go it!" and "Stick it!"

A cushion flew through the air and hit Janet on the shoulder. She threw it back. A girl raised her voice dolefully.

"Oh, do shut up! I want to hear the radio!"

Nobody took any notice. The girl shouted even more loudly: "I say. I WANT TO HEAR THE RADIO."

Somebody snapped off the record player, and the radio seemed to boom out even more loudly. There was dance music on it.

"Let's dance!" cried Fred, fox-trotting by, holding a cushion as if it were a partner. "Hallo, Mike, hallo Janet. Where on earth have you been? Come into our quiet, peaceful room, won't you? Don't stand at the door looking like two scared mice."

So into their common-room went the two children, at first quite scared of all the noise around them. But gradually they got used to it, and picked out the voices of the boys and girls they knew, talking, shouting, and laughing together. It was fun. It felt good to be there altogether like a big, happy family. The noise was nice too.

For an hour the noise went on, and then died down as the children became tired.

Books were got out, and puzzles. The radio was turned down a little. The supper-bell went, and the children trooped down into the dining-hall. The first day was nearly over. A quiet hour after supper, and then bed. Yes – it was going to be nice at St Rollo's!

CHAPTER III
A HAPPY TIME

Michael and Janet found things rather strange at first, but after two or three days St Rollo's began to seem quite familiar to them. They knew their way about by then – though poor Janet got quite lost the second day, looking for her classroom!

She opened the door of what she thought was her form-room – only to find a class of big boys and girls taking painting! They sat round the room with their drawing-boards in front of them, earnestly drawing or painting a vase of bright leaves.

"Hallo! What do you want?" asked the drawing-master.

"I wanted the second form classroom," said Janet, blushing red.

"Oh well, this isn't it," said the master. "Go down the stairs, turn to the right – and it's the first door."

"Thank you," said Janet, thinking how silly she was not to remember what floor her classroom was on. She ran down the stains, and tried to remember if the drawing-master had said turn to the left or to the right.

"I think he said left," said Janet to herself. So to the left she turned and opened the first door there. To her horror, it was the door of the junior mistresses' common-room! One or two of them sat there, making out time-tables.

"What is it?" said the nearest one.

"Nothing," said Janet, going red again. "I'm looking for my classroom – the second form. I keep going into the wrong room."

"Oh, you're a new girl, aren't you?" said the mistress, with a laugh. "Well, go along the passage and take the first door on the right."

So at last Janet found her classroom, and was very relieved. But when three or four days had gone by she couldn't imagine how she could have made such a mistake! The school building, big as it was, was beginning to be very familiar to her.

The second form settled down well. Janet and Mike were the only new children in it. Miss Thomas let them keep the desks they had chosen – but she looked with a doubtful eye on Tom, when he sat down at the desk in the back row, next to Janet.

"Oh," she said, "so you've chosen a desk in the back row again, Tom. Do you think it's worthwhile doing that? You know quite well that before a week has gone by you will be told to take a desk out here in front, where I can keep my eye on you."

"Oh, Miss Thomas," said Tom. "I'm turning over a new leaf this term. Really I am. Let me keep this desk. I'm trying to help the new children, so I'm sitting by them."

"I see," said Miss Thomas, who looked as if she didn't believe a word that Tom said. "Well – I give you not more than a week there, Tom. We'll just see!"

There were a good many children in Mike's form. Mike and Janet soon got to know them all. They were a jolly lot, cheerful and full of fun – except for the boy called Hugh, who hardly spoke to anyone and seemed very sullen.

Tom was a great favourite. He made the silliest jokes, played countless tricks, and yet was always ready to help anyone. The teachers liked him, though they were forever scolding him for his careless work.

"It isn't necessary for you to be bottom of *every* subject, *every* week, is it, Tom?" said Miss Thomas. "I mean – wouldn't you like to give me a nice surprise and be top in something just for once?"

"Oh, Miss Thomas – would it really give you a nice surprise?" said Tom. "Wouldn't it give you a shock, not a surprise! I wouldn't like to give you a shock."

"Considering that you spend half your time thinking out tricks to shock people, that's a foolish remark!" said Miss Thomas. "Now, open your books at page 19."

Janet and Mike found the work to be about the same as they had been used to. They both had brains, and it was not difficult for them to keep up with the others. In fact, Janet felt sure that if she tried very hard, she could be top of the form! She had a wonderful memory, and couldn't seem to forget anything she had read or heard. This was a great gift, for it made all lessons easy for her.

Doris, the girl with glasses, was easily top each week. Nothing seemed difficult to her. Even the hot-tempered French master beamed on Doris and praised her – though he seldom praised anyone else. Mike and Janet were quite scared of him.

"Monsieur Crozier looked as if he was going to shout at me this morning," said Janet to Mike. "Don't you think he did?"

"He will shout at you if you give him the slightest chance!" said Tom, with a grin. "He shouted at me so loudly last term that I almost jumped out of my skin. I just got back into it in time!"

"Idiot!" said Mike. "I bet you had played some sort of trick on him."

"He had," said Fred. "He put white paint on that front lock of his hair – and when Monsieur Crozier exclaimed about it, what do you suppose Tom said?"

"What?" said Janet and Mike together.

"He said, 'Monsieur Crozier, my hair is turning white with the effort of learning the French verbs you have given us this week',” said Fred. “And do you wonder he shouted at him after that?”

“I'll think out something to make old Monsieur sit up!” said Tom. “You wait and see.”

“Oh, hurry up, then,” begged the children around. They loved Tom's tricks.

A week or two passed by, and Mike and Janet settled down well. They loved everything. The work was not too difficult for them. The teachers were jolly. Hockey was marvellous. This was played three times a week, and everyone was expected to turn up. Gym was fine, too. Mike and Janet were good at this, and enjoyed the half-hours in the big gym with the others.

Their tuck-boxes were soon finished, and they had to be content with the ordinary school meals. These were very good, though the children always pretended that they were dreadful.

“Bacon and eggs again!” Tom would groan, when he saw the big steaming dishes coming in. “Dear me! Fancy expecting us to eat bacon and eggs for breakfast twice a week!”

But he would eat his share with the greatest appetite! All the children were hungry for any meal, and it was amazing how many plates of bread-and-butter they could empty at tea-time.

There were lovely walks around the school. The children were allowed to go for walks by themselves, providing that three or more of them went together. So it was natural that Tom, Mike and Janet should often go together. The other children made up threes too, and went off for an hour or so when they could. It was lovely on the hills around, and already the children were looking for ripe blackberries and peering at the nut trees to see if there were going to be many nuts.

“Doesn't Hugh ever go for a walk?” said Janet once, when she, Mike and Tom had come in from a lovely sunny walk, to find Hugh bent double over a book in a far corner of the common-room. He was alone. All the other children were out doing something – either practising hockey on the field, or gardening, or walking.

“Well, you have to be at least three to go for a walk,” said Tom in a low voice. “And no one ever asks Hugh, of course – and he wouldn't like to ask two others because he'd be pretty certain they'd say No.”

“Why does everyone dislike him so?” asked Janet. “He would be quite a nice-looking boy if only he didn't look so surly.”

“He was new last term,” said Tom. “He's not very clever, but he's an awful swot – mugs up all sorts of things, and always has his nose in a book. Won't join in things, you know. And when he cheated at the exams last term, that was the last straw. Nobody decent wanted to have anything to do with him.”

"What happened? How did he cheat?" asked Mike. But Tom didn't want to tell tales.

"Don't let's talk about it," he said. "It's over now. But Hugh thinks I told tales of him then, because I was the only one who knew he was cheating. So he has hated me ever since. But I didn't say a word. Miss Thomas found it out herself."

"He can't be very happy," said Janet, who was a kind-hearted girl, willing to be friends with anyone.

"Perhaps he doesn't deserve to be," said Tom.

"But even if you don't deserve to be happy, it must be horrid never to be," argued Janet.

"Oh, don't start being a ministering angel, Janet," said Mike impatiently. "Don't you remember how sorry you were for that spiteful dog next door, who was always being told off for chasing hens? Well, what happened when you went out of your way to be kind to him, because you thought he must be miserable? He snapped at you, and nearly took your finger off!"

"I know," said Janet. But that was only because be couldn't understand anyone being kind to him."

"Well, Hugh would certainly snap your head off if you tried any kind words on *him*," said Tom, with a laugh. "Look out – here he comes."

The children fell silent as Hugh got up from his seat and made his way to the door. He had to pass the three on his way, and he looked at them sneeringly.

"Talking about me, I suppose?" he said. "Funny how everyone stops talking when I come near!"

He bumped rudely into Janet as he passed and sent her against the wall. The two boys leapt at Hugh, but he was gone before they could hold him.

"Well, do you feel like going after him and being sweet?" said Tom to Janet.

She shook her head. She thought Hugh was horrid. But all the same she was sorry for him.

Mike and Janet wrote long letters to their mother and father. "We're awfully glad we came to St Rollo's," wrote Mike. "It's such fun to be with boys and girls together, and as Janet is in my form, we are as much together as ever we were. I shouldn't be surprised if she's top one week. The hockey is lovely. I'm good at it. Do send us some chocolate, if you can."

His mother and father smiled at his letters and Janet's. They could see that the two children were happy at the school they had chosen for them and they were glad.

"St Rollo's is fine," wrote Janet. "I *am* glad we came here. We do have fun!"

They certainly did – and they meant to have even more fun very soon!

CHAPTER IV
TOM IS UP TO TRICKS

Tom was always up to tricks. He knew all the usual ones, of course – the trick of covering a bit of paper with ink on one side, and handing it to someone as if it were a note – and then, when they took it they found their fingers all inky! He knew all the different ways of making paper darts. He knew how to flip a pellet of paper from underneath his desk so that it would land exactly where he wanted it to. There was nothing that Tom didn't know, when it came to tricks!

He lasted just four days in his desk at the back. Then Miss Thomas put him well in the front!

"I thought you wouldn't last a week at the back there," she said. "I feel much more comfortable with you just under my eye! Ah – that's better. Now I think you will find it quite difficult to fire off your paper pellets at children who are really trying to work."

The trick that had made Miss Thomas move him had caused the class a good deal of merriment. Miss Thomas had written history questions on the board for the form to answer in writing. Janet was hard at work answering them, for she wanted to get good marks, and Mike was working well too.

Suddenly Janet felt a nudge. She looked up. Tom had already finished answering the questions, though Janet felt certain that he had put "I don't know" to some of them! Tom nodded his head towards the window.

Janet looked there. Just outside was one of the gardeners, hard at work in a bed. He was a large man, red-faced, with a very big nose.

"What about giving old Nosey a shock?" said Tom, opening his desk to speak behind it. Janet nodded gleefully. She didn't know what Tom meant to do, but she was sure it would be funny.

Tom hunted in his desk till he found what he wanted. It was a piece of clay. The boy shut his desk and warmed the clay in his hands below it. It soon became soft and he picked off pieces to make hard pellets.

Janet and Mike watched him. Miss Thomas looked up. "Janet! Michael! Tom! Have you all finished your history questions? Then get out your text-book and learn the list of answers on page 23."

The children got out their books. Tom winked at Janet. He waited until Miss Thomas was standing at Fred's desk, with her back turned to him, and then, very deftly, he flicked the clay pellet out of the open window with his thumb.

It hit the gardener on the top of his hat. He thought something had fallen on him from above and he stood up, raising his head to the sky, as if he thought it must be raining. Janet gave a muffled giggle.

"Shut up," whispered Tom. He waited till the man had bent down again, and his big nose presented a fine target. Flick! A big pellet flew straight out of the window – and this time it hit the astonished man right on the tip of his nose, with a smart tap.

He stood up straight, rubbing his nose, glaring into the window. But all he saw were bent heads and innocent faces, though one little girl was certainly smiling very broadly to herself. That was Janet, of course. She simply could *not* keep her mouth from smiling!

The gardener muttered something to himself, glared at the bent heads, and bent over his work again. Tom waited his chance and neatly flicked out another pellet. It hit the man smartly on the cheek, and he gave a cry of pain.

All the children looked up. Miss Thomas gazed in surprise at the open window, outside which the gardener was standing.

"Now, look here!" said the angry man, staring in at the window. "Which of you did that? Hitting me in the face with peas or something! Where's your teacher?"

"I'm here," said Miss Thomas. "What is the matter? I don't think any of the children here have been playing tricks. You must have made a mistake. Please don't disturb the class."

"Made a mistake! Do you suppose I don't know when anyone is flicking peas or something at me?" said the gardener. He glared at Janet, who was giggling. 'Yes – and that's the girl who did it, too, if you ask *me*! She was giggling to herself before – and I'm pretty certain I saw her doing it."

"That will do, gardener," said Miss Thomas. "I will deal with the matter myself. I am sorry you have been hindered in your work."

She shut down the window. The man went off, grumbling. Miss Thomas looked at Janet, who was very red.

"Kindly leave the gardeners to do their work, Janet," she said in a cold voice. "Bring your things out of your desk, and put them in the empty front one. You had better sit there, I think."

Janet didn't know what to say. She couldn't give Tom away, and if she said she hadn't done it, Miss Thomas would ask who did, and then Tom would get into trouble. So, with a lip that quivered, Janet opened her desk and began to get out her things.

Tom spoke up at once. "It wasn't Janet," he said. "I did it. I didn't like the look of the gardener's nose – so I just hit it with a clay pellet or two, Miss Thomas. I'm sure you would have liked to do it yourself, Miss Thomas, if you had seen that big nose out there."

Everyone choked with laughter. Miss Thomas didn't even smile. She looked straight at Tom with cold eyes.

"I hope my manners are better than yours," she said. "If not, I don't know what I should feel inclined to do to you, Tom Young. Bring your things out here, please. You will be under my eye in future."

So, with many soft groans, Tom left his seat at the back beside Janet, and went to the front.

"Oh, what a pity," said Janet, later on, as the class was waiting for Monsieur Crozier to come. "Now you won't be able to do any more tricks, Tom. You're right at the front."

"Goodness, you don't think that will stop Tom, do you?" said Fred. And Fred was right. It didn't!

Monsieur Crozier was not a very good person to play about with, because he had such a hot temper. The class never knew how he was going to take a joke. Sometimes, if Tom or Marian said something sharp, he would throw back his grey head and roar with laughter. Yet at other times he could not see a joke at all, but would fly into a temper.

Few people dared to play tricks on the French master, but Tom, of course, didn't care what he did. One morning, Janet and Mike found him kneeling down in a far corner of the room, behind the teacher's desk. In this corner stood two or three rolled-up maps. Tom was hiding something behind the maps.

"Whatever are you doing?" asked Janet in surprise. Tom grinned.

"Preparing a little surprise packet for dear Monsieur Crozier," he said.

"What is it?" said Mike, peering down.

"Quite simple," said Tom. "Look – I've got two empty cotton-reels here – and I've tied thin black thread to each. If you follow the thread you'll see it runs behind this cupboard – behind that book-case, over the hot-water pipe, and up to my desk. Now, what will happen when I pull the threads?"

The cotton-reels will dance in their corner!" giggled Janet, "and Monsieur Crozier won't know what the noise is – because it's far from where anyone sits! What fun!"

Mike told everyone what was going to happen. It was a small trick, but might be very funny. The whole class was thrilled. In the French lesson that day they were to recite their French verbs, which was a very dull thing to do. Now it looked as if the lesson wouldn't be so dull, after all.

Monsieur Crozier came into the room, his spectacles on his nose. His thick hair was untidy. It was plain that he had been in a temper with somebody, for it was his habit to ruffle his hair whenever he was angry. It stood up well, and the class smiled to see it.

"*Asseyez-vous!*" rapped out Monsieur Crozier, and the class sat down at once. In clear French sentences the master told them what he expected of them. Each child was to stand in turn and recite the French verb he had been told to learn, and the others were to write them out.

"And this morning I expect HARD WORK!" said the French master. "I have had disgraceful work from the third form – disgrrrrrrraceful! I will not put up with the same thing from you. You understand?"

"Yes, Monsieur Crozier," chanted the class. Monsieur Crozier looked at Tom, who had on a most innocent expression that morning.

"And you, too, will work!" he said. "It is not necessary always to be bottom. If you had no brains I would say 'Ah, the poor boy – he cannot work'. But you have brains and you will not use them. That is bad, very bad."

"Yes, sir," said Tom. Monsieur Crozier gave a grunt and sat down. Fred stood up to recite his verbs. The rest of the class bent over their desks to write them.

They were all listening for Tom to begin his trick. He did nothing at first, but waited until Fred had sat down. There was silence for a moment, whilst the French master marked Fred's name in his book.

Then Tom pulled at the threads which ran to his desk. At once the cotton-reels over in the far corner began to jiggle like mad. Jiggle, jiggle, jiggle! they went. Jiggle, jiggle, jiggle!

Monsieur Crozier looked up, puzzled. He didn't quite know where the noise came from. He stared round at the quiet class. Everyone's head was bent low, for most of the children were trying to hide their smiles. Janet felt a giggle coming and she shut her mouth hard. She was a terrible giggler. Mike looked at her anxiously. Janet so often gave the game away by exploding into a tremendous laugh.

The noise stopped. Doris stood up to say her verbs. She was quite perfect in them. She sat down. Monsieur Crozier marked her name. Tom pulled at the threads and the cotton-reels jerked madly about behind the maps.

"What is that noise?" said the master impatiently, looking round. "Who makes that noise?"

"What noise, sir?" asked Tom innocently. "Is there a noise? I heard an aeroplane pass over just now."

"An aeroplane does not make a noise in this room!" said the master. "It is a jiggling noise. Who is doing it?"

"A jiggling noise, sir?" said Mike, looking surprised. "What sort of jiggling noise? My desk is a bit wobbly, sir – perhaps it's that you heard?"

Mike wobbled his desk and made a terrific noise. Everyone laughed.

"Enough!" cried Monsieur Crozier, rapidly losing his temper. "It is not your desk I mean. Silence! We will listen for the noise together."

There was a dead silence. Tom did not pull the threads. There was no noise at all.

But as soon as Eric was standing up, reciting his verbs in his soft voice, Tom jerked hard at his threads, and the reels did a kind of fox-trot behind the maps, sounding quite loud on the boards.

"There is that noise again!" said the master angrily. "Silence, Eric. Listen!"

Tom could not resist making the reels dance again as everyone listened. Jiggle-jiggle-jiggle-tap-tap-tap-jiggle-jiggle they went, and the class began to giggle.

"It comes from behind those maps," said the French master, puzzled. "It is very strange."

"Mice perhaps, sir," said Mike. Tom flashed him a grin. Mike was playing up well.

The French master did not like mice. He stared at the maps, annoyed. He did not see how the noise could possibly be a trick, for the maps were far from any child's desk.

"Shall I see, sir?" asked Tom, getting up. "I don't mind mice a bit. I think Mike may be right, sir. It certainly does sound like a mouse caught behind there. Shall I look, sir?"

Now, what Tom thought he would do was to look behind the maps, pocket the reels quickly after pulling the threads away, and then announce that there was no mouse there. But when he got to the corner, he couldn't resist carrying the trick a bit further. "I'll pretend there really *is* a mouse!" he thought. "That'll give the class a real bit of fun!"

So, when he knelt down and fiddled about behind the maps, pulling away the threads and getting hold of the cotton-reels, he suddenly gave a yell that made everyone jump, even the French master.

"It's a mouse! It's a mouse! Come here, you bad little thing! Sir, it's a mouse!"

The class knew perfectly well it wasn't. Janet gave a loud, explosive giggle that she tried hastily to turn into a cough. Even the surly Hugh smiled.

Tom knocked over all the maps, pretending to get the mouse. Then he made it seem as if the little creature had run into the classroom, and he jumped and bounded after the imaginary mouse, crawling under desks and nearly pulling a small table on top of him The whole class exploded into a gale of laughter that drowned Monsieur Crozier's angry voice.

"Come here, you!" yelled Tom, thoroughly enjoying himself. "Ah – got you! No, I haven't! Just touched your tail. Ah, there you are again. Whoops! Nearly got you that time. What a mouse! Oh, what a mouse! Whoops, there you go again!"

Mike got out of his desk to join him. The two boys capered about on hands and knees and nearly drove Monsieur Crozier mad. He hammered on his desk. But it was quite impossible for the class to be silent. They laughed till their sides ached.

And in the middle of it all Miss Thomas walked in, furious! She had been taking the class next door, and could not imagine what all the noise was. She had felt certain that no teacher was with the second form. She stopped in surprise when she saw Monsieur Crozier there, red in the face with fury.

The class stopped giggling when they saw Miss Thomas. She had a way of giving out rather unpleasant punishments, and the class somehow felt that she would not readily believe in their mouse.

"I'm sorry, Monsieur Crozier," said Miss Thomas. "I thought you couldn't be here."

"Miss Thomas, I dislike your class," said Monsieur Crozier, quite as ready to fly into a temper with Miss Thomas as with the children. "They are ill-disciplined, ill-behaved, ill-mannered. See how they chase a mouse round your classroom! Ah, the bad children!"

"A mouse!" said Miss Thomas, in the utmost surprise. "But how could that be? There are no mice in the school. The school cats see to that. Has anyone got a tame mouse then?"

"No, Miss Thomas," chorused the children together.

"We heard a noise behind the maps," began Tom – but Miss Thomas silenced him with a look.

"Oh, you did, did you?" she said. "You may as well know that I don't believe in your mouse, Tom. I will speak to you all at the beginning of the next lesson. Pardon me for coming in like this, Monsieur Crozier. I apologise also for my class."

The class felt a little subdued. The French master glared at them, and proceeded to give them so much homework that they would have groaned if they had dared. Tom got shouted at when he opened his mouth to protest. After that, he said no more. Monsieur Crozier was dangerous when he got as far as shouting!

Miss Thomas was very sarcastic about the whole affair when she next saw her class. She flatly refused to believe in the mouse, but instead, asked who had gone to examine the noise in the corner.

"I did," said Tom, who always owned up to anything, quite fearlessly.

"I thought so," said Miss Thomas. "Well, you will write me an essay, four pages long, on the habits of mice, Tom. Give it in to me this evening."

"But, Miss Thomas," began Tom, "you know it's the hockey-match this afternoon, and we're all watching it, and after tea there's a concert."

"That doesn't interest me at all," said Miss Thomas. "What interests me intensely at the moment is the habits of mice, and that being so, I insist on having that essay by seven o'clock. Not another word, Tom, unless you also want to write me an essay on, let us say, cotton-reels. I am not quite so innocent as Monsieur Crozier."

After that there was no more to be said. Mike and Janet gave up watching the hockey match in order to help Tom with his essay. Mike looked up the habits of mice, and Janet looked up the spelling of the words. With many groans and sighs Tom managed to write four pages in his largest handwriting by seven o'clock. "It *is* decent of you to help," he said gratefully.

"Well, we shared the fun, didn't we?" said Mike. "So we must share the punishment too!"

CHAPTER V
AN EXCITING IDEA

In the middle of that term Mike's birthday came. He was very much looking forward to it because he knew he would have plenty of presents sent to him, and he hoped his mother would let him have a fine birthday cake.

"I hope it won't be broken in pieces before it arrives," he said to Janet. "You know, Fred had a birthday last term, and he said his cake came in crumbs, and they had to eat it with a spoon. I'd better warn Mother to pack it very carefully."

But Mother didn't risk packing one. She wrote to Mike and told him to order himself a cake from the big cake shop in the town near by. "And if you would like to give a small party to your own special friends, do so," she said. " You can order what you like in the way of food and drink, and tell the shop to send me the bill. I can trust you not to be too extravagant, I know. Have a good time, and be sure your birthday cake has lots of icing on."

Mike was delighted. He showed the letter to Tom. "Isn't Mother decent?" he said. "Can you come down to the town with Janet and me today, Tom, and help me to order things?"

You're not going to ask all the boys and girls in the class to share your party, are you?" said Tom. "You know, that would cost your mother a small fortune."

"Would it?" said Mike. "Well – what shall I do, then? How shall I choose people without making the ones left out feel hurt?"

"Well, if I were you, I'd just ask the boys in your own dormitory, and the girls in Janet's," said Tom. "That will be quite enough children."

"Yes, that's a good idea," said Mike, pleased. "I wish we could have our party in a separate room, so that the others we haven't asked won't have to see us eating the birthday cake and the other things. That would make me feel rather mean."

"Well, listen," said Tom, looking excited. "Why not have a midnight feast? We haven't had one for two terms. It's about time we did."

"A midnight feast!" said Janet, her eyes nearly popping out of her head. "Oooh, that would be marvellous. I've read about them in books. Oh Mike, *do* let's have your party in the middle of the night. Do, do!"

Mike didn't need much pressing. He was just as keen on the idea as Janet and Tom. The three of them began to talk excitedly about what they would do.

"Shall we have it in one of our dormitories?" said Janet. "Yours or mine, Mike?"

"No," said Tom at once. "Mr Wills sleeps in the room next to ours – and Miss Thomas sleeps in the room next to yours, Janet. Either of them might hear us making a noise and come and find us."

"We needn't make a noise," said Janet. "We could just eat and drink."

"Janet! You couldn't possibly last an hour or two without going off into one of your giggling fits, you know you couldn't," said Mike. "And you make an awful noise with your first giggle. It's like an explosion."

"I know," said Janet. "I can't help it. I smother it till I almost burst – and then it comes out all of a sudden. Well – if we don't have the feast in one of our dormitories, where *shall* we have it?"

They all thought hard. Then Tom gave a grin. "I know the very place. What about the gardeners' shed?"

"The gardeners' shed!" said Mike and Janet together. "But why there?"

"Well, because it's out of the school and we can make a noise," said Tom. "And because it's not far from the little side-door we use when we go to the playing fields. We can easily slip down and open it to go out. And also, it would be a fine place to store the food in. We can put it into boxes and cover them with sacks."

"Yes – it does sound rather good," said Mike. "It would be marvellous to be out of the school building, because I'm sure we'd make a noise."

"Last time we had a midnight feast, we had it in a dormitory," said Tom. "And in the middle someone dropped a ginger-beer bottle. We got so frightened at the noise that we all hopped into bed, and the feast was spoilt. If we hold ours in the shed, we shan't be afraid of anyone coming. Let's!"

So it was decided to hold it there. Then the next excitement was going down to the town to buy the food.

They went to the big cake shop first. Mike said what he wanted. "I want a big birthday cake made," he said. "Enough for about twelve people, please. And I want it to be covered with pink icing, and written on it in white I'd like 'A happy birthday'. Can you do that?"

"Certainly," said the shopgirl, and wrote down Mike's name, and his mother's address, so that she might send her the bill. Then Mike turned to the others. "What else shall we have?" he said. "You help me to choose."

So Janet and Tom obligingly helped him, and between them they chose chocolate cakes, biscuits, shortbread and currant buns. Then they went to the grocer and asked for tinned sweetened milk, which everyone loved, sardines, tinned pineapple, and bottles of ginger-beer.

"I hope Mother won't think I've spent too much," said Mike anxiously. "But if she thinks I have, I'll give her some of my birthday money towards the bill. I'm sure to get some."

The shop promised to pack up the goods and have them ready for the children to collect on the morning of Mike's birthday. The children meant to go down immediately after morning school and fetch the things.

They felt very excited. Janet and Mike counted up the cakes and things they had ordered and felt sure they had bought enough to feed everyone very well indeed.

"And now we'll have to ask everyone," said Mike happily. "Isn't it fun to invite people, Janet?"

"I'll ask the girls in my dorm tonight," said Janet. "The rest of the class won't be there then, so they won't know. I vote we don't tell anyone except our guests that we're going to have a feast. We don't want it to get to the ears of any of the teachers. Tell the boys in your dorm to keep it quiet, Mike."

"Right," said Mike. Then he frowned. "I say, Janet," he said, "what about Hugh? Are we to ask him?"

Janet stared at Mike. She didn't know what to say. "Well, I suppose we'd better," she said at last. "It would be rather awful to leave him out as he belongs to your dormitory. No one likes him – but still he'd feel simply awful if he knew we were having a feast and hadn't been asked."

"All right," said Mike. "I'll ask him. But he's such a surly fellow that he'll be an awful wet blanket."

Tom agreed that Hugh must be asked too. "I don't want him," he said, "but, after all, he belongs to our dorm, and it would make him feel pretty dreadful to be left out when everyone else is going."

So Mike quite meant to ask Hugh too. But then, something happened to make him change his mind. It had to do with Tom, and it happened in Mr Wills's class.

Mr Wills was taking maths with the second form. Tom was bored. He hated maths, and seldom got a sum right. Mr Wills had almost given him up. So long as Tom sat quietly at his desk and didn't disturb the others, Mr Wills left him in peace. But if Tom got up to any tricks Mr Wills pounced on him.

Tom usually behaved himself in the maths class, for he respected Mr Wills, and knew that he would stand no nonsense. But that morning he was restless. He had slept very well the night before and was so full of beans that he could hardly sit still. He had prepared a trick for the French master in the next lesson, and was longing to play it.

The trick was one of his string tricks. He was marvellous at those. He had slipped into the classroom before school that morning and had neatly tied strong yellow thread to the pegs that held the blackboard on its easel. A jerk at the thread, and a peg would come out – and down would crash the blackboard!

Tom looked at Mr Wills. Mr Wills caught his eye and frowned. "Get on, Tom," he said. "Don't slack so. If you can't get a sum right, get it wrong. Then, at least, I shall know you've been doing something."

"Yes, Mr Wills," said Tom meekly. He scribbled down a few figures that meant nothing at all. His hand itched to pull away the peg. As his desk was at the front, he could easily leap forward and pick up the peg before Mr Wills could see that string was tied to it.

"It's a bit dangerous to try it on with Mr Wills," thought Tom. "But I'm so bored I must do something!"

He turned round and caught Mike's eye. Mike winked. Tom winked back. Then he winked twice with each eye in turn. That was his signal to Mike that a trick was about to be played. Mike nudged Janet. They both looked up eagerly. Hugh caught their eager looks and wondered what was up. He guessed that Tom was about to pay a trick and he watched him.

Mr Wills was at the back of the room, looking at Bertha's work. Tom jerked his thread. The peg of the easel flew out – one side of the blackboard slipped down – and then it fell with a resounding crash on to the floor, making everyone jump violently. Mike and Janet knew what had happened, and they tried not to laugh. Hugh also saw what had happened. Before anyone could do anything Tom was out of his desk in a flash, and had picked up the blackboard and peg and set them back in place. He wondered whether or not to remove the threads, but decided he would risk it again.

"Thank you, Tom," said Mr Wills, who hadn't for a moment guessed that it was a trick. "Get on with your work, everybody."

Most of the children guessed that it was Tom up to his tricks again. They watched to see if it would happen once more. Mr Wills went to see Hugh's work. He had done most of his sums wrong, and the master grumbled at him.

"You haven't been trying! What have you been thinking of to put down this sum like that! No one else in the class has so many sums wrong!"

Hugh flushed. He always hated being grumbled at in front of anyone. "I'm sure Tom has more sums wrong than I have," he said, in a low voice.

At that moment Tom jerked the two pegs neatly out of the easel, and the board fell suddenly, with an even greater crash than before. Everyone giggled, and Janet gave one of her explosions. The noise she made caused the children to laugh even more loudly.

"What's the matter with the board this morning?" said Mr Wills irritably.

"I should think Tom has something to do with it," said Hugh spitefully. "You'll find he hasn't got a single sum right – and has given all his attention to our blackboard instead. I have at least been working!"

There was a silence. Mr Wills went to the blackboard. He examined the pegs. But they now had no thread on them, for Tom had slipped it off and it was safely in his pockets.

But not very safely, after all! Mr Wills turned to Tom. "Just turn out your pockets, please," he ordered. Tom obeyed promptly – and there on the desk lay the tell-tale yellow thread, still with the little slipknots at one end.

"I'll see you after the class, Tom," said Mr Wills. "I can't make you do good work – but I can at least stop you from preventing the others from working. You should know by now that I don't stand any nonsense in my classes."

"Yes sir," said Tom dolefully.

"Maths is a most important subject," went on Mr Wills. "Some of the children here are working for scholarships and it is necessary they should get on well this term. If you disturb my classes once more I shall refuse to have you in them."

"Yes, sir," said Tom again, going red. Mr Wills had a very rough tongue. When the master had turned his back on the class to write something on the now steady blackboard, Tom turned round to get the comfort of a look from Mike and Janet. They nodded at him – and then Tom caught sight of Hugh's spiteful face.

Hugh wore a spiteful grin on his face. He was pleased to have got Tom into trouble.

"Sneak!" whispered Mike to Hugh.

"SILENCE!" said Mr Wills, not turning round. Mike said no more, but gave Hugh a look that said all his tongue longed to say!

"Wait till after school!" said the look. "Just wait till after school!"

CHAPTER VI
MIDNIGHT FEAST!

Tom got a tremendous scolding after class, and entered the French class four minutes late, with a very red face. Monsieur Crozier looked at him in surprise.

"And why are you so late?" he said. "It is not the custom to walk into my classes after they have started."

"Please, sir, I'm sorry," said Tom, "but Mr Wills was talking to me."

The French master guessed that Tom had been up for a scolding, and he said no more. Tom was very subdued that lesson. Mr Wills had said some cutting things to him, and the boy felt rather ashamed of himself. It was all very well to play tricks and have a good time – but there *was* work to do as well. So he sat like a lamb in the French class, and really listened to the lesson.

After school, Mike, Janet and Fred went after Hugh.

"Sneak!" said Mike furiously. "What did you want to go and give Tom away for?"

"Why shouldn't I?" said Hugh. "He sneaked on me last term."

"No, he didn't," said Mike. "He says he didn't – and you know as well as anybody that Tom's truthful. He doesn't tell lies. You're a beastly sneak!"

"Oh shut up," said Hugh rudely, and walked off. But the others walked after him, telling him all kinds of truthful but horrid things about himself. Hugh went into a music-room to practise and banged the door. He even turned the key in the lock.

"He really is a spiteful sneak," said Janet. "Mike, you're surely not going to ask him to our feast now, are you?"

"You bet I'm not," said Mike. "As if I'd have a sneaky creature like that on my birthday night! No fear!"

"Well, we'll ask all the others, and we'll warn them not to say a word to Hugh," said Janet. So they asked everyone else – Fred, Eric, small George, Marian, Bertha, Connie, Audrey and Doris. With Mike, Janet and Tom there would be eleven children altogether.

"And don't say a single word to anyone outside our dormitories," said Mike. "And don't say anything to Hugh, either. He's such a sneak that I'm not asking him. I'm sure if he got to know we were having a feast he'd prowl round and then tell about it, So, not a word, mind!"

Nobody said anything to Hugh. They were all excited about the feast, but what whispering they did was only done when Hugh was not there. They could talk freely about it when they went for walks, and it was then that all the plans were made.

Mike's birthday came. He had a lot of cards and many presents. A good deal of it was money and he meant to spend it in the holidays. His mother and father sent him a new paint-box and pencil-box with his name on them. His grandfather wrote to say that he had bought him a new bicycle, Janet gave him a box of writing-paper and stamps. The others gave him small presents – pencils, rubbers, sweets, and so on. Mike was very happy.

"After school, we'll pop down with baskets and get all those things," he said. "We'd better ask one or two of the others to come too. We'll never be able to carry all the stuff ourselves."

So Fred and Marian came too, and the five set off with giggles and talk. They came back with all the food and drink, and undid the birthday cake in the gardeners' shed. It was simply marvellous.

"A happy birthday" was written across it, and the pink icing was thick and not too hard. It was a fine big cake. The children were delighted. Mike put it carefully back into its box.

The gardeners' shed was a big place. It was piled with boxes, tools, pots, wood and so on. Actually it was not much used, for the gardeners had another, smaller shed they preferred, and they used the big shed mostly as a store-house. The children soon found a good hiding-place for their food and drink.

There was an enormous old crate, made of wood, at the back of the shed. They put everything into this and then put a board on top. On the board they piled rows of flower pots.

"There," said Mike. "I don't think anyone would guess what is under those pots! Now, let's arrange what we're going to sit on."

There were plenty of boxes and big flower pots. The children pulled them out and arranged them to sit on.

"We shall have to pin sacks across the windows," said Mike. "Else the light of our candles will be seen."

"Better do that this evening," said Tom. "It might make people suspicious if they came by and saw sacks across the windows."

So they left the windows uncurtained. There was nothing else they could do except smuggle in a few mugs and plates and spoons. Janet said she could do this with Marian. She knew where the school crockery was kept, and she could easily slip into the big cupboard after handwork that afternoon and get what was needed. They could wash it after the feast and put it back again.

"I think that's everything," said Mike happily. "I say – this is going to be fun, isn't it! Golly, I can hardly wait till tonight!"

The children felt sure they couldn't go to sleep that night. They had planned not to get up until midnight, because very often Mr Wills worked till half-past eleven, and they didn't want to bump into him as he was coming up to bed next door!

"I'll wake the girls in my dorm," said Janet, "and you wake the boys, Mike. Don't wake Hugh by mistake, though!"

Everything went off as planned. Janet fell asleep, but awoke just before midnight. She switched on her torch and looked at her watch. Five minutes to twelve! She slipped out of bed, put on shoes, stockings, vest, under her nightdress, and jersey over it. Then her dressing-gown on top. She woke the other girls one by one, shaking them and whispering into their ears.

"It's time! Wake up! The midnight feast is about to begin!"

The girls awoke, and sat up, thrilled. They began to put on vests and jerseys too. Meanwhile the boys were doing the same thing. Mike had awoken them all, except, of course, Hugh, and in silence they were dressing. They did not dare to whisper, as the girls could, because they were afraid of waking Hugh.

They all crept out of the dormitory, and found the six girls waiting for them in the passage outside. Janet was trying to stop her giggles.

"For goodness' sake don't do one of your explosions till we're out in the shed," said Mike anxiously. So Janet bit her lips together and waited. They all went down the stairs and out of the little side-door. Then across to the big shed. Mike opened the door and everyone filed in. Once the door was shut, the children felt safe and began to talk in loud whispers.

Mike and Tom quickly put sacks across the three windows, and then lighted three candles. Their wavering light made strange shadows in the shed, and everything looked rather mysterious and exciting. The other children watched Mike and Tom go to the box at the back and lift off the flower pots arranged there.

And then out came the good things to eat and drink. How the children gaped for joy to see them. They all felt terribly hungry, and were pleased to see so much to eat and drink.

Mike set the birthday cake down on a big box. All the children crowded round to look at it. They thought it was marvellous. "We'll cut it the very last thing," said Mike. "And don't forget to wish, everybody, because it's a birthday cake!"

They made a start on sardines and cake. It was a lovely mixture. Then they went on to currant buns and biscuits, pineapple and tinned milk. They chattered in low voices and giggled to their hearts' content. When Fred fell off his box and upset tinned, sticky milk all over himself, there was a gale of laughter. Fred looked so funny with his legs in the air, and milk dripping all over him!

"Sh! Sh!" said Tom.
"Honestly, we'll wake up the whole school! Shut up, Janet! Your giggles make everyone worse still. You just make me want to giggle myself."

That was the worst of Janet's giggles. They set everyone giggling, too. Janet tried to stop – and then she got hiccups. That made her giggle again, and every time she stopped, she gave a loud hiccup. The eleven children held their sides and laughed till they ached.

"This is the best feast we've ever had," said Tom, helping himself to a large piece of chocolate cake. "Any more ginger-pop, Mike?"

"Yes," said Mike. "Help yourself – and now, what about cutting the grand birthday cake?"

"It looks big enough for the whole school," giggled Marian. "I say – I wish Hugh knew what he was missing! Wouldn't he be wild! I expect he is still sound asleep in his bed."

But Hugh wasn't. He had awakened about half-past twelve, and had turned over to go to sleep again.

And then something strange had struck him. There was something missing in the dormitory. It was quite dark there and the boy could see nothing. But he lay there, half-asleep, wondering what was missing.

Then he suddenly knew. There was no steady breathing to be heard. There was no sound at all. Hugh sat up, alarmed. Why was nobody breathing? That was the usual sound to be heard at night, if anyone woke up. What had happened?

Hugh switched on his torch and got out of bed. He looked round the curtains that separated his cubicle from the next boy's. The bed was empty!

Hugh looked at all the beds. Every one was empty. Then the boy guessed in a flash what was happening.

"It's Mike's birthday – and he's having a midnight party somewhere. The beast! He's asked everyone else, and not me! I bet Janet's dormitory is empty too."

He slipped out to see. It was as he had guessed – quite empty. All the beds were bare, their coverings turned back. The boy felt angry and hurt. They might have asked him. It was hateful to be left out like this.

"I'm always left out of everything!" he thought, hot tears pricking his eyelids. "Always! Do they think it will make me behave any better to them if they treat me like this? How I hate them! I'll jolly well spoil their feast for them. That will serve them right!"

CHAPTER VII
A SHOCK FOR THE FEASTERS

Hugh wondered how to spoil the feast. Should he go and knock on Mr Wills's door and tell him that the dormitories were empty? No – Mr Wills didn't look too kindly on tale-bearing. Well, then, he had better find out where the children were feasting and spoil it for them. He looked out of the window, and by chance he caught sight of a tiny flicker outside. It came from a corner of the big window of the shed. The sack didn't quite cover the glass.

Hugh stood and looked at it, wondering where the light came from.

"It's from the big shed," he thought. "So that's where they're feasting. I'll go down and find out!"

Down he went, out of the door, which the children had left open, and into the yard. He went across to the shed, and at once heard the sounds of laughter and whispering inside. He put his eye to the place in the window where the light showed, and saw the scene inside. It was a very merry one.

Fred was acting the donkey, as he knew very well how to, and everyone was laughing at him. All the children had enormous slices of birthday cake in their hands. It made Hugh hungry to see them!

Empty bottles of ginger-beer lay around. Empty tins stood here and there, and crumbs were all over the place. It was plain that the two dormitories had had a marvellous time. Hugh's heart burned in him. He felt so angry and so miserable that he could almost have gone into the shed and fought every child there!

But he didn't do that. He knew it would be no use. Instead, he took up a large stone and crashed it on to the window! The glass broke at once, with a very loud noise. All the children inside the shed jumped up in a fright, their cake falling from their fingers.

"What's that?" said Mike in a panic. "The window is broken. Who did it?"

There was another crash as the second window broke under Hugh's stone. The children were now really afraid. They simply couldn't imagine what was happening.

"The noise will wake everyone up!" cried Mike, in a loud whisper. "Quick, we'd better get back to our dormitories. Leave everything. There isn't time to clear up."

Hugh didn't wait to break the third window. He had seen a light spring up in Mr Wills's room above and he knew the master would be out to see what was happening before another minute had gone by. So he sped lightly up the stairs, and was in his bed before the door of Mr Wills's room opened.

The eleven children opened the door of the shed and fled into the school. They went up the stairs and into the passage where their dormitories were – and just as they were passing Mr Wills's door it opened. Mr Wills stood there in his dressing-gown, staring in amazement at the procession of white-faced children slipping by.

"What are you doing?" he asked. "What was all that noise?"

The children didn't wait to answer. They fled into their rooms and hopped into bed, half-dressed as they were, shoes and all. Mr Wills went into the boys' dormitory, switched on the light and looked sternly round. He pulled back the curtains from those cubicles that had them drawn around, and spoke angrily.

"What is the meaning of this? Where have you been? Answer me!"

Nobody answered. The boys were really frightened.

Hugh's bed was nearest to Mr Wills, and the master took hold of Hugh's shoulder, shaking him upright.

"You, boy! Answer me! What have you been doing?"

"Sir, I've been in bed all the evening," said Hugh truthfully. "I don't know what the others have been doing. I wasn't with them."

Mr Wills glared round at the other beds. "I can see that you are half-dressed," he said in an icy voice. "Get out and undress, and then get back into bed. I shall want an explanation of this in the morning. You can tell the girls, when you see them, that I shall want them too. It seems to me that this is something the Heads should know about. Now then – quick – out of bed and undress!"

The boys, all but Hugh, got out of bed and took off their jerseys and other things. Mr Wills told Hugh to get out of bed too.

"But I'm not half-dressed," said Hugh. "I've only got my pyjamas on, sir. I wasn't with the others."

But Mr Wills wasn't believing anyone at all that night. He made Hugh get out too, and saw that he was in his pyjamas as he said. He did not notice one thing – and that was that Hugh had his shoes on! But Mike noticed it.

He was puzzled. Why should Hugh have his shoes on in bed? That was a funny thing to do, surely. And then the boy suddenly guessed the reason.

"Hugh woke up – saw the beds were empty – put on his shoes and slipped down to find us. It was he who broke the windows, the beast! He's got us all into this trouble!"

But he said nothing then. He would tell the others in the morning. He slipped back into bed and tried to go to sleep.

All the eleven children were worried when the morning came. They couldn't imagine what Mr Wills was going to do. They soon found out. Mr Wills had gone to the two Heads, and it was they that the children were to see, not Mr Wills. This was worse than ever!

"You will go now," said Mr Wills, after prayers were over. " I don't want to hear any explanations from you. You can tell those to the Heads. But I may as well tell you that I went down into the shed last night and found the remains of your feast, the candles burning – and the windows smashed. I understand the feast part – but why you should smash the windows is beyond me. I am ashamed of you all."

"We didn't smash . . ." began Mike. But Mr Wills wouldn't listen to a word. He waved them all away. Hugh had to go, too, although he kept saying that he hadn't been with the others. Mike had told the others what he suspected about Hugh, and every boy and girl looked at him with disgust and dislike.

They went to see the Heads. Their knees shook, and Bertha began to cry. Even Janet felt the tears coming. All the children were tired, and some of them had eaten too much and didn't feel well.

The Heads looked stern. They asked a few questions, and then made Tom tell the whole story.

"I can understand your wanting to have some sort of a party on Michael's birthday," said Miss Lesley, "but to end it by smashing windows is disgusting behaviour. It shows a great lack of self-control."

"I think it was Hugh who broke the windows," said Mike, not able to keep it back any longer. "We wouldn't have done that, Miss Lesley. For one thing we would have been afraid of being caught if we did that – it made such a noise. But, you see, we left Hugh out of the party – and I think that out of spite he smashed the windows to give us a shock, and to make sure we would be caught."

"Did you do that, Hugh?" asked the headmaster, looking at the red-faced boy.

"No, sir," said Hugh, in a low voice. "I was in bed asleep. I don't know anything about it."

"Well, then, why was it you had your shoes on in bed when Mr Wills made you get out last night?" burst out Tom. "Mike saw them!"

Hugh said nothing, but looked obstinate. He meant to stick to his story.

The punishment was very just. "As you have missed almost a night's sleep, you will all go to bed an hour earlier for a week," said Miss Lesley.

"And you will please pay for the mending of the windows," said the headmaster. "You too, Hugh. I am not going to go into the matter of how the windows got broken — but I think Michael is speaking the truth when he says that he would not have thought of smashing windows because of the noise. All the same, you will all twelve of you share for the mending of the windows. I will deduct it from your pocket-money."

"And please remember, children, that although it is good to have fun, you are sent here to work and to learn things that will help you to earn your living later on," said Miss Lesley. "There are some of you here working for scholarships, and you will not be able to win them if you behave like this."

The children went out, feeling very miserable. It was hateful to go to bed early — earlier even than the first formers. And they felt bitter about the payment for the windows, because they themselves had not broken them.

"Though if we hadn't held the feast, the windows wouldn't have been broken," said Mike. "So in a way it was because of us they got smashed. But I know it was Hugh who did it, out of spite. Let's not say a word to him. Let's send him to Coventry and be as beastly as we can."

So Hugh had a very bad time. He was snubbed by the whole of his class. The first and third formers joined in too, and nobody ever spoke a word to him, unless it was a whispered: "Sneak Tell-tale Sneak!" which made him feel worse than if he had not been spoken to.

He worried very much over the whole thing. It was awful to have no friends, terrible to be treated as if he were a snake. He knew it was stupid and wrong to have broken the windows like that. He had done it in a fit of spiteful temper, and now it couldn't be undone.

He couldn't sleep at night. He rose the next day looking white and tired. He couldn't do his work, and the teachers scolded him, for he was one of the children who were going in for the scholarship. He couldn't remember what he had learnt, and although he spent hours doing his prep, he got poor marks for it.

Hugh knew that he must win the scholarship, for his parents were not well-off and needed help with his schooling. He had brothers and a sister who were very clever, and who had won many scholarships between them. Hugh didn't want to let his family down. He mustn't be the only one who couldn't do anything.

"The worst of it is, I haven't got good brains, as they have," thought the boy, as he tried to learn a list of history dates. "Everything is hard to me. It's easy to them. Daddy and Mother don't realise that. They think I must be as clever as the rest of the family, and I'm not. So they get angry with me when I'm not top of my form, though, goodness knows, I swot hard enough and try to be."

The children all paid between them for the windows. They were mended and the remains of the feast were cleared away. The week went by, and the period for early going to bed passed by too. The children began to forget about the feast and its unfortunate ending. But they didn't forget their dislike for Hugh.

"I shan't speak a word to him for the rest of the term," said Fred. And the others said the same. Only Janet felt sorry for the boy, and noticed how white and miserable he looked. But she had to be loyal to the others, and so she said nothing to him too, and looked away whenever he came near.

"I can't stick this!" Hugh thought to himself. "I simply can't. I wish I could run away! I wish I was old enough to join a ship and go to sea. I hate school! I hate everyone and everything!"

CHAPTER VIII
A SHOCK FOR TOM – AND ONE FOR HUGH

The days slipped by, and each one was full of interest. Janet and Mike liked their work, and loved their play. They loved being friends with Tom, and they liked all the others in their form, except Hugh.

The great excitement now was handwork. The boys were doing carpentering, and the things they were making were really beginning to take shape. The girls were doing raffia-work and were weaving some really lovely baskets. Janet couldn't help gloating over the basket she was making. It was a big work-basket for her mother, in every bright colour Janet could use. Mike was making a very fine pipe-rack for his father.

But the finest thing of all that was being made in the carpentery class was Tom's. The boy was mad on ships, and he had made a beautiful model. He was now doing the rigging, and the slender masts were beginning to look very fine indeed, set with snowy sails and line thread instead of ropes.

There were wide window-sills in the handwork and carpentering room, and on these the children set out their work, so that any other form could see what they were doing. They all took a deep interest in what the others were making. Tom's ship was greatly admired and the boy was really very proud of it.

"I think this is the only class you really work in, Tom, isn't it?" the woodwork master said, bending over Tom's model. "My word, if you worked half as hard in the other classes as you do in mine, you would certainly never be bottom. You're an intelligent boy – yes, very intelligent – and you can use your brains well when you want to."

Tom flushed with pleasure. He gazed at his beautiful ship and his heart swelled with pride as he thought of how it would look on his mantelpiece at home, when it was quite finished. It was almost finished now – he was soon going to paint it. He hoped there would be time to begin the painting that afternoon.

But there wasn't. "Put your things away," said the master. "Hurry, Fred. You mustn't be late for your next class."

The children cleared up, and put their models on the wide window-sills. The master opened the windows to let in fresh air, and then gave the order to file out to the children's own classroom, two floors below. The handwork rooms were at the top of the school, lovely big light rooms, with plenty of sun and air.

The next lesson was geography. Miss Thomas wanted a map that was not in the corner and told Hugh to go and get it from one of the cupboards on the top landing. The children stood up to answer questions whilst Hugh was gone.

In the middle of the questions, something curious happened. A whitish object suddenly fell quickly past the schoolroom windows and landed with a dull thud on to the stone path by the bed. The children looked round in interest. What could it have been? Not a bird, surely.

Mike was next to the window. He peeped out to see what it was – and then he gave a cry of dismay.

"What's the matter?" asked the teacher, startled.

"Oh, Miss Thomas – it looks as if Tom's lovely ship is lying broken on the path outside," said Mike. Tom darted to the window. He gave a wail of dismay.

"It *is* my ship! Somebody has pushed it off the window-sill, and it's smashed. All the rigging is spoilt! The masts are broken!"

The boy's voice trembled, for he had really loved his ship. He had spent so many hours making it. It had been very nearly perfect.

There was a silence in the room. Everyone was shocked, and felt very sorry for Tom. In the middle of the silence the door opened and Hugh came in, carrying the map.

At once the same thought flashed into everyone's mind. Hugh had been to the top of the school to get the map – the cupboard was opposite the woodwork room – and Hugh had slipped in and pushed Tom's ship out of the window to smash it!

"You did it!" shouted Mike. Hugh looked astonished.

"Did what?" he asked.

"Smashed Tom's ship!" cried half a dozen voices.

"I don't know what you're talking about," said Hugh, really puzzled.

"That will do," said Miss Thomas. "Tom, go and collect your ship. It may not be as badly damaged as you think. Hugh, sit down. Do you know anything about the ship?"

"Not a thing," said Hugh. "The door of the woodwork room was shut when I went to get the map."

"Story-teller!" whispered half a dozen children.

"Silence!" rapped out Miss Thomas. She was worried; She knew that Tom had been hated by Hugh ever since last term, and she feared that the boy really had smashed up the ship. She made up her mind to find out about it from Hugh himself after the lesson. She felt sure she would know if the boy were telling her the truth or not, once she really began to question him.

But it was not Miss Thomas that Hugh feared. It was the children! As soon as morning school was over they surrounded him and accused him bitterly, calling him every name they could think of.

"I didn't do it, I didn't do it," said Hugh pushing away the hands that held him. "Don't pin everything on to me simply because I have done one or two mean things. I didn't do that. *I* liked Tom's ship, too."

But nobody believed him. They gave the boy a very bad time, and by the time that six o'clock came, Hugh was so battered by the children's looks and tongues that he crept up to his dormitory to be by himself. Then the tears came and he sobbed to himself, ashamed because he could not stop.

"I'm going away," he said. "I can't stay here now. I'm going home. Daddy and Mother will be angry with me, but I won't come back here. I can't do anything right. I didn't smash that lovely ship. I liked it just as much as the others did."

He began to stuff some of his clothes into a small case. He hardly knew what he was doing. He knew there was a train at a quarter to seven. He would catch that.

The other children wondered where he was. "Good thing for him he's not here," said Fred. "I've thought of a few more names to call him, the horrid beast!"

They were all in their common-room, discussing the affair. Tom's ship stood on the mantelpiece, looking very sorry for itself. The woodwork master came to see it.

"It's not as bad as it might be," he said cheerfully. "Just a bit dented here. Those masts can easily be renewed, and you can do the rigging again. You're good at that. Cheer up, Tom!"

The master went out. "All very well for him to talk like that," said Tom gloomily. "But it isn't his ship. I don't feel the same about it now it's spoilt."

There came a knock at the common-room door. It was such a timid, faint knock that at first none of the children heard it. Then it came again, a little louder.

"There's someone knocking at the door," said Audrey, in astonishment, for no one ever knocked at their door.

"Come in!" yelled the whole form. The door opened and a first former looked in. It was a small boy, with a very white, scared face.

"Hallo, Pete, what's up?" said Fred.

"I w-w-w-want to speak to T-t-t-tom," stammered the small boy, whose knees were knocking together in fright.

"Well, here I am," said Tom. "Don't look so scared. I shan't eat you!"

The small boy opened and shut his mouth like a fish, but not another word came out. The children began to giggle.

"Peter, whatever's the matter?" cried Janet. "Has somebody frightened you?"

"N-n-n-no," stammered Pete. "I want to tell Tom something. But I'm afraid to."

"What is it?" asked Tom kindly. He was always kind to the younger ones, and they all liked him. "What have you been doing? Breaking windows or something?"

"No, Tom — m-m-m-much worse than that," said the boy, looking at Tom with big, scared eyes. "It's — it's about your lovely ship. That ship there," and he pointed to the mantelpiece.

"Well, what about it?" said Tom, thinking that Pete was going to tell him how he had seen Hugh push it out of the window.

"Oh Tom, it was my fault it got broken!" wailed the little boy, breaking into loud sobs. "I was in the woodwork room with Dick Dennison, and we were fooling about. And I fell against the window-sill — and — and . . ."

"Go on," said Tom.

"I put out my hand to save myself," sobbed Pete, "and it struck your lovely ship — and sent it toppling out of the open window. I was so frightened, Tom."

There was a long silence after this speech. So Hugh hadn't anything to do with the ship, after all! No wonder he had denied it so vigorously. All the children stared at the white-faced Pete.

"I d-d-d-didn't dare to tell anyone," went on the small boy. "Dick swore he wouldn't tell either. But then we heard that you had accused Hugh of doing it — and we knew we couldn't do anything but come and own up. So I came because it was me that pushed it out — quite by accident, Tom."

"I see," said Tom slowly. He looked at the scared boy and gave him a kindly push. "All right. Don't worry. You did right to come and tell me. Come straight away another time you do anything, old son — you see, we've done an injustice to somebody else – and that's not good. Go along back to your common-room. I daresay I can manage to mend the ship all right."

The small boy gave Tom a grateful look out of tearful eyes, and shot out of the room at top speed. He tore back to his common-room, feeling as if a great load had been taken off his heart.

When he had gone, the children looked at one another. "Well, it wasn't Hugh after all," said Janet, saying what everyone else was thinking.

"No," said Tom. "It wasn't. And I called him a good many beastly names. For once they were unjust. And I hate injustice."

Everyone felt uncomfortable. "Well, anyway, he's done things just as horrid," said Fred. "It's no wonder we thought it was him. Especially as he just happened to be by the woodwork room at the time."

"Yes," said Mike. "That was unlucky for him. What are we going to do about it?"

Nobody said anything. Nobody wanted to apologise to Hugh. Tom stared out of the window.

"We've got to do something," he said. "Where is he? We'd better find him and get him here, and then tell him we made a mistake. We were ready enough to be beastly – now we must be ready to be sorry."

"I'll go and find him," said Janet. She had remembered Hugh's startled face as the others had suddenly accused him when he had come into the room carrying the map. She thought, too, of his miserable look when they had all pressed round him after tea, calling him horrid names. They had been unjust. Hugh had done many mean things – but not that one. Janet suddenly wanted to say she was sorry.

She sped into the classroom. Hugh wasn't there. She ran to the gym. He wasn't there either. She looked into each music-room, and in the library, where Hugh often went to choose books. But he was nowhere to be found.

"Where can he be?" thought the little girl. "He can't be out. His clothes are hanging up. What has he done with himself?"

She thought of the dormitory. She ran up the stairs, and met Hugh just coming out, carrying a bag, with the marks of tears still on his face. She ran up to him.

"Hugh! Where have you been? What are you doing with that bag? Listen, we want you to come downstairs."

"No, you don't," said Hugh. "You none of you want me. I'm going home."

"Hugh! What do you mean?" cried Janet, in alarm. "Oh, Hugh, listen. We know who broke Tom's ship. It was little Pete. He pushed it out of the window by accident! Don't go home, Hugh. Come down and hear what we have to say!"

CHAPTER IX
THINGS ARE CLEARED UP!

But Hugh pushed past Janet roughly. He did not mean to change his mind. Janet was scared. It seemed a dreadful thing to her that Hugh should run away because of the unkindness he had received from his class. She caught hold of the boy and tried to pull him back into the dormitory.

"Don't," said Hugh. "Let me go. You're just as bad as the others, Janet. It's no good your trying to stop me now."

"Oh, do listen to me, Hugh," said Janet. "Just listen for half a minute. Pete came and owned up about the ship. He pushed it out of the window when he was fooling about. And now you can't think how sorry we are that we accused you."

Hugh went back into the dormitory, and sat on the bed. "Well," he said bitterly, "you may feel pretty awful about it — but just think how I must feel always to have you thinking horrid things about me, and calling me names, and turning away when you meet me. And think how I felt when I woke up the other night and found everyone had gone to a midnight feast — except me! *You've* never been left out of anything. Everyone likes you. You don't know what it's like to be miserable."

Janet took Hugh's cold hand. She was very troubled. "Hugh," she said, "we did mean to ask you to our feast. Mike and Tom and I planned that we would. We didn't want you to be left out."

"Well, why didn't you ask me then?" demanded Hugh. "It would have made all the difference in the world to me if only you had. I'd have felt terribly happy. As it was you made me lose my temper and do something horrid and spiteful. I've been ashamed of it ever since. I spoilt your feast — and got you all into trouble. I wanted to do that, I know — but all the same I've been ashamed. And now that I'm going to run away, I want you to tell the others something for me."

"What?" asked Janet, almost in tears.

"Tell them I *did* break the windows, of course," said Hugh, "and tell them that I want to pay for them. They had to pay a share — well, give them this money and let them share it out between them. I wanted to do that before, only I kept saying I hadn't broken the windows, so I couldn't very well offer to pay, could I? But now I can."

Hugh got out his leather purse and took out some silver. He counted it and gave it to Janet. "There you are," he said. "I can't do much to put right what I did, but I can at least do this. Now goodbye, Janet, I'm going."

"No, don't go, Hugh, please don't," said Janet, her voice trembling. "Please come down and let us all tell you we're sorry. Don't go."

But Hugh shook off her hand and went quickly down the stairs, carrying his little bag. Janet flew down to the common-room, tears in her eyes and the money in her hand. She burst in at the door, and everyone turned to see what she had to say.

"I found him," said Janet. "He's – he's running away. Isn't it dreadful? He says he's ashamed of himself now for breaking the windows, and he's given me the money to give you, to pay for the whole amount, And oh Mike, oh Tom, somehow I can understand now why he broke those windows – he was so miserable at being left out!"

Everyone stared at the silver in Janet's hand. They all felt scared and most uncomfortable. It was one thing to tease a boy and give him a bad time – but it was quite another to make him run away. The Heads would soon know about that.

"I do wish we hadn't accused him unjustly," began Fred. "It's an awful pity he cheated last term like that. He seemed quite a decent chap till then – but somehow we got it into our heads after that that he was a dreadful boy and we didn't really give him a chance."

"Look here – I'm going after him," said Tom suddenly. "If the Heads get to know about this, we'll all get into awful trouble, and goodness knows what will happen to Hugh. What's the time? Half-past six? I can catch him then, before he gets on the train."

"You can't, Tom! You can't get to the station in fifteen minutes," said Marian.

"Yes, I can," said Tom. "I shall borrow Mr Wills's bike. I know where it is."

"He won't let you," said George.

"He won't be asked," said Tom. "I'll just take it. I know I shouldn't – but in a matter like this I can't stop to think of things like that. I'll get Hugh before he reaches the station, you see if I don't."

He rushed out of the room. The others stared after him. They couldn't help admiring Tom. He always knew his own mind, and when he decided to do a thing, he did it. Tom had plenty of character!

He ran out of the school building and went to the shed where Mr Wills's bicycle was kept. He wheeled it out and jumped on it. He didn't stop to light the lamp.

Down the drive he went and out of the great school gates.

He pedalled fast, for it was quite a way to the station. He kept his eyes open for Hugh, but it was not until he had almost come to the station that he saw the boy. Hugh was running fast. He had been running all the way, because he had been so afraid of missing the train.

Tom rode up close to him, jumped off the bicycle, clutched Hugh's arm and pulled him to the side of the road. He threw the bicycle against the hedge, and then dragged the astonished boy into a nearby field.

"What's up? Oh, it's you, Tom! Let me go. I'm going home."

"No, you're not," said Tom. "Not until you hear what I've got to say, anyway. Listen, Hugh. We're ashamed of ourselves. We really are. It's true you've been pretty beastly and spiteful – but it was partly because of us. I mean, we made you behave like that. I see that now. If we'd behaved differently you might have, too. You were a decent chap till the end of last term. We all liked you."

"I know," said Hugh, in a low voice. "I was happy till then. Then I cheated. I know there's no excuse for cheating – but I had a reason for my cheating. It seemed a good reason to me then, but I see it wasn't now."

"What was the reason?" asked Tom.

"Somehow or other I had to pass that exam," said Hugh. "All my brothers and my sister are clever and pass exams and win scholarships, and my father said I mustn't let the family down. I must pass mine too. Well, I'm not really clever. That is why I have to swot so hard, and never have time to play and go for walks as the rest of you do. So, as I was afraid I'd not pass the exam, I cheated a bit. And you gave me away."

"I didn't," said Tom. "I saw you'd cheated, but I didn't give you away. Why don't you believe that? Miss Thomas found it out."

"Do you swear you didn't give me away?" said Hugh.

"I swear I didn't!" said Tom. "You've never known me to sneak, have you, or to tell lies? I do a lot of silly things and play the fool, but I don't do mean things."

"All right. I believe you," said Hugh. "But I can't tell you how the thought of that cheating, and knowing that you all knew it, weighed on my mind. You see, I'm not really a cheat."

"I see," said Tom. "It's really your parents' fault for trying to drive you too hard. You're silly. You should tell them."

"I'm going to," said Hugh. "That's one thing I'm going home to say now. And I've been so miserable this term that what brains I have won't work at all! So it's no good me trying for the scholarship anyhow. Somehow things aren't fair. There's you with brains, and you don't bother to use them. There's clever Janet and Mike, and they fool about and don't really try to be top, when they could. And there's me, with poor brains, doing my very best and getting nowhere."

Tom suddenly felt terribly ashamed of all his fooling and playing. He felt ashamed of making Mike and Janet do bad work too, for they none of them really tried their hardest. He bit his lip and stared into the darkness.

"I've done as much wrong as you have," he said at last. "You cheated because you hadn't got good enough brains – and I've wasted my good brains and not used them. So I've cheated too, in another way. I never thought of it like that before. Hugh, come back with me. Let's start again. It's all been a stupid mistake. Look – give us a chance to show you we're sorry, won't you?"

"You didn't give *me* a chance," said Hugh.

"I know. So you can feel awfully generous if you will give *us* a chance!" said Tom. "And look here, old son – I'm not going to waste my good brains any more and cheat the teachers out of what I could really do if I tried – I'm going to work hard. I'll help you, if you'll help me. I don't know how to work hard, but you can show me – and I'll help you with my brains. See?"

Just then a loud whistle came from the station and then a train puffed out. Hugh looked at the shower of sparks coming from the funnel.

"Well, the train's gone," he said. "So I can't go with it. I'll have to come back with you. Let me sleep over it and see how I feel in the morning. I don't want to see any of you again tonight. I should feel awkward. If I make up my mind I can begin all over again, I'll nod at you when we get up – and just let's all act as if nothing had happened. I can't stand any more of this sort of thing. I simply MUST work if I'm going to enter for that scholarship."

The two boys went back together. Hugh went straight upstairs to his dormitory, telling Tom to say that he didn't want any supper. But before he went, Hugh held out his hand.

"You're a good sort"' he said to Tom. "Shake hands with me and let's be friends."

There was a warm hand-shake between the two of them and then Tom went soberly back to the common-room, wondering what to say. The children crowded round him and Tom explained what had happened.

When they heard what Hugh had said about how he was expected to do as well as his brothers and sister, and how he knew he hadn't good enough brains, they were silent. They knew then why Hugh had swotted so much. They even understood why he had been tempted to cheat. Every child knew how horrid it was to disappoint parents or let their family down.

"Well, let's hope he'll make up his mind to stay," said Tom. "And listen – I feel quite a bit ashamed of *my* behaviour too. My parents pay for me to learn things here, and I never try at all – except in woodwork. I just fool about the whole time, and make you laugh. Well, from now on, I'm going to do a spot of work. And so are you, Mike and Janet. You've neither of you been top once this term, and you could easily be near it, and give Doris a shock!"

"All right," said Janet, who had been thinking quite a lot too, that night. "I'll work. Miss Thomas said today she would give me a bad report because I've not been doing my best. I don't want that. Mike will work too. We always do the same."

Hugh was asleep when the children went up to bed. For the first night for a long time he was at peace, and slept calmly without worrying. Things had been cleared up. He was happier.

In the morning the boys got up when the bell went. Tom heard Hugh whistling softly to himself as he dressed, and he was glad. Then a head was put round Tom's curtains, and Tom saw Hugh's face. It was all smiles, and looked quite different from usual.

Tom stared at the smiling head. It nodded violently up and down and disappeared. Tom felt glad. Hugh was doing the sensible thing – starting all over again, and giving the others a chance to do the same thing!

And what a change there was for Hugh that morning when the boys and girls met in their common-room! He was one of them now, not an outcast – and everyone felt much happier because of it.

CHAPTER X
END OF TERM

Miss Thomas and the other teachers had a pleasant shock that week. For the first time since he had been at St Rollo's Tom began to work! The teachers simply couldn't understand it. Not only Tom worked, though – Mike and Janet did too.

"Something's happened that we don't know about," said Miss Thomas to Mr Wills. "And do you notice how much happier that boy Hugh looks? It seems as if the others have decided to be nicer to him. It's funny how Tom seems to have made friends with him all of a sudden. They even seem to be working together!"

So they were. They did their prep together, and learnt many things from each other. Tom's quick brains were useful at understanding many things that Hugh's slow brain did not take in – and Hugh's ability for really getting down to things, once he understood them, was a fine example for the rather lazy Tom.

"You make a good team," said Miss Thomas approvingly. "I am pleased with you both. Tom, I think it would be a good idea to move you away from that front desk, and put you beside Hugh. You can help one another quite a lot."

"Oooh, good," said Tom, his eyes gleaming. "It does rather cramp my style, Miss Thomas, to be under your eye all the time, you know."

The class laughed. They had been surprised at Tom's sudden change of mind regarding his work. But they were afraid that he might no longer fool about as he used to do. He always caused so much amusement – it would be sad if he no longer thought of his amazing tricks.

"Don't worry," said Tom, when Mike told him this. "I shall break out at times. I can't stop thinking of tricks even if I'm using my brains for my work too!"

He kept his word, and played one or two funny tricks on poor Monsieur Crozier, nearly driving him mad. Tom provided him with a pen on his desk, which, on being pressed for writing, sent out a stream of water from its end. The French master was so angry that he threw the blackboard chalk down on the floor and stamped on it.

This thrilled the class immensely, and was talked of for a long time. In fact, that term, on the whole, was a very exciting one indeed. Mike and Janet got quite a shock when they realised that holidays would begin in a week's time!

"Oh! Fancy the term being so nearly over!" said Janet dolefully.

"Gracious, Janet, don't you want to be home for Christmas?" said Marian.

"Yes, of course," said Janet. "But it's such fun being at St Rollo's. Think of the things that have happened this term!"

Miss Thomas overheard her. She smiled. "Shall I tell you what is the most surprising thing that has happened?" she said.

"What?" asked the children, crowding round. Miss Thomas held the list of marks for the last week in her hand. She held it up.

"Well, for the first time this term Tom Young isn't bottom!" she said. "I couldn't believe my eyes when I added up the marks – in fact I added them all up again to make sure. And it's true – he actually isn't bottom. Really, the world must be coming to an end!"

Everyone roared with laughter. Tom went red. He was pleased.

"I suppose I'm next to bottom, though," he said, with a twinkle.

"Not even that!" said Miss Thomas. "You are sixth from the top – simply amazing. And Hugh has gone up too – he is seventh. And as for Mike and Janet –

well, wonders will never cease! They tie in second, only two marks behind Doris!"

Mike, Janet, Tom and Hugh were delighted. It really was nice to find that good work so soon showed results. Hugh took Tom's arm.

"I can't tell you how you've helped me," he said. "Not only in my work – in other ways too. I feel quite different."

The children thought that Hugh looked different too. He smiled and laughed and joked with the others, and went for walks as they did. Who would have thought that things could possibly have turned out like that, after all?

The term came quickly to an end. There were concerts and handwork exhibitions – and, not quite so pleasant, exams as well! All the children became excited at the thought of Christmas, pantomimes, presents and parties, and the teachers had to make allowances for very high spirits.

The last day came. There was a terrific noise everywhere, as packing went on in each dormitory, and boys and girls rushed up and down the stairs, looking for pencil-boxes, books, boots, shoes and other things. There were collisions everywhere, and squeals of laughter as things rolled down the stairs with a clatter.

"I suppose all this noise is necessary," sighed Mr Wills, stepping aside to avoid somebody's football, which was bouncing down the stairs all by itself, accompanied above by a gale of laughter. "Dear me – how glad I shall be to say goodbye to all you hooligans! What a pity to think you are coming back next term!"

"Oh no, sir – we're glad!" shouted Mike, rushing down after the football. "We shall love the holidays – but it will be grand to come back to St Rollo's!"

Goodbyes were said all round. Some of the children were going home by train, some by car.

"Good!" said Janet. "We don't need to say our goodbye till we get to London. Look – there's our coach at the door. Come on!"

They all piled into the big coach, with about twenty other children. It set off to the station. The children looked back at the big grey building.

"Goodbye St Rollo's," said Mike. "See you next term. Goodbye! Goodbye!"

"WELL, MY FATHER SAYS . . ."

≈ ILLUSTRATED BY ≈

Stanley Lloyd

Enid created many adventures set in co-educational or girls' boarding schools but here, unusually, we have a tale about a boys' boarding school.

Alan Richards stuck his hands into his pockets and glared at the boys round him.

"You're beasts," he said. "Absolute beasts. Jealous because you haven't got a father like mine!"

He swung round and strode off, trying to take as long steps as he could. His face was red and angry, but in his mind he was puzzled and dismayed.

He went into the house-study and sat down. There was nobody there, thank goodness. Alan sat by the window and looked out on the lively scene below.

Boys, boys, boys . . . some playing games, some walking along with books, some rushing off on a message, some playing the fool.

"I thought I'd like it all so much," he said to himself. "After all, I'm fair at most things, and I can *do* most things, and I'm not bad in class either – not top, but pretty near it. Then why are the boys so nasty to me? What have I *done*?"

Alan was at West Dunnett School, famous for its work and its games, too. It was where his father had been before him, and Alan had been looking forward to going there for years. Now he wished he had gone anywhere else but West Dunnett!

His father had been a very famous pilot in the war. He was a V.C., a D.S.O. and had won the D.F.C. as well. So Alan was very proud of him, thought him the greatest hero in the world, and was determined that everyone should know it.

This was his first term at West Dunnett. He remembered how he had set off with such high hopes, and how his father had clapped him on the back and said "Well, Alan, old man, remember all the things I've told you, and you won't go far wrong!"

And, so far as Alan knew, he *had* remembered all the things; and everything had gone wrong!

He thought back to the first week. He had been one of four or five new boys. An older boy had come up and offered to show them round the school, which was enormous.

"Thanks," said Alan. " I feel as if I know every corner already. You see, my father was here."

"So was mine – and my grandfather too," said the older boy. "And also my great-grandfather."

"Well, my father says the school was only founded a hundred years ago, so I don't see how your great-grandfather could . . ." began Alan.

"Cut it out," said the bigger boy. " If you go on like that on your first day goodness knows where you'll end. This school is jolly old."

"Yes, but my father says . . ." went on Alan again, and then was annoyed because the boy rudely turned his back on him and walked away, whistling loudly.

Another group of boys came up and asked the new boys their names.

"Mine's Thomson." "Mine's Richards." "Mine's Harrison."

Then came the next question. "What's your father?"

"Mine's a banker." " Mine's a doctor." "And mine," said Alan proudly, "is the most famous pilot of the last war. He's a V.C. and a D.S.O. and . . ."

"Gosh – is Peter Richards your father?" said the now admiring group of boys. Alan sunned himself in the glow of admiration.

"My father says . . ." he began, and went on to repeat many things he had heard his father say. But new boys were not allowed to talk so much.

"Not so much gas," said an older boy, and as soon as Alan opened his mouth again, they all talked nonsense at the tops of their voices so that he couldn't make himself heard at all.

When Alan had settled down a bit, and had got to know his form-master, and the games-master, and the other boys of his form, he began to enjoy himself. But alas, it didn't last very long.

He just *couldn't* stop himself from bringing his father into everything. When the boys were discussing cricket, he butted in at once. "Well, *my* father says that Bradman was . . ."

"Oh, shut up," said Terry. "Who cares what your father says? Keep him out of it."

And when, in class, the master began to tell the boys about the modern developments of science, and asked them to tell him what they thought were among the most marvellous inventions, up went Alan's hand.

"Yes, Richards?" said the master.

"Sir, *my* father says that . . ."

"I didn't ask what your father thought. I asked what you yourself thought," said the master, who was getting just as tired as everyone else of Alan's father.

"My father says! My father says! My father says!" chanted the class, under their breath, and Alan flushed red.

"Silence," said the master. "We will now leave Richards to thoughts of his father, and go on to the next boy. Walker!"

Alan sat angrily silent in the class. How dare anyone snub his father, that great hero? People ought to welcome hearing what his father thought about things. Anyway, *he* wasn't going to be disloyal to him. He was going to go on following his example in every way he could, and he wasn't going to stop telling people about him either, or quoting his ideas.

So, very obstinately and persistently, Alan went on with his everlasting "Well, *my* father says . . ." "Well, *my* father doesn't think . . ." " Well, *my* father . . ."

Soon the boys made up a hateful chant that floated to Alan's ears wherever he was. "*His* father says he's a little angel-bud, but *my* father says he's an awful little dud!"

This silly rhyme was chanted whenever poor Alan came near, and he hated it. The boys laughed to see him go red and clench his teeth, and sang it all the more.

"It's not *fair*," Alan said to his only friend, William Forest, "my father has never said I was a marvel or anything like that — and I'm *not* a dud!"

"Well, why don't you just shut up about your father?" asked William. "Let the boys forget him, and they'll stop ragging you. And don't rise to their ragging, you idiot. When you do that red-faced act, and grind your teeth and clench your fists, that's just what they want!"

The next day the form held a meeting about starting a chess-club.

"What about you, Richards?" called Terry, his pencil hovering over Alan's name. "Do you play chess? And if not, would you like to learn?"

"Oh, I know chess," said Alan, at once. "I learnt to play years ago, with Dad. My father says it's a . . ."

There was a howl of delight. "My father says – oh, my father says!"

"*His* father says Alan's very good at chess, but *my* father says he's a nasty little mess," yelled Terry, making up the silly rhyme on the spur of the moment. Everyone thought it was marvellous and they took it up at once.

"*His* father says Alan's very good at chess, but *my* father says he's a nasty little mess!" chanted the whole form.

Alan flushed bright red, got up and walked out. "Beasts!" he said to himself. "Absolute beasts!"

And after that the boys waited every day for that "Well, my father says . . ." which Alan invariably produced, and then some wag would immediately make up an idiotic, rude rhyme, and the whole class would chant it in unison. It was maddening. It was hateful. It spoilt everything for Alan. He began to slack at his work. He wouldn't try at games. He crossed his name off the chess list. He crossed it off the bird-watching list. He refused to go in for the swimming matches each week, In fact he was stubborn and sulky and, except for the faithful William Forest, quite friendless.

He slid almost to the bottom of the form. He got ticked off by the games captain three times in public. His form-master became more and more impatient with him. The boys ragged him unmercifully, and one afternoon Alan snatched up a heavy ruler and struck Terry hard on the head with it.

Crash! The ruler came down hard, and Terry sat down suddenly on a chair, looking dazed. Fortunately he had a very hard head, and except for an enormous bump that came up immediately, no real damage had been done.

"Now look here, young Richards, this is just about the limit!" said the head boy of the form, James Walker. "If you can't take a bit of ragging you'll never be any good. And let me tell you this, too – that your father would be jolly well ashamed of you, the way you've been behaving these last few weeks! You may have got a V.C. for a father, a D.S.O. and goodness knows what – but *he's* got a jolly rotten son. I shall report you for that crack at Terry. You might have knocked him right out!"

And then it was that Alan had stuck his trembling hands into his pockets and glared at the boys around him. "You're beasts!" he said. "Absolute beasts. Jealous because you haven't got a father like mine!"

Then he had stalked off, trying to take long strides. Now here he was in the house-study on a fine afternoon when he should be playing games, and yelling and laughing with the others – and he was miserable and alone, expecting to be reported for a cowardly blow. It *was* a cowardly blow. Alan couldn't think how he could have done such a thing. He was ashamed and scared, and he hated every minute he was at West Dunnett!

"I shan't stay," he thought, suddenly. "I'll run away. I'll pack my bag, sneak out, and catch the train to Leaton. Then I'll get out and go to farm and ask for some work to do. I'm big and strong. I won't stay at this hateful place a day longer!"

He went up to the room where the trunks and night-cases were kept. He found his own first-night case and pulled it down. He went to his dormitory, which was empty, and shoved a few things into the case. He did not stop to think any more. For one thing he knew that he had chosen to do a stupid thing, but he wasn't going to tell himself it was silly. He wanted to think he was doing a daring and a fine thing.

Everything was really very easy. All the boys and masters seemed to be out on the playing-fields that afternoon. Alan stole downstairs with his bag, went to a side-door, let himself out, and ran to the bus-stop. A bus came up almost at once and he got in. He remembered that it met a train that came in at the station.

"It's a Leaton train, too," he thought. "I can catch it easily."

He got his ticket at the station and then thought he saw someone he knew. Was it

Matron? He darted behind the book-stall in case it was. He stayed there till the train thundered into the station. Then he made a dash for a carriage.

He jumped in and slammed the door. He peered out. Ah, it wasn't Matron after all. It was somebody rather like her. He sat down and heaved a sigh of relief.

Then he saw that there was somebody else in the carriage, someone who must have got in just before him. He stared at him in dismay. It was Mr Luton, the singing master. Mr Luton nodded at him, drawing on his pipe to make it start.

"Hallo, young Richards! Taking an afternoon off, like me?"

Alan went scarlet. He really didn't know *what* to say. And there was his case on the seat beside him too! Whatever would Lutey think he was doing?

He mumbled something. Mr Luton went on puffing at his pipe, and looked rather thoughtful. He had seen the bag beside young Richards. Now what was the young scamp up to? Where was he going?

Mr Luton only saw Alan in singing lessons, which Alan did not much enjoy, for he was not very good at music. But Mr Luton had heard quite a lot about him and his "My father says . . ."

"I suppose you've got leave to go off this afternoon, instead of playing games?" said Mr Luton, still puffing away.

Alan hesitated, He was usually a truthful boy, but somehow lately he had been changing into all kinds of boys he really wasn't. He decided on a lie.

"Yes, sir, I got leave," he said, at last.

Mr Luton said nothing for a moment. Then he said in a casual voice, "I knew your father well. He and I were in the same squadron in the war. A very fine fellow."

Alan glowed. "Yes, isn't he?" he said, eagerly. "You know he's a V.C., sir, as well as a D.S.O. and he's got the D.F.C. too."

"Oh, yes, I know all that," said Mr Luton. "And if ever a man deserved the whole lot, he did. And yet he was the most modest fellow I ever knew – never boasted, never pushed himself forward – and although, you know, he was sometimes afraid, before we went up on a bombing raid . . ."

"My father afraid! Never!" cried Alan. "Do you suppose he'd ever have got all those decorations for bravery if he'd been afraid for one moment?"

"It is a much, much finer thing to be brave when you are afraid, than to be brave when you are not afraid at all," said Mr Luton. "Didn't you know that, Richards? I tell you, I knew your father well. Sometimes he was as scared as some of us others were – but where we might give in, or run away, he never would. He always stuck things out to the last. That's why his men worshipped him so – they guessed he was scared just as they were, sometimes – but they knew he'd stick things out, and dare anything to bring them and the plane back safely."

"I see," said Alan.

"He must be very pleased to think you're at West Dunnett, his old school," went on Mr Luton, pressing the burning tobacco down into the bowl of his pipe and not looking at Alan at all. "You know – carrying on the old tradition – doing good work, playing good games, adding a bit more to the fame of his old school."

Alan said nothing. This was awful. Didn't Mr Luton know he'd been an idiot this last few weeks, a real slacker?

"It's nice to be proud of your father, isn't it?" said Mr Luton. "And it must be just as good a feeling to be proud of your son. Grand to know he'd never be a coward, or run away from things."

Alan swallowed hard. He wished Mr Luton would stop talking. He was saying just the very things that Alan had been trying hard not to think of.

Then he suddenly burst out with a few words that surprised him. He hadn't meant to say them at all and yet he did.

"Well, I'm a coward, Mr Luton," he heard himself saying. "I'm running away!"

"I rather thought you were," said Mr Luton, puffing away again. "Things have got too much for you, I suppose. You're afraid of them. So you're running away. Well, that's the difference between your father and you, you see. He was afraid, but he didn't run away. *You* are afraid, so you do run away. No V.C.s for you, my boy! It takes a fellow like your father to win those."

Then Mr Luton picked up a paper, and began to read it. All that Alan could see was the top of his head and clouds of thick smoke. Alan's thoughts were muddled, but gradually one thing became quite clear. He was not going to be a coward. He would never be as brave as his father, but at least he need not run away.

When the train drew in at the next station, Alan got up. Mr Luton looked at him over the top of his paper.

"Mr Luton, sir," said Alan, his voice sounding rather shaky. "Thanks for what you said, and for not scolding me. I'm not running away. I'm catching the next train back."

"A chip off the old block after all!" said Mr Luton, and he grinned widely at Alan. He pulled him down on the seat. "Don't get out here. Come and spend the afternoon with me. I can make things right about that when we get back. I'd like a good old talk about the days when your father and I were in the R.A.F."

Alan sat down again, and the train pulled out of the station. And then he talked to his heart's content about his hero-father, the things he had done and the things he had said.

Mr Luton listened quietly, as the boys at school had never done. He added a bit now and again. They got out at Leaton, and Mr Luton put Alan's bag into the cloakroom there.

"I'm going for a good long walk," he said. "And you're coming with me. We'll get things straight."

They did get things straight, and when Alan went back he knew quite clearly that what mattered at school was not what your father did or said, but what you yourself did and said. And he also knew that the main difference between a coward and a real hero was that although they might both be scared stiff of things, one ran away and the other didn't.

"Gosh, it's easy to be a coward, isn't it?" he said to Mr Luton. "But honestly I thought I was doing something rather grand and bold and heroic, rushing off like that to find work on a farm."

"Cowards usually wrap up their real reasons so that they may think themselves heroes!" said Mr Luton. "By the way, I'll let you into a secret if you promise not to tell anyone till it's made public. Your father's coming down for Speech Day – and he's going to be the Speaker!"

And with that Mr Luton waved his pipe at Alan and went off to the Masters' quarters.

Alan stood absolutely still. His father coming down for Speech Day – and making the Speech! How simply super. He wanted to yell for joy.

Then he went very soberly indeed to put his bag away. Suppose he *had* run away as he had meant to do? Suppose he had caused a frightful lot of trouble and annoyance and disgust? His father would not have liked to come down at Speech Day – he would have felt ashamed and sad.

"What a narrow squeak I've had," thought Alan. "Gosh, I'll always think twice and three times and four times in future before I act like an idiot!"

He went down to where the boys were gathered round the notice-board looking at the games list for the following day. Terry saw him.

"*His* father says he's a little angel-bud, but *my* father says he's an awful little dud!" he chanted, and everyone took up the refrain. Alan went scarlet as usual, but to everyone's immense surprise, he opened his mouth and joined in the chant.

The boys fell silent and stared at him in surprise. Alan spoke to Terry. "Terry, I apologise for hitting you. If you'd like to give me a good conk back with the same ruler, you can."

Terry was a generous, straightforward boy when it came to things like this. He grinned and rubbed the enormous bump on his head. "Apology accepted. I'll give you a conk all right though – here it comes!"

And he slapped Alan on the back and made him gasp. Then, suddenly, things were all right. Forest slipped his arm through Alan's and began talking about cricket. Nobody went on with the chant. Terry called to him to come and practise catching a cricket ball. It was really most extraordinary.

Alan hugged his secret to him. What would the boys say when they knew his father was coming on Speech Day? He wouldn't say a single word more about him. He wouldn't boast, or quote his words, or even mention him. His father could speak for himself, when Speech Day came!

The chanting did not stop all at once. There was quite a lot of "*His* father says, *my* father says," and one or two rhymes were made up. But Alan always joined in the chant himself, so there didn't seem to be any point in it after a time. Also, Alan never now said "*My* father says," which used so often to start the boys off.

Gradually the chanting stopped. Alan was pleased. He began to work hard and play hard. He wanted his father to get a good report of him, when he spoke to the Head on Speech Day. He would be sure to want to know how his son was getting on. Alan thought with surprise how very, very right Mr Luton had been in all the things he said. It was nice for a son to be proud of his father – but it was just as important to the father that he should be proud of his son.

The boys were thrilled when they knew that the famous V.C. was coming to talk to them on their Speech Day. "He's your father, isn't he?" said the Head Boy of the school to Alan. He had never addressed one word to him before, and Alan was proud. He stopped himself boasting just in time.

"Yes. He's my father," was all he said.

The famous V.C. arrived at his old school on Speech Day. He was cheered to the echo, and Alan had to blink away some most unexpected tears when he heard the cheering. And what a speech the V.C. made! A fine, man-to-man, straight-from-the-shoulder talk, one that every boy understood and responded to. Alan was prouder than he had ever been in his life before

Afterwards he showed his father round. Mr Luton came up to them. "Congratulations on the speech, old man," he said. "Finest we've ever had. Hallo, young Richards. Showing your father round the place, as if he didn't know every corner already?"

"It's good to have a son at my old school," said Alan's father.

"Well, he's a chip off the old block," said Mr Luton. "I've told you that before sometime, haven't I, young Richards?"

"Yes, sir, you have," said Alan, and went his usual bright scarlet.

After supper, when the boys were talking over the events of the day, Terry spoke to Alan.

"I say, your father's super, isn't he? I spoke to him, and do you know, your father says . . ."

"Well, what does my father say?" said Alan, with a grin. "Go on – you tell *me* for a change! I'll listen to you all right."

"Your father says . . . your father says . . . your father says . . ." Alan went to sleep that night with the words ringing in his ears. And then the words changed to "A chip off the old block." Yes, that was better still!

In fact, as far as Alan was concerned, it was the best thing of all.

THE CHEAT

≈ ILLUSTRATED BY ≈

Stanley Lloyd

This story shows what happens when a schoolgirl who is suffering badly from examination stress thinks she can overcome her problems by cheating.

Susan was swotting up for the exam. Her hands were over her ears, and she was repeating dates to herself with her eyes shut, opening them every now and again to see if she was right.

"Susan! SUSAN! Look at her swotting away like that when we want her for rehearsal. Pull her hands from her ears, somebody!"

Mollie pulled Susan's hands away and she jumped. "What's up?" she said. "Can't you see I'm working?"

"Well, the exam's not till next week," said Pam. "For goodness' sake stop working and come and join the rehearsal."

"I know my part. Let somebody else take my place this evening," said Susan. "I really must get on with this."

"No, you come," said Pam. "You've been cramming hard all week. What's the sense? You know you'll pass all right. We're all in the same boat anyway."

"No, you're not," said Susan. "This is a scholarship exam, and it doesn't matter to you whether you win the scholarship or not – but it does to me. I can't go on to college unless I get it."

"Well, for goodness' sake, do help us just for once," said Molly. "You backed out of the rehearsal last week. You can't keep on doing that, or we'll get somebody else for your part, and you won't like that."

"It's only just till the exam's over," said Susan. "That's one more week. It's really my duty to swot up now, if I want to get the scholarship."

"It's your duty to come to rehearsal and not make things difficult for the others," said Pam, flaring up. "Come on."

So, rather sulkily, Susan went. But as she would keep repeating all the dates she had learnt whenever she was not on the stage, the others got very bored with her.

"We won't ask you to come to any rehearsal or meetings or anything till the exam's over," said Pam, crossly. "You're just no use at all. But let me tell you this – you're an absolute idiot to cram like this, all day and half the night, and not take any time off – it won't do your exam work a bit of good!"

"I'm the best judge of that," said Susan, stiffly. "But all the same I'll be glad not to waste time on rehearsals and meetings for one more week."

So the girls left her alone, and she worked very hard indeed. She *must* win that scholarship, she must. She did so badly want to go to college. She had good brains, she could do well. So she missed out games and any social gathering all that week, and kept her nose glued to her work.

And, just as Pam had warned her, her work suddenly began to suffer because she slogged at it too hard. She felt very tired. She couldn't remember all she wanted to remember. She began to have headaches, and worse still she found it quite impossible to go to sleep at night.

"This is awful," thought Susan, in a panic. "I shall do frightfully badly. Oh dear – it's so dreadful to have to go over the whole of the term's history and geography and maths and literature – when all we shall be asked is just a few questions on bits of it!"

"Don't you wish you knew what the examiners are going to ask us?" said Mollie to Susan. "We could just swot up those answers then, instead of working hard like this."

"Yes. If only we knew!" said Susan, and put her hands over her ears again, whilst she read through her French grammar.

By the time the day before the exam came Susan was almost in a panic. She couldn't seem to remember anything at all! She would never be able to answer a single question. She would be bottom. She wouldn't have a chance of getting the scholarship.

"Nobody is to work tonight," said Miss Lesley, the form mistress. "I have already warned you of that, but I am telling you again in case there is anyone foolish enough to tire herself out on the evening before the exam."

Susan gazed at her in despair. "But Miss Lesley, I simply *must* go over my geography again. Just once, please. It won't take me long."

"Not even once," said Miss Lesley, firmly. She looked at Susan's pale face and made up her mind that she would keep an eye on her, and not let her slip off anywhere to work unseen.

"I want somebody to take these things to Matron for me," she said, looking round. "Susan, you might as well. Wait for Matron to give you the mended clothes, and then give them out to the right girls."

There was nothing to do but obey. Sulkily Susan got up and took the laundry bag that Miss Lesley held out. She went to Matron and gave it to her.

"Thank you," said Matron. "Now you wait a minute whilst I get all the mended things in a pile. Where's that tunic? Oh, here it is. Bless us all, what in the world did Pamela do to get a tear like that? Now, there's the stockings . . . and the ankle socks . . ."

Susan stood impatiently whilst Matron talked and sorted out things. Oh dear — she could have gone halfway through her geography by now! Never mind. Perhaps when she got back she could slip away with her book. She took the mended things back and gave them out. Then she went to get her geography book, seeing that Miss Lesley was talking to Pam.

But almost at once Miss Lesley called to Susan. "Susan! I want you to do something else for me."

"Blow, blow, blow!" said Susan under her breath. She shut her locker and went to Miss Lesley.

"Go to our form-room," said Miss Lesley, "and see if you can find my bottle of red ink. I may have left it on the mantelpiece. I want you to underline some words for me in red — lines in the play we're doing."

Feeling really exasperated Susan went to her form-room and looked for the red ink. It wasn't on the mantelpiece. She looked on the window-sill. It wasn't there either. Blow Miss Lesley – why couldn't she remember where she put things?

Perhaps it was on her desk. Susan went to the big desk and looked. Yes, there it was. She picked it up. And then her eye fell on something, and she stood quite still.

The exam papers were there for the next day! They lay in a neat pile. The history questions were on top. Question 1. What do you know of . . . Question 2. Write an essay about the . . . Question 3. Give a short account of . . .

Susan gave a little gasp. She rubbed her hand across her forehead and thought quickly. The exam questions were actually there, under her nose! She could read every single one of them.

"But it would be cheating," she whispered to herself. "I should be a cheat. I never have cheated, never, though I've often wanted to."

Yes, she had often wanted to. Perhaps other girls had too? But they all were so very, very scornful of cheating. It couldn't have been a temptation to them, as it sometimes had been to Susan.

She set the red ink down on the desk and went to the window, so that if anyone came in she could be right away from the desk, pretending to look for the red ink. She had to think, think, think.

"I've never cheated. Never. I oughtn't to begin. Mother says once you begin a wrong thing it's much easier to do it next time, and then you just slide down and down. If I read those questions I *shall* be a cheat. It's no good deceiving myself. I *shall* be a cheat."

She pressed her forehead against the cold glass. She did need that scholarship so very badly.

"None of the others do. They'll go to college anyhow. I shan't. Mother couldn't afford it. And I've got such good brains, I don't want to waste them."

Somebody came up the corridor, humming. Susan began to pretend to hunt around for the ink. She half hoped that whoever it was coming along would come

into the classroom – then she couldn't possibly cheat. Her mind would be made up for her. She couldn't cheat with somebody else there.

But the person passed by the classroom and went up the stairs. Susan's cheeks began to feel very hot, and her hands trembled as she still pretended to hunt for the ink. Then she went to the door and looked up and down the long corridor.

There was nobody about at all. If she didn't make up her mind quickly Miss Lesley would send somebody after her – she might even think that Susan had found the exam papers and was reading them!

Susan went back to the desk. She picked up the exam papers one after another and read them through. She read the geography questions, the history, the maths, the literature, every single one of them.

"Some of these questions aren't fair!" she thought angrily. "They ought to keep to the things we've studied. What's the use of asking a question about North West America when we didn't take that in our work for the exam?"

She went to the door again. Still there was nobody about. Taking a pencil and a slip of paper from her desk Susan quickly jotted down a few of the questions to look up. Then she replaced the papers neatly in their exact order, and went out, her face still flaming.

She hoped the cool air in the corridor would make her face less red. Miss Lesley must not notice anything peculiar about her. She walked into the common-room, where all the others were talking noisily.

Miss Lesley was not there! "She's gone to Matron," said Pam. "Matron didn't give you half the things she ought to have done."

Susan was thankful Miss Lesley could not see her flaming face. She set the bottle of ink down on the table and then went out of the room.

She wanted to bathe her face and cool it down. And she wanted to think how she could look up all the answers to those questions.

In the bathroom a thought kept trying to rise up to the surface. "I'm a cheat. I've done it at last. I've cheated." But she forced down the unwelcome thought and began to plan how she might get hold of some books and do a little looking up.

When she went back to the common-room Miss Lesley was back. She glanced at Susan and smiled. "You found the ink then. Thank you. Look, here are the lines I want marked — all those with a cross beside them."

Susan sat down with the red ink. It was plainly no use hoping to do any work with Miss Lesley there. She must smuggle her books up to bed, take out her torch, and work in bed.

She managed to smuggle the books upstairs before the girls went up to bed. She put them under her pillow. She found her torch and put that there too.

"Ooooh! The exam begins tomorrow," said Pam, as she undressed. "I'm shaking with nerves, girls."

Everyone laughed except Susan. "You're looking rather mouldy, Sue — anything up?" asked Pam.

"No," said Susan. "Just a bit tired, that's all."

"Well, don't worry about the exam," said Mollie. "You'll probably be top anyhow. I heard Miss Lesley say so. She said your work's better than anyone's, and she doesn't see how you can *fail* to be top. So there's a nice little tit-bit for you to sleep on, Susan!"

"Thank you, Mollie," said Susan. She was surprised. Was her work really as good as all that? It was true she was nearly always top of the weekly form marks. But exams were so different from ordinary weekly work. Suppose she might have been top of the scholarship exam anyhow, suppose she could have won it without cheating? But now she would never know. She had cheated. She knew the questions. Even if she didn't look up the answers, she could go over and over the questions in her mind and take her time in remembering the answers.

Everyone got into bed. Lights were switched off. Miss Lesley put her head in. "Not a word to be spoken tonight," she said. "Sleep well, and you'll do some marvellous papers tomorrow!"

"Goodnight, Miss Lesley," said the girls, and settled themselves to sleep. All except Susan. She was going to wait until everyone was asleep, and then she meant to put on her torch, get out her books, and read them under the sheets by the light of the torch. She would look up the answers to every single question. Whether she could or could not win the scholarship without cheating she didn't know — but certainly she would win it if she could — and cheating would make it absolutely certain.

When she was sure that everyone was asleep Susan cautiously pulled the sheet over her head. She put on her torch, and pulled the books down from under her pillow. She opened her geography book first.

She worked hard. She looked up the answer to every question in the exam papers. Then, her head aching and her eyes burning, she put out her torch, and tried to go to sleep.

But she couldn't. A curious little voice began in her mind. "Susan's a cheat! Isn't it dreadful? I thought she was such a nice girl, didn't you? Well, she's not, she's a cheat. Do you know her mother? Whatever would she say if she knew that Susan cheated?"

At once a picture of her mother slid into Susan's mind. Her mother was not pretty at all, but she had a kind sweet face that lighted up when she smiled. But she was not smiling now. She was crying.

"I'm being silly and imagining things," thought Susan, crossly. "I really must go to sleep." But the little voice began again. "Susan's a cheat! Isn't it awful? She's probably *always* been a cheat!"

But Susan interrupted the small voice at once. "I haven't, I haven't. It was only tonight – for the very first time . . . I'll never, never do it again."

"Yes, you will," went on the small voice. It was a very determined little voice. "You will. It's the first time that matters. After that it's easy to do it again and again. Then you'll be found out – and your good name will be gone – and perhaps one day you might even go to prison for dishonesty of some sort. Once you begin this sort of thing you slide down and down . . . and down . . . and down . . ."

Susan gave a groan and sat suddenly up in bed, feeling cold and shivery. What had

she done? Yes, cheated for the first time – but it wasn't going to stop there – it never did. Why had she started? She'd been strong enough not to for years and years. And now, just those two minutes in the form-room had made her into a cheat.

"I wish I hadn't! I'd give anything now not to have done it. What was I *thinking* of, to let myself do such a thing – with a mother like mine too, who has always shown me the right things to do. I'll never be able to look her in the face again. I've spoilt everything, absolutely everything. I shall hate myself for ever and ever."

She lay down again, and tears began to trickle over her pillow. She couldn't undo what she had done now. She knew the answers to all the exam questions. Whatever she did she would not be able to win the scholarship fairly. If she confessed, she wouldn't be able to go in for the exam, and the Head would despise her terribly and perhaps expel her. Perhaps she could answer the questions wrongly and stupidly? Then she would be bottom, and her mother would be grieved and puzzled. All the girls would laugh.

"If I could only be given another chance!" thought Susan, wildly. "I'd never cheat again. But there isn't any other chance I can have – there's nothing to be done. Either I go on with cheating and win the scholarship – or I confess and lose it – or I answer the questions wrongly and lose it. I've got no other choice. Oh, why did I do it?"

She got out of bed and went to the window. The moon was shining brightly. She heard a movement near her and saw that Janet, one of the girls she had thought was asleep, was awake.

"What's the matter, Susan? Aren't you well?" asked Janet, sleepily.

"Oh, Janet – something awful's happened to me," said Susan, and stopped in horror. She hadn't meant to say that – especially not to Janet, of all people. Janet was religious and good, and would think her simply dreadful if she said any more.

"What?" asked Janet, and sat up. "Why, you're crying, Sue. What's the matter, old thing?"

There was such kindness in Janet's voice that Susan couldn't stop herself from saying a great deal more, and soon she had poured everything out to Janet.

Janet listened without a word.

"There," said Susan, at last. "*Now* what do you think of me? And whatever can I do? I'm caught. I *might* have won the scholarship fairly – but now either I win it by cheating, or I lose it because I can't bear to cheat after all. I know I oughtn't to go in for it, because I know the answers."

Janet was horrified to hear this story poured out to her. She had never thought that Susan could cheat. She took her cold hand.

"I don't believe you *are* really a cheat," she said. "You were tired and did something you wouldn't do in the ordinary way. But honestly I don't see any way out for you, poor Sue. You're caught in a trap!"

"Oh Janet – it's frightful," said Susan. "What would *you* do in my place?"

"It's no good telling you that," said Janet. "You'd laugh."

"I shouldn't," said Susan. "I never felt less like laughing in my life."

"Well then – I'd go into the school chapel, and I'd jolly well kneel down and ask for help," said Janet. "I'd beg for another chance."

"But what would be the use of that?" asked Susan. "You can see there's nothing that would help me – and I can't possibly get another chance. I've done for myself."

"Well, either you believe or you don't," said Janet, settling down. "I told you it wouldn't be any good my telling you what I'd do."

Oh Janet – I'll do it, I will," said Susan. "I might feel a bit happier perhaps. I do despise myself so dreadfully now."

"Well, hurry up and get back to bed," said Janet. "You're shivering."

But before she went back to bed Susan did go down to the school chapel. She put on her dressing-gown and stole down quietly. The little chapel looked lovely, full of moonlight. It was where the school went to hear the services every Sunday. Susan was used to gabbling the Lord's Prayer there, without thinking. She was often bored listening to the sermons.

But tonight was different. She thought hard about every word she said. "What I want is a miracle," she thought, sadly. "A miracle that would put everything right and give me another chance. Oh, help me, and give me another chance if it's possible."

Then, still shivering, she went back to bed, a little comforted. She fell asleep and did not wake till the dressing-bell clanged loudly.

It was a miserable Susan that dressed and went down to a breakfast she could hardly eat. Janet glanced at her anxiously, but Susan would not look at her. She felt sure that Janet must be disgusted with her.

Prayers. Roll call. Take your places. The exam papers will be given out. Susan felt as if things were happening to her in a dream. Now – she must make up her mind what she was going to do – answer the questions rightly or wrongly. A miracle had not happened, and anyway she didn't deserve that it should.

She would answer all the questions wrongly. That was the only thing to do. She would lose the scholarship, get into disgrace and grieve her mother. But it couldn't be helped. It was the only decent thing to do. Susan's heart felt much lighter when she had made this decision.

Pam was giving out the exam papers – geography – history – maths – all of which were to be done that morning. Everyone began to study them, with sighs and groans. Miss Lesley tapped on her desk.

"Girls! You may begin. You will have three quarters of an hour for each paper. Read the questions carefully before you begin."

Susan looked at the geography paper. Then she frowned and looked again. Was this the *right* paper? The questions were quite different from the ones she had read in the pile of papers the evening before. Quite different!

Susan read down them quickly. Then she turned to the history paper.

Why, this was quite different too – and so were the maths questions. What had happened? Susan gazed round in bewilderment. Everyone had begun writing.

She looked at the papers again. It was odd, very, very odd. Not a single question was the same. And yet, stamped across the top were the words "Form III, Exam Papers."

A girl came into the room and spoke to Miss Lesley. "Please, Miss Lesley, may I have the exam papers for Form IV? Miss Robinson says she thinks she must have left them in your room yesterday."

"Ah – here they are," said Miss Lesley, and picked up a little pile. "Yes – Form IV. Funny I didn't notice them. They must have been here all night! I kept Form III's under lock and key."

Susan sat back, feeling suddenly out of breath. She could hardly believe what had happened! Why – the papers she had read belonged to *Form IV* – not to her form at all! Her own exam papers had been safely locked up. She hadn't seen them. She hadn't seen *any* of the questions she was supposed to answer.

She had made a mistake. She had tried to be a cheat, but she wasn't. It wasn't exactly a miracle that had happened, but it seemed just like one to Susan. She had got another chance after all. She could answer the questions in front of her quite honestly. She needn't cheat, she needn't lose the scholarship.

"I asked for help and I asked for another chance, and I got both," thought Susan, happily. She felt a different girl. She took up her pen and began to write feverishly. She knew all the answers! She could do the papers well.

She went to find Janet afterwards and told her what had happened. Janet was glad. Her kind face glowed.

"Well – you've got the second chance you wanted," she said. "Good luck to you!"

"I've had a dreadful lesson," said Susan. "I know what it's like to be a cheat and to feel like one – and I never want to be one again. I wasn't really one, as things turned out – but I meant to be. I don't really deserve a second chance."

"You *did* deserve one, or you wouldn't have got it," said Janet. "Well – I hope you win the scholarship!"

FRED'S FORGETTERY

Written with younger children in mind, this story is set in a day school for boys.

A TALE FOR ROBIN

There was once a boy who had a very bad memory. He didn't even *try* to remember anything, which made things even worse!

"Fred, you haven't got a memory, you've only got a forgettery!" his mother said to him, many times. "Didn't I remind you three times to call at the shoemaker's for your shoes and *now* you haven't remembered!"

"Oh Mother, I quite forgot," said Fred.

"But did you *try* to remember?" asked his mother. "No, you didn't. Now you will have to wear your old shoes with your new suit when you go to see Granny. That really is a pity."

One day the circus came to Fred's town. It really was a marvellous one. It was Mr Phillippino's, and there were elephants, a giraffe, monkeys, and the funniest clowns you ever saw.

Some of the children went, and they really loved it. Fred wanted to go, but as he had really been very silly that week, his mother said no.

"You forgot to take your books to school yesterday, and lost a good mark for that," she said. "And on Monday you forgot I had asked you to stay at school for lunch and you came home, and made a great fuss because I was out and there was no one to get you your meal. And this very morning I asked you to call at the paper shop and bring me back my paper, and you didn't. No, you don't deserve a ticket for the circus. That forgettery of yours is playing all kinds of tricks this week!"

Now, on Thursday evening Fred had to go to a nearby friend's house to borrow a school book he had forgotten. As he came back with it he saw an old man hurrying to catch the post.

"The post has gone!" thought Fred. "I saw the postman collecting the letters as I came by. The old man has missed the post."

The man stopped by the pillar-box and looked at the post-times, as he held up the letter to the slit in the red box. Then he gave a cry of annoyance, for he saw that there was no collection until the next day. He had missed the last post.

"What a nuisance!" Fred heard him say. "Missed the post! Now the letter won't get there until Saturday morning if I post it. I'd better deliver it myself."

He stopped Fred as the boy came by. "Do you know where Rockland School is?" he asked. "Is it far?"

"Yes, a good way," said Fred. "It's my school. I go there every day. You go down there and turn to the left and . . ."

"Wait a minute, wait a minute – did you say you go to Rockland School?" asked the old man. "Well, I wonder if you'd mind taking this letter with you tomorrow morning, without fail, and giving it to the headmaster?"

"Oh yes, of course," said Fred, and he held out his hand for the note. "I can easily do that."

"Thanks very much," said the man. "Now don't forget, will you? You'll be sorry if you do!"

Fred didn't tell the old fellow what a forgettery he had! He took the note, quite meaning to give it to the headmaster the next morning.

He didn't think to himself, "Now I must remember this – I will carry it home in my hand, and put it on my dressing-table so that I shall see it tomorrow morning. Then if I carry it in my hand all the way to school, I simply won't be able to help remembering to deliver it!"

No – he didn't try to remind himself at all that he had something to do for somebody else. He just put it in his pocket – and forgot ALL about it.

He didn't once think of the letter that evening. He didn't think of it the next

morning. He forgot all about it when he got to school and took off his coat. There was the letter, safe in his coat pocket, hanging up in the cloakroom, and nobody knew it was there.

Friday came and went. Saturday morning came. That was the very last day of the circus! Fred asked his mother again if he could go, but she shook her head.

"I should think not, Fred! Do you know you forgot to call in and ask how poor old Mrs Jones was yesterday, and I reminded you six times at least. The poor old

thing was very hurt. Certainly you can't have treats if you don't even *try* to remember something."

Fred went out to play with his friends. They went to peep in between the railings round the field where the circus camp was. It did look so exciting. The boys wished and wished they could see it.

"The tickets are expensive," said one boy. "Usually they are half-price for children, but this circus has done so well, and been so crowded every night, that there have been no half-price tickets. I think the circus-owner must be jolly mean!"

Saturday went and Sunday came. That day the circus moved off. Some of the boys watched it. It was fun to see the elephants move away, dragging caravans behind them. The clowns no longer looked like clowns, for they were dressed in ordinary old jerseys and trousers. The horses were not so beautiful without their waving plumes. All the same, it was exciting to watch, as the big procession slowly made its way out of the field.

Monday morning came. All the boys went back to school again, and gathered together in the big hall for prayers and roll-call. They were about to go to their classrooms when the headmaster stood up again. He had something to say.

"One moment, boys," he said. "I have something to tell you. I have had a letter, this morning, from the owner of the circus that was here last week. I will read it to you."

The boys stood still, listening. The head began to read the letter.

"Dear Mr Kenley,

I was astonished not to see the boys of your school at the circus on Saturday evening. I had hoped that you would allow them all to come and take the front seats, as I had offered them to you free. I hope you got the invitation safely. I gave it to one of your boys on Thursday evening to deliver to you for me as I had missed the post. He promised to do this.

Yours faithfully,

Phillippino."

The headmaster folded up the letter and looked down from the platform at the surprised boys. They were nudging one another and whispering.

"We could have gone — gone for nothing!"

"Who took the note? Why didn't he give it to the head?"

"What a shame. The circus has gone now and we can't see it."

One boy stood without saying a word, his face as red as a beetroot. That boy was

Fred! Of course – that old man by the letter-box was Phillippino, the owner of the circus – and he had given the invitation to Fred – and he had forgotten all about it.

"I've robbed all the boys of the chance of seeing the circus for nothing!" thought Fred, with horror. "Oh, why didn't I *try* to remember?"

"Well, boys," said the headmaster, putting the letter into his pocket. "If Mr Phillippino is right, one of you took the invitation from him, and forgot to deliver it. Who was it?"

Fred was frightened to say it was he who had forgotten. The boys would be so angry. He stood there, saying nothing, his face still red.

"Come, come!" said the headmaster impatiently. "It must have been one of you. It is bad enough to forget to deliver a letter, but a great deal worse not to be brave enough to own up to it. I've no doubt it was quite by accident that the note was not delivered to me, but please don't make matters worse by not owning up."

Fred was terribly ashamed of himself. Was he a coward as well as a careless forgetter? Yes, he was a coward – but he'd put a stop to *that*! He would own up.

He heard his own voice, rather shaky and small.

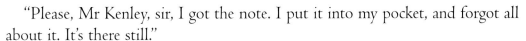

"Please, Mr Kenley, sir, I got the note. I put it into my pocket, and forgot all about it. It's there still."

There was a silence. The boys glared at Fred in anger, and then began whispering, calling the boy all kinds of names because he had made them miss going to the circus.

"Fetch the note," said the Head. Fred went out and brought the letter back. The Head opened it and read it out loud.

"Dear Mr Kenley,

It is my custom, when my circus has done well during the week, to offer on the last Saturday of the show the front seats free to any school in the district whose boys seem to me to be the best-behaved. I would be glad to welcome your lads on Saturday evening, and will keep one hundred of the front seats reserved for them.
Yours faithfully,
Phillippino."

"Well!" said the headmaster, folding up the note. "I'm afraid Fred has spoilt the treat for you. Fred, will you kindly write an explanation and an apology to Mr Phillippino today. Dismiss!"

Fred had a bad time that day. Every boy was disgusted, disappointed and angry.

"Can't you remember anything? You're not stupid, just lazy!"

"It's all very well to forget things that only concern yourself, but when you spoil something for other people it's different!"

"Let's leave him out of games. Who wants a boy who can't even remember to deliver a note for an old man!"

It was a tremendous shock for Fred. He must get rid of his forgettery! He must remind himself to remember things in all sorts of ways, even if it was a nuisance. He must tie knots in his handkerchief, write out notes and stick them in his dressing-table mirror so that he could read them in the morning and remember. He must keep saying to himself, "What did Mother tell me today? What did Mr Kenley ask me to do?"

"I must get back my memory and lose my forgettery," said Fred. "Then perhaps the boys will forget what I have done, and forgive me. It's so horrid having no friends at school."

So he is trying hard, but it's very difficult. What's *your* memory like? I do hope it's not a forgettery like Fred's!

SHE HADN'T ANY FRIENDS

The heroine of this day school tale seems younger than the girls at Enid's fictional boarding schools, but just like some of them she also has problems "fitting in" with the group.

There was once a girl called Linda who hadn't any friends. She was an only child, so, as she had no brothers or sisters, and no friends either, you can guess she was lonely.

Nobody asked her out to tea. Nobody asked her to play on Saturday mornings in their garden. Nobody wanted to walk home with her from school.

This was rather odd, because there was nothing really the matter with Linda. She wasn't rough or rude or spiteful or boastful – she wasn't any of the things that make children dislike somebody. She spoke nicely and she had good manners, and she was quite a pretty child, too.

"It's strange," said her mother. "Linda is quite a nice little girl – and yet nobody likes her. Nobody makes friends with her. So, poor child, she is terribly shy and hardly knows how to play at all!"

But the person who worried about it most of all was poor Linda herself! When she saw Mary and Joan running off together, she felt ready to cry. They never shared a joke with *her*. And when George asked Anne to tea, and told her he was going to have his clockwork railway out especially for her, Linda simply longed and longed to see it too. But George didn't ask her once.

One day Kenneth came to school with a lovely new pencil that had a screw top. If you screwed it one way the pencil wrote red. If you screwed it the other way it wrote blue. Kenneth showed it to everyone. But he didn't show it to Linda. Linda was longing to see it. She kept at the back, hoping Kenneth would say, "Linda, look!" But he didn't.

"Now why didn't Kenneth show me his pencil?" wondered Linda sadly. "There must be something dreadfully wrong with me, because I've no friends at all. Not a single one! I'll have to do something about it."

Now, you know, the world is made up of two different kinds of people. One kind just sit down and mope and do nothing when difficulties come – and the other kind think about them hard, and find some way of beating them. And luckily for Linda, she belonged to the second kind of people.

So she sat down and thought about it. "I don't know, myself, why I've no friends – and Mother doesn't know, or she would help me," thought Linda. "If I could find somebody who did know, they might be able to tell me what to do. I can't go on and on never having any friends – it's too lonely and miserable."

Now Linda's teacher at school was Miss Brown, who was very nice indeed. She was strict, very fair, and always kind and patient. Linda liked her, though she was just a bit afraid of her.

"Miss Brown knows a tremendous lot about everything," said Linda to herself. "She really does. I'll go and tell her my worries. She might be able to tell me what to do."

So after tea that evening Linda ran along the road to Miss Brown's house. She knocked at the door. Miss Brown opened it. She was surprised to see Linda.

"Come along in," she said. "What's the matter? Anything wrong?"

"There is, rather," said Linda. "I don't know quite how to tell you – but oh, Miss Brown, it does worry me dreadfully that I haven't any friends at all. I think and think about it. Is there anything horrid about me?"

Miss Brown laughed. She took Linda into her sitting-room. She was sorting out all kinds of tangled silks for the sewing class the next day. She went on with her work, and listened to Linda.

"But *is* there anything horrid about me?" asked Linda. "Please, please do tell me if there is. I could alter it perhaps."

"There is nothing horrid about you," said Miss Brown. "Nothing at all. But there isn't anything very nice either! You're an in-between person, Linda – not nice, and not nasty either. Just a little in-between."

"Oh," said Linda, puzzled. "I don't quite know what you mean! How can I

be nice if nobody is nice to me?"

"Now listen carefully, Linda," said Miss Brown in her kind voice, as she sorted out the silks. "There is only one way in this world to make friends – yes, only ONE way – the way to make friends, Linda, is to BE one. Be a good friend to everybody, and they will be good friends to you. You are never unkind enough to push anyone over – but on the other hand, you are never kind enough to rush to help somebody up when they have fallen. You leave someone else to do that."

"I see," said Linda. "It isn't enough to sit back and wait for other people to be friendly. I've got to go right out and be friendly myself."

"That's right," said Miss Brown. "Now look – here am I, sitting sorting out tangled silks.

If Mary or Joan had been here they would have said "*I'll* help you, Miss Brown," and I should have felt so warm and friendly towards them. But you, silly little girl, sit there with your hands in your lap and say nothing about helping me – so you don't make me full of warm, kindly feelings towards you. That's not my fault – it's yours."

"Oh, Miss Brown!" said poor Linda, going red with shame. "I *did* think of helping you – but I thought you'd say no."

"Well, you might have given me a chance to say no or yes," said Miss Brown. "Don't be a little in-between any more – neither nasty nor nice. Even if people say no to you, never mind. You will at least have *tried* to be nice. Now, think of Margery – she's a naughty, untidy, careless little girl, not nearly so good-mannered or neat as you are, and yet all the children love her. She rushes to everyone's help. She's interested in everybody. She takes books and toys to children who are ill. She just *will* be a friend to everyone, so everyone is a friend to her. Now what about you trying to do the same thing?"

"Will people be friends with me if I do?" asked Linda, who was now busy sorting out the silks, and quite enjoying it.

"I can't promise you that," said Miss Brown. "But at least they will take some notice of you. We haven't any idea what you are really like, you see. You just sit at the back of the class and say 'Yes, Miss Brown,' and 'No, Miss Brown,' and I don't believe that some of the children think you are real! Be a real person for a week, and see what happens. Don't mind being laughed at, and don't mind being pushed aside. Just make up your mind to be friends with everyone, no matter what they say or do."

"I will," said Linda, and she went home feeling excited and pleased. Now at last she was going to find out if she could get any friends. It seemed so simple when she thought about it.

"The only way to make friends is to BE one," she said again and again to herself. "Why didn't I think of that before?"

Linda felt quite excited when she got up the next morning. She rushed off to school early. On the way she met Billy and John. Billy was telling John about his new kitten. Neither of the boys took any notice of Linda.

"Do you know, my kitten climbed up on to the bookcase where Mummy keeps her bowl of goldfish — and it put its paw in to catch the fish!" said Billy. Linda walked beside Billy, listening.

"Tell me some more of the naughty things it does," she said.

Billy stared at her in surprise. "Do you like kittens, then?" he asked.

"I love them," said Linda. "Tell me all the things your kitten does."

Well, Billy was quite ready to do that. All the way to school he told about the bad things his kitten did, and Linda listened.

"You ought to come and see my kitten," said Billy, as they went in at the school gates. "I haven't got a name for it yet. You could think of one perhaps. Come after tea and see it, will you?"

Linda's heart jumped for joy. That was the very first time anyone had ever said "Come and see it."

"I'd love to," she said.

As they all took their things off in the cloakroom, untidy little Margery came in, panting because she was late. She flung her satchel down on the form — and it burst open. Out flew all her pencils, rulers, pen, books, and everything. "Oh dear, I'll be later than ever!" she said, and knelt down to pick them up.

Linda flew to help. "I'll pick them up while you hang up your things," she said. "Then you won't be late."

"Oh, thanks awfully, Linda," said Margery. "You *are* a brick!"

Linda went red. It was a funny thing to be called a brick, but she liked it. She picked all the things up and put them back into the satchel. Then she went off to the big hall. Margery came after her and slipped her arm in hers. "I should have been late if it hadn't been for you!" she said.

Nobody had ever slipped their arm through Linda's before. It was a lovely feeling.

There was painting that morning. Somebody always had to put out the water in the little pots. Linda put up her hand when the painting lesson came.

"May I fill the water-pots for you, Miss Brown?" she said, feeling quite nervous at hearing her own voice.

"Thank you, Linda. That would be kind of you," said Miss Brown at once.

Linda got the water in a little jug, and filled each pot without spilling a drop. It was really nice to be doing a job for the class. She had never offered to do one before.

"I'm getting on," she thought. "It's not as hard as I thought it would be." But the next thing that happened wasn't quite so easy.

It was playtime, in the middle of the morning. The children were going to play policemen and robbers. Kenneth was the head of the policemen, and he called out the names of the children he wanted. Mary was the head of the robbers.

"I'll be a policeman, Kenneth," said Linda eagerly. Kenneth looked at her.

"I don't want you," he said. "You wouldn't be any good."

Linda went red and felt very small. She went to Mary.

"Can I be on *your* side?" she asked.

"No, thanks," said Mary. "You're no good at games."

Well, that was rather dreadful. "But I suppose it's my own fault for never joining in before," thought Linda. She stood watching the others play. It looked so exciting. One of the robbers came squealing by her. It was Joan. As she went by, she caught her foot on something and fell over. Down she went with a crash!

Linda ran up to her, hoping that Joan wouldn't push her away.

"Oh, you've hurt your knee," she said. "Come with me and I'll bathe it for you."

Joan was crying. She was glad to lean on Linda's arm. She limped into the cloak-room and Linda bathed the knee for her. "Have you got a hanky?" she asked Joan.

"No, I've lost it," said Joan.

"Well, I'll lend you mine," said Linda. "It's one of my best ones, but never mind!" She bound up Joan's knee very well indeed.

"I never knew you were so kind before, Linda," said Joan, surprised. "Thank you. I'll bring back your hanky quite clean. I can't play policemen and robbers any more. Let's go and play a quiet game together in the garden."

So the two of them played together. Joan took Linda's arm when the bell went. "If my mother says you can, will you come to tea with me tomorrow?" she asked. Linda beamed joyfully.

"Oh *yes!*" she said. "Thank you."

Linda felt happy for the rest of the morning. After school the children went to their cloakrooms to get their coats and hats. Linda wondered if any of the children would ask her to walk home with them. She didn't quite like to ask anybody herself, for they all had their own special friends. But nobody asked her. It was disappointing.

"Still, I can't expect to have everything all at once," thought Linda. She was just going to leave, when she saw John rushing back.

"Linda! Have you seen my scarf? Mother said she'd be very cross if I didn't bring it home – and I nearly forgot it."

"No, I haven't seen it," said Linda, and was just going to walk off when she noticed how worried John looked. She stopped. "I'll help you to look for it if you like," she said.

"Oh, I say, thanks!" said John, and the two of them began to hunt around. Linda found the scarf at last, hung up on somebody else's peg. John was so pleased.

"You've saved me from getting into a row," he said, as he wound it round his neck. "I didn't know you were so nice, Linda. Walk with me on the Nature ramble this afternoon, will you?"

Linda sped home, delighted. She was going to see Billy's kitten after tea. She was going to walk with John in the afternoon. And she might be going to tea with Joan the next day. Her mother was most surprised to see such a happy face. Linda usually looked so very solemn and serious.

"Mother! Can I help you to lay the dinner?" cried Linda, ready to do anything for anybody, she felt so happy.

"Oh, darling, how sweet of you to want to help me," said her mother in surprise. "Yes – get the plates and the glasses, will you?"

As Linda ate her dinner she thought happily of the other children. Why, they were as nice and friendly as could be, after all! Miss Brown was quite right. She looked at her mother, a splendid idea coming into her head.

"Mother! Do you think I could give a little party soon?" she asked. "I've got some money left over from my birthday – I could buy a balloon for each child, and perhaps a box of crackers, if you can't afford to."

Linda's mother was astonished. Why, Linda had always said she had no friends to have at a party before – and now here she was, asking for one!

"Of course you can have a party," she said. "It would be lovely if you could buy balloons and crackers. I'll buy the cakes and the sweets and make lemonade for you."

"I'll ask the children this afternoon," said Linda. So she did. Everyone was surprised, but oh, how pleased! Boys and girls do so love parties, and Linda had never given one before.

"I'd love to come," said Hilary. "Thank you awfully."

"And I'd love to come too," said Robert. "And you must come to mine. It's on the twenty-third. Don't forget."

"And when I have *my* birthday party, I'll ask you too," said Margery, slipping her arm through Linda's. "Linda, you seem quite a different person this week. You're just as nice as anyone else!"

Linda asked Miss Brown to come too. Miss Brown looked at the little girl and smiled.

"Yes, I'll come," she said. "I shall like to see you giving balloons to all your friends. How does it feel to have plenty of friends, Linda, after having none at all?"

"It's wonderful," said Linda, slipping her hand into Miss Brown's. "It wasn't very difficult either, Miss Brown. I'm glad you told me what to do!"

And today is Linda's first party. She has spent all her money on colourful balloons, two boxes of crackers, and a little present for everyone, even Miss Brown. You should just see her in her blue party-frock, looking pretty and happy, standing at the door to welcome her friends.

"Yes, my *friends!*" she thought. "I've plenty now. Oh, how I wish I could tell everybody that the quickest way to make friends is to BE one. I'd so like everyone to know."

Well, I'm telling everybody for her. It's a very good idea, isn't it?

VERY MYSTERIOUS

When all kinds of things begin to disappear at school, it is hard to identify the culprit.

"Has anyone seen my silver pencil?" said Ted. "The little one that I won for swimming last Sports Day?"

"No. Where did you put it last?" asked Ruth.

"On my desk here, just by the window," said Ted. "I left it there after arithmetic, when we went out to play."

"Well, we've only just come back and nobody's been in the classroom," said Connie. "It must be somewhere about."

They hunted everywhere, but it couldn't be found. "Somebody might have passed the open window and seen your pencil on the desk," said Tessie. "It would be easy to put in a hand and take it."

"Who's been by the window?" asked Ted at once.

"I saw Mark going by here, when we were playing," said Hetty, after a pause.

"It *couldn't* have been Mark," said Connie. "He wouldn't do a thing like that."

"How do you know?" said Tessie. "He's often admired Ted's pencil. He hasn't got many things of his own, not even a paint-box."

"Well — we won't say anything more about it," said Ted, looking uncomfortable. "We've no proof. We can't go about accusing people unless we have proof. The pencil will turn up. But it really is very mysterious."

It didn't turn up. And then something else vanished, just after sewing lesson. It was Mary-Lou's little pair of scissors. Everyone loved them because they were so tiny and yet so sharp.

"Has anyone borrowed my scissors?" said Mary-Lou. No, nobody had.

"Look in your work-bag," said Miss Hicks. "They may be there, Mary-Lou. Perhaps you put them there when we went out for a nature lesson in the garden."

They weren't there. Mary-Lou was upset. "They belong to my Granny," she said. "She just lent me them for sewing lessons. I *must* find them."

But no, they were gone. Then Tessie whispered something to Mary-Lou. "I think Mark took them. He had to come to the classroom next to this to fetch something. I saw him walking down the passage."

"Oh, *no* – Mark wouldn't do that!" said Mary-Lou, shocked.

"Well, we think he took Ted's silver pencil, so why shouldn't he take something else?" said Tessie.

"Yes, why shouldn't he?" said Hetty, nodding her head. "*Some*body must have taken them."

So, when Mark next came into the classroom, the girls looked at him curiously. Had he taken Mary-Lou's scissors – and Ted's pencil?

"We'll wait and see if anything else goes, shall we?" said Connie. "Perhaps nothing will."

The next day Janet came hunting for her little tie-pin. It was in the shape of a fox's head, and she was very fond of it. "Has anyone seen it? I took it off when we changed for dancing," she said. "Now I can't find it anywhere. It should be in the changing-room but it isn't. It's really very mysterious."

Hetty looked at Tessie, and the same thought was in their minds. Was Mark anywhere near the changing-room while they had been dancing?

"I'll ask him," said Hetty. So, when she saw Mark, she called to him. "Mark – where were you while we girls were at our dancing-lessons?"

"Why do you want to know?" said Mark, surprised. "Well – let me see – I was doing some gardening – all the boys were. I was weeding by the changing-room – and I got awfully pricked by thistles, look!"

He held out his hands but Hetty didn't even look at them. She went to find Tessie.

"It *was* Mark," she said. "He was weeding by the changing-room – and he must have popped in there, taken the little foxhead tie-pin, and put it into his pocket."

"Can't we ask him to turn out his pockets?" asked Tessie. "Let's go and tell the others and see what they say."

Soon they had told everyone, and some of the children were shocked, others were angry, and all were quite disgusted. Fancy taking things like that from your friends. How horrid Mark must be!

"Oughtn't we to tell Miss Reader, the headmistress?" said Tessie. Ted shook his head.

"No. I don't think so. Nobody *saw* Mark — and my father says that you must never accuse anyone of anything like that unless you've got real proof."

"Well, we must watch him, then," said Tessie. "If we all keep an eye on him we're sure to see him doing something deceitful some time. Then we'll pounce!"

So the children kept an eye on Mark. Wherever he went somebody was sure to be behind him, or just nearby. Whenever he looked round, somebody's eyes were watching him. He began to feel uncomfortable.

"Don't they like me?" he thought. "They aren't nearly as nice to me as they used to be. Have I done something they don't like?"

For a whole week nothing disappeared. "He knows we're watching him," whispered Hetty to Tessie. "He daren't take anything at the moment. But you'll see — he will when he sees a chance!"

Then something else vanished. This time it was money! George had a coin given him for his bus-fares, and when he found that he had a hole in his pocket, he took out the coin, and put it on his desk for safety. And when he came back from Break, it was gone!

"I say — my money's gone!" said George. "Anyone being funny? It's my bus fare, so give it back, please."

But nobody gave it back. George couldn't help looking at Mark. Had *he* taken it?

"What are you looking at me like that for?" said Mark, going red. "You don't suppose *I've* taken it, do you?"

Nobody said anything to that — but some of them remembered that Mark hadn't been with them during the whole of Break. Where had he gone to?

I bet he took George's money," said Hetty. "What a pity we weren't watching him! We could have crept behind him and watched what he did. Then we should have caught him properly."

"Did you see how red he went when George looked at him?" said Tessie. "He's a thief! I really DO think we ought to tell Miss Reader!"

"Well — she takes Scripture lesson this afternoon," said Ted. " Perhaps we could tell her about all the things that have disappeared – and make Mark own up. I must say I'd like to get my silver pencil back."

So it was decided that Ted should stand up in Scripture lesson that afternoon and tell Miss Reader how worried they all were about their things disappearing. They would say that they felt sure it was one of their own number who was guilty – and leave it to Miss Reader to do the rest.

Mark felt very unhappy that day. Why did all the children look at him so oddly? Why wouldn't they walk with him? Why didn't they chatter with him as they did with one another? He looked very gloomy indeed.

Scripture lesson came. Miss Reader appeared, Bible in hand, and all the children stood.

"Sit," said Miss Reader, and they sat. The children looked at Ted. Now was the time they had planned for him to get up and make his speech. He put up his hand.

"Please, Miss Reader, may I say something – something serious?"

Miss Reader looked surprised. "Certainly," she said. " What is it?"

Then Ted told about the missing things – how they had suddenly vanished and not been found. Some of the children looked at Mark as Ted related all the things – the pencil, the scissors, the tie-pin, the coin. Mark saw them staring at him, and he went bright red, and looked miserable. The children nudged one another, and Hetty whispered to Tessie.

"Look at him – he looks guilty, doesn't he? He will just *have* to own up now!"

Miss Reader listened, looking grave. When Ted came to the end of his story, she spoke in a solemn voice. "Do you think that one of your number has taken these things? Think before you answer, please. This is a very serious thing."

Ted opened his mouth to answer – and at that very moment there came a knock at the door. In came – the gardener!

"Excuse me, Mam, for interrupting you – but I've come to show you what I've found," said the old gardener. He opened his brown, wrinkled hand – and  in it were all the things that had vanished! Yes, the pencil, the scissors, the tie-pin and the coin.

Everyone stared at them in amazement. "Dear me – this is very remarkable," said Miss Reader. "Where did you find them?"

"Well, Mam, there's been a jackdaw about the school lately," said the old man. "And I've been keeping an eye on him, for they be dreadful thieves, as you know. I saw him a-poking about in my shrubbery, hiding something under the dead leaves there, and off I went to poke in them myself!"

"Yes. Go on," said Miss Reader.

"Well, what did I find but all these things," said the gardener. "And I says to the jackdaw, "Ah, you be a rascal, taking the children's things. One of these days somebody else will be accused of taking them and get into trouble. And I took them and brought them, Mam, in case anyone had got into trouble already!"

"Thank you, Twigg," said Miss Reader. "Put the things on my desk. No one has got into trouble – but I think you came only just in time!"

And now every child in the class was red in the face except Mark. He was rather white. He gazed round, guessing that the others had thought he was the thief. But he wasn't. It was the artful old jackdaw who had popped in and out of the classroom!

"I don't think we need discuss the vanished things any more," said Miss Reader, looking round. "They are here again – and the jackdaw is the guilty one. I am sure that there is nobody in this room who would do what the jackdaw did, so we will leave it at that. BUT – if there is any one of you here who has thought false thoughts of anyone else, I hope you will show that you are sorry, in some good way."

Then the lesson went on as usual. But, dear me, how shocked and ashamed the children were, to think that almost – *almost* – they had accused Mark of being a thief!

"I must show I'm sorry," they thought, every single one of them. And goodness me, what a wonderful time Mark had that week! The children brought him sweets and little presents, they asked him out to tea, they begged him to walk with them to and from school, they couldn't do enough for him.

Mark was very happy. Everything was all right again. He called loudly to the jackdaw when he saw him. "Hey, you rascal! You nearly got me into trouble. Don't you do *that* again!"

"Chack-chack-chack," said the jackdaw, and flew off to see what else he could find. Whoever would have thought that *he* was the thief!

THE WORST BOY IN THE FORM

Sports day excitements provide the background for this day school adventure.

Now please remember," said the Headmaster to the whole school, "the Sports begin in Mr Williams' field at two o'clock sharp – so you must all be there at a quarter-to, and not a minute after. Otherwise you will be disqualified, and not allowed to run, jump or enter for anything. That's understood, is it?"

"Yes, sir," said the listening children, and all of them made up their minds to be there at half-past one, and not run any risk of being out of the sports.

"Very well. Dismiss!" said the Head, and the boys and girls marched out of the assembly hall.

They were all excited. Sports Day was such fun. Their parents came to see them, everything was free and easy, there was plenty of shouting, plenty of rushing about, and an enormous amount of clapping and cheering whenever anyone did anything really good.

"I'm going to go straight home to my dinner now and gobble it up," said Alec. "Then I'm going to change into my sports things and come straight back."

"I hope my mother will have *my* dinner ready," said Susan. "Sometimes it's late."

"Well, if mine's late I shall go without it," said Henry. "I wouldn't be out of the sports for anything. I mean to win the running!"

"Well, you won't," said Jeff. "I'm going to win the quarter-mile race. I've been practising like anything."

"I bet you won't be at the field at a quarter-to-two!" said Henry. "You're always late – and I bet you'll forget to put on a clean shirt!"

"And *I* bet Jeff will have a puncture in that awful old bike of his at the very last minute," said Pam. "You're never in time for anything, are you Jeff? You're always losing marks or being late, or careless and forgetful."

Jeff grinned. He was very good-tempered. "I know. I'm untidy and never remember a thing. I'm never in time, I don't wash properly, I lose my shoes – go on, let me hear it all. I'm the worst boy in the form, I let the school down – I've heard it all before! Still – I'll be punctual this afternoon all right – because I'm going to win the quarter-mile race!"

"You're not," said Henry. But secretly he was afraid that Jeff *might* win. He certainly had practised a great deal.

They all went home, some walking, some by bus, some on their bicycles. They had been sent back early that morning, so that they could all be back in good time for the sports.

"Mother!" yelled Jeff, as soon as he got home. "Is my dinner ready? I've got to get back early for the sports today."

"Oh dear – I forgot," said his mother. "I've a memory just like yours, Jeff. Well, you'll have to scrape round the larder and see what you can find."

"Did you wash and iron my other white shirt?" asked Jeff. "You said you would. We've all got to look clean and tidy today. Extra special!"

"There now – I did wash your shirt, but I haven't ironed it," said his mother. She was just like Jeff – rather untidy, forgetful and very careless. No wonder Jeff was like that too! The neighbours all turned up their noses at her and her family.

"What a home!" they said. "Not a clean spot in it! And if she plans to cook meat for dinner she can't because she's probably forgotten to fetch the joint! And why doesn't somebody weed the garden? Really, they let the whole street down!"

"Look, Mother – you iron my shirt now," said Jeff getting some bread and cheese out of the larder. "I've just *got* to be in time today. It won't take you long, will it?"

"Oh no – I'll do it straightaway," said his mother, switching on the electric iron. Jeff set up the ironing board for her. He chattered away to his mother as she ironed.

"Can you come along at about three o'clock and see me win the quarter-mile?" he asked. "Put on your nicest frock, and come and clap me!"

"Well, I might, if I've got time," said his mother. "There – your shirt's finished. There's a button missing – I'll just put it on – or does it matter?"

"Oh, Mother – yes, of course, I must have a button on for the *sports*," said Jeff. "And do remember to put on a nice dress when you come along this afternoon. What a dreadful family we are! No wonder people point their fingers at us and say we're a disgrace!"

He set off at just after half-past one. He had to go the same way as Henry and Susan, and he was sure they were already a long way ahead of him. He only *just* had time to get to the Sports field at a quarter-to-two.

Henry and Susan were a long way ahead. Susan had left her house in very good time, because she had to walk, and she went quickly down the long lane from her home to Mr Williams' field.

Halfway down she stopped and looked round and about. What was that she heard? It sounded like someone crying.

Yes, it was. The noise came from the little wood that lay near the lane. She called out.

"What's the matter? Who's crying?"

A weak voice answered. "Come and help me! I'm Robin Holt."

"Susan stepped into the wood. It was dark there, for the sun hardly pierced the thick trees. "Where are you?" she called.

"Here!" said the voice, and Susan saw a small boy lying beside a bush. He had a black eye and his nose was bleeding.

"I was walking through the wood and two big boys set on me and fought me and knocked me down. Then they took my wrist watch and some money I had, and my new torch. When I fell down I hurt my ankle and I can't walk on it."

"Oh dear!" said Susan, in alarm, looking all round her. "Are the boys anywhere near?"

"They've only just gone," said Robin, wiping away his tears. "Can you help me?"

Susan heard the sound of trees rustling in the wind and stared round her in a panic. Was it those two boys coming again? Her heart thumped as she ran back to the lane at once.

"I'll tell somebody to come and help you," she called. "I'll tell somebody!"

And she ran down the lane to make up for the time she had lost. She couldn't possibly stop and help Robin – those boys might come back and knock her down too!

A few minutes later Henry came riding by on his bicycle. Robin heard him whistling as he came, and shouted as loudly as he could.

"Help! Help!"

Henry stopped. Who was that calling? He jumped off his bicycle and went to see. He soon came to Robin, and heard his tale.

Henry was not afraid of the two boys who had hurt and robbed Robin – but he was in a great hurry! He looked at his watch. Goodness, he couldn't possibly spare ten minutes to get this kid out of the wood and home!

"Look here – someone is sure to come along again soon," he said. "You just stay here and yell when you hear anyone. I can't stop. Sorry and all that – but I don't think you're *very* badly hurt!"

And he left Robin and went to his bicycle. He was soon riding quickly down the road to make up for lost time.

Robin felt very miserable. He tried to stand up but his ankle hurt so much that he fell down again, looking suddenly white. Then he heard someone else coming along the lane, on a bicycle that made a rattling, clanking noise. He called out.

"Help! Help me, somebody!"

It was Jeff on the bicycle, in his nice clean shirt, racing along at top speed. When he heard the voice he put on his brakes and came to a sudden stop. He threw his bicycle into the hedge and ran to the little wood.

"What's up? Who's calling?" he cried – and then he saw Robin, and heard his tale.

"Golly – they did give you a bang!" said Jeff, looking at the boy's black eye and bleeding nose. "And what's this cut on your head?"

"I did that when I fell down," said Robin. "I think I hit it on a stone. Is it bleeding?"

"Rather!" said Jeff and took out his nice clean hanky. He tied it round the boy's head. "Now I'll help you up," he said. "You can lean on me. Where do you live?"

"At Granger's Farm," said Robin, gratefully. "But aren't you on the way to school? The others would not stop, they were in such a hurry."

"What others?" said Jeff, surprised. "Do you mean to say two children saw you and didn't stop to help?"

Robin nodded. He was now leaning on Jeff, hopping on his good foot and dragging his hurt one. Jeff glanced at his wrist watch. Almost a quarter-to-two! He'd never get to the Sports Field in time! Would the sports master listen to his tale, and excuse him for being late when he knew what had happened?

"I expect he will," thought Jeff. "Anyway, I can't help it. I've got to take this kid home. He doesn't look at all well to me."

Jeff helped the boy to where he had left his bicycle, and then sat Robin on the saddle. He wheeled him to his home at Granger's Farm. A worried-looking woman came to the door.

"Robin! I've been looking for you. Whatever's happened?"

"Two boys set on him," said Jeff. "I found him lying near the lane. Can I do anything more? If not, I must rush off."

Robin's mother put her arm round her son and looked at Jeff gratefully. "You've been kind," she said. "But don't stop now. You go to Hallam's School, don't you? I can see by your cap – and it's their Sports Day, I know."

"My uncle's going," said Robin. "Is he here, Mummy? He said he'd take me to see the sports, but I can't go now."

Jeff saw that it was now two o'clock. He really MUST go, and he did hope that the sports master would excuse him. He raised his cap to Robin's mother and leapt on his bicycle. He pedalled away at top speed, scaring the hens in the drive and making them run clucking away.

The sports master frowned when he saw Jeff ride into the field and fling his bicycle down on the grass. The boy came running up, panting.

"Sir! I couldn't help it. I had to help a—"

"I'm not listening to any excuses from a boy who is over twenty minutes late," said Mr James. "You can consider yourself out of the sports today, Jeff."

"But, sir – if you'd just listen, you'd see that I couldn't—" began Jeff again. But Mr James turned away.

"There's no more to be said," he grunted, annoyed that the best runner in the school should be so unpunctual. Jeff went red and turned away too. He put his hands deep down into his pockets, and glared at Henry, who had just come up.

"You *are* a fathead to come so—" began Henry – but for once in a way Jeff did not feel good-tempered, and he shoved past him, and went to the back of the crowd. Out of the sports! And he had so hoped to win the quarter-mile race! Mr James *might* have listened to him. He wouldn't watch anything! He would go home and kick a ball round the garden.

But he didn't. He heard shouts and yells, and knew that a race had begun – what was it – the three-legged race? He went to watch. Soon he forgot that he had meant to go home and stood clapping with the rest.

At three o'clock there was a stir among the grown-ups who sat watching – the parents, their friends, the masters and mistresses. Somebody was arriving.

"It's Mr Reynolds – he's to give the prizes at the end of the afternoon," said the children. "He's the man who once won medals at the Olympic Games! Give him a clap!"

So they clapped and cheered, and Mr Reynolds stood smiling and waving. The Headmaster led him to a seat, and he sat down. Soon the two men were talking hard.

Henry watched them. He was very glad that Jeff was out of the big race. Now he would win it easily – and Mr Reynolds, the Olympic runner, would present him with his prize. His mother and father were there – they would watch and clap like anything.

The next event was a long jump. Jeff had meant to go in for this too, though he was not a good jumper. He watched the others with interest.

As he watched, a tap came on his shoulder. Jeff turned and saw one of the masters. "The Head wants to see you," he said.

Jeff's heart thumped. What had he done *now*? Surely the Head wasn't going to scold him this afternoon while the sports were on? He followed the master to where the Head sat with Mr Reynolds.

"Jeff," said the Head, "why aren't you joining in the sports? We have been watching for you to compete, because Mr Reynolds wanted to see you."

"Oh," said Jeff, astonished. "Well – you see, sir, I was late – and Mr James wouldn't let me go in for any of the events. That's why."

"Why were you late?" said the Head.

Jeff hesitated. Should he tell him or not? But Mr Reynolds spoke suddenly.

"I can tell why you were late!" he said. "It was you who helped my nephew Robin, wasn't it? It was you who bandaged him, set him on your bicycle and took him home? And that made you late for the sports."

Jeff went red. "Yes, sir," he said. "That *is* what happened. But how did you know?"

"I was at Granger's Farm for lunch with my sister, Robin's mother," said Mr Reynolds. "Robin told me all about you – and his mother knew your name. So I came to the sports, not only to present the prizes, but to see you and thank you for helping the small boy. I told the Head about it, and he said he would point you out to me in some of the races – but to our surprise you weren't in any."

"No, sir. I was late, so Mr James wouldn't let me join in," said Jeff. "I don't mind about the three-legged race and the long jump – I wouldn't have had much chance in those, anyway – but I was sorry about the quarter-mile. I might have won that."

"You can go in for any event you like!" said the Head, and Jeff beamed. "Apparently two children from this school saw Robin and wouldn't help him – but you came by and although you knew it would make you very late, you did all you could for him. You're a credit to the school!"

"And I wish you luck in the quarter-mile race!" said Mr Reynolds, smiling. "Go along now – it's just about due. The boys are lining up!"

Well! Jeff sped off to the boys, hardly believing it could all be true. He lined up, laughing to see Henry's surprised face. The pistol cracked – they were off!

Did Jeff win? Yes, of course he did, beating Henry, who was second, by ten yards. You should have heard the cheers and shouts! Jeff might have a lot of faults – but all the children liked him for his kindness of heart.

Jeff nearly burst with pride when Mr Reynolds presented him with the prize – a brand-new cricket bat! And will you believe it, the Head stood up and added a few words too, telling how Jeff had been late – and why.

"I am sorry to say that two other children from this school had the chance of helping Robin," he said, "but they didn't. They went on their way and left him there."

Henry's face went scarlet and so did Susan's. They simply didn't know where to look!

Jeff carried his bat off proudly to show the boys. "May you make hundreds of runs with it!" Mr Reynolds called after him.

He will! He has made five hundred and twenty-seven runs already this season. Well done, Jeff!

SOMETHING WENT WRONG!

≈ ILLUSTRATED BY ≈

Marjorie L. Davies

The boys in this story realise that it's better to do their own work than to rely on others.

Alan! Wait!" said a voice from the hedge, as Alan came along on his way to school. Alan looked round. It was Ted, lying in wait for him.

"What do you want?" said Alan. "I'm not telling you any of the homework answers, if that's what you're after!"

"Oh, come on, Alan!" said Ted, coming out of the hedge. "I didn't have time to work out those sums last night. Tell me the answers quickly, and I'll write them down."

"No. Why should I?" said Alan. You're a cheat, always copying other people's work. Do your *own* work!"

"I'm not a cheat," said Ted. "I could work out all those sums and get the right answers — but I just can't be bothered. All I want you to do is to let me put down the answers you've got — mine would be exactly the same if I worked them out myself, you know they would."

"*No,*" said Alan. "You cribbed my geography answers last week — and you copied my history dates. You jolly well work out your own sums!"

Ted suddenly leapt at Alan and tore his satchel off his shoulder. He ripped it open and took out his arithmetic book. Alan tried to grab it but Ted fended him off. He was no bigger than Alan but he was strong and determined.

"Go on — be a sport," he said. "I'll give you half my Saturday pocket-money. I shan't be a tick copying out your answers. I've got my sums all written down — I only want the answers."

"I've a good mind to tell our teacher what you do," said Alan.

"No, you won't. You're not a tell-tale," said Ted, busily copying down the figures he wanted. "There – that's all. Thanks awfully, Alan. Good thing you always get your sums right, or I should be in trouble!"

"One of these days you'll be sorry," said Alan, taking back his book. " But *I* shall be glad if you're stopped doing this kind of thing. And *keep* your pocket-money – *I* don't want any of it. I'd be as bad as you if I took it!"

"Now don't be cross," said Ted, and he slipped his arm through Alan's. "If ever you want to copy any of *my* homework, you're welcome."

"Thanks – but as I've told you a dozen times I'm not a cheat," said Alan. "You'll make a mistake one of these days and get into a mess!"

"No. I'm not silly enough for *that*," said Ted and laughed. He was clever and sly, hardly ever in trouble, and often top of the form. He didn't *need* to copy other people's work, but there were times when he just couldn't be bothered to do his own.

The two boys were soon at school. They gave in their homework as usual, and then settled down to morning lessons. Ted yawned. He had been up very late the night before and he was sleepy. He glanced at the exercise book of the boy next to him. It would be easier to copy from him than to work out answers himself – but it would be dangerous, because Peter's answers were often wrong! Ted gave a sigh and settled down to work them out.

Soon it was time for the arithmetic lesson, and the master took up the pile of homework books. He opened them rapidly and looked down the answers, calling out marks as he did so.

"Ronald – all sums correct save one – 9 marks out of 10. Leslie, only six right. Four to be done again, 6 out of ten. Alan – all correct. Excellent – 10 out of 10."

Ted smiled. Aha! If Alan's sums were all right, then his would be too, for he had copied each answer carefully. He would get 10 out of 10 too. The master went on reading out the results.

"Wilfrid – five out of ten. Come to me after school. John, nine out of ten correct – good. Ted . . . er . . . Ted – good gracious, *every single sum is wrong*! This won't do, Ted. You have been extremely careless! You will stay in and do them all again. Nought out of 10!"

"But sir – I *know* they're right!" cried Ted, amazed.

"Then you know wrong," said the master. "Not one correct."

"But — but you said *Alan's* were right!" said Ted, still looking astonished.

"What has that got to do with *your* sums?" said the teacher, sharply. "Because Alan has worked *his* out correctly doesn't therefore mean that you have, too!"

"But it *does!*" argued Ted, quite bewildered. Hadn't he copied Alan's answers down, figure by figure — well then, how *could* his be wrong? He glanced round at Alan and saw that he was grinning from ear to ear. So were some of the other boys. Why? What was so funny?

"Come here," said the teacher, beginning to lose his temper. Ted went to his desk and looked where the master was pointing with his pencil. He had Alan's book open before him and also Ted's "Perhaps you will believe me when you see these two books side by side," said the master, grimly — and Ted saw to his horror that all his answers were quite different from Alan's.

"Explain this nonsense, please," said the master. "You can't? I thought not. Stay in for an extra hour, and do them all again — *and* an extra twelve as well. And I shall also expect an explanation of your curious statement that if Alan's sums are right, then yours must be. Go back to your seat."

Ted went back, his face red, trying not to see the grins of the other boys. They were glad he had got into trouble. But whatever had gone wrong? He ought to have got 10 out of 10 if Alan had!

At break, he went to Alan. "Look here," he began — but Alan laughed loudly. The other boys came round too, all grinning and enjoying the joke.

"It's your own fault, Ted," said Alan. "I told you that your cheating would get you into trouble one day — and it has. How was *I* to know that you'd got my book open at last week's page and were copying down the answers to *last week's* sums, instead of this week's! It serves you right — and just you be careful I don't play the same trick again, now that I see how it works!"

"Did you *mean* me to copy the wrong answers?" asked Ted, fiercely.

"No — *I* didn't know you'd got the wrong page!" said Alan. "Ha ha! Who's got to stay in and do an hour's work — and what explanation are you going to give to our teacher about it all? I bet he guesses what's happened!"

That was the end of Ted's copying other boys' work. He was much too afraid of trying it again in case the boys played him the same trick! Still, he's top of the form and finds it easy to keep there.

"Better to be top by your own efforts, than by somebody else's, Ted!" said his teacher, with an odd little smile. " Funny things happen when you trust someone else to do *your* job, don't they?"

"Yes, sir — but they won't happen to *me* again!" said Ted. "*I* didn't think it was at all funny!"

FIRST TERM AT MALORY TOWERS

AN EXTRACT

≈ ILLUSTRATED BY ≈

Stanley Lloyd

Twelve-year-old Darrell Rivers is just about to start her first term at Malory Towers, a boarding school set on the Cornish coast. With a tall tower at each corner, Malory Towers looks just like a medieval castle. The towers house the dormitories and Darrell is to be a North Tower girl, which means that from her dormitory window she will have a wonderful view out to sea. Here we meet Darrell waiting for the taxi to take her to London where she will board the special train taking the Malory Towers girls to Cornwall . . .

CHAPTER I
OFF TO BOARDING SCHOOL

Darrell Rivers looked at herself in the mirror. It was almost time to start for the train, but there was just a minute to see how she looked in her new school uniform.

"It's jolly nice," said Darrell, turning herself about. "Brown coat, brown hat, orange ribbon, and a brown tunic underneath with an orange belt. I like it."

Her mother looked into Darrell's room, and smiled.

"Admiring yourself?" she said. "Well, I like it all too. I must say Malory Towers has a lovely school uniform. Come along, Darrell. We don't want to miss the train your very first term!"

Darrell felt excited. She was going to boarding school for the first time. Malory Towers did not take children younger than twelve, so Darrell would be one of the youngest there. She looked forward to many terms of fun and friendship, work and play.

"What will it be like?" she kept wondering. "I've read lots of school stories, but I expect it won't be quite the same at Malory Towers. Every school is different. I do hope I make some friends there."

Darrell was sad at leaving her own friends behind her. None of them was going to

Malory Towers. She had been to a day school with them, and most of them were either staying on there or going to different boarding schools.

Her trunk was packed full. On the side was painted in big black letters DARRELL RIVERS. On the labels were the letters M.T. for Malory Towers. Darrell had only to carry her tennis racket in its press, and her small bag in which her mother had packed her things for the first night.

"Your trunks won't be unpacked the first evening," she said. "So each girl has to take a small hand-bag with her nighty and tooth-brush and things like that. Here is your ten-pound note. You must make that last a whole term, because no girl in your form is allowed to have more pocket-money than that."

"I shall make it do!" said Darrell, putting it into her purse. "There won't be much I have to buy at school! There's the taxi waiting, Mother. Let's go!"

She had already said goodbye to her father, who had driven off to his work that morning. He had squeezed her hard and said, "Goodbye and good luck, Darrell. You'll get a lot out of Malory Towers, because it's a fine school. Be sure you give them a lot back!"

Now they were off at last, the trunk in the taxi too, beside the driver. Darrell put her head out to take a last look at her home. "I'll be back soon!" she called, to the big black cat who sat on the wall, washing himself. "I'll miss you all at first but I'll soon settle down. Shan't I, Mother?"

"Of course," said her mother. You'll have a lovely time! You won't want to come home for the summer holidays!"

They had to go up to London to catch the train for Cornwall, where Malory Towers was. "There's a special train always, for Malory Towers," said Mrs Rivers. "Look, there's a notice up. Malory Towers. Platform 7. Come along. We're in nice time. I'll stay with you a few minutes and see you safely with your house-mistress and her girls, then I'll go."

They went on to the platform. A long train was drawn up there, labelled Malory Towers. All the carriages were reserved for the girls of that school. The train had different labels stuck in the windows. The first lot said "North Tower". The second lot said "South Tower". Then came compartments labelled "West Tower" and others labelled "East Tower".

"You're North Tower," said her mother. "Malory Towers has four different boarding houses for its girls, all topped by a tower. You'll be in North Tower, the Head Mistress said, and your house-mistress is Miss Potts. We must find her."

Darrell stared about her at the girls on the crowded platform. They all seemed to be Malory girls, for she saw the brown coats and hats, with the orange ribbons, everywhere. They all seemed to know one another, and laughed and chattered at the tops of their voices. Darrell felt suddenly shy.

"I shall never never know all these girls!" she thought, as she stared round. "Gracious, what big ones some of them are! They look quite grown-up. I shall be terrified of them."

Certainly the girls in the top forms seemed very grown-up to Darrell. They took no notice at all of the little ones. The younger girls made way for them, and they climbed into their carriages in a rather lordly manner.

"Hallo, Lottie! Hallo, Mary! I say, there's Penelope! Hi, Penny, come over here. Hilda, you never wrote to me in the hols, you mean pig! Jean, come into our carriage!"

The happy voices sounded all up and down the platform. Darrell looked for her mother. Ah, there she was, talking to a keen-faced mistress. That must be Miss Potts. Darrell stared at her. Yes, she liked her – she liked the way her eyes twinkled – but there was something very determined about her mouth. It wouldn't do to get into her bad books.

Miss Potts came over and smiled down at Darrell. "Well, new girl!" she said. "You'll be in my carriage going down – look, that one over there. The new girls always go with me."

"Oh, are there new girls besides me – in my form, I mean?" asked Darrell.

"Oh, yes. Two more. They haven't arrived yet. Mrs Rivers, here is a girl in Darrell's form – Alicia Johns. She will look after Darrell for you, when you've said goodbye."

"Hallo," said Alicia, and two bright eyes twinkled at Darrell. "I'm in your form. Do you want to get a corner-seat? If so, you'd better come now."

"Then I'll say goodbye, dear," said Mrs Rivers, cheerfully, and she kissed Darrell and gave her a hug. "I'll write as soon as I get your letter. Have a lovely time!"

"Yes, I will," said Darrell, and watched her mother go down the platform. She didn't have time to feel lonely because Alicia took complete charge of her at once, pushed her to Miss Potts' carriage, and shoved her up the step. "Put your bag in one corner and I'll put mine opposite," said Alicia. "Then we can stand at the door and see what's happening. I say – look over there. Picture of How Not to Say Goodbye to your Darling Daughter!"

Darrell looked to where Alicia nodded. She saw a girl about her own age, dressed in the same school uniform, but with her hair long and loose down her back. She was clinging to her mother and wailing.

"Now what that mother should do would be to grin, shove some chocolate at her and go!" said Alicia. "If you've got a kid like that, it's hopeless to do anything else. Poor little mother's darling!"

The mother was almost as bad as the girl. Tears were running down her face too. Miss Potts walked firmly up to them.

"Now you watch Potty," said Alicia. Darrell felt rather shocked. Potty! What a name to give your house-mistress. Anyway, Miss Potts didn't look in the least potty. She looked thoroughly all-there.

"I'll take Gwendoline," she said to the girl's mother. "It's time she went to her carriage. She'll soon settle down there, Mrs Lacey."

Gwendoline appeared ready to go, but her mother clung to her still. Alicia snorted. "See what's made Gwendoline such an idiot?" she said. "Her mother! Well, I'm glad mine is sensible. Yours looked jolly nice too – cheerful and jolly."

Darrell was pleased at this praise of her mother. She watched Miss Potts firmly disentangle Gwendoline from her mother and lead her towards them.

"Alicia! Here's another one," she said, and Alicia pulled Gwendoline up into the carriage.

Gwendoline's mother came to the carriage too and looked in. "Take a corner-seat, darling," she said. "And don't sit with your back to the engine. You know how sick it makes you. And . . ."

Another girl came up to the carriage, a small, sturdy girl, with a plain face and hair tightly plaited back. "Is this Miss Potts's carriage?" she asked.

"Yes," said Alicia. "Are you the third new girl? North Tower?"

"Yes. I'm Sally Hope," said the girl.

"Where's your mother?" asked Alicia. "She ought to go and deliver you to Miss Potts first, so that you can be crossed off her list."

"Oh, Mother didn't bother to come up with me," said Sally. "I came by myself."

"Gracious!" said Alicia. "Well, mothers are all different. Some come along and smile and say goodbye, and some come along and weep and wail – and some just don't come at all."

"Alicia – don't talk so much," came Miss Potts's voice. She knew Alicia's wild tongue. Mrs Lacey suddenly looked annoyed, and forgot to give any more instructions to Gwendoline. She stared at Alicia angrily. Fortunately the guard blew his whistle just then and there was a wild scramble for seats.

Miss Potts jumped in with two or three more girls. The door slammed. Gwendoline's mother peered in, but alas, Gwendoline was on the floor, hunting for something she had dropped.

"Where's Gwendoline!" came Mrs Lacey's voice. "I must say goodbye. Where's . . ."

But the train was now puffing out. Gwendoline sat up and howled.

"I didn't say goodbye!" she wailed.

"Well, how many times did you want to?" demanded Alicia. "You'd already said it about twenty times."

Miss Potts looked at Gwendoline. She had already sized her up and knew her to be a spoilt, only child, selfish, and difficult to handle at first.

She looked at quiet little Sally Hope. Funny little girl, with her tight plaits and prim, closed-up face. No mother had come to see her off. Did Sally care? Miss Potts couldn't tell.

Then she looked at Darrell. It was quite easy to read Darrell. She never hid anything, and she said what she thought, though not so bluntly as Alicia did.

"A nice, straightforward, trustable girl," thought Miss Potts. "Can be a bit of a monkey, I should think. She looks as if she has good brains. I'll see that she uses them! I can do with a girl like Darrell in North Tower!"

The girls began to talk. "What's Malory Towers like?" asked Darrell. "I've seen a photograph of it, of course. It looked awfully big."

"It is. It's got the most gorgeous view over the sea, too," said Alicia. "It's built on the cliff, you know. It's lucky you're in North Tower — that's got the best view of all!"

"Does each Tower have its own schoolrooms?" asked Darrell. Alicia shook her head.

"Oh, no! All the girls from each of the four Tower houses go to the same classrooms. There are about sixty girls in each house. Pamela is head of ours. There she is over there!

Pamela was a tall, quiet girl, who had got into the carriage with another girl about her own age. They seemed very friendly with Miss Potts, and were eagerly discussing with her the happenings planned for the term.

Alicia, another girl called Tessie, Sally and Darrell chattered too. Gwendoline sat in her corner and looked gloomy. Nobody paid her any attention at all, and she wasn't used to that!

She gave a little sob, and looked at the others out of the corner of her eye. Sharp Alicia saw the look and grinned. "Just putting it on!" she whispered to Darrell. "People who really do feel miserable always turn away and hide it somehow. Don't take any notice of our darling Gwendoline."

Poor Gwendoline! If she had only known it, Alicia's lack of sympathy was the best thing for her. She had always had far too much of it, and life at Malory Towers was not going to be easy for her.

"Cheer up, Gwendoline," said Miss Potts, in a cheerful tone, and immediately turned to talk to the big girls again.

"I feel sick," announced Gwendoline at last, quite determined to be in the limelight and get sympathy somehow.

"You don't look it," said the downright Alicia. "Does she, Miss Potts? I always go green when I feel sick."

Gwendoline wished she could really be sick! That would serve this sharp-tongued girl right. She leaned back against the back of the seat, and murmured faintly. "I really do feel sick! Oh, dear, what shall I do?"

"Here, wait a bit – I've got a paper bag," said Alicia, and fished a big one out of her bag. "I've got a brother who's always sick in a car, so Mother takes paper bags with her wherever she goes, for Sam. I always think it's funny to see him stick his nose in it, poor Sam – like a horse with a nose-bag!"

Nobody could help laughing at Alicia's story. Gwendoline didn't, of course, but looked angry. That horrid girl, poking fun at her again. She wasn't going to like her at all.

After that Gwendoline sat quiet, and made no further attempt to get the attention of the others. She was afraid of what Alicia might say next.

But Darrell looked at Alicia with amusement and liking. How she would like her for a friend! What fun they could have together!

CHAPTER II
MALORY TOWERS

It was a long journey to Malory Towers, but as there was a dining-car on the train, and the girls took it in turns to go and have their midday meal, that made a good break. They had tea on the train too. At first all the girls were lively and chattery, but as the day wore on they fell silent. Some of them slept. It was such a long journey!

It was exciting to reach the station for Malory Towers. The school lay a mile or two away, and there were big motor coaches standing outside the station to take the girls to the school.

"Come on," said Alicia, clutching hold of Darrell's arm. "If we're quick we can get one of the front seats in a coach, beside the driver. Hurry! Got your bag?"

"I'll come too," said Gwendoline. But the others were gone long before she had collected her belongings. They climbed up into front seats. The other girls came out in twos and threes, and the station's one and only porter helped the drivers to load the many trunks on to the coaches.

"Can we see Malory Towers from here?" asked Darrell, looking all round.

"No. I'll tell you when we can. There's a corner where we suddenly get a glimpse of it," said Alicia.

"Yes. It's lovely to get that sudden view of it," said Pamela, the quiet head-girl of North Tower, who had got into the coach just behind Alicia and Darrell. Her eyes shone as she spoke. "I think Malory Towers shows at its best when we come to that corner, especially if the sun is behind it."

Darrell could feel the warmth in Pamela's voice as she spoke of the school she loved. She looked at her and liked her.

Pamela saw her look and laughed. "You're lucky, Darrell," she said. "You're just beginning at Malory Towers! You've got terms and terms before you. I'm just ending. Another term or two, and I shan't be coming to Malory Towers any more – except as an old girl. You make the most of it while you can."

"I shall," said Darrell, and stared ahead, waiting for her first glimpse of the school she was to go to for at least six years.

They rounded a corner. Alicia nudged her arm. "There you are, look! Over there, on that hill! The sea is behind, far down the cliff, but you can't see that, of course."

Darrell looked. She saw a big, square-looking building of soft grey stone standing high up on a hill. The hill was really a cliff that fell steeply down to the sea. At each end of the gracious building stood rounded towers. Darrell could glimpse two other towers behind as well, making four in all. North Tower, South, East and West.

The windows shone. The green creeper that covered parts of the wall climbed almost to the roof in places. It looked like an old-time castle.

"My school!" thought Darrell, and a little warm feeling came into her heart. "It's fine. How lucky I am to be having Malory Towers as my school-home for so many years. I shall love it."

"Do you like it?" asked Alicia, impatiently.

"Yes. Very much," said Darrell. "But I shall never never know my way about it! It's so big."

"Oh, I'll soon show you," said Alicia. "It's surprising how quickly you get to know your way round."

The coach turned another corner and Malory Towers was lost to sight. It came into view again, nearer still, round the next corner, and it wasn't very long before all the

coaches roared up to the flight of steps that led to the great front door.

"It's just like a castle entrance!" said Darrell.

"Yes," said Gwendoline, unexpectedly, from behind them. "I shall feel like a fairy princess, going up those steps!" She tossed her loose golden hair back over her shoulders.

"You would," said Alicia, scornfully. "But you'll soon get ideas like that out of your head when Potty gets going on you."

Darrell got down and was immediately lost in a crowd of girls, all swarming up the steps. She looked round for Alicia, but she seemed to have disappeared. So up the steps went Darrell, clutching her small bag and racket, feeling rather lost and lonely in the chattering crowd of girls. She felt in quite a panic without the friendly Alicia!

After that things were rather a blur. Darrell didn't know where to go and she didn't know what to do. She looked vainly for Alicia, or Pamela, the head-girl. Was she supposed to go straight to North Tower? Everyone seemed to know exactly what to do and where to go, except poor Darrell!

Then she saw Miss Potts, and felt a wave of relief. She went up to her, and Miss Potts looked down, smiling. "Hallo! Feeling lost? Where's that rascal of an Alicia? She ought to look after you. All North Tower girls are to go there and unpack their night-bags. Matron is waiting for you all."

Darrell had no idea which way to go for North Tower, so she stood by Miss Potts, waiting. Alicia soon reappeared again, accompanied by a crowd of girls.

"Hallo!" she said to Darrell. "I lost you. These are all girls in our form, but I won't tell you their names just now. You'll only get muddled. Some are North Tower girls, but some belong to the other houses. Come on, let's go to North Tower and see Matron. Where's darling Gwendoline?"

"Alicia," said Miss Potts, her voice stern, but her eyes twinkling. "Give Gwendoline a chance!"

"And Sally Hope. Where's she?" said Alicia. "Come on, Sally. All right, Miss Potts, I'll take them along to North Tower, and nurse them a bit!"

Sally, Gwendoline and Darrell followed Alicia. They were in a big hall that had doors leading off on either side, and a wide staircase curving upwards.

"The assembly hall, the gyms, the lab, the art rooms, and the needlework room are all on this side," said Alicia. "Come on, we'll cross the Court to get to our tower."

Darrell wondered what the Court was. She soon found out. Malory Towers was built round a large oblong space, called the Court. Alicia took her and the others out of a door opposite the entrance they had come in by, and there lay the Court surrounded on all sides by the buildings.

"What a lovely place!" said Darrell. "What's that sunk piece in the middle?"

She pointed to a great circle of green grass sunk a good way below the level of the Court. Round the sloping sides of the circle were stone seats. It looked like an open-air circus ring, the ring sunk low, and the stone seats rising upwards around it, Darrell thought.

"That's where we act plays in the summer," said Alicia. "The players perform in the ring, and the audience sit round on those stone seats. We have good fun."

Round the sunk circle, on the level, was a beautifully set out garden, with roses and all kinds of flowers planted there. Green lawns, not yet cut by the gardeners, were set between the beds.

"It's warm and sheltered in the Court," said Darrell.

"It's too hot in the summer," said Alicia, steering them all across the Court to the opposite side. "But you should see it in the Easter term! When we come back, in January, leaving our own homes in frost and maybe snow, we find snowdrops and aconites and primroses blooming in all the beds here, in the sheltered Court. It's gorgeous. Well, look at the tulips coming out here already, a nd it's only April!"

At each end of the hollow oblong of buildings was a tower. Alicia was making for North Tower. It was exactly like the other three. Darrell looked at it. It was four storeys high. Alicia stopped short just outside.

"On the ground floor there's our dining-hall, our common-rooms, where we go when we're not in class, and the kitchens. On the second floor are the dormies, where we sleep – dormitories, you know. On the third floor are more dormies. On the top floor are the bedrooms of the staff, and the box rooms for our luggage."

"And each house is the same, I suppose?" said Darrell, and she looked up at her tower. "I wish I slept right at the top there, in the tower itself. What a lovely view I'd have!"

Girls were going in and out of the open door at the bottom of North Tower. "Buck up!" they called to Alicia. "Supper's in a few minutes' time – something good by the smell of it!"

"We always get a jolly good supper the day we arrive," said Alicia. "After that – not so good! Cocoa and biscuits, something like that. Come on, let's find Matron."

Each of the Tower houses had its own matron, responsible for the girls' health and well-being. The matron of North Tower was a plump, bustling woman, dressed in starched apron and print frock, very neat and spotless.

Alicia took the new girls to her. "Three more for you to dose and scold and run after!" said Alicia, with a grin.

Darrell looked at Matron, frowning over the long lists in her hand. Her hair was neatly tucked under a pretty cap, tied in a bow under her chin. She looked so spotless that Darrell began to feel very dirty and untidy. She felt a little scared of Matron, and hoped she wouldn't make her take nasty medicine too often.

Then Matron looked up and smiled, and at once Darrell's fears fell away. She couldn't be afraid of a person who smiled like that, with her eyes and her mouth and even her nose too!

"Now let me see – you're Darrell Rivers," said Matron, ticking off her name on a list. "Got your health certificate with you? Give it to me, please. And you're Sally Hope."

"No, I'm Gwendoline Mary Lacey," said Gwendoline.

"And don't forget the Mary," said Alicia, pertly. "Dear Gwendoline Mary."

"That's enough, Alicia," said Matron, ticking away down her list. "You're as bad as your mother used to be. No, worse, I think."

Alicia grinned. "Mother came to Malory Towers when she was a girl," she told the others. "She was in North Tower too, and Matron had her for years. She sent you her best love, Matron. She says she wishes she could send all my brothers to you too. She's sure you're the only person who can manage them."

"If they're anything like you, I'm very glad they're not here," said Matron. "One of the Johns family at a time is quite enough for me. Your mother put some grey hairs into my head, and you've certainly done your bit in adding a few more."

She smiled again. She had a wise, kindly face, and any girl who fell ill felt safe in Matron's care. But woe betide any pretender, or any lazy girl or careless one! Then Matron's smile snapped off, her face closed up, and her eyes glinted dangerously!

A big gong boomed through North Tower. "Supper," said Matron. "Unpack your things afterwards, Alicia. Your train was late and you must all be very tired. All first formers are to go to bed immediately after supper tonight."

"Oh, Matron!" began Alicia, groaning. "Can't we just have ten minutes after . . ."

"I said immediately, Alicia," said Matron. "Go along now. Wash your hands quickly and go down. Hurry!"

And in five minutes' time Alicia and the others were sitting down, enjoying a good supper. They were hungry. Darrell looked round at the tables. She was sure she would never know all the girls in her house! And she was sure she would never dare to join in their laugh and chatter either.

But she would, of course — and very soon too!

CHAPTER III
FIRST NIGHT AND MORNING

The next morning Darrell and the other new girls go to see Miss Grayling, the headmistress, whose words of welcome make a great impression on Darrell.

The new girls stood in a row before the Head, and Miss Grayling looked at them all closely. Darrell felt herself going red, she couldn't imagine why. Her knees felt a bit wobbly too. She hoped Miss Grayling wouldn't ask her any questions, for she was sure she wouldn't be able to say a word!

Miss Grayling asked them their names, and spoke a few words to each girl. Then she addressed them all solemnly.

"One day you will leave school and go out into the world as young women. You should take with you eager minds, kind hearts, and a will to help. You should take with you a good understanding of many things, and a willingness to accept responsibility and show yourselves as women to be loved and trusted. All these things you will be able to learn at Malory Towers – if you *will.* I do not count as our successes those who have won scholarships and passed exams, though these are good things to do. I count as our successes those who learn to be good-hearted and kind, sensible and trustable, good, sound women the world can lean on. Our failures are those who do not learn these things in the years they are here."

These words were spoken so gravely and solemnly that Darrell hardly breathed. She immediately longed to be one of Malory Towers' successes.

"It is easy for some of you to learn these things, and hard for others. But easy or hard, they must be learnt if you are to be happy, after you leave here, and if you are to bring happiness to others."

There was a pause. Then Miss Grayling spoke again, in a lighter tone. "You will all get a tremendous lot out of your time at Malory Towers. See that you give a lot back!"

"Oh!" said Darrell, surprised and pleased, quite forgetting that she had thought she wouldn't be able to speak a word, "that's *exactly* what my father said to me when he said goodbye, Miss Grayling!"

"Did he?" said Miss Grayling, looking with smiling eyes at the eager little girl. "Well, as you have parents who think in that way, I imagine you will be one of the lucky ones, and will find that the things I have been speaking of will be easy to learn. Perhaps one day Malory Towers will be proud of you."

A few more words and the girls were told to go. Very much impressed, they walked out of the room. Not even Gwendoline said a word. Whatever they might do, in the years to come at Malory Towers, each girl wanted, at that moment, to do her best. Whether or not that wish would last, depended on the girl.

Then they went to the Assembly Hall for Prayers, found their places, and waited for Miss Grayling to come to the platform.

Soon the words of a hymn sounded in the big hall. The first day of term had begun. Darrell sang with all her might, happy and excited. What a lot she would have to tell her mother when she wrote!

SECOND FORM AT MALORY TOWERS
AN EXTRACT

≈ ILLUSTRATED BY ≈

Stanley Lloyd

Gwendoline, a spoilt and selfish girl, has made friends with Daphne, a boastful newcomer to Malory Towers who has been helped with her French by the timid and friendless Mary-Lou. Gwen becomes jealous but is reassured when Daphne tells her that she is only pretending to like Mary-Lou so that she will continue to give her help. One morning Daphne needs a parcel sent off urgently, and Mary-Lou decides to help, with almost tragic consequences . . .

CHAPTER XVII
RUMOURS AND TALES

Look, we've got ten minutes, haven't we," said Daphne. "I've got a most important parcel to send off this morning, and I can't find any string anywhere. Be a dear and get me some. I've got the brown paper."

Mary-Lou sped off, wondering what the important parcel was. She couldn't seem to find any string at all. It was astonishing, the total lack of any string that morning. When at last she got back to Daphne, the bell went for the next lesson.

"Haven't you got any string?" said Daphne, disappointed. "Oh, blow! Well, I'll see if I can find some after the morning lessons, and then I'll slip down to the post with the parcel this afternoon. I've got half an hour in between two lessons, because my music mistress isn't here today."

"Is it so very important?" asked Mary-Lou. "I could take it for you, if you like."

"No. You'd never get there and back in time," said Daphne. "It's a long way by the inland road. You could manage it by the coast road, but there's such a gale again today you'd be blown over the top! I'll go in between lessons this afternoon."

But she couldn't go after all, with her "important parcel", whatever it was, for the music mistress turned up, and Daphne was called away to her lesson. She left the parcel in her desk.

"Oh dear!" she said at teatime, to Gwen and Mary-Lou. "I did so badly want to take my parcel to the post – and I had to have my music-lesson after all – and now I've got to go to Miss Parker after tea for a returned lesson, and after that there's a rehearsal for that silly French play."

"What's so urgent about the parcel?" asked Gwen. "Somebody's birthday?"

Daphne hesitated. "Yes," she said. "That's it. If it doesn't go today it won't get there in time!"

"Well, you'll have to post it tomorrow!" said Gwen. Mary-Lou looked at Daphne's worried face. What a pity she, Mary-Lou, couldn't take it for her. She always liked doing things for Daphne, and getting that charming smile in return.

She began to think how she might do it. "I'm free at seven, after prep," she thought. "I'll have half an hour before supper. I could never get to the post-office and back if I take the inland road – but I could if I took the coast road. Would I dare to – in the dark and rain?"

She thought about it as she sat in afternoon school. "People don't mind what they do for their friends," she thought. "They dare anything. Daphne would be so thrilled if I went to the post and got her birthday parcel off for her. How kind she is to want it to get there on the day. Just like her. Well – if it isn't too dark and horrible, I might run along tonight for her. I mustn't tell anyone though, because it's against the rules. If Sally got to know, she'd forbid me!"

So timid little Mary-Lou planned to do something that even not one of the seniors would do on a dark, windy night – take the coast road on the cliff, whilst a gale blew wildly round!

CHAPTER XVIII
MARY-LOU

After prep that night Mary-Lou scuttled back to the second form room, which was now empty except for Gwendoline, who was tidying up. Mary-Lou went to Daphne's desk. Gwendoline looked at her jealously. "What do you want in Daphne's desk? I can take her anything she's forgotten. I wish you wouldn't suck up to her so much, Mary-Lou."

"I don't," said Mary-Lou. She opened the desk-lid and fished for the brown-paper parcel, now neatly tied up with string. "I'm going to the post with this for Daphne. But don't go and split on me, Gwen. I know it's against the rules."

Gwendoline stared at Mary-Lou in surprise. "*You* breaking the rules!" she said. "I don't believe you ever did that before. You're mad to think you can get to the post and back in time."

"I shall. I'm taking the coast road," said Mary-Lou, valiantly, though her heart failed her when she said it. "It's only ten minutes there and back by that road."

"Mary-Lou! You must be daft!" said Gwendoline. "There's a gale blowing and it's dark as pitch. You'll be blown over the cliff as sure as anything."

"I shan't," said Mary-Lou, stoutly, though again her heart sank inside her. "And, anyway, it's only a small thing to do for a friend. I know Daphne particularly wants this parcel to go today."

"Daphne isn't your friend," said Gwendoline, a flare of jealousy coming up in her again.

"She is," said Mary-Lou, with such certainty that Gwendoline was annoyed.

"Baby!" said Gwendoline, scornfully. "You're too silly even to see that Daphne only uses you because you can help her with her French. That's the only reason she puts up with you hanging round her. She's told me so."

Mary-Lou stood looking at Gwendoline, the parcel in her hand. She felt suddenly very miserable. "It's not true," she said. "You're making it up."

"It *is* true!" said Gwendoline, spitefully. "I tell you Daphne has said so herself to me heaps of times. What would a girl like Daphne want with a mouse like you! You're just useful to her, that's all, and if you weren't so jolly conceited you'd know it without being told!"

Mary-Lou felt as if it must be true. Gwendoline would never say such a thing so emphatically if it wasn't. She picked up the parcel, her mouth quivering, and turned to go.

"Mary-Lou! You don't mean to say you're going to bother with that parcel after what I've just told you!" called Gwendoline, in surprise. "Don't be an idiot."

"I'm taking it for Daphne because I'm *her* friend!" answered Mary-Lou, in a shaky voice. "She may not be mine, but if I'm hers I'll still be willing to do things for her."

"Stupid little donkey!" said Gwendoline to herself, and began to slam books back on to shelves and to make a terrific cloud of dust with the blackboard duster.

She didn't tell Daphne that Mary-Lou had gone off into the darkness with her parcel. She was feeling rather ashamed of having been so outspoken. Daphne might not like it. But after all it was nearly the end of the term, and there would be now no need for Mary-Lou to help Daphne. She would probably be glad to be rid of Mary-Lou when she no longer needed her help with her French.

Half-past seven came and the supper-bell rang. Girls poured out of the different rooms and went clattering down to the dining-room. "Oooh! Coffee tonight for a change! And jammy buns and rolls and potted meat!"

They all sat down and helped themselves, whilst Miss Parker poured out big cups of coffee. She glanced round the table. "Two empty chairs! Who's missing? Oh, Ellen, of course. Who's the other?"

"Mary-Lou," said Sally. "I saw her just after prep. She'll be along in a minute, Miss Parker."

But five minutes, ten minutes went by and there was no sign of Mary-Lou. Miss Parker frowned.

"Surely she must have heard the bell. See if you can find her, Sally."

Sally sped off and came back to report that Mary-Lou was nowhere to be found. By this time Gwendoline was in a great dilemma. She and she only knew where Mary-Lou was. If she told, she would get Mary-Lou into trouble. Surely she would be back soon? Maybe she had had to wait at the post-office!

Then she suddenly remembered something. The post-office shut at seven! It wouldn't be any use Mary-Lou trying to post a parcel there, because it would be shut. Why hadn't she thought of that before? Then what had happened to Mary-Lou?

A cold hand seemed to creep round Gwendoline's heart and almost stop her breathing. Suppose – suppose that the wind had blown little Mary-Lou over the cliff? Suppose that even now she was lying on the rocks, dead or badly hurt! The thought was so terrible that Gwendoline couldn't swallow her morsel of bun and half-choked.

Daphne thumped her on the back. Gwendoline spoke to her in a low, urgent voice.

"Daphne! I must tell you something as soon after supper as possible. Come into one of the practice-rooms where we shall be alone."

Daphne looked alarmed. She nodded. When supper was finished she led the way to one of the deserted practice-rooms and switched on the light. "What's the matter?" she asked Gwendoline. "You look like a ghost."

"It's Mary-Lou. I know where she went," said Gwendoline.

"Well, why on earth didn't you tell Miss Parker then?" asked Daphne, crossly. "What *is* the matter, Gwen?"

"Daphne, she took your precious parcel to the post just after seven o'clock," said Gwendoline. "She took the coast road. Do you think anything's happened to her?"

Daphne took this in slowly. "Took my parcel to the post? What*ever* for? At this time of night, too."

"She went all soppy and said that although it meant her going out in the dark and the wind, she'd do it because you were her friend," said Gwendoline.

"Why didn't you stop her, you idiot?" demanded Daphne.

"I did try," said Gwendoline. "I even told her that you were *not* her friend – you only found her useful for helping you with your French, as you've often and often told me, Daphne – and you'd think that would stop anyone from going off into the dark on a windy night, wouldn't you, to post a silly parcel?"

"And didn't it stop her?" said Daphne, in an odd sort of voice.

"No. She just said that she would take it for you because she was *your* friend," said Gwendoline, rather scornfully. "She said you might not be her friend, but she was yours, and she'd still be willing to do things for you."

Gwendoline was amazed to see tears suddenly glisten in Daphne's eyes. Daphne never cried! "What's up?" said Gwendoline in surprise.

"Nothing that you'd understand," said Daphne, blinking the tears away savagely. "Good heavens! Fancy going out on a night like this and taking the coast road – just because she wanted to take that parcel for me. And the post-office would be shut too! Poor little Mary-Lou! What can have happened to her?"

"Has she fallen over the cliff, do you think?" asked Gwendoline.

Daphne went very white. "No – no, don't say that!" she said. "You can't think how awful that would be. I'd never, never forgive myself!"

"It wouldn't be *your* fault if she did," said Gwendoline, surprised at this outburst.

"It would, it would! You don't understand!" cried Daphne. "Oh, poor kind little Mary-Lou! And you sent her out thinking I didn't like her – that I only just used her! I *do* like her. I like her ten times better than I like you! She's kind and generous and unselfish. I know I used her at first, and welcomed her just because she could help me – but I couldn't help getting fond of her. She just gives everything and asks nothing!"

"But – you told me heaps of times you only put up with her because she was useful," stammered Gwendoline, completely taken aback by all this, and looking very crestfallen indeed.

"I know I did! I was beastly. It was the easiest thing to do, to keep you from bothering me and nagging me about Mary-Lou. Oh, I shall never, never get over it if anything has happened! I'm going after her. I'm going to see if I can find her!"

"You can't!" cried Gwendoline, in horror. "Hark at the wind. It's worse than ever!"

"If Mary-Lou can go out into that wind to post a stupid parcel for me, surely *I* can go out into it to find her!" said Daphne, and a look came into her pretty, pale face that Gwendoline had never seen before – a sturdy, determined look that gave her face unexpected character.

"But, Daphne," protested Gwendoline, feebly, and then stopped. Daphne had gone out of the little music room like a whirlwind. She ran up to the dormy and got her mackintosh and sou-wester. She tore down to the cloakroom and put on her wellingtons. Nobody saw her. Then out she went into the night, flashing on her torch to see her way.

It was a wild night, and the wind howled round fiercely. It took Daphne's breath away as she made her way to the coast road up on the cliff. Whatever would it be like there! She would be almost blown away.

She flashed her torch here and there. There was nothing to be seen but a few bent bushes, dripping with rain.

She went a little farther and began to call loudly and desperately. "Mary-Lou! Mary-LOU! Where are you?"

The wind tore her words out of her mouth and flung them over the cliff. She called again, putting her hands up to her mouth. "Mary-Lou! MARY-LOU! MARY-LOU!"

And surely that was a faint call in answer. "Here! Here! Help me!"

CHAPTER XIX
A HEROINE!

Daphne stood quite still and listened. The cry came again on the wind, very faint. "Here! Here!" It seemed to come from somewhere in front. Daphne struggled on against the wind, and then came to a place where the cliff edge swung inwards. She followed the edge round cautiously, not daring to go too near,

for the wind was so strong. Still, it seemed to be dying down a little now.

She suddenly heard Mary-Lou's voice much nearer. "Help! Help!"

Daphne was afraid of being blown over the cliff if she went too near the edge. But the voice seemed to come from the edge somewhere. Daphne sat down on the wet ground, feeling that the wind would not then have so much power over her, and began to edge herself forward, holding on to the tufts of grass.

She came to where the cliff had crumbled away a little and made a series of ledges, going steeply down to the sea. She crawled to this place, lay down flat and shone her light over the broken cliff.

And there, a few feet below, was poor Mary-Lou, clinging for dear life to a ledge, her white face upturned to the glare of the torch.

"Help!" she called again, feebly, seeing the torch. "Oh, help me! I can't hold on much longer!"

Daphne was horrified. She could see that if Mary-Lou did leave go, she would hurtle down to the rocks a long way below. Her heart went cold at the thought. What could she do?

"I'm here, Mary-Lou!" she called. "Hold on. I'll fetch help."

"Oh – Daphne! Is it you! Don't go away, Daphne. I shall fall in a minute. Can't you do something?"

Daphne looked down at Mary-Lou. She felt that it would not be the slightest use leaving her and going for help, for it was clear that Mary-Lou might leave go at any moment. No, she must think of something else and do it at once.

She thought of her mackintosh belt, and her tunic belt. If she tied those both together and let them down, Mary-Lou might hold them and drag herself up. But would they reach?

She undid her mackintosh belt and took off her tunic belt with fingers that fumbled exasperatingly. All the time she kept up a comforting flow of words.

"I'll save you, don't you worry! I'll soon have you up here! I'm making a rope with my belts and I'll let it down. Hold on, Mary-Lou, hold on, and I'll soon save you!"

Mary-Lou was comforted and held on. She had been so frightened when the gale took her and rolled her over to the edge of the cliff. How she had managed to hold on to the tufts of grass she didn't know. It had seemed ages and ages till she heard Daphne's voice. Now Daphne was here and would rescue her. Whatever Gwendoline said, Daphne was her friend!

Daphne lay down flat again. She found a stout gorse bush behind her and she pushed her legs under it till her feet found the sturdy root-stem growing out of the ground. Heedless of scratches and pricks, she wound her two feet firmly round the stem, so that she had a good hold with her legs and would not be likely to be pulled over the cliff by Mary-Lou.

A frantic voice suddenly came up to her. "Daphne! This tuft of grass is giving way! I shall fall! Quick, quick!"

Daphne hurriedly let down the rough rope, made of her two belts. Mary-Lou caught at it and looped the end firmly round her wrists. Daphne felt the pull at once.

"Are you all right?" she called, anxiously. "You won't fall now, will you?"

"No. I don't think so. My feet have got quite a firm hold," called back Mary-Lou, much reassured by the belt round her wrists. "I shan't pull you over, shall I, Daphne?"

"No. But I don't think I'm strong enough to pull you up!" said Daphne, in despair. "And the belts might break and let you fall. I don't see that we can do anything but just hang on to each other till somebody finds us."

"Oh, poor Daphne! This is awful for you," came back Mary-Lou's voice. "I wish I'd never thought of taking that parcel."

"It was kind of you," said Daphne, not knowing how to get the words out. "But you're always kind, Mary-Lou. And Mary-Lou, I'm your friend. You know that, don't you? Gwen told me the beastly things she said. They're not true. I think the world of you, I do really. I've never been fond of anyone before."

"Oh, I knew Gwen told me untruths, as soon as I heard your voice and knew you'd come to look for me," said Mary-Lou, out of the darkness. "I think you're a heroine, Daphne."

"I'm not," said Daphne. "I'm a beastly person. You simply don't know how beastly."

"This is a funny conversation to be having on a cliff-side in a stormy night, isn't it?" said Mary-Lou, trying to sound cheerful. "Oh dear — I am so sorry to have caused all this trouble. Daphne, when will people come to look for us?"

"Well, only Gwen knows I've come out," said Daphne. "If I don't come back soon, surely she will tell Nosey Parker, and they'll send out to look for us. I do hope she'll have the sense to tell someone."

Gwendoline had. She had felt very worried indeed about first Mary-Lou and now Daphne. When Daphne had not come back after half an hour, Gwendoline had gone to Miss Parker. She told her where Mary-Lou had gone and that Daphne had gone to look for her.

"What! Out on the coast road at night! In this weather! What madness!" cried Miss Parker, and rushed off to Miss Grayling at once.

In two or three minutes a search-party was out with lanterns, ropes and flasks of hot cocoa. It was not long before the two girls were found. Miss Grayling gave an agonised exclamation as she saw them. "They might both have been killed!"

Daphne's arms were almost numb with strain when the search-party came up. They saw her lying flat on ground, her legs curled tightly round the stem of the prickly bush, holding the two belts down the cliff-side — and there, at the other end, holding on for dear life, was Mary-Lou, the sea pounding away far below her.

A rope was let down to Mary-Lou, slipped right over her head, and tightened over her arms and shoulders. Another one looped tightly round her waist. Daphne got up thankfully, her legs almost asleep, and Miss Parker caught hold of her. "Steady now! Hold on to me!"

Mary-Lou was pulled up safely by a hefty gardener. She lay on the ground, crying with relief. The gardener undid the ropes and lifted her up. "I'll carry her," he said. "Give her a drink, Mam, she's freezing!"

Both girls felt glad of the hot cocoa. Then, holding on to Miss Parker, Daphne staggered back to school, followed by the gardener carrying Mary-Lou, and then by the rest of the party.

"Put both girls to bed," Miss Grayling said to Matron. "They've had a terrible experience. I only hope they don't get pneumonia now! Daphne, you saved little Mary-Lou's life, there's no doubt about that. I am very proud of you!"

Daphne said nothing at all, but, to Miss Grayling's surprise, hung her head and turned away. She had no time to puzzle over this, but helped Matron to get Mary-Lou undressed and into bed. Both girls were soon in warm beds, with hot food and drink inside them. They each felt extremely sleepy, and went off to sleep quite suddenly.

The second formers were in bed, worried and sleepless. Gwen had told them about Mary-Lou going off, and Daphne following her to see if she could find her. They knew that a search-party had gone out. All kinds of horrible pictures came into their minds as they lay in bed and listened to the wind.

They talked long after lights out. Sally did not forbid them. This was not a usual night – it was a night of anxiety, and talking helped.

Then, after a long time, they heard Miss Parker's quick footsteps coming along the corridor. News! They all sat up at once.

She switched on the light and looked round at the seven waiting girls. Then she told them the story of how Mary-Lou and Daphne had been found, and how Daphne, by her ingenious idea, had saved Mary-Lou. She described how she had laid herself down on the wet ground, her feet curled round the gorse bush stem, and had held the belts down to Mary-Lou until help came.

"Daphne's a heroine!" cried Darrell. "I never liked her – but, Miss Parker, she's been marvellous, hasn't she! She's a real heroine!"

"I think she is," said Miss Parker. "I did not guess that she had it in her. She's in bed now, in the San, but I think she'll soon be all right again. We'll give her three cheers and a clap when she comes back to class."

She switched off the light and said good night. The girls talked excitedly for a few minutes more, thankful that they knew what had happened. Fancy Daphne turning out like that! And doing it for Mary-Lou! Why, Gwen had always said that Daphne only put up with Mary-Lou because she helped her with her French.

"Daphne must be fond of Mary-Lou," said Darrell, voicing what everyone thought. "I'm glad. I always thought it was mean to use Mary-Lou and not really like her."

"I wonder what became of the parcel," said Belinda. "Mary-Lou can't have posted it, because the post-office was shut. I bet nobody thought of the precious parcel."

"We'll go and hunt for it tomorrow," said Sally. "I say – what a small dormy we are tonight – only seven of us. Ellen gone – and Daphne and Mary-Lou in the San. Well, thank goodness they're there and not out on the cliff."

The wind rose to a gale again and howled round North Tower. The girls snuggled down closer into the beds. "I do think Daphne was brave," said Darrell, "and I can't *imagine* how timid little Mary-Lou could possibly have dared to go out in this gale. *Mary-Lou* of all people."

"People are odd," said Irene. "You simply never can tell what a person will do from one day to the next."

"You never said a truer word!" chuckled Darrell. "Today you put your French grammar away in the games cupboard and tried to put your lacrosse stick into your desk – and goodness knows what you'll do tomorrow!'

THIRD YEAR AT MALORY TOWERS

AN EXTRACT

≈ ILLUSTRATED BY ≈

Stuart Tresilian

An American girl named Zerelda has joined the school. She dresses very old for her age and wears make-up when she thinks she can get away with it. Zerelda dislikes all sports and gym but has a big passion for films and hopes one day to be a film-star. She believes that she is a fine actress and expects to be chosen for the main role when she sees that rehearsals are to begin for a production of Romeo and Juliet . . .

CHAPTER XII
THE DAYS GO BY

The next excitement was a notice put up on the board to say that Miss Hibbert, the English mistress, was going to start rehearsals for "Romeo and Juliet". All third formers were to go to the art room to be tried out for parts.

"Blow!" said Gwendoline, who didn't like Miss Hibbert because she had so often ticked her off for being affected and silly in her acting. "I was hoping she had forgotten about the play. It's such a waste of time."

"Oh *no*, it isn't," said Zerelda, who had brightened up very much at the notice. "Acting is marvellous! That's a thing I really *can* do! I did Lady Macbeth over in . . ."

"Yes, we know you did," interrupted Daphne. "We ought to know by now, anyway! You tell us often enough."

"I suppose you fancy yourself in one of the chief parts, Daphne?" said Alicia. "What a disappointment you'll get! Anyway, if Zerelda's so good, she'll play Juliet – if she can get rid of that American drawl!"

Zerelda looked alarmed. "Do you think my way of speaking will stop me having a good part?" she asked.

"Well – I can't imagine Shakespeare's Juliet talking with a pronounced American accent," said Alicia. "Still – if you act the part well enough I don't see why you shouldn't get it!"

Zerelda had been rather subdued lately, but now she came to life again, with the hope of starring in "Romeo and Juliet"! She paid a tremendous amount of attention to her appearance and spent as much time as she dared in front of her looking-glass. She also tried to get rid of her American drawl!

This amused the class very much. Zerelda had never made the slightest attempt before to speak in the English way and had laughed at the English accent and called it silly. Now she badgered everyone to tell her how to pronounce the words the way they did.

"Well, try to say 'won*d*erful' with a D in the middle, instead of 'wunnerful', for a start," said Darrell. "And say 'twen*ty* four' with the T in the middle, instead of 'twe*nny* four'. And couldn't you say 'stop' instead of 'starp' and 'shop' instead of 'sharp'? Or can't you hear the difference?"

Zerelda patiently tried to master the English way of speaking, much to Miss Peters' astonishment. She had felt quite pleased with Zerelda's efforts to keep up with the work of the form, but she was still annoyed with the girl's constant attention to her hair and appearance. Nor did she like Zerelda's still grown-up air, and her habit of appearing to look down on the others just because they were schoolgirls.

"Now I'll show them all!" thought Zerelda, studying the part of Juliet with great attention. "Now they'll see what I mean when I say I'm going to be one of the greatest of all film-stars!"

CHAPTER XIII
ZERELDA'S UNFORTUNATE REHEARSAL

Miss Hibbert took a great deal of trouble in producing the school plays. She gave her time to each form in turn, and really achieved some excellent results. This term it was the third form's turn. They were to give the play towards the end of the term. They were thankful not to be doing French plays. Both the Mam'zelles took a hand in producing those, and as they had quite different ideas about acting, it was a little trying for the actors.

"Does Miss Hibbert choose the characters the first time?" asked Zerelda.

"Oh no – she tries us all out in almost every part several times," said Darrell. "She does that for two reasons – she says that in that way she really does find the right actor for every part – and we all get to know every part of the play and work better as a team."

"Gee, that's wunnerful – I mean, won*derful*," said Zerelda. "I've been studying Juliet's part. It's a lovely one. Would you like to hear me do some of the lines?"

"Well – I'm just going out to my lacrosse practice," said Darrell. "Sorry! Look – ask Alicia. She's got nothing to do this period."

But Alicia was not going to admire Zerelda's Juliet. She got up hastily. "Sorry! I've got to go to a meeting, Zerelda. But I'm sure you'd be just wunnerful!"

"I'll hear you, Zerelda," said Gwendoline, glad of an opportunity to please the American girl. "Let's go into one of the empty music practice-rooms, where you won't be disturbed. It will be lovely to see you act. I'm sure you must be awfully good. As good as – what's the star you like so much – oh yes, Lossie Laxton!"

"Well, maybe I'm not up to her standard yet," said Zerelda, fluffing up her hair in the way Lossie did on the films. "OK, Gwen – we'll go to a practice-room."

But they were all full, and music sounded from each of them, with the exception of one at the end. Irene was there, poring over a music score.

"I say, Irene," said Gwen, going in, "can you . . ."

"Go away," said Irene, fiercely. "I'm busy. Can't you see?"

"Well, you're not needing the piano, are you?" said Zerelda. "Can't you do your work, whatever it is, somewhere else?"

"No, I can't. I shall want to try it out on the piano in a minute," said Irene. "Go away. Interrupting me like that!"

Zerelda was surprised. She had never seen Irene so annoyed before. But Gwendoline had. She knew that Irene could not bear to be disturbed when she was concentrating on her music, whether it was writing it out, or playing it on the piano.

"Come on," she said to Zerelda. "Let's go."

"Yes. GO!" said Irene, with a desperate expression on her face. "You've stopped me just when it was all coming beautifully. Blow you both!"

"Well, really, Irene, I do think you might let us use this room if you're only playing about with pencil and paper," began Zerelda. "I want to recite some lines of Juliet and . . ."

Then Irene went quite mad. She threw her music, her pencil and her music-case at the alarmed Zerelda. "You're daft!" she shouted. "Give up my music-hour for your silly acting! Oh yes, I know you're going to be a wonderful film-star, parading about in marvellous clothes, thinking of third-rate things if ever you *do* have a thought in your head – but what's all that compared to music! I tell you I'm . . ."

But Zerelda and Gwen did not wait to hear any more. They saw Irene looking round for something else to throw and as there was a vase of flowers on the little mantelpiece Gwen thought the sooner they went out of the room the better.

"*Well!*" said Zerelda. "If that doesn't beat all! Irene's mad!"

"Not really," said Gwen. "It's only when she feels sort of inspired, and music comes welling up into her mind and she has to write it down. She's got the real artistic temperament, I suppose."

"Well, so have I," said Zerelda at once. "But I don't go mad like that. I wouldn't have believed it of her."

"She can't help it," said Gwendoline. "It's only when she's interrupted. Look – there's Lucy going out of one of the practice-rooms. We can have that one if we're quick."

They slipped into the room that Lucy had just left. Gwendoline sat down, ready to listen for hours if she could please Zerelda and make her feel really friendly towards her. Zerelda struck a lovesick attitude and began.

> "*Wilt thou be gone? It is not yet near day;*
> *It was the nightingale and not the lark,*
> *That pierced the fearful hollow of thine ear;*
> *Nightly she sings on yon pomegranate-tree;*
> *Believe me, love, it was the nightingale.*"

Gwendoline listened with a rapt and admiring expression on her face. She had no idea at all whether Zerelda was good or not, but that made no difference to her praise.

"It's marvellous!" she said, when Zerelda at last stopped for breath. "However have you learnt such a lot? My goodness, you do act well. And you really look the part, Zerelda, with your hair and all."

"Do I?" said Zerelda, pleased. She always enjoyed herself when she was acting. "I

know what I'll do. I'll shake my
hair loose. And I'll wrap this
tablecloth round me. No – it's not
big enough. The curtain will do!"

To Gwendoline's amusement
Zerelda took down the blue
curtain and swathed it round
herself over her brown school
tunic. She undid her brilliant hair
and shook it all over her
shoulders. She decided to put the
tablecloth round her too. Ah –
now she felt more like Juliet.
Holding her hands out pathetical-
ly in front of her she began
another speech. It sounded really a
little strange because Zerelda tried
very hard to speak in the English
way but kept lapsing into her
usual drawl, so that the whole
effect was rather funny.

Gwendoline wanted to laugh
but she knew how offended
Zerelda would be. The American
girl paraded up and down,
declaiming her speeches most dra-
matically, the blue curtain

dragging behind her like a train, her hair almost hiding one eye.

Someone looked in. It was Bessie, a second former. She had come to practise.
But seeing two third formers there, she fled. Then a fourth former came. She was
not scared of third formers, but was very much astonished to see Zerelda and her
strange raiment.

"I've got to practise," she said, coming in. "Clear out."

Zerelda stopped indignantly. "Clear out yourself!" she said. "Gee, of all the nerve!
Can't you see I'm rehearsing?"

"No, I can't," said the fourth former. "And wait till a mistress sees you in that
curtain – you'll be for it, Zerelda Brass. Clear out now, both of you. I'm late
already."

Zerelda decided to go all temperamental like Irene. She caught up her book of

Shakespeare's plays and threw it at the fourth former. Most unfortunately at that moment Matron came by, and, as she always did, glanced into the practice-rooms to see that each girl there was practising. She was filled with astonishment to see somebody wearing a curtain and a tablecloth, with hair all over her face, throwing a book at a girl about to sit down at the piano.

She opened the door sharply, making everyone jump. "What's all this? What are you doing? Oh, it's *you*, Zerelda. What on earth have you got the curtain round you for? Are you quite mad? And what has happened to your hair? It looks a hundred times worse than usual. Janet, get on with your practising. Gwendoline, you shouldn't be here when a fourth former is practising. As for you, Zerelda, If I see any more tempers like that, I shall report you to Miss Grayling! Throwing books at one another indeed! A third former too! You'll go down into the first form if you behave like that!"

The girls couldn't get a word in, for Matron fired all this off at top speed. She pushed Janet firmly down on the stool, shooed Gwendoline out as if she was a hen, and took Zerelda firmly by the shoulder.

"You'll just come with me and let me find out if you've torn the cloth or the curtain," she said. "If you have you'll sit down in my room under my eye and mend it. And while I think of it – if you don't darn your stockings better than you have been doing, I shall have to ask you to come to me for darning lessons."

Angry and embarrassed, poor Zerelda had to walk down the corridor after Matron, trying to take the curtain and cloth away from her shoulders and waist, and wishing she could tie her hair back.

But Matron would give her no time to rearrange or tidy herself. This stuck-up, affected American girl had annoyed Matron so often – now Matron was getting a bit of her own back! Let everyone see Zerelda in this rumpled, ridiculous state!

And most unfortunately for Zerelda they met a whole batch of giggling second formers, who stared at Zerelda in delighted amazement.

"What's she done? Where's Matron taking her? Doesn't she look *awful!*" poor Zerelda heard the twelve-year-olds say. She blushed miserably and looked round for Gwen. But Gwen had gone. She knew Matron in this mood, and she wasn't going to go near her if she could help it!

They met Mam'zelle at the bend of the stairs, and Mam'zelle exclaimed in surprise. "*Tiens!* What is this? Zerelda! Your hair!"

"Yes. I'm dealing with her, Mam'zelle," said Matron firmly. She and Mam'zelle were usually at war with one another, so Matron did not stop to talk, but swept Zerelda along to her room at top speed, leaving Mam'zelle to gape and wonder.

Fortunately for Zerelda, Matron could find no damage done to either the tablecloth or the curtain. She was quite disappointed! She did Zerelda's hair for her herself, and Zerelda was so overcome by Matron's briskness and ability to talk without stopping that she submitted without saying a word.

Matron plaited Zerelda's hair into two fat plaits! Zerelda had never had her hair plaited in her life. She sat there, horror-struck. This awful school! Whatever would happen to her next?

"There," said Matron, satisfied at last, tying the ends of the plaits with blue tape. She stepped back. "Now you look a proper schoolgirl, Zerelda – and very sensible and nice too. Why you want to go about pretending you are twenty, I don't know."

Zerelda got up weakly. She caught a glimpse of herself in the mirror. How *awful!* Could that really be herself? Why, she looked a nobody – just like all the other English girls. She crept out of Matron's room and fled up to the dormy to try and put her hair right.

She met Miss Peters, who stared at her as if she didn't know her. Zerelda smiled a weak smile and tried to get by without a word.

"Well – *Zerelda!*" she heard Miss Peters say, as if she couldn't believe her eyes. Zerelda shot down the corridor, praying that she would not meet anyone else.

Gwendoline was in the dormy, and she too stared at Zerelda as if she was seeing a ghost.

"Did Matron do that to you?" she asked. "Oh, Zerelda – you look like a real schoolgirl now – not a bit like yourself. Oh, I *must* tell the others Matron plaited your hair."

"If you dare to repeat such a thing I'll never speak to you again!" said Zerelda, in such a fierce voice that Gwen was quite scared. She shook her hair free of the plaits. "This horrible school! I'll never forgive Matron, never!"

UPPER FOURTH AT MALORY TOWERS
AN EXTRACT

≈ ILLUSTRATED BY ≈

Stanley Lloyd

Clarissa, a new girl to Malory Towers, has been to see her old Nurse, Mrs Lucy, who lives close to the school. Mrs Lucy had thought that the entire form was to visit her and prepared a huge quantity of food. So that the food is not wasted, the girls plan to have a midnight feast around the natural, sea-filled swimming pool at the school. Unfortunately Alicia, a strong-willed member of the form, has told two of her friends in different dormitories of their plans so that they can slip along and join the fun. Others too seem to have heard rumours of the feast and soon things begin to get out of hand . . .

CHAPTER XII
THAT EVENING

"For goodness' sake don't let Potty or Mam'zelle guess there's anything planned for tonight," said Darrell to the others after supper. "I saw Mam'zelle looking very suspicious. Come into the common-room now, and we'll arrange the details. How gorgeous to have so much food given to us — Clarissa, many thanks!"

Clarissa blushed, but was too nervous to say anything. She was delighted to think that she could provide a feast for the others.

They all went to the common-room and sat about to discuss their plans. "It's such a terrifically hot evening that it really will be lovely down by the pool," said Sally. "There mustn't be any of the usual screeching or yelling though — sounds carry so at night, and although the pool is right down on the rocks, it's quite possible to hear noises from there if the wind is right."

Alicia was pleased to hear Sally say this. It would make it seem natural for Betty and Eileen and Winnie to come and say they had heard sounds from the pool.

"I and Sally will keep awake tonight," planned Darrell. "Then when we hear the clock strike twelve, we will wake you all, and you can get into dressing-gowns and bring your bathing-things. We'd better fetch them from the changing-rooms now, or else we may wake up one of the staff, if we rummage about late at night."

"Is all the food safely down by the pool?" asked Bill, who was very much looking forward to this adventure. It was the first time she had ever been to a midnight feast!

"Yes. Safely locked in the cubby-hole on the left," said Alicia. "I've got the key."

"We'll have a bathe first and then we'll feast," said Darrell. "It's a pity we haven't anything exciting to drink."

"I bet if I went and asked old Cookie for some lemonade, she'd leave us some ready," said Irene, who was a great favourite with the kitchen staff.

"Good. You go then," said Darrell. "Ask her to make two big jugfuls, and stand them on the cold larder floor. We'll fetch them when we're ready."

Irene sped off. Then Alicia was sent with Mavis to fetch the bathing-things from the changing-room. Everyone began to feel tremendously excited. Clarissa could hardly keep still.

"I wish I hadn't had so much supper," said Gwendoline. "I'm sure I shan't feel hungry by midnight."

"Serves you right for being a pig," said Belinda. "You had five tomatoes at supper. I counted!"

"A pity you hadn't anything better to do," said Gwendoline, trying to be sarcastic.

"Oh, it's wonderful to watch your nice little ways," said Belinda, lazily. "No wonder you're getting so fat, the way you gobble everything at meals. Dear me, what a wonderful drawing I could make of you as a nice fat little piggy-wig with blue eyes and a ribbon on your tail."

Everyone roared. "Do, do!" begged Sally. Gwendoline began to scowl, saw Belinda looking at her, and hastily straightened her face. She wished she hadn't tried to be sarcastic to Belinda. She always came off badly if she did!

Alicia and Mavis came back, giggling, with the bathing-things. "Anyone spot you?" asked Darrell, anxiously.

"I don't think so. That pestiferous young cousin of mine, June, was somewhere about, but I don't think she'd spot anything was up," said Alicia. "I heard her whistling somewhere, when we were in the changing-room."

Irene came back from the kitchen, grinning all over her face. "I found Cookie, and she was all alone," she said. "She'll have two thumping big jugs of lemonade ready for us on the floor of the larder, any time after eleven o'clock tonight. The staff go to bed then, so she says any time after that will be safe for us to get it."

"This is going to be super," said Alicia. "What exactly did you say the food was, Clarissa?"

Clarissa explained, with Gwen prompting her proudly. Gwen really felt as if she had provided half the feast herself, and she basked in Clarissa's reflected glory.

"Did you ever have midnight feasts at your last school, Ruth?" asked Darrell, seeing that Ruth looked as excited as the others.

Connie answered for her as usual. "No. We tried once, but we got caught — and my word we did get a wigging from the Head."

"I asked Ruth, not you," said Darrell, annoyed with Connie. "Don't keep butting in. Let Ruth answer for herself." She turned to Ruth again.

"Was your last head very strict?" she asked. Connie opened her mouth to answer for Ruth again, caught the glint in Darrell's eye, and shut it.

Ruth actually answered, after waiting for a moment for Connie. "Well," she said, "I think probably *you* would call her very strict. You see . . ."

"Oh, not *very* strict, Ruth," interrupted Connie. "Don't you remember how nice she was over . . ."

"I'M ASKING RUTH," said Darrell, exasperated.

What would have happened next the form would dearly have loved to know — but there came an interruption that changed the subject. Matron popped her head in and said she wanted Gwendoline.

"Oh, *why*, Matron?" wailed Gwendoline. "What haven't I done now that I ought to have done? Why do you want me?"

"Just a little matter of darning," said Matron.

"But I've *done* the beastly darning you told me to," said Gwen, indignantly.

"Well then — shall we say a little matter of *unpicking* and *re*-darning?" said Matron, aggravatingly. The girls grinned. They had seen Gwen's last effort at darning a pair of navy-blue knickers with grey wool, and had wondered if Matron would notice.

Gwendoline had to get up and go, grumbling under her breath. "I could do her darning for her," suggested Clarissa to Darrell. "I don't play games or do gym — I've plenty of time."

"Don't you dare!" said Darrell at once. "You help her too much as it is — she's always copying from you."

Clarissa looked shocked. "Oh – she doesn't *copy*," she said loyally, going red at the idea of her daring to argue with Darrell.

"Don't be such a mutt," said Alicia, bluntly. "Gwendoline's a turnip-head – and she's always picked other people's brains and always will. Take off your rose-coloured glasses and see Gwen though your proper eyes, my dear Clarissa!"

Thinking that Alicia really *meant* her to take off her glasses for some reason, Clarissa removed her spectacles most obediently! The girls were about to laugh loudly, when Darrell bent forward in surprise.

"Clarissa! You've got real green eyes! I've never seen proper green eyes before! You must be related to the pixiefolk – people with green eyes always are!"

Everyone roared – but on looking closely at Clarissa's eyes, they saw that they were indeed a lovely clear green, that somehow went remarkably well with her wavy auburn hair.

"My word – I wish I had stunning eyes like that," said Alicia enviously. "They're marvellous. How sickening that you've got to wear glasses."

"Oh, it's only for a time," said Clarissa, putting them on again, looking rather shy but pleased at Alicia's admiration. "I'm glad you like my green eyes! Gwendoline thinks it's awful to have green eyes like a cat."

"If all cats have green eyes, then our dear Gwendoline certainly ought to have them," said Belinda at once.

Clarissa looked distressed. "Oh, but Gwendoline has been very kind to me," she began, and then everyone shushed her. Gwen was coming in, scowling, holding a pair of games knickers and a pair of games stockings in her hands.

"I do think Matron's an absolute *beast*," she began. "I spent *hours* darning these last week – and now I've got to unpick all my darns and re-do them."

"Well, don't darn navy knickers with grey wool, or red stockings with navy wool this time," said Alicia. "Anyone would think you were colour-blind."

Clarissa longed to help Gwen, but after Darrell's remark she didn't like to offer, and Gwen certainly didn't dare ask for help. The girls sat about, yawning, trying to read, longing for bed because they really felt tired. But not too tired to wake up at twelve and have a bathe and a feast.

They didn't take long getting into bed that night. Even slow Gwendoline was quick. Irene was the quickest of the lot, much to Darrell's surprise. But it was discovered that she had absentmindedly got into bed half-undressed, so out she had to get again.

The bathing-things were stacked in someone's cupboard, waiting. Dressing-gowns and slippers were set ready on the end of each bed.

"Sorry for you, Darrell, and you, too, Sally, having to keep awake till twelve!" said Irene, yawning. "Good night, all – see you in a little while!"

Sally said she would keep awake for the first hour, and then wake Darrell, who would keep awake till twelve. Then each would get a little rest.

Sally valiantly kept awake, and then shook Darrell, who slept in the next bed. Darrell was so sound asleep that she could hardly open her eyes. But she did at last, and then decided she had better get out of bed and walk up and down a little, or she might fall off to sleep again – and then there would be no feast, for she was quite certain no one else would be awake at twelve!

At last she heard the clock at the top of the Tower striking twelve. Good. Midnight at last! She woke up Sally and then the two of them woke everyone else up. Gwendoline was the hardest to wake – she always was. Darrell debated whether or not to leave her, as she seemed determined not to wake – but decided that Clarissa might be upset – and after all, it was Clarissa's feast!

They all put on dressing-gowns and slippers. They got their bathing-things out of the cupboard and sent Irene and Belinda for the jugs of lemonade. The dormy was full of giggles and whisperings and shushings. Everybody was now wide awake and very excited.

"Come on – we'll go down to the side-door, out into the garden, and through the gate to the cliff-path down to the pool," whispered Darrell. "And for GOODNESS' sake don't fall down the stairs or do anything idiotic."

It wasn't long before they were down by the pool, which was gleaming in the moonlight, and looked too tempting for words. Irene and Belinda had the jugs of lemonade.

"Let's get out the food and have a look at it," said Sally. "I'm longing to see it!"

"Alicia! Where's the key of the cubby-hole?" said Darrell.

"Blow!" said Alicia. "I've left it in my tunic pocket. I'll skip back and get it. Won't be half a minute!"

CHAPTER XIII
MIDNIGHT FEAST!

Alicia ran up the cliff-path, annoyed with herself for forgetting the key. She slipped in at the side-door of the Tower and went up the stairs. As she went along the landing where the first form dormy was, she saw a little white figure in the passage, looking out of the landing window. "Must be a first former!" thought Alicia. "What's she out this time of night for? Little monkey!"

She walked softly up to the small person looking out of the window and grasped her by the shoulder. There was a loud gasp.

"Sh!" said Alicia. "Good gracious, it's *you*, June! What are you doing out here at midnight?"

"Well, what are *you*?" said June, cheekily.

Alicia shook her. "None of your cheek," she said. "Have you forgotten the trouncing I gave you last summer hols for cheeking me and Betty, when you came to stay with me?"

"No. I haven't forgotten," said June, vengefully. "And I never shall. You were a beast. I'd have split on you if I hadn't been scared. Spanking me with a hair-brush as if I was six!"

"Served you jolly well right," said Alicia. "And you know what would have happened if you *had* split – Sam and the others would have trounced you, too!"

"I know," said June, angrily. She was scared of Alicia's brothers. "You wait, though. I'll get even with you some time!"

Alicia snorted scornfully. "You could do with another spanking, I see," she said. "Now – you clear off to bed. You know you're not supposed to be out of your dormy at night."

"I saw you all go off with bathing-things tonight," said June, slyly. "I guessed you were up to something, you fourth formers, when I spotted you and somebody else getting bathing-dresses in the changing-room tonight. You thought I didn't see you, but I did!"

How Alicia longed for a hair-brush to spank June with – but she dared not even raise her voice.

"Clear off to bed," she ordered, her voice shaking with rage.

"Are you having a midnight feast, too?" persisted June, not moving. "I saw Irene and Belinda with jugs of lemonade."

"Nasty little spy," said Alicia, and gave June a sharp push. "What we fourth formers do is none of your business. Go to bed!"

June resisted Alicia's hand, and her voice grew dangerous. "Does Potty know about your feast?" she asked. "Or Mam'zelle? I say, Alicia, wouldn't it be rotten luck on you if somebody told on you?"

Alicia gasped. Could June really be threatening to go and wake one of the staff, and so spoil all their plans? She couldn't believe that anyone would be so sneaky.

"Alicia, let me come and join the feast," begged June. "Please do."

"No," said Alicia, shortly, and then, not trusting herself to say any more, she left June standing by the window and went off in search of the key to the cubby-hole. She was so angry that she could hardly get the key out of her tunic pocket. To be cheeked like that by a first former – her own cousin! To be threatened by a little pip-squeak like that! Alicia really hated June at that moment.

She found the key and rushed back to the pool with it. She said nothing about meeting June. The others were already in the water, enjoying themselves.

"Pity the moon's gone in," said Darrell to Sally. "Gosh, it *has* clouded up, hasn't it? Is that Alicia back? Hey, Alicia, what a time you've been. Got the key?"

"Yes, I'm unlocking the cubby-hole," called back Alicia. "Clarissa is here. She'll help me to get out the things. Pity it's so dark now – the moon's gone."

Suddenly, from the western sky, there came an ominous growl – thunder! Blow, blow, blow!

"Sounds like a storm," said Darrell. "I thought there might be one soon, it's so terrifically hot today. I say, Alicia, do you think we ought to begin the feast now, in case the storm comes on?"

"Yes," said Alicia. "Ah, here's the moon again, thank goodness!"

The girls clambered out of the water and dried themselves. As they stood there, laughing and talking, Darrell suddenly saw three figures coming down the cliff-path from the school. Her heart stood still. Were they mistresses who had heard them?

It was Betty, of course, with Eileen and Winnie. The three of them stopped short at the pool and appeared to be extremely astonished to see such a gathering of the Upper Fourth.

"I say! Whatever are you doing?" said Betty. "We *thought* we heard a noise from the pool. It made us think that a bathe would be nice this hot night."

"We're going to have a feast!" came Alicia's voice. "You'd better join us."

"Yes, do – we've got plenty," said Irene, and the others called out the same. Even Darrell welcomed them, too, for it never once occurred to her that Betty had heard about the feast already and had come in the hope of joining them.

Neither did it occur to her that there was a strict rule that girls from one tower were never to leave their own towers at night to meet anyone from another. She just didn't think about it at all.

They all sat down to enjoy the feast. The thunder rumbled again, this time much nearer. A flash of lightning lit up the sky. The moon went behind an enormous cloud and was seen no more that night.

Worst of all, great drops of rain began to fall, plopping down on the rocks and causing great dismay.

"Oh dear – we'll have to go in," said Darrell. "We'll be soaked through, and it won't be any fun at all sitting and eating in the rain. Come on – collect the food and we'll go back."

Betty nudged Alicia. "Shall *we* come?" she whispered.

"Yes. Try it," whispered back Alicia. "Darrell hasn't said you're not to."

So everyone, including Betty, Eileen and Winnie from West Tower, gathered up the food hurriedly, and stumbled up the cliff-path in the dark.

"Where shall we take the food?" panted Darrell to Sally. "Can't have it in our common-room because it's got no curtains and the light would shine out."

"What about the first form common-room?" asked Sally "That's not near any staff-room, and the windows can't be seen from any other part."

"Yes. Good idea," said Darrell, and the word went round that the feast was to be held in the first form common-room.

Soon they were all in there. Darrell shut the door carefully and put a mat across the bottom so that not a crack of light could be seen.

The girls sat about on the floor, a little damped by the sudden storm that had spoilt their plans. The thunder crashed and the lightning gleamed. Mary-Lou looked alarmed, and Gwen went quite white. Neither of them liked storms.

"Hope Thunder's all right," said Bill, tucking into a tongue sandwich. Her horse was always her first thought.

"I should think . . ." began Alicia, then she stopped dead. Everyone sat still. Darrell put up her finger for silence.

There came a little knocking at the door. Tap-tap-tap-tap! Tap-tap-tap-tap!

Darrell felt scared. Who in the world was there? And why knock? She made another sign for everyone to keep absolutely still.

The knocking went on. Tap-tap-tap. This time it was a little louder.

Still the girls said nothing and kept quite silent. The knocking came again, sounding much too loud in the night.

"Oh dear!" thought Darrell. "If it gets any louder, someone will hear, and the cat will be out of the bag!"

Gwendoline and Mary-Lou were quite terrified of this strange knocking. They clutched each other, as white as a sheet.

"Come in," said Darrell, at last, in a low voice, when there was a pause in the knocking.

The door opened slowly, and the girls stared at it, wondering what was coming. In walked June – and behind her, rather scared, was Felicity!

"June!" said Alicia, fiercely.

"*Felicity!*" gasped Darrell, hardly believing her eyes.

June stared round as if in surprise.

"Oh," she said, "it's you, is it! Felicity and I simply *couldn't* get to sleep because of the storm, and we came to the landing window to watch it. And we found these on the ground!"

She held up three hard-boiled eggs! "We were awfully surprised. Then we heard a bit of a noise in here and we wondered who was in our common-room – and we thought whoever it was must be having a good old feast – so we came to bring you your lost hard-boiled eggs."

There was a silence after this speech. Alicia was boiling! She knew that June had watched them coming back because of the storm – had seen them going into the first form common-room – and had been delighted to find the dropped eggs and bring them along as an excuse to join the party!

"Oh," said Darrell, hardly knowing what to say. "Thanks. Yes – we're having a feast. Er . . ."

"Why did you use our common-room?" asked June, innocently, and she broke the shell off one of the eggs. "Of course it's an honour for us first formers to have you Upper Fourth using our room for a feast. I say – this egg's super! I didn't mean to nibble it, though. So sorry."

"Oh, finish it if you like," said Darrell, not finding anything else to say.

"Thanks," said June, and gave one to Felicity, who began to eat hers, too.

It ended, of course, in the two of them joining in the feast, though Darrell really felt very uncomfortable about it. Also, for the first time she realised that the three girls from West Tower were still there, in North Tower where they had no business to be! Still, how could she turn them out now? She couldn't very well say, "Look here, you must scram! I know we said join the feast when we were down by the pool – but we can't have you with us now." It sounded too silly for words.

Darrell did not enjoy the feast at all. She wanted to send June and Felicity away, but it seemed mean to do that when the feasters were using their common-room, and June had brought back the eggs. Also she felt that Alicia might not like her to send June away. Little did she know that Alicia was meditating all kinds of dire punishments for the irrepressible June. Oh dear – the lovely time they had planned seemed to have gone wrong somehow.

And then it went even more wrong! Footsteps were heard overhead.

CHAPTER XIV
THINGS HAPPEN FAST

Did you hear that?" whispered Sally. "Someone is coming! Quick, gather everything up, and let's go!"

The girls grabbed everything near, and Darrell caught up the brush by the fireplace and swept the crumbs under a couch. She put out the light and opened the door. All was dark in the passage outside. There seemed to be nobody there.

Who could have been walking about overhead? That was where the first form dormy was.

June and Felicity were scared now. They shot away at once. Betty, Eileen and Winnie disappeared to the stairs, running down them to the side-door. They could then slip round to their own tower. The others, led by Darrell, went cautiously upstairs to find their own dormy.

A slight cough from somewhere near, a familiar and unmistakable cough, brought them to a stop. They stood, hardly daring to breathe, at the top of the stairs. "That was Potty's cough," thought Darrell. "Oh blow – did she hear us making a row? But we really were quite quiet!"

She hoped and hoped that Betty and the other two West Tower girls had got safely to their own dormy without being caught. It really was counted quite a serious offence for girls of one tower to meet girls in another tower at night. For one thing there was no way to get from one tower to another under cover. The girls had to go outside to reach any other tower.

What could Potty be doing? Where was she? The girls stood frozen to the ground, waiting for the sign to move on.

"She's in the third form dormy," whispered Darrell, at last. "Perhaps somebody is ill there. I think we had better make a dash for it, really. We can't stand here for hours."

"Right. The next time the thunder comes, we'll run for it," said Sally, in a low voice. The word was passed along, and the girls waited anxiously for the thunder. The lightning flashed first, showing up the crouching line of girls very clearly – and then the thunder came.

It was a good long, rumbling crash, and any sound the girls made in scampering along to their dormy was completely deadened. They fell into bed thankfully, each girl stuffing what she carried into the bottom of her cupboard, wet bathing-suits and all.

No Miss Potts appeared, and the girls began to breathe more freely. Somebody *must* have been taken ill in the third form dormy. Potty still seemed to be there. At last the Upper Fourth heard the soft closing of the third form dormy, and Miss Potts' footsteps going quietly off to her own room.

"Had we better take the lemonade jugs down to the kitchen now?" whispered Irene.

"No. We won't risk any more creeping about tonight," said Darrell. "You must take them down before breakfast, as soon as the staff have gone into the dining-room, even though it makes you a bit late. And we'll clear out all the food left over before *we* go down, and hide it somewhere till we can get rid of it. *What* a pity that beastly storm came!"

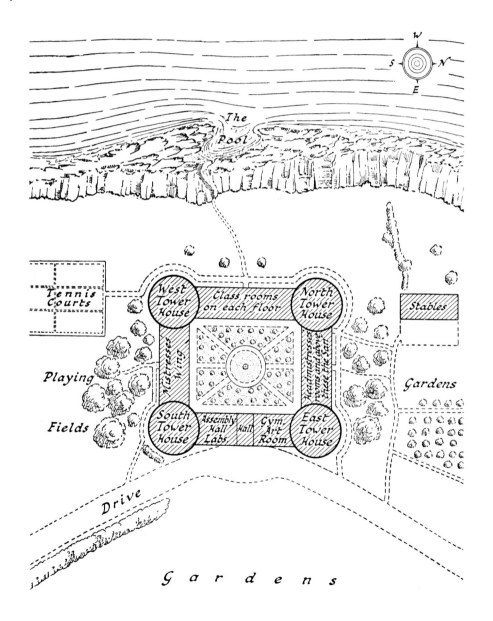

IN THE FIFTH AT MALORY TOWERS
AN EXTRACT

≈ ILLUSTRATED BY ≈

Stuart Tresilian

The Malory Towers girls are always playing tricks on Mam'zelle Dupont, one of their two French teachers, but the tables are turned when Mam'zelle decides to get her own back on the girls with a 'treek' of her own!

CHAPTER XX
THINGS HAPPEN

Mam'zelle sat down at her desk in Miss Potts' room one day, and announced her intention of turning it out. "About time, too," said Miss Potts, dryly. "You'll probably find the year before last's exam papers there, I should think. I never saw such a collection of rubbish in anyone's desk in my life."

"Ha, Miss Potts! You wish to be funny?" said Mam'zelle, huffily.

"No," said Miss Potts. "Merely truthful."

Mam'zelle snorted, and took hold of about a hundred loose papers in her desk. She lifted them out and they immediately fell apart and slithered all over the floor. One booklet floated to Miss Potts' feet. She looked at it with interest, for there was a very brightly coloured picture on the cover, showing a conjurer doing tricks. "New tricks. Old tricks. Tricks to play on your enemies. Tricks to play on your friends," she read out loud. She glanced at Mam'zelle in astonishment. "Since when did you think of taking up tricks to play?" she inquired.

"I do not think of it," said Mam'zelle, depositing another hundred papers on the floor. "*Tiens!* Here is the programme of the play the third formers gave six years ago!"

"What did I tell you?" said Miss Potts. "You'll probably find the Speeches made at the Opening of Malory Towers if you look a little further into your desk."

"Do not tizz me," said Mam'zelle. "I do not like being tizzed."

"I'm not teasing," said Miss Potts. "I'm quite serious. I say — *where* did you get these trick and conjuring lists from? Look at this one — I'm sure it's got in it all the tricks that Alicia and Betty ever played on you!"

Mam'zelle took the booklets. She was soon completely absorbed in them. She chuckled. She laughed. She said *"Tiens!"* and "Oh, *là là*," a dozen times. Miss Potts went on with her work. She was used to Mam'zelle's little ways.

Mam'zelle had never read anything so enthralling in all her life as these booklets that described tricks of all sorts and kinds. She was completely lost in them. She read of machines that could apparently saw people's fingers in half without hurting them – cigarettes with glowing ends that were not really alight – ink spots and jam-clots that could be placed on table-cloths to deceive annoyed mothers or teachers into thinking they were real.

The booklets blandly described these and a hundred others. Mam'zelle was absolutely fascinated. She came to one trick that made her laugh out loud. "Ah, now listen, Miss Potts," she began.

"*No*, Mam'zelle," said Miss Potts, sternly. "I've twenty-three *disgraceful* maths papers to mark that the first form have had the nerve to give in today – and I do NOT want to listen to your recital of childish tricks."

Mam'zelle sighed and went back to the booklets. She read over again the thing that had so intrigued her, There were two photographs with the description of the trick. One showed a smiling man with ordinary teeth – the other showed the same man – with trick teeth! He looked horrible.

Mam'zelle read the description over again. "These trick teeth are cleverly made of celluloid, and are shaped to fit neatly over the wearer's own teeth – but project forwards and downwards, and so alter the expression of the wearer's face considerably as soon as he smiles, giving a really terrifying and exceedingly strange appearance."

Mam'zelle studied the photographs. She tried to imagine herself wearing teeth like that – and suddenly flashing them at the girls with a smile. Ha! They had dared her to do a trick on them! Mam'zelle had a very very good mind to write for this teeth trick. Perhaps she would wear them at a lacrosse match out in the field – or maybe take the girls for a walk, and keep showing her trick teeth.

Mam'zelle shook with laughter. Ha ha – so many "treeks" had those bad girls played on her, it was time their poor old Mam'zelle played a "treek" on them too. How they would be astonished! How they would stare. How they would laugh afterwards.

Mam'zelle scuffled about among her untidy papers and found her writing pad. In her slanting French handwriting she wrote for the "teeth trick" and sent a cheque with the letter. She was delighted. She would not tell even Miss Potts

"No. I will not tell her. I will suddenly smile at her – like this," said Mam'zelle to herself – and did a sudden fierce grin – "and I shall look so strange that she will start back in fright at my horrible teeth."

CHAPTER XXI
MAM'ZELLE'S "TREEK"

The trick teeth arrive and Mam'zelle decides to use them as soon as possible.

There was a house-match that afternoon – North Tower girls against West Tower. Mam'zelle decided she would appear as a spectator at the match – with her teeth!

Ah, those teeth! Mam'zelle had tried them on. They might have been made for her! They fitted over her own teeth, but were longer, and projected slightly forward. They were not noticeable at all, of course, when she had her mouth shut – but when she smiled – ah, how sinister she looked, how strange, how fierce!

Mam'zelle had shocked even herself when she had put in the extraordinary teeth and smiled at herself in the mirror.

"*Tiens!*" she said, and clutched her dressing-table. "I am a monster! I am truly terrible with these teeth . . ."

That afternoon she put them in carefully over her others and went downstairs to the playing-fields, wrapping herself up warmly in coat, scarf and turban. Darrell saw her first, and made room for her on the form she was on.

"Thank you," said Mam'zelle, and smiled at Darrell. Darrell got a tremendous shock. Mam'zelle had suddenly looked altogether different – quite terrifying. Darrell stared at her – but Mam'zelle had quickly shut her mouth.

The next one to get the Smile was little Felicity who came up with Susan. Mam'zelle smiled at her.

"Oh!" said Felicity in sudden horror, and Susan stared. Mam'zelle shut her mouth. A desire to laugh was gradually working up inside her. No, no – she must not laugh. Laughing spoilt tricks.

She did not smile for some time, trying to conquer her urge to laugh. Miss Linnie, the sewing-mistress, passed by and nodded at Mam'zelle. Mam'zelle could not resist showing her the teeth. She smiled.

Miss Linnie looked amazed and horrified. She walked on quickly. "Was that *really* Mam'zelle?" she wondered. "No, it must have been someone else. What awful teeth!"

Mam'zelle felt that she must get up and walk about. It was too cold to sit – and besides she so badly wanted to laugh again. Ah, now she understood why the girls laughed so much and so helplessly when they played their mischievous tricks on her.

She walked along the field, and met Bill and Clarissa. They smiled at her and she smiled back. Bill stood still, thunderstruck. Clarissa hadn't really noticed.

"Clarissa!" said Bill, when Mam'zelle had gone. "What's the matter with Mam'zelle this afternoon? She looks *horrible!*"

"Horrible? How?" asked Clarissa in great surprise.

"Well, her *teeth!* Didn't you see her teeth?" asked Bill. "They seem to have changed or something. Simply awful teeth she had – long and sticking-out."

Clarissa was astonished. "Let's walk back and smile at her again," she said. So back they went. But Mam'zelle saw their inquisitive looks, and was struggling against a fit of laughter. She would not open her mouth to smile.

Matron came up. "Oh, Mam'zelle – do you know where Gwen is? She's darned her navy gym pants with grey wool again. I want her indoors this afternoon!"

Mam'zelle could not resist smiling at Matron. Matron stared as if she couldn't believe her eyes. Mam'zelle shut her mouth. Matron backed away a little, looking rather alarmed.

"Gwen's over there," said Mam'zelle, her extra teeth making her words sound rather thick. Matron looked even more alarmed at the thick voice and disappeared in a hurry. Mam'zelle saw her address a few words to Miss Potts. Miss Potts looked round for Mam'zelle.

"Aha!" thought Mam'zelle, "Matron has told her I look terrible! Soon Miss Potts will come to look at my Smile. I shall laugh. I know I shall. I shall laugh without stopping soon."

Miss Potts came up, eyeing Mam'zelle carefully. She got a quick glimpse of the famous teeth. Then Mam'zelle clamped her mouth shut. She would explode if she didn't keep her mouth shut! She pulled her scarf across her face, trying to hide her desire to laugh.

"Do you feel the cold today, Mam'zelle?" asked Miss Potts anxiously. "You – er – you haven't got toothache, have you?"

A peculiar wild sound came from Mam'zelle. It startled Miss Potts considerably. But actually it was only Mam'zelle trying to stifle a squeal of laughter. She rushed away hurriedly. Miss Potts stared after her. What *was* up with Mam'zelle?

Mam'zelle strolled down the field by herself, trying to recover. She gave a few loud gulps that made two second formers wonder if she was going to be ill.

Poor Mam'zelle felt she couldn't flash her teeth at anyone for a long time, for if she did she would explode like Irene. She decided to go in. She turned her steps towards the school – and then, to her utter horror, she saw Miss Grayling, the head mistress, bearing down on her with two parents! Mam'zelle gave an anguished look and hurried on as fast as she could.

"Oh – there's Mam'zelle," said Miss Grayling's pleasant voice. "Mam'zelle, will you meet Mrs Jennings and Mrs Petton?"

Mam'zelle was forced to go to them. She lost all desire for laughter at once. The trick teeth suddenly stopped being funny, and became monstrosities to be got rid of at once. But how? She couldn't spit them into her handkerchief with people just about to shake hands with her.

Mrs Jennings held out her hand. "I've heard so much about you, Mam'zelle Dupont," she said, "and what tricks the naughty girls play on you, too!"

Mam'zelle tried to smile without opening her mouth at all, and the effect was rather peculiar – a sort of suppressed snarl. Mrs Jennings looked surprised. Mam'zelle tried to make up for her lack of smile by shaking Mrs Jennings' hand very vigorously indeed.

She did the same with Mrs Petton, who turned out to be a talkative mother who wanted to know *exactly* how her daughter Teresa was getting on in French. She smiled gaily at Mam'zelle while she talked, and Mam'zelle found it agony not to smile back. She had to produce the suppressed snarl again, smiling with her mouth shut and her lips firmly over her teeth.

Miss Grayling was startled by this peculiar smile. She examined Mam'zelle closely. Mam'zelle's voice was not quite as usual either – it sounded thick. "As if her mouth is too full of teeth," thought Miss Grayling, little knowing that she had hit on the exact truth.

At last the mothers went. Mam'zelle shook hands with them most vigorously once more, and was so relieved at parting from them that she forgot herself and gave them a broad smile.

They got a full view of the terrible teeth, Miss Grayling, too. The head stared in the utmost horror – *what* had happened to Mam'zelle's teeth? Had she had her old ones out – were these a new, false set? But how TERRIBLE they were! They made her look like the wolf in the tale of Red Riding Hood.

The two mothers turned their heads away quickly at the sight of the teeth. They hurried off with Miss Grayling who hardly heard what they said, she was so concerned about Mam'zelle's teeth. She determined to send for Mam'zelle that evening and ask her about them. Really – she couldn't allow any of her staff to go about with teeth like that! They were monstrous, hideous!

Mam'zelle was so thankful to see the last of the mothers that she hurried straight into a little company of fifth formers going back to the school, some to do their piano practice and some to have a lesson in elocution.

"Hallo, Mam'zelle!" said Mavis. "Are you coming back to school?"

Mam'zelle smiled. The fifth formers got a dreadful shock. They stared in silent horror. The teeth had slipped a little, and now looked rather like fangs. They gave Mam'zelle a most sinister, big-bad-wolf look. Mam'zelle saw their alarm and astonishment. Laughter surged back into her. She felt it swelling up and up. She gasped. She gulped. She roared.

She sank on to a bench and cried with helpless laughter. She remembered Matron's face – and Miss Grayling's – and the faces of the two mothers. The more she thought of them the more helplessly she laughed. The girls stood round, more alarmed than ever. What *was* the matter with Mam'zelle? What was this enormous joke?

Mam'zelle's teeth slipped out altogether, fell on to her lap, and then to the ground. The girls stared at them in the utmost amazement, and then looked at Mam'zelle. She now looked completely normal, with just her own small teeth showing in her laughing face. She laughed on and on when she saw her trick teeth lying there before her.

"It is a treek," she squeaked at last, wiping her eyes with her handkerchief. "Did you not give me a dare? Did you not tell me to do a treek on you? I have done one with the teeth. They are treek teeth. Oh, *là là*. – I must laugh again. Oh my sides, oh my back!"

She swayed to and fro, laughing. The girls began to laugh, too. Mam'zelle Rougier came up, astonished to see the other French mistress laughing so much.

"What is the matter?" she asked, without a smile on her face.

Irene did one of her explosions. She pointed to the teeth on the ground. "Mam'zelle wore them – for a trick – and they've fallen out and given the game away!"

She went off into squeals of laughter again, and the other girls joined in. Mam'zelle Rougier looked cold and disapproving.

"I see no joke," she said. "It is not funny, teeth on the grass. It is time to see the dentist when that happens."

She walked off, and her speech and disapproving face sent everyone into fits of laughter again. It was altogether a most successful afternoon for Mam'zelle, and the "treek" story flew all through the school immediately.

Mam'zelle suddenly found herself extremely popular, except with the staff. "A little *undignified*, don't you think?" said Miss Williams.

"Not a thing to do *too* often, Mam'zelle," said Miss Potts, making up her mind to remove the trick booklets from Mam'zelle's desk at the first opportunity.

"Glad you've lost those frightful teeth," said Matron, bluntly. "Don't do that again without warning me, Mam'zelle. I got the shock of my life."

But the girls loved Mam'zelle for her "treek", and every class in the school, from top to bottom, worked twice as hard (or so Mam'zelle declared) after she had played her truly astonishing "treek"!

THE TWINS AT ST CLARE'S
AN EXTRACT

≈ ILLUSTRATED BY ≈

W. Lindsay Cable and Jenny Chapple

Pat and Isabel O'Sullivan are twins who look exactly alike, although they have very different personalities. At their old school, Redroofs, they were "top dogs", but they have left because it only took girls up to the age of 14. Their parents decide to send the twins to St Clare's, which is more robust and democratic than the exclusive Redroofs. St Clare's is a spacious and friendly school, with large playing fields and gardens, and a wonderful country setting. But now that Pat and Isabel are just very junior first formers they have difficulty settling in. They are helped by becoming friends with the straightforward Janet Roberts and their form-leader, Hilary Wentworth. Here the first form is in disgrace after they have thrown bangers into the classroom fire . . .

CHAPTER VIII
THE GREAT MIDNIGHT FEAST

Miss Roberts kept a very tight hand indeed on her form for the next week or two, and they squirmed under her dry tongue. Pat and Isabel hated being spoken to as if they were nobodies, but they did not dare to grumble.

"It's simply awful being ticked off as if we were in the kindergarten, when we've been used to bossing the whole school at Redroofs," said Isabel. "I shall never get used to it!"

"I hate it too," said Pat. "But all the same, I can't help liking Miss Roberts, you know. I do respect her awfully, and you can't help liking people you respect."

"Well, I wish she'd start respecting *us*, then," said Isabel gloomily. "Then maybe she'd like us, and we wouldn't get such a hard time in class. Golly, when I forgot to take my maths book to her this morning you'd have thought she was going to phone up the police station and have me sent to prison!"

Pat laughed. "Don't be an idiot," she said. "By the way, don't forget to give a pound towards buying Miss Theobald something on her birthday. I've given mine in."

"Oh, my!" groaned Isabel. "I hope I've got a pound! I had to give something towards the sweep, and I gave a pound to the housemaid for cleaning my tunic for me in case Matron ticked me off about it – and we had to give something to the Babies' Convalescent Home last week. I'm just about broke!"

She went to her part of the shelf in the common-room and took down her purse. It was empty!

"Golly!" said Isabel in dismay "I'm sure I had a pound in my purse. Did you borrow it, Pat?"

"No," said Pat. "Or I'd have told you. It must be in your coat pocket, silly"

But the money was nowhere to be found. Isabel decided she must have lost it, and she had to borrow some money from Pat to give towards buying the head a present.

Then Janet had a birthday and everyone went down to the town to buy a small present for her – all but Hilary, who discovered, to her dismay, that the money that her granny had sent her, had disappeared out of her pocket!

"Oh, my, a whole ten pounds!" wailed Hilary. "I was going to buy all sorts of things with it. I really must get some new shoelaces, and my lacrosse stick wants mending. Where in the world has it gone?"

Joan lent Hilary some money to buy a present for Janet, and on her birthday Janet was most delighted to find so many gifts. She was very popular, in spite of her bluntness. The finest gift she had was from Kathleen Gregory, who presented her with a gold brooch, with her name inscribed at the back.

"I say! You shouldn't have done that!" said Janet, in amazement. "Why, it must have cost you a mint of money, Kathleen! I really can't accept it. It's too generous a gift."

"But you *must* accept it, because it's got your name inside," said Kathleen. "It's no use to anyone else!"

Everyone admired the little gold brooch and read the name inscribed on the back. Kathleen glowed with pleasure at the attention that her gift produced, and when Janet thanked her again, and slipped her arm through hers, she was red with delight.

"It was very generous of Kathleen," said Janet to the twins, as they went to the classroom. "But I can't understand why she went such a splash on me! Usually she's awfully mean with her gifts — either gives nothing at all, or something that costs fifty pence! It isn't as if she likes me such a lot, either. I've gone for her heaps of times because she's such a goof!"

Janet had a marvellous hamper sent to her for her birthday, and she and Hilary and the twins unpacked it with glee. "All the things I love!" said Janet. "A big chocolate cake! Shortbread biscuits! Sardines in tomato sauce! Nestlé's milk. And look at these peppermint creams! They'll melt in our mouths!"

"Let's have a midnight feast!" said Pat, suddenly. "We once had one at Redroofs, before we were head girls. I don't know why food tastes so much nicer in the middle of the night than in the daytime, but it does! Oh, Janet — don't you think it would be fun?"

"It might be rather sport," said Janet. "But there's not enough food here for us all. The rest of you will have to bring something as well. Each girl had better bring one thing — a cake or ginger beer – or chocolate. When shall we have the feast?"

"Tomorrow night," said Isabel, with a giggle. "Miss Roberts is going to a concert. I heard her say so. She's going to stay the night with a friend and get a train that brings her back in time for prayers."

"Oh, good! Tomorrow's the night then!" said Janet. "Let's tell everyone!"

So the whole form was told about the Great Feast, and everyone promised to bring something.

Pat bought a jam sponge sandwich. Isabel, who again had to borrow from Pat, bought a bar of chocolate. Joan brought candles, because the girls were not allowed to put on the electric light once it was turned out except for urgent reasons, such as illness.

The most lavish contribution was Kathleen's! She brought a really marvellous cake, with almond icing all over it, and pink and yellow sugar roses on the top. Everyone exclaimed over it!

"Golly, Kathleen! Have you come into a fortune or something!" cried Janet. "That cake must have cost you all your pocket-money for the rest of the term! It's marvellous."

"The prettiest cake I've ever seen," said Hilary. "Jolly decent of you, Kathleen."

Kathleen was red with pleasure. She beamed round at everyone, and enjoyed the smiles that she and her cake received.

"I wish I could have got something better than my silly little bar of chocolate," said Isabel. "But I even had to borrow from Pat to get that."

"And I can only bring a few biscuits I had left from a tin that Mother sent me a fortnight ago," said Hilary "I'm quite broke since I lost my money."

"Anyway, we've got heaps of things," said Janet, who was busy hiding everything at the bottom of a cupboard just outside the dormitory. "Golly, I hope Matron doesn't suddenly take it into her head to spring-clean this cupboard! She *would* be surprised to see what's in it. Goodness – who brought this pork pie? How marvellous!"

The whole form was in a state of excitement that day. It was simply gorgeous to have a secret and not to let any of the other forms know. Hilary knew that the upper third had had a midnight feast already that term, and it had been a great success. She meant to make theirs even more of a success!

Miss Roberts couldn't think why the first form girls were so restless. As for Mam'zelle, she sensed the underlying excitement at once, and grew excited too.

"Ah, now, *mes petites*, what is the matter with you today!" she cried, when one girl after another made a mistake in the French translation. "What is in your thoughts? You are planning something – is it not so? Tell me what it is."

"Oh, Mam'zelle, whatever makes you think such a thing!" cried Janet. "What should we be planning?"

"How should I know?" said Mam'zelle. "All I know is that you are not paying attention. Now, one more mistake and I send you to bed an hour earlier than usual!"

Mam'zelle did not mean this, of course – but it tickled the girls, who were all longing for bedtime that night, and would have been quite pleased to go early. Janet giggled and was nearly sent out of the room.

At last bedtime came, and everyone undressed.

"Who's going to get the stuff out of the cupboard?" said Pat.

"You and I and Hilary and Isabel," said Janet. "And for goodness' sake don't drop anything. If you drop the pork pie on the floor there *will* be a mess."

Everyone laughed. They snuggled down into bed. They all wanted to keep awake, but it was arranged that some of them should take it in turns to sit up and keep awake for half an hour, waking the next girl when it was her turn. Then, at midnight, they should all be awakened and the Feast would begin!

First Janet sat up in bed for half an hour, hugging her knees, and thinking of all the things in the cupboard outside. She was not a bit sleepy. She switched on her torch to look at the time. The half hour was just up. She leant across to the next bed and awoke Hilary.

At midnight everyone was fast asleep except for the girl on watch, who was Pat. As she heard the big clock striking from the west tower of the school, Pat crept out of bed. She went from girl to girl, whispering in her ear and shaking her.

"Hilary! It's time! Wake up! Isabel! It's midnight! Joan! The Feast is about to

begin. Kathleen! Kathleen! Do wake up! It's twelve o'clock!"

At last every girl was awake, and with many smothered giggles, they put on their dressing-gowns and slippers.

The whole school was in darkness. Pat lighted two candles, and placed them on a dressing-table in the middle of the dormitory. She had sent Isabel to waken the rest of the form in the next dormitory, and with scuffles and chuckles all the girls crept in. They sat on the beds nearest to the candles, and waited whilst Pat and the others went to get the things out of the cupboard.

Pat took her torch and shone it into the cupboard whilst the others took out the things. A tin of sweetened milk dropped to the floor with a crash. Everyone jumped and stood stock still. They listened, but there was no sound to be heard – no door opened, no one switched on a light.

"Idiot!" whispered Janet to Isabel. "For goodness' sake don't drop that chocolate cake. Where did that tin roll to? Oh, here it is."

At last all the eatables were safely in the dormitory, and the door was shut softly. The girls looked at everything, and felt terribly hungry.

"Golly! Pork pie and chocolate cake, sardines and Nestlé's milk, chocolate and peppermint creams, tinned pineapple and ginger beer!" said Janet. "Talk about a feast! I bet this beats the upper third's feast hollow! Come on – let's begin. I'll cut the cake."

Soon every girl was munching hard and thinking that food had never tasted quite so nice before. Janet took an opener and opened a ginger beer bottle. The first one was quite all right and Janet filled two tooth-glasses. But the next ginger beer bottle fizzed out tremendously and soaked the bed that Janet was sitting on. Everyone giggled. It went off with a real pop, and sounded quite loud in the silence of the night.

"Don't worry! No one will hear that," said Janet. "Here, Pat – open the sardines. I've got some bread and butter somewhere, and we'll make sandwiches."

The bread and butter was unwrapped from its paper. Janet had brought it up from the tea-table. Every girl had taken a piece from the plate at tea-time, and hidden it to give to Janet.

"Look – take a bite of a sardine sandwich, and then a bite of pork pie, and then a spoonful of Nestlé's milk," said Pat. "It tastes gorgeous."

The chocolate was saved till last. By that time the girls were all unable to eat any more and could only suck the sweets and the chocolate. They sat about and giggled at the silliest jokes.

"Of course, the nicest thing of the whole feast was Kathleen's marvellous cake," said Hilary. "The almond icing was gorgeous."

"Yes – and I had one of the sugar roses," said Joan. "Lovely! However much did you pay for that cake, Kath? It was jolly decent of you."

"Oh, that's nothing," said Kathleen. "I'm most awfully glad you liked it."

She looked very happy. There had not been quite enough cake to go round and Kathleen hadn't even tasted the marvellous cake. But she didn't mind at all. She sat quite happily watching the others feast on it.

Then the girls began to press Doris to do her clown dance. This was a dance she had learnt during the holidays at some special classes, and it was very funny. Doris was full of humour and could make the others laugh very easily. The clown dance was most ridiculous, because Doris had to keep falling over herself She accompanied this falling about with many groans and gurgles, which always sent the audience into fits of laughter.

"Well, don't laugh too loudly this time," said Doris, getting up. "You made such a row last time I did it in the common-room that Belinda Towers came in and ticked me off for playing the fool."

She began the dance with a solemn face. She fell over the foot of the bed, on purpose of course, and rubbed herself with a groan. The girls began to chuckle, their hands over their mouths.

Doris loved making people laugh. She swayed about, making comical faces, then pretended to catch one leg in another, and fell, clutching at Pat with a deep groan.

With a giggle Pat fell too, and knocked against the dressing-table. The table shook violently, and everything on it slid to the floor! Brushes, combs, photograph frames, tooth-mugs, a ginger beer bottle – goodness, what a crash!

The girls stared in horror. The noise sounded simply terrific!

"Quick! Clear everything up and get into bed," cried Janet, in a loud whisper, "Golly! We'll have half the mistresses here."

The girls belonging to the next dormitory fled out of the door at once. The others cleared up quickly, but very soon heard the sound of an electric light being switched on in the passage.

"Into bed!" hissed Hilary, and they all leapt under the sheets. They pulled them up to their chins and lay listening. Hilary remembered that they had left two ginger beer bottles out in the middle of the floor – and they hadn't had time to clear up the remains of the pork pie either. Pork pies were so untidy, and *would* scatter themselves in crumbs every time a bite was taken!

The door opened, and someone was outlined against the light from the passage outside. Pat saw who it was – old Kenny! What bad luck! If she discovered anything she would be sure to report it after the bad behaviour of the form. But perhaps she wouldn't switch on the dormitory light.

Miss Kennedy stood listening. One of the girls gave a gentle snore, making believe that she was fast asleep – but that was too much for Kathleen, who was already very strung up. She gave a smothered giggle, and Miss Kennedy heard it. She switched on the light.

The first thing she saw were the two ginger beer bottles standing boldly in the middle of the floor. Then she saw the remains of the pork pie. She saw the paper from the chocolate. She guessed immediately what the girls had been up to.

A little smile came over her face. What monkeys girls were! She remembered the thrill of a midnight feast herself — and how she and the others had been caught and severely punished. She spoke in a low voice to Hilary, the head of the dormitory.

"Hilary! Are you awake?"

Hilary dared not pretend. She answered in a sleepy voice. "Hallo, Miss Kennedy! Is anything wrong?"

"I thought I heard a noise from this dormitory," said Miss Kennedy. "I'm in charge of it tonight as Miss Roberts isn't here. But I may have been mistaken."

Hilary sat up in bed and saw the ginger beer bottles. She glanced at Miss Kennedy and saw a twinkle in her eye.

"Perhaps you *were* mistaken, Miss Kennedy," she said. "Perhaps — perhaps — it was mice or something."

"Perhaps it was," said Miss Kennedy. "Er — well, I don't see that there's anything to report to Miss Roberts — but as you're head of the dormitory, Hilary, you might see that it's tidy before Matron does her rounds tomorrow morning. Good night."

She switched off the light, shut the door and went back to her room. The girls all sat up in bed at once and began to whisper.

"My goodness! Kenny's a sport!"

"Golly! She saw those awful ginger beer bottles all right! And fancy agreeing that that terrific noise we made might have been *mice!*"

"And she as good as said we were to remove all traces of the feast, and she promised not to report anything to Miss Roberts."

"Though old Roberts is a sport too, in her way," said Doris.

"Yes, but we're in her bad books at the moment, don't forget, and anything like this would just about finish things!" said Isabel. "Good old Kenny!"

CHAPTER IX
A LACROSSE MATCH – AND A PUZZLE

The only bad effects of the Great Midnight Feast, as it came to be called, were that Isabel, Doris and Vera didn't feel at all well the next day. Miss Roberts eyed them sharply.

"What have you been eating?" she asked.

"Only what the others have," answered Doris, quite truthfully.

"Well, go to Matron and she'll dose you," said Miss Roberts. The three girls went off dolefully. Matron had some most disgusting medicine. She dosed the girls generously and they groaned when she made them lick the spoon round.

Then Joan and Kathleen felt ill and they were sent to Matron too.

"I know these symptoms," said Matron. "You are suffering from Midnight Feast Illness! Aha! You needn't pretend to me! If you *will* feast on pork pies and sardines, chocolate and ginger beer in the middle of the night, you can expect a dose of medicine from me the next day."

The girls stared at her in horror. How did she know?

"Who told you?" asked Joan, thinking that Miss Kennedy had told tales after all.

"Nobody," said Matron, putting the cork back firmly into the enormous bottle. "But I haven't been Matron of a girls' school for twenty-five years without knowing a *few* things! I dosed your mother before you, Joan, and your aunt too. They couldn't stand midnight food any more than you can. Go along now – don't stare at me like that. I shan't tell tales – and I always say there's no need to punish girls for having a midnight feast, because the feelings they get the next day are punishment enough!"

The girls went away. Joan looked at Kathleen. "You know, I simply loved the pork pie and the sardines last night," she said, gloomily, "but the very thought of them makes me feel sick today. I don't believe I'll ever be able to look a sardine in the face again."

But everyone soon forgot their aches and pains, and the feast passed into a legend that was told throughout the school. Even Belinda Towers heard about it and chuckled when she was told how everything fell off the dressing-table at the last.

It was Kathleen who told Belinda. It was rather strange how Kathleen had altered during the last few weeks. She was no longer nervous and apologetic to everyone, but took her place happily and laughed and joked like the rest. She could even talk to tall Belinda Towers without stammering with nervousness! She was waiting on Belinda that week, and rushed about quite happily, making toast, running errands and not even grumbling when Belinda sent for her in the middle of a concert rehearsal.

Kathleen was to play in an important lacrosse match that week, and so was Isabel. They were the only first form girls chosen – all the others were second formers. At first Pat had been by far the better of the two, but Isabel soon learnt the knack of catching and throwing the ball in the easiest way, and had outstripped her twin. The match was to be against the second form of a nearby day school, and the girls were very keen about it.

"Kathleen's goalkeeper," said Pat to Isabel. "Belinda told her today. I say, isn't Kath different? I quite like her now."

"Yes – and she's so generous!" said Isabel. "She bought some sweets yesterday and shared the whole lot round without having even one herself. And she bought some chrysanthemums for Vera – they must have cost a lot!"

Vera was in the sickbay, recovering from a bad cold. She had been very surprised and touched when Kathleen had taken her six beautiful yellow chrysanthemums. It was so unlike Kathleen, who had always been rather mean before.

Kathleen got Isabel to practise throwing balls into the goal, so that she might get even better at stopping them. She was very quick. Then she and Isabel practised catching and throwing the ball and running with it and dodging each other.

"If only, only I could shoot two or three goals on Saturday," Isabel said a dozen times a day. Hilary laughed. Isabel asked her why.

"I'm laughing at *you*," said Hilary. "Who turned up her nose at lacrosse a few weeks ago? You did! Who said there wasn't any game worth playing except hockey? You did! Who vowed and declared she would never try to be any good at a silly game like lacrosse? You did. That's why I'm laughing! I have to sit and hear you raving about lacrosse now, talking about it all day long. It sounds funny to me."

Isabel laughed too, but she went rather red. "I must have seemed rather an idiot," she said.

"You *were* a bit of a goof," said Janet, joining in. "The stuck-up twins! That's what we used to call you."

"Oh," said Isabel, ashamed. She made up her mind to play so well on Saturday that her whole form would be proud of her. The stuck-up twins! What a dreadful name! She and Pat must really do something to make the form forget that.

Saturday came, a brilliantly fine winter's day. The first form were excited. The girls from the day school were coming to lunch and they had to entertain them. Dinner was to be sausages and mashed potatoes, with treacle pudding to follow, a very favourite meal.

"Now look here, Isabel and Kathleen, just see you don't eat too much," ordered Hilary. "We want you to play your best. You're the only ones from the first form who are playing – all the rest are second formers. We'll stuff the other school all right – give them so much to eat that they won't be able to catch a ball!"

"Oh, I say! Can't I have two sausages?" said Isabel in dismay. "And I always have two helpings of treacle pudding."

"Well, you won't today," said Janet, firmly. "But if you play well and we win, the whole form will stand you cream buns at tea-time. See?"

So Isabel cheered up and went without a second helping of treacle pudding quite amiably. It was a pleasant lunch. The guests were all jolly, friendly girls, and how they laughed when they were told the story of the Great Feast!

"We can't have fun like that," said one of the day girls. "We always go home at night. What's your lacrosse team like? Any good? We've beaten you each time we've played you so far."

"And I bet we'll beat them again," cried the captain, a tall girl with flaming red hair.

"Cream buns for you if you stop their goals, Kathleen!" cried Janet, and everyone laughed.

All the first, second and third forms turned out to watch the match. The fourth form were playing a match of their own away from home, and the sixth rarely bothered to watch the juniors. Some of the fifth turned up, among them Belinda Towers, who arranged all the matches and the players, for she was sports captain, and very keen that St Clare's should win as many matches as possible.

The players took their places. Isabel was tremendously excited. Kathleen was quite cool and calm in goal. The match began.

The day girls made a strong team, and were splendid runners. They got the ball at once, and passed it from one to another whenever they were tackled. But Isabel jumped high into the air and caught the ball as it flew from one day girl to another!

Then she was off like the

wind, racing down the field. A girl came out to tackle and tried to knock the ball off Isabel's net – but Isabel jerked it neatly over her head into the waiting net of another St Clare's – girl and she was off down the field too. Isabel sped behind and caught the ball again neatly as the other girl threw it when tackled.

But a very fast girl was after Isabel and took the ball from her. Back the other way raced the day girl, making for the goal. She passed the ball to another girl, who passed it to a third – and the third one shot straight at the goal, where Kathleen stood on guard. Swift as lightning Kathleen put her net down towards the ball, caught it and threw it to Isabel who was waiting not far off

"Jolly well saved, Kathleen!" roared every one of the St Clare's girls, and Kathleen went red with excitement and delight.

So the match went on till half-time, when lemon quarters were taken round on plates to all the hot and panting players. How they loved sucking the cool sour lemon!

"The score is three-one," said the umpire. "Three to the day girls of St Christopher's and one to St Clare's."

"Play up, St Clare's!" cried Belinda. "Play up. Now, Isabel, score, please!"

The second half of the match began. The players were not quite so fast now, for they were tired. But the excitement ran very high, especially when St Clare's shot two goals in quick succession, one of them thrown by Isabel.

Kathleen hopped about on one leg as the play went on down the other end of the field. She had saved seven goals already. Down the field raced the players, the ball flying from one to another with grace and ease. Kathleen stood tensely, knowing that a goal would be tried.

The ball came down on her, hard and swift. She tried to save the goal, but the ball shot into the corner of the net. Goal! Four-three – and only five minutes to go!

Then St Clare's scored a most unexpected goal in the next two minutes and that made the score equal.

"Only one and a half minutes more!" panted Isabel to a St Clare's girl as she passed her the ball. "For goodness' sake, let's get another goal and win!"

The ball came back to her. A day girl thundered down on Isabel, a big, burly girl. Isabel swung round and dodged, the ball still in her net. She passed it to another girl, who neatly passed it back as soon as she was tackled. And then Isabel took a look at the goal, which, although a good way away, was almost straight in front. It was worth a shot!

She threw the ball hard and straight down the field. The goalkeeper stood ready – but somehow she missed the ball and it rolled into the net, just before the whistle went for time! How the St Clare's girls cheered! Pat leapt up and down like a mad thing. Belinda yelled till she was hoarse, and Hilary and Janet thumped one another on the back, though neither of them quite knew why!

"Good old Isabel! She saved the match just in time!" cried Pat. "Cream buns for her!"

Hot and tired and happy, all the girls trooped off the field to wash and tidy themselves before tea. Janet ran to get her purse to rush off on her bicycle to buy the cream buns.

But her purse only had a few pence inside! How strange! Janet knew quite well that it had had five pounds in it that very morning – and she certainly hadn't spent any of it.

"I say! My money's gone!" she said in dismay. "I can't get the cream buns. Dash! Where's it gone?"

"Funny," said Isabel. "Mine went a little while ago – and so did Hilary's. Now yours has gone."

"Well, don't discuss it now," said Joan. "We've got to entertain the day girls. But it's a pity about the cream buns."

"*I'll* buy them!" said Kathleen. "I'll give you the money, Janet."

"Oh, no!" said Janet. "We wanted to buy them for you and Isabel because you did so well in the match. We can't let you buy them for yourselves!"

"Please do," said Kathleen, and she took some money from her pocket. "Here you are. Buy buns for everyone!"

"Well – it's jolly decent of you," said Janet, taking the money. "Thanks awfully." She sped off on her bicycle whilst the other girls got ready for tea.

"Well played, kids," said Belinda Towers, strolling up. "You stopped some pretty good goals, Kathleen – and you just about saved the match, Isabel, though all the rest did jolly well too."

Everyone glowed at the sports captain's praise. Then they sat down to tea, and soon the big piles of bread and butter and jam, currant buns and chocolate cake disappeared like magic. Janet was back in a few minutes with a large number of delicious-looking cream buns. The girls greeted them with cheers.

"Thanks, Kathleen! You're a brick, Kathleen," everyone cried, and Kathleen beamed with delight.

"Well, I *did* enjoy today!" said Isabel to Pat, as they went off to the common-room together, after seeing the day girls off. "Simply marvellous! Every bit of it."

"Not quite every bit," said Pat, rather gravely. "What about Janet's money? Somebody took that, Isabel. And that's pretty beastly. Who in the world could it be?"

"I simply can't imagine," said Isabel.

Neither could anyone else. The girls talked about it together, and wondered who had been near Janet's coat. She had hung it on a peg in the sports pavilion, and most of the first and second form had been in and out. But surely, surely no St Clare's girl could possibly do such a thing!

"It's stealing, just plain stealing," said Hilary. "And it's been going on for some time too, because I know others besides myself and Janet and Isabel have lost money. Belinda lost ten pounds too. She made an awful row about it, but she never found it."

"Could it be one of the staff?" said Joan.

"Shouldn't think so," said Hilary. "They've been here for years. Well – we must all be careful of our money, that's all, and, if we can't *find* the thief, we'll make it difficult for her to *be* one!"

CHAPTER X
A VERY MUDDLED GIRL

One afternoon Rita George, one of the older girls, sent for Kathleen to give her some instructions about a nature ramble she was getting up. Kathleen was head of the nature club in her form. She asked Pat to finish winding the wool that Isabel was holding for her, and ran off.

"Shan't be long," she said, and disappeared. Pat wound the wool into balls and then threw them into Kathleen's work-basket. She looked at her watch.

"I hope Kath won't be long," she said. "We are due for gym in five minutes. I'd better go and remind her. Coming, Isabel?"

The twins went out, and made their way to Rita's study, meaning to see if Kathleen was still there. But when they arrived they stood still in dismay.

Someone was sobbing and crying inside! Someone was saying, "Oh, please forgive me! Oh, please don't tell anyone! Please, please, don't!"

"Gracious! That's not Kathleen, is it?" said Pat, horrified. "What's happened?"

They did not dare to go in. They waited, hearing more sobs, pitiful, heartbroken sobs, and they heard Rita's rather deep voice, sounding very stern. They could not hear what she said.

Then the door opened and Kathleen came out, her eyes red, and her cheeks tear-stained. She sobbed under her breath, and did not see the twins. She hurried towards the stairs that led to her dormitory.

Pat and Isabel stared after her. "She's forgotten about gym," said Pat. "I don't like to go to her in case she hates anyone seeing her cry."

"Oh, let's go and comfort her," said Isabel. "We'll get into a row for being late for gym – but it's awful to see anyone in trouble like that and not see if we can help."

So they ran up the stairs to the dormitory. Kathleen was lying on her bed, her face buried in her pillow, sobbing.

"Kathleen! Whatever's happened?" asked Isabel, putting her hand on Kathleen's shoulder. Kathleen shook it off.

"Go away!' she said. "Go away! Don't come peeping and prying after me."

"We're not," said Pat, gently. "What's the matter? We're your friends, you know."

"You wouldn't be, if I told you what had happened," sobbed Kathleen. "Oh, do go away. I'm going to pack my things and leave St Clare's! I'm going this very night!"

"Kathleen! Do tell us what's happened!" cried Isabel "Did Rita tick you off for something? Don't worry about that."

"It's not the ticking off I'm worrying about – it's the thing I did to *get* the ticking off," said Kathleen. She sat up, her eyes swollen and red. "Well, I'll tell you – and you can go and spread it all round the school if you like – and everyone can laugh and jeer at me – but I'll not be here."

She began to cry again. Pat and Isabel were very much upset. Isabel slipped her arm round the sobbing girl. "All right – tell us," she said. "We won't turn on you, I promise."

"Yes, you will, yes you will! What I've done is so dreadful!" sobbed Kathleen. "You won't believe it! I hardly believe it myself. I'm – I'm – I'm a thief."

"Kathleen! What do you mean?" asked Pat, shocked. Kathleen stared at her defiantly. She wiped her eyes with a hand that shook.

"*I* took all the money that's been missing!" she said. "Every bit of it – even yours, Isabel. I couldn't bear never having any money of my own, and saying no when people wanted subscriptions, and not giving any nice birthday presents to anyone, and being thought mean and selfish and ungenerous. I did so want to be generous to everybody, and to make friends. I do so love giving things and making people happy."

The twins stared at Kathleen in surprise and horror. They could hardly believe what she said. She went on, pouring out her troubles between her sobs.

"I haven't a mother to send me money as you and the other girls have. My father is away abroad and I only have a mean old aunt who gives me about a penny a week. I hated to own up to such a miserable bit of money – and then one day I found a pound belonging to someone and I bought something for somebody with it – and they were so terribly pleased – and I was so happy. I can't tell you how dreadful it is to want to be generous and not to be able to be!"

"Poor Kathleen!" said Isabel, and she patted her on the shoulder "Nobody would have minded at all if only you had told them you hadn't any money. We could all have shared with you."

"But I was too proud to let you do that," said Kathleen. "And yet I wasn't too proud to steal. Oh, I can't think how I did it now! I took Janet's money – and Hilary's – and even Belinda's. It was all so easy. And then this afternoon I – I – I . . ."

She began to cry so bitterly that the twins were quite frightened. "Don't tell us if you'd rather not," said Pat.

"Oh, I'll tell you everything now I've begun," said poor Kathleen. "It's a relief to tell somebody. Well, this afternoon when I went to Rita's study, she wasn't there – but I saw her coat hanging up and her purse sticking out of it. And I went to it – and oh, Rita came in quietly and caught me! And she's going to Miss Theobald about it, and I will be known all over the school as a thief, and I'll be expelled and . . ."

She wept again, and the twins looked at one another helplessly. They remembered all Kathleen's sudden generosity – her gifts – the marvellous cake with sugar roses on it – the fine chrysanthemums for Vera – and they remembered too Kathleen's flushed cheeks and shining eyes when she saw her friends enjoying the things she had bought for them.

"Kathleen – go and wash your face and come down to gym," said Pat at last.

"I'm not going to," said Kathleen, obstinately. "I'm going to stay here and pack. I don't want to see anybody again. You two have been decent to me, but I know in your heart of hearts that you simply despise me!"

"We don't, Kath dear," said Isabel. "We're terribly, terribly sorry for you – and we do understand why you did it. You so badly wanted to be generous – you did a wrong thing to make a right thing, and that's never any good."

"Please go, and leave me alone," said Kathleen. "Please go."

The twins went out of the dormitory. Halfway to the gym Isabel stopped and pulled at Pat's arm.

"Pat! Let's go and find Rita if we can. Let's say what we can for poor old Kathleen."

"All right," said Pat. The two of them went to Rita's study, but it was empty. "Blow!" said Pat. "I wonder if she's gone to Miss Theobald already."

"Well, come on – let's see," said Isabel. So to the head's room they went – and coming out of the door, looking very grim indeed, was Rita George!

"What are you two kids doing here?" she said, and went on her way without waiting for an answer. Pat looked at Isabel.

"She's told Miss Theobald," she said. "Well – dare we go in and speak to the head about it? I do really think Kathleen isn't an ordinary kind of thief – and if she gets branded as one, and sent away, she may really become one, and be spoilt for always. Come on – let's go in."

They knocked, and the head called them to come in. She looked surprised to see them.

"Well, twins," she said. "What is the matter? You look rather serious."

Pat didn't quite know how to begin. Then the words came in a rush and the whole story came out about how Kathleen had stolen all the money, and why.

"But oh, Miss Theobald, Kathleen didn't spend a penny on herself," said Pat. "It was all for us others. She certainly took our money — but we got it back in gifts and things. She isn't just an ordinary, contemptible sort of thief. She's terribly, terribly upset. Oh, could you possibly do anything about it — not send her away — not let the school know? I'm quite sure Kathleen would try to repay every penny, and Isabel and I would help her all we could never to do such a thing again."

"You see, it was all because Kathleen got hardly any pocket-money and she was too proud to say so — and she hated to be thought mean and selfish because really she's terribly generous," said Isabel.

Miss Theobald smiled a very sweet smile at the earnest twins. "My dears," she said, "you tell me such a different story from Rita, and I'm so very glad to hear it. Rita naturally sees poor Kathleen as a plain thief. You see her as she is — a poor muddled child who wants to be generous and chooses an easy but a very wrong way. I am sure I would not have got any explanation from Kathleen, and I might have written to her aunt to take her away. And then I dread what might have happened to her, poor, sensitive child!"

"Oh, Miss Theobald! Do you mean that you will let Kathleen stay?" cried Pat.

"Of course," said the head. "I must talk to her first, and get her to tell me all this herself. I shall know how to deal with her, don't worry. Where is she?"

"In her dormitory, packing," said Pat.

Miss Theobald stood up. "I'll go to her," she said. "Now you go off to whatever lesson you are supposed to be at, and tell your teacher please to excuse your being late, but that you have been with me. And I just want to say this — I am proud of you both! You are kind and understanding, two things that matter a great deal."

Blushing with surprise and pleasure, the twins held open the door for Miss Theobald to go out. They looked at each other in delight.

"Isn't she a sport?" said Pat. "Oh, how glad I am we dared to come in and tell her. I believe things will be all right for Kath now!"

They sped off to gym, and were excused for being late.

They wondered and wondered how Kathleen was getting on with Miss Theobald. They knew after tea when Kathleen, her eyes still red, but looking very much happier, came up to them.

"I'm not going," she said. "I'm going to stay here and show Miss Theobald I'm as decent as anyone else. She's going to write to my aunt and ask for a proper amount of pocket-money to be paid to me – and I shall give back all the money I took – and start again. And if I can't be as generous as I'd like for a little while, I'll wait patiently till I can."

"Yes – and don't be afraid of owning up if you haven't got money to spare," said Pat. "Nobody minds that at all. That's just silly pride, to be afraid of saying when you can't afford something. Oh, Kath – I'm so glad you're not going. Isabel and I had just got to like you very much."

"You've been good friends to me," said Kathleen, squeezing their arms as she walked between them. "If ever I can return your kindness, I will. You *will* trust me again, won't you? It would be so awful not to be trusted. I couldn't bear that."

"Of course we'll trust you," said Pat. "If you go on like that I'll get a hundred pounds out of the bank and ask you to keep it for me! Don't be such a silly-billy!"

THE O'SULLIVAN TWINS
AN EXTRACT

≈ ILLUSTRATED BY ≈

W. Lindsay Cable and Jenny Chapple

In their second term at St Clare's, Pat and Isabel have to cope with Erica, a spiteful 'tell-tale' who resents their popularity, and Margery Fenworthy, a big athletic new girl who is unfriendly and rude to everyone. When Erica plays underhand tricks, Margery gets blamed for them. Pat, Isabel, and their cousin Alison have found out that Margery has been expelled from one or two previous schools, but they agreed not to mention this to the other girls so that Margery might have a chance to make good at St Clare's . . .

CHAPTER XIV
MARGERY MAKES A DISCOVERY

The twins felt most uncomfortable about Margery. Yet they could not blame their cousin for telling the girl's secret. Alison had been very indignant about the trick that had been played on Pat, and it was her way of backing up her cousin, to talk against Margery.

"I say – you don't think Margery will run away or anything like that, do you?" said Pat, to Isabel. "You know, Isabel – if that sort of thing happened to me, I couldn't stay one moment more at St Clare's. I simply couldn't. I'd have to go home."

"Maybe Margery hasn't much of a home to go to," said Isabel. "You know, she never talks about her home as we all do – she never says anything about her mother and father, or if she has any brothers or sisters. Does she? It seems rather strange to me."

"I don't think we can leave things like this," said Lucy Oriell, looking grave. "I think Miss Theobald must have known all about Margery – and her bad reputation – and I think she must have said she would let her try here, at St Clare's. And I think something else too – I think that all the mistresses were in the secret, and knew about Margery – and that they have been asked to be lenient with her to give her a chance."

The girls stared at Lucy's serious little face. She was such a sweet-natured girl that everyone listened to her willingly. No one had ever known Lucy say anything horrid about anyone.

"I think you're right, Lucy," said Pat. "I've often wondered why Margery seemed to get away with rudeness and carelessness – whilst we got into hot water if we did the same things. I knew of course it wasn't favouritism, for no mistress could possibly *like* Margery. Now I understand."

"Yes – Lucy's right," said Hilary. "All the mistresses were in the secret, and were trying to help Margery, hoping she'd turn over a new leaf, and be all right at St Clare's. What a hope!"

"It's this meanness I can't stand," said Pat. "I can put up with bad manners and rudeness and even sulkiness, but I just hate meanness,"

"Yes, I agree with you there," said Janet. "You can't do much with a mean nature. Well – what are we going to do about Margery? Lucy, you said we couldn't leave things as they are now. What do you suggest doing?"

"I suggest that we all sleep on it, and then one or more of us should go to Miss Theobald tomorrow and tell all we know," said Lucy "If Margery can't face us after what has happened, then she ought to be given the chance to go. But if she still wants to stay, and face it out, then she ought to have the chance to do that. But Miss Theobald ought to decide – not us. We don't know enough. Miss Theobald probably knows the reason for Margery's funny behaviour. We don't."

"All right. Let's sleep on it," said Janet. "My mother always says that's a good thing to do. Things often seem different after a night's sleep. Well – we'll do that – and tomorrow we'll go to Miss Theobald and tell her all we know."

"Lucy must go," said Hilary. "She's good at that sort of thing. She's got no spite in her and can tell a story fairly. Pat and Isabel had better go too – because after all, it's against Pat that these hateful tricks have been directed."

"All right," said Lucy. "I'd rather *not* go really, because I hate being mixed up in this sort of thing. But somebody's got to go. Well, that's decided then."

But although the girls had laid their plans seriously and carefully, they were not to be put into action. For something happened that night that upset them completely, and that changed everything in a few hours.

The girls all went to bed as usual. Erica had complained of a sore throat and had been sent to Matron. Matron had taken her temperature, and found that it was a hundred. So into the sickbay went Erica, where two other girls were, with bad chills.

"You've just got a chill too," said Matron. "Now drink this, and settle down quickly into bed. I'll pop in and see you later. You'll probably be normal tomorrow, and can go back to school the next day if you're sensible."

Erica didn't mind at all. She rather liked missing lessons for a day or two – and she felt that it was lucky to be away when all the fuss was being made about Margery. Erica was a mean soul – but even she had been horrified at the look on Margery's face when she had overheard what the girls were saying about her.

"I wouldn't have played those tricks and made it seem as if they'd been done by Margery if I'd known the girls were going to find out about her being expelled – and blame the tricks on to her as well as despise her for her disgrace," thought Erica, her conscience beginning to prick her for the first time. "I wish I hadn't done them now. But I do hate that horrid Pat. It does serve her right to have her jumper spoilt and all her nature books!"

Erica got undressed and into bed. She was alone in a little room at the top of the sickbay, which was a separate building on the west side of the school. Here were put any infectious cases, any girls with measles and so on, or who had perhaps sprained an ankle. Here Matron looked after them and kept them under her eye until they were well enough to go back to their forms.

Erica was put into a room alone because Matron was not quite sure if her cold was going to turn to something infectious. There had been a case of measles among the Oakdene girls who had played the match against St Clare's, and the mistresses had been on the watch in case any of their own girls should have caught it from the Oakdene girl.

So Erica was not put with the two girls who had chills, in case by any chance she was beginning measles, which she hadn't had.

It was a nice little room, tucked away at the top of the sickbay. Erica looked out of the window before she got into bed and saw a sky full of stars. She drew back the curtains so that the sun could come in the next morning and then got into bed.

Matron came along with a hot-water bottle and some hot lemon and honey. Erica enjoyed it. Then Matron tucked her up, switched off the light, and left her to go to sleep.

Erica was soon asleep. Her conscience did not keep her awake, for it was not a very lively one. If Pat or Isabel had done the things that Erica had done lately, neither of them would have been able to sleep at night because of feeling mean and wretched. But Erica went sweetly off to sleep, and slept as soundly as any of the girls in her form.

But one girl did not sleep that night. It was Margery. She lay in her dormitory, wide awake, thinking of what she had heard the girls say about her. Always, always, wherever she went, her secret was found out, and sooner or later she had to go. She didn't want to be at school. She didn't want to stay at home. She wished with all her might that she could go out into the world and find a job and earn her own living. It was dreadful going from school to school like this, getting worse every time!

The other girls slept soundly. Someone snored a little. Margery turned over to her left side and shut her eyes. If only she could go to sleep! If only she could stop thinking and thinking! What was going to happen tomorrow? Now that all the girls knew about her, things would be terrible.

She couldn't go home. She couldn't run away because she didn't have much money. There was simply nothing she could do but stay and be miserable – and when she was miserable she didn't care about anything in the world, and that made her rude and careless and sulky.

"There isn't any way out for me," thought the girl. "There's simply nothing I can do. If only there was something – some way of escape from all this. But there isn't."

She turned over on to her right side, and shut her eyes again. But in a moment they were wide open. It was impossible to go to sleep. She tried lying on her back, staring up into the dark. But that didn't make her sleepy either She heard the school clock chime out. Eleven o'clock. Twelve o'clock. One o'clock. Two o'clock. Was there ever such a long night as this? At this rate the night would never never be over.

"I'll get myself a drink of water," said Margery, sitting up. "Maybe that will help me to go to sleep."

She put on her dressing-gown and slippers and found her torch. She switched it on. Its light showed her the sleeping forms of the other girls. No one stirred as she went down between the cubicles to the door.

She went out into the passage. There was a bathroom not far off, with glasses. She went there and filled a glass with water She took it to the window to drink it.

And it was whilst she was standing there, drinking the icy-cold water, that she saw something that puzzled her She forgot to finish the water, and set the glass down to peer out of the window.

The bathroom window faced the sickbay, which was a four-storey building, tall and rather narrow. It was in complete darkness except at one place.

A flickering light showed now and again from high up on the third storey. It came from a window there. Margery puzzled over it. She tried to think what it could be.

"It looks like flickering firelight," she thought. "But who is sleeping on the third storey, I wonder? Wait a minute – surely that isn't the window of a bedroom? Surely it's the little window that gives light to the stairway that goes up to the top storey?"

She watched for a little while, trying to make certain. But in the darkness she couldn't be sure if it was the staircase window or a bedroom window. The light flickered on and on, exactly as if it were the glow of a bedroom fire, sometimes dancing up into flames and sometimes dying down.

"I'd better go back to bed," said Margery to herself, shivering. "It's probably the room where Erica is – and Matron has given her a fire in her bedroom for a treat. It's the flickering glow I can see."

So back to bed she went – but she kept worrying a little about that curious light – and in the end she got out of bed once more to see if it was still there.

And this time, looking out of the bathroom window, she knew without any doubt what it was. It was Fire, Fire, Fire!

CHAPTER XV
A WONDERFUL RESCUE

As soon as Margery saw the light for the second time, she gave a shout. The whole of the staircase window was lit up, and flames were shooting out of it! "Fire!" yelled Margery, and darted off to Miss Roberts's room. She hammered on her door.

"Miss Roberts! Miss Roberts! Quick, come and look! The sickbay is on fire! Oh, quick!"

Miss Roberts woke with a jump. Her room faced on to the sickbay and she saw at once what Margery had just seen. Dragging on a dressing-gown she ran to the door. Margery clutched hold of her.

"Miss Roberts! Shall I go across and see if Matron knows! I'm sure she doesn't!"

"Yes, run quickly!" said Miss Roberts. "Don't wake any of the girls in this building, Margery – there's no need for them to know. Hurry now. I'll get Miss Theobald and we'll join you."

Margery tore down the stairs and undid the side door. She raced across the piece of grass that separated the sickbay from the school. She hammered on the door there and shouted.

"Matron! Matron! Are you there!"

Matron was fast sleep on the second floor. She didn't wake. It was Queenie, one of the girls in bed with a chill, who heard Margery shouting. She ran to the window and looked out.

"What is it, what is it?" she cried.

"The sickbay is on fire!" shouted Margery. "Flames are coming out on the storey above you. Wake Matron!"

The girl darted into the Matron's room. She shook her hard, calling to her in fright. Matron woke up in a hurry and pulled on a coat.

Miss Theobald appeared with some of the other mistresses. Someone had telephoned for the fire-engine. Girls appeared from everywhere, in spite of mistresses' orders to go back to bed.

"Good gracious! Go back to bed when there's a perfectly good fire on!" said Janet who, as usual, was eager to enjoy any experience that came her way. "Golly, I've never seen a fire before! I'm going to enjoy this one. Nobody's in any danger!"

Girls swarmed all over the place. Matron tried to find the three who had had chills – Queenie, Rita, and Erica. "They mustn't stand about in this cold night air," she said, very worried. "Oh, there you are, Queenie. You are to go at once to the second form dormitory and get into the first bed you see there. Is Rita with you – and where is Erica?"

"Rita's here," said Queenie, "and I think I saw Erica somewhere."

"Well, find her and take her to bed at once," ordered Matron. "Where are the two nurses? Are they safe?"

Yes – they were safe. They were shivering in their coats nearby, watching the flames getting bigger and bigger

"Matron, is everyone out of the sickbay?" asked Miss Theobald. "Are you sure? All the girls? The nurses? Anyone else?"

"I've seen Queenie," said Matron, "and Rita – and Queenie said she saw Erica. Those are the only girls I had in. And the two nurses are out. They are over there."

"Well, that's all right then," said Miss Theobald, in relief. "Oh, I wish that fire-engine would hurry up. I'm afraid the fourth storey will be completely burnt out."

Queenie had not seen the right Erica. She *had* seen a girl called Erica, who was in the fourth form, and she had not known that Matron meant Erica of the second form. Erica was still in the sickbay.

No one knew this at all until suddenly Mam'zelle gave a scream and pointed with a trembling hand to the window of the top storey.

"*Oh, que c'est terrible!*" she cried. "There is someone there!"

Poor Erica was at the window. She had been awakened by the smell of smoke, and had found her bedroom dark with the evil-smelling smoke that crept in under and around her door. Then she had heard the crackling of the flames.

In a terrible fright she had jumped up and tried to switch on her light. But nothing happened. The wires outside had been burnt and there was no light in her room. The girl felt for her torch and switched it on.

She ran to the door – but when she opened it a great roll of smoke unfolded itself and almost choked her. There was no way out down the staircase. It was in flames.

The fire had been started by an electric wire which had smouldered on the staircase, and had kindled the dry wood nearby. The staircase was old and soon burnt fiercely. There was no way out for Erica. She tried to run into the next room, from whose window there was a fire-escape – but the smoke was so thick that it choked her and she had to run back into her own room. She shut the door and rushed to the window.

She threw it open, and thankfully breathed in the pure night air. "Help!" she shouted, in a weak voice. "Help!"

No one heard her – but Mam'zelle saw her. Everyone looked up at Mam'zelle's shout, and a deep groan went up as they saw Erica at the window.

Miss Theobald went pale, and her heart beat fast. A girl up there! And the staircase burning!

"The fire-engine isn't here," she groaned. "If only we had the fire-engine to run up its ladder to that high window! Oh, when will it come?"

Someone had found the garden-hose and was spraying water on the flames. But the force of water was feeble and made little difference to the fire. Erica shouted again.

"Help! Save me! Oh, save me!" She could see all the crowd of people below and she could not think why someone did not save her. She did not realise that the fire-engine had not yet come, and that there was no ladder long enough to reach her.

"Where is the long garden ladder?" cried Margery, suddenly, seeing a gardener nearby. "Let's get it. Maybe we can send a rope up or something, even if the ladder isn't long enough!"

The men ran to get the longest ladder. They set it up against the wall and one of them ran up to the top. But it did not nearly reach to Erica's window

"It's no good," he said, when he came down. "It's impossible to reach. Where's that fire-engine? It's a long time coming."

"It's been called out to another fire," said one of the mistresses, who had just heard the news. "It's coming immediately."

"Immediately!" cried Margery "Well, that's not soon enough! Erica will soon be trapped by the flames."

Before anyone could stop her, the girl threw off her dressing-gown and rushed to the ladder. She was up it like a monkey, though Miss Theobald shouted to her to come back.

"You can't do anything, you silly girl!" cried the head mistress. "Come down!"

Everyone watched Margery as she climbed to the very top of the ladder. The flames lit up the whole scene now, and the dark figure of the climbing girl could be clearly seen,

"What *does* she think she can do?" said Miss Roberts in despair. "She'll fall!"

But Margery had seen something that had given her an idea. To the right side of the ladder ran an iron pipe. Maybe she could swarm up that and get to Erica's window. What she was going to do then she didn't know — but she meant to do *something*!

She reached the top of the ladder. She put out a hand and caught hold of the strong iron pipe hoping that it was well nailed to the wail. Fortunately it was. Margery swung herself from the ladder to the pipe, clutching hold of it with her knees, and holding for dear life with her hands.

And now all her training in the gym stood her in good stead. All the scores of times she had climbed the ropes there had strengthened her arms and legs, and made them very steady and strong. It was far more difficult to climb an unyielding pipe than to swarm up a pliant rope, but Margery could do it. Up the pipe she went, pulling herself by her arms, and clinging with her knees and feet. Erica saw her coming.

"Oh, save me!" cried the girl, almost mad with fright. Margery came up to the window. Now was the most difficult part. She had to get safely from the pipe to the window-sill.

"Erica! Hold on to something and give me a hand!" yelled Margery, holding out her hand above the window-sill. "If you can give me a pull I can get there."

Erica gave her hand to Margery. She held on to a heavy book-case just inside the room, and Margery swung herself strongly across to the sill from the pipe. She put up a knee, grazing it badly on the sill, but she did not even feel the pain. In half a moment she was inside the room. Erica clung to her, weeping.

"Now don't be silly," said Margery, shaking herself free and looking round the room, filled with dense black smoke. The flames were already just outside the door and the floor felt hot to her feet. "There's no time to lose. Where's your bed?"

Erica pointed through the smoke to where her bed was. Margery ran to it, choking, and dragged the sheets and blankets off it. She ran back to the window, and leant her head outside to get some fresh air. Then she quickly tore the sheets in half.

"Oh, what are you doing?" cried Erica, thinking that Margery was quite mad. "Take me out of the window with you!"

"I will in a moment," said Margery, as she knotted the sheet-strips firmly together. There were four long strips. Margery looked for something to tie one end to. As she looked, the door fell in with a crash, and flames came into the room.

"Oh, quick, quick!" cried Erica. "I shall jump!"

"No, you won't," said Margery. "You're going to be saved – and very quickly too. Look here – see how I've knotted this sheet – and tied it to the end of your bed. Help me to drag the bed to the window. That's right."

Margery threw the other end of the sheet-strips out of the window. The end almost reached the top of the ladder! There was no need to climb down the pipe this time! Margery sat herself on the window-sill and made Erica come beside her. Below, the crowds of girls and mistresses were watching what was happening, hardly daring to breathe. One of the gardeners had gone up the ladder, hoping to help.

"Now do you think you can climb down this sheet-rope I've made?" said Margery to the trembling Erica. "Look – it should be quite easy."

"Oh, no, I can't, I can't," sobbed Erica, terrified. So Margery did a very brave thing. She took Erica on her back, and with the frightened girl clinging tightly to her, her arms holding fast, she began to climb down the sheet-rope herself. Luckily the sheets were new and strong, and they held well.

Down went Margery and down, her arms almost pulled out of their sockets with Erica's weight. She felt with her feet for the ladder, and oh, how thankful she was when at last she felt the top rung, and a loud voice cried, "Well done, miss! I've got you!"

The gardener at the top of the ladder reached for Erica, and took hold of her. He helped the weeping girl down, and Margery slid down the few remaining feet of the sheet-rope.

What happened next nobody ever knew. It was likely that Margery was tired out with her amazing climb and equally amazing rescue, and that her feet slipped on the ladder – for somehow or other she lost her balance, and half slid, half fell down the ladder. She fell on the gardener, who helped to break her fall a little – but then she slid right off the ladder to the ground seven or eight feet below.

People rushed over to her – but Margery lay still. She had struck her head against something and was quite unconscious. Careful hands carried her into the big school just as the fire-engine rumbled up with a great clangour of its big bell. In one minute strong jets of water were pouring on to the flames, and in five minutes the fire was under control.

But the top storey, as Miss Theobald had feared, was entirely burnt out. The room where Erica had been sleeping was a mass of black charred timbers.

The girls were ordered back to bed, and this time they went! But there was one name on everyone's lips that night – the name of a real heroine.

"Margery! Wasn't she wonderful! She saved Erica's life. Fancy her climbing that pipe like that. Let's pray she isn't much hurt. Margery! Well, wasn't she *wonderful!*"

CHAPTER XVI
A CONFESSION

The next morning everyone wanted to know how Margery was. A few remembered to ask about poor Erica, but it was Margery that people worried about.

"She's broken her leg! Poor old Margery! And she's hurt her head too, but not very badly. She's in the dressing-room off Miss Theobald's own bedroom. Miss Theobald is terribly proud of her!"

"I don't wonder!" said Janet, who always intensely admired bravery of any sort. "I

don't care now what Margery has been like in the past few weeks. I've forgotten it all! A girl who can do a big thing like that can be as rude and sulky as she likes, for all I care!"

"And now I find it more difficult than ever to think that Margery can have played any mean tricks!" said Lucy. "I simply can't help thinking we made a mistake over that. It *must* have been someone else! Courage of the sort that Margery showed last night never goes with a mean nature — never, never, never! It's impossible."

"I wish we knew for certain," said Alison, who was now feeling very guilty because she had told Margery's secret, and had let the girls know that she had been expelled from so many schools.

They did know, very soon, who was the guilty one. It was

200

Lucy who found out. She went to see Erica who was in a little room off one of the dormitories, not much the worse for her adventure except that she was very sorry for herself.

Something had happened to Erica besides the fire. She had lain awake all that night, thinking of it – and thinking of Margery, who had rescued her.

And her conscience had come very much alive! To think that the girl who had so bravely saved her life was the girl who had been taking the blame for Erica's own meanness! Erica's cheeks burnt when she thought of it. She wished it had been any other girl but Margery who had rescued her.

Lucy came to see her at the end of morning school. Nobody had been allowed to see Margery, who was to be kept quite quiet for a few days. No one had wanted very much to see Erica – but kind-hearted Lucy, as usual, thought of the girl lying alone in the little room, and asked Matron if she could see her.

"Yes, of course," said Matron. "She's normal this morning and there's nothing wrong with her except a bit of a cold and shock. It will do her good to see you."

So Lucy went into the little room and sat down beside Erica. They talked for a while, and then Erica asked about Margery. She did not look at Lucy as she asked, for she felt very guilty.

"Haven't they told you about Margery?" said Lucy, in surprise. "Oh, poor thing, she's broken her right leg. That means no more gym or games for her for some time – and as they are the only things she cares about, she's going to have a pretty thin time. She hit her head on something too, but not very badly. She *was* a heroine, Erica!"

Erica was terribly upset. She had thought that Margery was quite all right, and had pictured her receiving the praise of the whole school. And now after all she was in bed with a broken leg and a bad head!

Erica turned her face to the wall, trying to think the matter out. She looked so miserable that Lucy was touched. She didn't like Erica, but misery of any kind must be comforted.

She took Erica's hand. "Don't worry about it," she said. "Her leg will mend – and she will be quite all right again. We are all very proud of her."

"Do you – do you still think she did those mean things?" asked Erica, not looking at Lucy.

"No, I don't," said Lucy at once. "Those kind of tricks don't go with a strong and fearless nature like Margery's. She's got plenty of faults – and bad ones too – but she has no petty, mean faults, as far as I can see."

Matron popped her head round the door. "Come along now, Lucy," she said. "Your ten minutes is up."

"Oh, don't go yet, don't go yet!" said Erica, clutching Lucy's hand, and feeling that she did not want to be left alone with her own thoughts. But Lucy had to go.

And then Erica had a very bad time indeed. It is hard enough when anyone thinks contemptuously of us — but far worse if we have to despise ourselves. And that is what poor Erica found herself doing. She saw herself clearly — a mean, small, spiteful little creature, insincere and dishonest, and she didn't like herself at all.

She turned her face to the wall. She would not eat any dinner at all, and Matron took her temperature, feeling worried. But it was still normal.

"Are you worrying about something?" she asked. Erica's eyes filled with tears at the kind voice.

"Yes," she said desperately. "I'm worrying terribly. I can't stop."

"Tell me all about it," said Matron, gently.

"No," said Erica, and turned her face to the wall again. But she knew she could not keep all her thoughts to herself much longer. She had to tell someone, she simply had to. She called to Matron as she was going out of the room.

"Matron! I want Lucy!"

"My dear child, she's in class!" said Matron. "She can come and see you at tea-time, if you like."

Erica burst into floods of tears, and sobbed so heart-rendingly that Matron hurried over to her.

"Whatever *is* the matter?" she said.

"Matron, fetch Lucy," sobbed Erica. "Oh, do fetch Lucy."

Matron went out of the room and sent someone for Lucy. There was something strange about Erica's face, and the sooner she told somebody what was worrying her, the better! Lucy came along in surprise.

"Erica has something on her mind, Lucy," said Matron. "Try to get her to tell you, will you? Her temperature will shoot up and she'll be really ill if she goes on like this."

Lucy went into the little room and sat down on Erica's bed. Erica had stopped crying, and her face was white and pinched. She stared dry-eyed at Lucy.

"What's up, old girl?" asked Lucy, her kind little face glowing with friendliness.

"Lucy! I've got to tell somebody or I'll go quite mad!" said Erica, desperately. "*I* did all those awful things to Pat. It wasn't Margery. It was me."

"Oh, Erica!" said Lucy, deeply shocked. "Poor, poor Margery!"

Erica said nothing. She turned her face to the wall again and lay still. She felt ill.

Lucy sat for a moment, taking in what Erica had said. Then, with an effort, she took Erica's cold hand. She knew that she must try to be kind to the girl, though she could hardly bring herself to be, because of her pity for what Margery must have gone through.

"Erica! I'm glad you told me. You know that I must tell the others, don't you? They mustn't for one moment more think that Margery did those things. We have accused her most unjustly, and treated her very unfairly. You see that I must tell the others, don't you?"

"Must you?" said Erica, her eyes filling with tears again. "But how can I face them all, if you do?"

"I don't know. Erica," said Lucy. "That's for you to decide. You have been awfully mean and spiteful. Why don't you tell Miss Theobald, now that you've told me, and see what she says?"

"No. I daren't tell her," said Erica, trembling as she thought of Miss Theobald's stern face. "You tell her, Lucy. Oh, Lucy – I want to leave here. I've done so badly. Nobody has ever liked me much – and nobody will ever, ever like me now. And there won't be a chance for me to try properly if nobody feels friendly towards me. I'm a coward, you know. I can't stand up to things."

"I know," said Lucy gravely. "But sooner or later, you'll have to learn to face things that come along, Erica, and you'll have to get that meanness and spite out of your character, or you'll never be happy. I'll see Miss Theobald. Now don't worry too much. I'm very glad you told me all you did."

Lucy left Erica to her thoughts. She went to Matron. "Matron," she said, "Erica has told me what's worrying her – but it's something I ought to tell Miss Theobald. Can I go now?"

"Of course," said Matron, thinking that Lucy Oriell was one of the nicest girls who had ever come to St Clare's. "Hurry along now. I'll send a message to Miss Roberts for you."

And so it came about that Lucy went to Miss Theobald with Erica's guilty secret, and related it all to the head mistress in her clear, friendly little voice. Miss Theobald listened gravely, not interrupting her at all,

"So Margery was accused wrongly," she said. "Poor Margery! She is a most unlucky child! But she did behave amazingly last night. What a plucky girl she is! She has two sides to her character – and the finer side came out very strongly yesterday."

"Miss Theobald, we know that Margery has been expelled from many schools," said Lucy, looking the head straight in the eyes. "And we have guessed that the mistresses have been asked to be lenient with her to give her a chance at St Clare's. And although I'm a new girl too I do see that any girl with a bad record would have a fine chance here to do better, because there's a wonderful spirit in this school. I've felt it and loved it. I'm so very glad my parents chose this school to send me to."

Miss Theobald looked at Lucy's honest and sincere face. She smiled one of her rare sweet smiles.

"And I too am glad that your parents sent you here," she said. "You are the type of girl that helps to make the spirit of the school a living powerful thing, Lucy."

Lucy flushed with pleasure, and felt very happy. Miss Theobald went back to the matter they had been discussing.

"Now we have to decide one or two things," she said, and at that word "we", Lucy felt proud and delighted. To think that she and Miss Theobald together were going to decide things!

"About Margery. You shall go and see her and tell her what you have told me. She must know as soon as possible that you have all been wrong about her, and that you know it and are sorry. She must know it was Erica too. How strange that the girl she rescued should be the girl who did her so much wrong! Erica must have felt very upset about it."

"This will make a great difference to Margery," said Lucy, her eyes shining. "Everyone will think of her as a heroine now, instead of as a sulky, rude girl. What a chance for Margery!"

"Yes – I think things may be easier for her now," said Miss Theobald. "You may have guessed that Margery's home is not quite a normal one, Lucy, and that has made things hard for her. I can't tell you any more. You must just be content with that! And now – what about Erica?"

They looked at one another gravely, and Lucy felt pride swell up in her as she saw how Miss Theobald trusted her opinion.

"Miss Theobald – things won't be easier for Erica," said Lucy. "She's awfully weak, you know. She won't be able to stand up to the girls' unfriendliness after this. If she only could, it would be the making of her. But I'm quite sure she can't. I think it would be better for her to go away and start all over again at another school. I don't mean expel her in disgrace – but couldn't something be arranged?"

"Yes, of course," said the head mistress. "I can explain things to her mother – she has no father, you know – and suggest that Erica goes home for the rest of the term, and then is sent to a fresh school in the summer – perhaps with the determination to do a great deal better! Poor Erica! What a good thing she at least had the courage to tell you."

Lucy left the head mistress feeling contented. It was good to know that someone wise and kindly had the handling of matters such as these. By this time it was tea-time and Lucy went to the dining-hall feeling terribly hungry.

"Where *have* you been?" cried a dozen voices, as she came in. "You missed painting – and you love that!"

"Oh dear – so I did!" said Lucy, sadly. "I forgot about that. Well – I couldn't help it."

"But, Lucy, where have you been and what have you been doing?" asked Pat. "Do tell us! You look all excited somehow."

"I've heard some interesting things," said Lucy, helping herself to bread and butter and jam. "I'll tell you in the common-room after tea. I'm too hungry to talk now. You must just wait!"

SUMMER TERM AT ST CLARE'S

AN EXTRACT

≈ ILLUSTRATED BY ≈

W. Lindsay Cable and Jenny Chapple

New girls at St Clare's in the summer term include Prudence, a mean-spirited and snobbish character; Roberta ("Bobby"), who is outspoken and fond of practical jokes; and dark, intense Carlotta . . .

CHAPTER VIII
CARLOTTA IS SURPRISING

Prudence was careful not to come up against Bobby and Janet more than she could help. Bobby settled in so well that to the old first formers it seemed as if she had belonged to St Clare's for years. Carlotta too settled down in some sort of fashion, though she was a bit of a mystery to the girls.

"She seems such a common little thing in most ways," said Pat, overhearing Carlotta talking to Pam in her curious half-cockney, half-foreign voice. "And she's so untidy and hasn't any manners at all. Yet she's so natural and truthful and outspoken that I can't help liking her. I'm sure she'll come to blows with Mam'zelle some day! They just can't bear each other!"

Mam'zelle was not having an easy time with the first form that term. The girls who were to go up into the second form were not up to the standard she wanted them to be, and she was making them work very hard indeed, which they didn't like at all. Pam was excellent at French, though her accent was not too good. Sadie Greene was hopeless. She didn't care and she wasn't going to try! Prudence seemed to try her hardest but didn't do very well. Bobby was another one who didn't care — and as for Carlotta, she frankly detested poor Mam'zelle and was as nearly rude to her as she dared to be.

So Mam'zelle had a bad time. "Do you wonder we called her 'Mam'zelle Abominable' the first term we were here?" said Pat to Bobby. "She has called you and your work *abominable* and *insupportable* about twenty times this morning, Bobby! And as for Carlotta, she has used up all the awful French names she knows on her!

But I must say Carlotta deserves them! When she puts on that fierce scowl, and lets her curls drip all over her face, and screws up her mouth till her lips are white, she looks like a regular little tornado."

Carlotta was really rather a surprising person. Sometimes she gave the impression that she was really doing her best to be good and to try hard – and then at other times it seemed as if she wasn't in the classroom at all! She was away somewhere else, dreaming of some other days, some other life. That would make Mam'zelle furious.

"Carlotta! What is there so interesting out of the window today?" Mam'zelle would inquire sarcastically. "Ah – I see a cow in the distance. Is she so enthralling to you? Do you wait to hear her moo?"

"No," Carlotta said, in a careless voice. "I'm waiting to hear her bark, Mam'zelle."

Then the class would chuckle and wait breathlessly for Mam'zelle's fury to descend on Carlotta's head.

It was in gym that Carlotta was really surprising. Since Margery Fenworthy had gone up into the second form, there had been nobody really good at gym left in the first form. Carlotta had done the climbing and jumping and running more or less as the others had done, though with less effort and with a curious suppleness – until one day in the third week of the term.

The girl had been restless all the morning. The sun had shone in at the classroom window, and a steady wind had been blowing up the hill. Carlotta could not seem to keep still, and paid no attention at all to the lessons. Miss Roberts had really thought the girl must be ill, and seriously wondered if she should send her to Matron to have her temperature taken. Carlotta's eyes were bright, and her cheeks were flushed.

"Carlotta! What *is* the matter with you this morning?" said Miss Roberts. "You haven't finished a single sum. What are you dreaming about?"

"Horses," said Carlotta at once. "My own horse, Terry. It's a day for galloping far away."

"Well, I think differently," said Miss Roberts. "I think it's a day for turning your attention to some of the work you leave undone, Carlotta! Pay attention to what I say!"

Fortunately for Carlotta the bell went for break at that moment and the class was free to dismiss. After break it was gym. Carlotta worked off some of her restlessness in the playgrounds, but still had plenty left by the time the bell went for classes again.

Miss Wilton, the sports mistress, was gym mistress also. She had to call Carlotta to order several times because the girl would climb and jump out of her turn, or do more than she was told to do. Carlotta sulked, her eyes glowing angrily.

"It is such silly baby stuff we do!" she said.

"Don't be stupid," said Miss Wilton. "You do most advanced things considering you are the lowest form, I suppose you think you could do all kinds of amazing things that nobody else could possibly do, Carlotta."

"Yes, of course I could," said Carlotta. And to the astonishment of the entire class the dark-eyed girl suddenly threw herself over and over, and performed a series of the most graceful cart-wheels that could be imagined! Round and round the gym she went, throwing herself over and over, first on her hands, then on her feet, as easily as any clown in a circus! The girls gasped to see her.

Miss Wilton was most astonished. "That will do, Carlotta," she said. "You are certainly extremely good at cart-wheels – better than any girl I have known."

"Watch me climb the ropes as they should be climbed!" said Carlotta, rather beside herself now that she saw the plain admiration and amazement in the eyes of everyone around. And before Miss Wilton could say yes or no, the little monkey had

swung herself up a rope to the very top. Then she turned herself completely upside down there, and hung downwards by her knees, to Miss Wilton's complete horror.

"Carlotta! Come down at once. What you are doing is extremely dangerous!" ordered Miss Wilton, terrified that the girl would fall and break her neck. "You are just showing off. Come down at once!"

Carlotta slid down like lightning, turned a double somersault, went round the gym on hands and feet again and then leapt lightly upright. Her eyes shone and her cheeks were blazing. It was plain that she had enjoyed it all thoroughly.

The girls gazed openmouthed. They thought Carlotta was marvellous,

and every one of them wished that she could do as Carlotta had done. Miss Wilton was just as surprised as the girls. She stared at Carlotta and hardly knew what to say.

"Shall I show you something else?" said Carlotta, breathlessly. "Shall I show you how I can walk upside down? Watch me!"

"That's enough, Carlotta," said Miss Wilton in a firm voice. "It's time the others did something! You certainly are very supple and very clever – but I think on the whole it would be best if you did the same as the others, and didn't break out into these odd performances."

The gym class went on its usual way, but the girls could hardly keep their eyes off Carlotta, hoping she would do something else extraordinary. But the girl seemed to sink into her dreams again, and scarcely looked at anyone else. After the class was over the girls pressed round her.

"Carlotta! Show us what you can do! Walk on your hands, upside-down."

But Carlotta wasn't in the mood for anything more. She pushed her way through the admiring girls, and suddenly looked rather depressed.

"I said I wouldn't – and I have," she muttered to herself, and disappeared into the passage. The girls looked at one another.

"Did you hear what she said?" said Pat. "I wonder what she meant. Wasn't she marvellous?"

It seemed to have done Carlotta good. She was much better in her next classes after her curious performance in the gym, quieter and happier. She lost her scowl and was not at all rude to Mam'zelle in French conversation.

The girls begged her to perform again when the gym was empty, but she wouldn't. "No," she said. "No. Don't ask me to."

"Carlotta, wherever did you learn all that?" asked Isabel, curiously "You did all those things just as well as any clown or acrobat in a circus! The way you shinned up that rope! We always thought Margery Fenworthy was marvellous – but you're far better!"

"Perhaps Carlotta has relations who belong to a circus," said Prudence, maliciously. She didn't like the admiration and attention suddenly given to the girl, and she was jealous. She thought Carlotta was common and she wanted to hurt her.

"Shut up, Prudence," said Bobby. "Sometimes you make me think how lovely it would be to teach you a lesson."

Prudence flushed angrily The other girls grinned. They liked seeing Prudence taken down a peg or two.

"Come on to the tennis-court," said Pat to Bobby, seeing that a quarrel was about to begin. "We've got to practise our serving, Miss Wilton said. Let me serve twenty balls to you, and you serve back to me. Next month there are going to be matches against St Christopher's and Oakdene, and I jolly well want to be in the team from the first form."

"Well, I'll come and let you practise on *me*," said Bobby, with a last glare at Prudence, "but it's not a bit of good me hoping to be in any tennis team. Come on. Let's leave old Sour Milk behind."

How Prudence hated that name! But whenever she made one of her unkind remarks, someone was sure to whisper "Sour Milk". Prudence would look round quickly, but everyone would look most innocent, as if they hadn't said a single word.

Prudence hated Bobby because she had begun the nickname, but she was afraid of her. She would dearly have loved to give Bobby a clever, unkind name too — but she couldn't think of one. And in any case Bobby was "Bobby" to the whole school. Even the mistresses presently ceased calling her Roberta, and gave her her nickname. Much to Prudence's anger, Bobby was one of the most popular girls in the form!

CHAPTER X
AN UPROAR IN MAM'ZELLE'S CLASS!

Prudence continues to look down on Carlotta. She spies on her and, when a circus is encamped near the school, sees Carlotta talking to a groom who works there. He lets Carlotta ride one of the horses and then, standing up, she balances on its back while it trots round the field . . .

The next thing that happened was an uproar in Mam'zelle's French class. The term was getting on, and many of the first formers seemed to have made no progress in French at all. The weather was very hot just then, and most of the girls felt it and were disinclined to work hard. Girls like Pam Boardman and Hilary Wentworth, both of whom had brains, a steady outlook on their work, and a determination to get on, worked just as well as ever — but the twins slacked, and as for Sadie and Bobby, they were the despair of all the teachers.

But it was Carlotta who roused Mam'zelle's anger the most. When Carlotta disliked anyone she did not hide it. Neither did she hide her *liking* for any girl or teacher — she would do anything for a person she liked. The twins, and Janet and Bobby, found her generous and kind, willing to do anything to help them. But she thoroughly disliked Alison, Sadie, Prudence, and one or two others.

Carlotta's idea of showing her dislike for anyone was childish. She would make faces, turn her back, even slap. She would stamp her foot, call rude names, and often lapse into some foreign language, letting it flow out in an angry stream from her crimson lips. The girls rather enjoyed all this, though Hilary, as head of the form, often took the girl to task.

"Carlotta, you let yourself down when you act like this," she said, after a scene in which Carlotta had called Alison and Sadie a string of extraordinary names. "You let your parents down too. We are all more or less what our parents have made us, you know, and we want them to be proud of us. Don't let your people down."

Carlotta turned away with a toss of her head. "I don't let my parents down!" she said. "They've let *me* down. I wouldn't stay here if I hadn't made a promise to someone. Do you suppose I would ever choose to be in a place where I had to see people like Alison and Sadie and Prudence every day? Pah!"

The girl almost spat in her rage. She was trembling, and Hilary hardly knew what else to say.

"We can't like everyone," she said at last. "You *do* like some of us, Carlotta, and we like you. But can't you see that you only make things worse for yourself when you act like this? When you live in a community together, you have to behave as the others do. I'm head of the form, and I just can't let you go around behaving like a four year old, After all, you are fifteen."

Carlotta's rage vanished as suddenly as it had appeared. She genuinely liked the steady responsible Hilary. She put out her hand to her.

"I know you're right, Hilary," she said. "But I haven't been brought up in the same way as you have – I haven't learnt the same things. Don't dislike me because I'm different."

"Idiot!" said Hilary, giving her a clap on the shoulder. "We like you because you *are* so different. You're a most exciting person to have in the form. But don't play into the hands of people like Prudence, who will run to Miss Roberts if you bring out some of your rude names. If you really want to let off steam, let it off on people like me or Bobby, who won't mind!"

"That's just it," said Carlotta. "I *can't* go for you – you're too decent to me. Hilary, I'll try to be calmer. I really will. I'm getting on a bit better with Miss Roberts now – but Mam'zelle always drives me into a rage. I'll have to be extra careful in her class."

It was Bobby who really began the great uproar in Mam'zelle's class one morning. Bobby was bored. She hated French verbs, which had an irritating way of having different endings in their past tenses. "Just as if it was done on purpose to muddle us," thought Bobby, with irritation. "And I never can remember when to use this stupid subjunctive. Ugh!"

Nearby Bobby was a vivarium, kept by the first formers. It was a big cage-like structure, with a glass front that could be slipped up and down. In it lived a couple of large frogs and a clumsy toad. With them lived six large snails. The first formers regarded these creatures with varying ideas.

Kathleen, who loved animals, was really attached to the frogs and toad, and vowed she could tell the difference between the six snails, which she had named after some of the dwarfs in the story of Snow White. The rest of the form could only recognise Dopey, who never seemed to move, and who had a white mark on the spiral of his shell.

The twins liked the frogs and toad, and Isabel often tickled the frog down his back with a straw because she liked to see him put his front foot round, with its funny little fingers, and scratch himself. Some of the class were merely interested in the creatures, the rest loathed them.

Sadie and Alison couldn't bear them, and Prudence shuddered every time she saw the frogs or toad move. Doris disliked them intensely too. Bobby neither liked nor disliked them, but she had no fear of the harmless creatures as Prudence and the others seemed to have, and she handled them fearlessly when their vivarium needed to be cleaned or rearranged.

On this morning Bobby was bored. The French class seemed to have been going on for hours, and seemed likely to continue for hours too, though actually it was only a lesson lasting three-quarters of an hour. A movement in the vivarium caught the girl's eye.

One of the frogs had flicked out its tongue at a fly that had ventured in through the perforated zinc window at the back. Bobby took a quick look at Mam'zelle. She was writing French sentences on the blackboard, quite engrossed in her task. The girls were supposed to be reading a page of French, ready to translate it when she was ready.

Bobby nudged Janet. Janet looked up. "Watch me!" whispered Bobby with a grin. Bobby slid the glass front of the vivarium to the back and put in her hand. She took one of the surprised frogs out and then shut the glass lid.

"Let's set him hopping off to Prudence!" whispered Bobby. "It'll give her an awful fright!"

No one else had noticed Bobby's performance. Mam'zelle was irritable that morning, and the class were feverishly reading over their page of French, anxious not to annoy her more than they could help. Bobby reached over to set the frog on Prudence's desk.

But the poor creature leapt violently out of her hands on to the floor near Carlotta. The girl caught the movement and turned. She saw the frog on the floor, and Bobby nodding and pointing to show her that it was meant for the unsuspicious Prudence.

Carlotta grinned. She had been just as bored as Bobby in the French class, and the page of French had meant nothing to her at all. She hardly understood one word of it.

She picked up the frog and deposited it neatly on the edge of Prudence's desk. The girl sat next to her, so it was easy. Prudence looked up, saw the frog and gave such a scream that the whole class jumped in fright.

Mam'zelle dropped her chalk and the book she was holding, and turned round with an angry glare.

"PRUDENCE! What is this noise?"

The frog liked Prudence's desk. It hopped over her book and sat in the middle of it, staring with unwinking brown eyes at the horrified girl. She screamed loudly again and seemed quite unable to move. She was really terrified.

The frog took a leap into the air, and landed on Prudence's shoulder. It slipped down to her lap, and she leapt up in horror, shaking it off.

"Mam'zelle! It's the frog! Ugh, I can't bear it, I can't bear it! Oh, you beast, Carlotta! You took it out of the vivarium on purpose to give me a fright! How I hate you!" cried Prudence, quite beside herself with rage and fright.

Most of the class were laughing by now, for Prudence's horror was funny to watch. Mam'zelle began to lose her temper. The frog leapt once more and Prudence screamed again.

"*Taisez-vous*, Prudence!" cried Mam'zelle. "Be silent. This class is a garden of bears and monkeys. I will not have it. It is *abominable!*"

More giggles greeted this outburst. Prudence turned on Carlotta again and spoke to her with great malice in her voice.

"You hateful creature! Nothing

but a nasty little circus girl with circus-girl ideas! Oh you think I don't know things about you, but I do! *I* saw you take the frog out of the vivarium to make him leap on me. I saw you!"

"*TAISEZ-VOUS*, Prudence," almost shouted Mam'zelle, rapping on her desk. "Carlotta, leave the room. You will go straight to Miss Theobald and report what you have done. That such things should happen in my class! It is not to be believed!"

Carlotta did not hear a word Mam'zelle said. She had sprung up from her seat and was glaring at Prudence. Her eyes were flashing, and she looked very wild and very beautiful. Like a beautiful warrior, Isabel thought.

She began to speak – but not one of the girls could understand a word, for Carlotta spoke in Spanish. The words came pouring out like a torrent, and Carlotta stamped her foot and shook her fist in Prudence's face. Prudence shrank back, afraid. Mam'zelle, furious at being entirely disregarded by Carlotta, advanced on her with a heavy tread.

The whole class watched the scene, breathless. There had been one or two Big Rows, as they were called, in the first form at times, but nothing to equal this. Mam'zelle took Carlotta firmly by the arm.

"*Vous êtes in-sup-por-table!*" she said, separating the syllables of the word to make it even more emphatic. Carlotta shook off Mam'zelle's hand in a fury. She could not bear to be touched when she was in a rage. She turned on the astonished French mistress, and addressed her in a flow of violent Spanish, some of which Mam'zelle unfortunately understood. The mistress went pale with anger, and with difficulty prevented herself from giving Carlotta a box on the ears.

In the middle of this the door opened and Miss Roberts came in. It was time for the lesson to end, but everyone had been far too engrossed in the scene to think of the time. Miss Roberts had been surprised to find the classroom door shut, as usually it was held open for her coming by one of the class. She was even more astonished to walk in and see Mam'zelle and Carlotta apparently about to have a free fight!

Mam'zelle recovered herself a little when she saw Miss Roberts. "Ah, Miss Roberts!" she said, her voice quite weak with all the emotion she had felt during the last few minutes. "You come in good time! This class of yours is shocking – yes, most shocking and wicked. That girl Carlotta, she has defied me, she has called me names, she has – oh, *là là*, there is the frog again!"

Everyone had forgotten the frog – but it now made a most unexpected appearance again and leapt on to Mam'zelle's large foot. Mam'zelle had no liking for frogs. All insects and small creatures filled her with horror. She gave a squeal and stumbled backwards, falling heavily on to a chair.

Miss Roberts had taken everything in at a glance. Her face was extremely stern. She looked at Mam'zelle. She knew Mam'zelle's hot temper, and she felt that the best thing to do was to get the angry French mistress out of the class before making any inquiries herself.

"Mam'zelle, your next class is waiting for you," she said in her clear cool tones. "I will look into this matter for you and report to you at dinner-time. You had better go now and leave me to deal with everything."

Mam'zelle could never bear to be late for any class. She got up at once and left the room, giving Carlotta one look of fury before she went. Miss Roberts nodded to Hilary to shut the door and then went to her own desk. There was a dead silence in the room, for there was not a girl there who did not dread Miss Roberts when she was in this kind of mood.

Carlotta was still standing, her hair rumpled over her forehead, her fists clenched. Miss Roberts glanced at her. She knew Carlotta's fiery nature by now, and felt that it was of no use at all to attack her in that mood. She spoke to her firmly and coldly.

"Carlotta, please go and do your hair. Wash your inky hands too."

The girl stared at her teacher, half mutinous, but the direct order calmed her and she obeyed it. She left the room and there was a sigh of relief. Carlotta was exciting – but this time she had been a little *too* exciting.

"Now please understand that I am not encouraging any tale-bearing," said Miss Roberts, looking round her class with cold blue eyes, "but I am going to insist on finding out what this extraordinary scene is about. Perhaps you, Hilary, as head of the class, can tell me."

"Miss Roberts, let *me* tell you!" began Prudence, eager to get her word in before anyone else. "Carlotta opened the vivarium and took out the frog, and . . ."

"I don't want any information from you until I ask for it, Prudence," said Miss Roberts, in such a cutting tone that the girl sank back into her seat, flushing. "Now, Hilary – tell me as shortly as you can."

"Well, apparently someone took a frog out of the vivarium and put it on Prudence's desk," said Hilary reluctantly. Bobby got up, red in the face.

"Excuse me interrupting, Miss Roberts," she said. "I took the frog out."

"It was that beast Carlotta who played the trick on me!" exclaimed Prudence. "You're shielding her."

"Prudence, you'll leave the room if you speak again," said Miss Roberts. "Go on, Bobby."

"I was bored," said Bobby, honestly. "I took out the frog to make it jump on to Prudence for a bit of fun, because she's scared of frogs. But it leapt out of my hand on to the floor – and so I nodded to Carlotta to pick it up and put it on the desk — and she did. But I was the one to blame."

Bobby sat down. "Now you go on with this extraordinary tale, Hilary," said Miss Roberts, wondering if her class could really be in its right senses that morning.

"Well, Miss Roberts, there isn't much else to tell except that Prudence got an awful fright and screamed and Mam'zelle was angry, and Prudence blamed it all on to Carlotta and said some pretty horrid things to her, and Carlotta flared up as she does — and when Mam'zelle ordered her from the room she wouldn't go — I really think she didn't even *hear* Mam'zelle! Then Mam'zelle was furious because Carlotta didn't obey her and went over to her — and Carlotta turned on her and said something in Spanish that made Mam'zelle even more furious. And then *you* came in," finished Hilary.

"And spoilt your fun, I suppose," said Miss Roberts in the sarcastic voice that the class hated. "A very entertaining French lesson, I must say. You appear to have begun it all, Bobby — Carlotta certainly had a hand in it — and the rest of the tale appears to be composed of bad tempers on the part of several people. I imagine that everyone was simply delighted, and watched with bated breath. I'm disgusted and ashamed. Bobby, come to me at the end of the morning."

"Yes, Miss Roberts," said Bobby, dismally. Prudence looked round at Bobby with a pleased expression, delighted that the girl had a punishment coming to her. Miss Roberts caught sight of the look. She could not bear Prudence's meanness, nor her habit of tale-bearing and gloating over others' misfortunes. She snapped at her so suddenly that Prudence jumped.

"Prudence! You are not without blame, either! If you *can* make trouble for others, you invariably do. If you had not made such a stupid fuss none of this would have happened."

Prudence was deeply hurt. "Oh, Miss Roberts!" she said, in an injured tone, "that's not fair Really I . . ."

"Since when have I allowed you to tell me what is fair and what is not?" inquired Miss Roberts. "Hold your tongue and sit down. And while I think of it — your last essay was so bad that I cannot pass it. You will do it again this evening."

Prudence flushed. She knew that Miss Roberts definitely meant to be unkind at that moment, and she felt that all the girls, except perhaps Pam, silently approved of Miss Roberts's sharp tongue, and were pleased at her ticking-off. Her thoughts turned to Carlotta, and she brooded with bitterness over the fiery girl and what she had said. Miss Roberts had said nothing about punishing that beast Carlotta! Surely she wasn't going to let her go scot-free! Think of the things she had said to Mam'zelle! Carlotta was strange and bad — see how she broke the rules of the school and went off riding other people's horses!

The class was in a subdued mood for the rest of that morning. Bobby went to Miss Roberts and received such a scolding that she almost burst into tears – a thing that Bobby had not done for years! She also received a punishment that kept her busy for a whole week – a punishment consisting of writing out and learning all the things that Miss Roberts unaccountably appeared to think that Bobby didn't know. It is safe to say that at the end that week Bobby knew a good deal more than at the beginning!

Carlotta appeared to receive no punishment at all, which caused Prudence much anger and annoyance. Actually, as Pat and Isabel knew, Carlotta had been sent to the head, Miss Theobald, and had come out of that dread sitting-room in tears, looking very subdued and unlike herself. She told no one what had passed there, and nobody dared to inquire.

Mam'zelle received a written apology from Bobby and from Carlotta – and, much to Prudence's anger, one from Prudence herself too! Miss Roberts had demanded it, and would not listen to any objections on Prudence's part. So the girl had not dared to disobey but had written out her apology too.

"I'll pay Carlotta out for this!" she thought. "I'll go and find that man she was talking to – and ask him all about that horrid beast of a Carlotta! I'm sure there's something funny about her."

CHAPTER XI
CARLOTTA'S SECRET

The first chance that Prudence had of going for a walk over to the circus camp was two days later. She sought out Pam and asked her to go with her.

"Oh, Prudence! I did so badly want to finish reading this book," said Pam, who was in the middle of a historical novel dealing with the class's period of history. It was quite a joke with the first form that Pam never read any book unless it had to do with some of the classwork.

"Pam, do come," begged Prudence, slipping her hand under Pam's arm. Pam had had very little affection shown to her in her life and she was always easily moved by any gesture on Prudence's part. She got up at once, her short-sighted eyes beaming behind their big glasses. She put away her book and got her hat. The two girls set off, going the same way as before.

In half an hour's time they reached the camp. "Why, we've come the same way that we came last week!" said Pam.

"Yes," said Prudence, pretending to be astonished too. "And look – the circus camp is still there – and those lovely horses are still in the field. Let's go down to the camp and see if we can see any elephants or exciting things like that."

Pam wasn't at all sure that she wanted to find elephants, for she was nervous of animals, but she obediently followed Prudence. They went into the field, where the caravans and cages were arranged. No one took any notice of them.

After a while Prudence's sharp eyes found the untidy-haired man that she had seen Carlotta talking to. She went up to him.

"Does it matter us looking round the camp a bit?" she asked, with her sweetest smile.

"No, you go where you like, missy," said the man.

"Are those the circus horses in that field over there?" asked Prudence, pointing to the field where she had seen Carlotta riding.

"They are," said the man, and he went on polishing the harness that lay across his knees.

"I wish we could ride them like Carlotta," said Prudence, gazing at the horses with an innocent expression. The man looked at her sharply.

"Ay, she's a fine rider," he said. "Fine girl altogether, I say."

"Have you known her long then?" said Prudence, still looking very innocent indeed.

"Since she was a baby," said the man.

"She's had an awfully interesting life, hasn't she?" said Prudence, pretending that she knew far more than she did. "I love to hear all her stories."

Pam stared at Prudence open-mouthed. This was news to her! She wondered uncomfortably if Prudence was telling one of her fibs – but why should she do that?

"Oh, she's told you about her life, has she?" said the man, looking rather surprised. "I thought she wasn't . . ."

He stopped short. Prudence felt excited. She really was discovering something now. She looked at the untidy man, her eyes wide open with a most honest expression in them. No one could beat Prudence at looking innocent when she wasn't!

"Yes, I'm her best friend," said Prudence. "She told me to come over here and look round the camp. She said you wouldn't mind."

Pam was now quite certain that Prudence was telling dreadful untruths. In great discomfort the girl went off to look at a nearby caravan. She felt that she could not listen any more. She could not imagine what Prudence was acting like this for. She had so little spite in her own nature that it did not occur to her to think that Prudence was trying to find out something that might damage Carlotta.

Prudence was pleased to see Pam go off. Now she could get on more quickly! She felt certain somehow that Carlotta really had been connected with circus life in some way, so she took the plunge and asked the man the question.

"I expect Carlotta loved circus life, didn't she?"

The man apparently saw nothing odd about the question. He plainly thought that Carlotta had told Prudence a great deal about herself. He nodded his head.

"She oughtn't to have left it," he said. "My brother, who was in the same show as Carlotta was, said it would break her heart. That girl knew how to handle horses better than a man. I was glad to let her have a gallop when she came over here the other day. We move tomorrow – so you tell her when you get back that if she wants another gallop, she'll have to come along pretty early tomorrow morning, like she did two weeks ago."

Prudence was almost trembling with excitement. She had found out all she wanted to know. That nasty little Carlotta was a circus girl – a horrid, common, low-down little circus girl! How dare Miss Theobald accept a girl like that for her school! Did she really expect girls like Prudence, daughter of a good family, to mix with circus girls?

She called Pam and the two set off to go back to the school. Both were silent. Pam was still feeling very uncomfortable about Prudence's untruths to the man in the camp – and Prudence was thinking how clever she had been. She did not realise that it was not real cleverness – only shameful cunning.

She wondered how she could get the news round among the girls. Should she drop a hint here and there? If she could get hold of that foolish Alison, she would soon bleat it out everywhere! She went to find Alison that evening in the common-room. The girl was sitting doing a complicated jigsaw. She loved jigsaws, although she was very bad at them, and usually ended in losing half the pieces on the floor.

It was an interesting jigsaw. Four or five girls came to see how Alison was getting on. Bobby picked up a piece.

"Doesn't that go there?" she said, and tried it. Then Hilary picked up another piece, and in trying to make it fit, pushed the half-finished picture crooked.

"Oh!" cried Alison, exasperated. "If there's one thing I hate more than anything else it's having people help me with a jigsaw puzzle. First it's Bobby, then it's Hilary, then it's somebody else. I could finish it much more quickly if only people didn't help me!"

"I've never seen you finish a jigsaw puzzle yet, Alison," said Pat, teasingly.

"Why don't you do it properly?" said Doris who, however poor she was at lessons, was astonishingly quick at jigsaws. "You always begin by putting little bits together here and there. What you should do is begin with the outside pieces. You see, they've got a straight edge, and . . ."

"I know all that," said Alison, impatiently, "but Sadie says . . ."

Immediately the chorus was taken up in the greatest delight by the girls around. "Sadie says – oh Sadie says – Sadie, Sadie, Sadie SAYS!"

The girls at the back of the room took up the chorus too, and Sadie good-naturedly lifted her pretty head. "Don't you mind them, Alison," she said. But Alison did. She never could take teasing well. She muddled up her half-made jigsaw in peevishness, piled it into its box, dropped two or three pieces on the floor and went out of the room.

Prudence followed her, thinking she might drop a few words into Alison's ear. "Alison!" she called. "What a shame to tease you like that! Come out into the garden with me. It's a lovely evening."

"No, thanks," said Alison, half rudely, for she did not like Prudence. "I'm not in the mood to hear nasty things about half the girls in the form!"

Prudence flushed. It was true that she lost no chance of telling tales about the girls, trying to spread mischief among them – but she had not realised that the girls themselves knew it. It was plainly no use trying to get Alison to listen to tales about Carlotta.

"I'll have to think of some other way," said Prudence to herself. But she did not have to think – for the whole thing came out that same evening far more quickly than Prudence had ever expected.

She went back into the common-room. Carlotta was there, laughing as she told some joke in her half-foreign voice, which was rather fascinating to listen to. The girls were grouped around her, and Prudence felt a sharp twinge of jealousy as she saw them.

Her face was so sour as she looked at Carlotta that Bobby laughed loudly. "Here comes old Sour Milk!" she said, and everyone giggled.

"Sour Milk!" said Carlotta. "That is a very good name. Why have you gone sour, Prudence?"

Prudence was suddenly full of spite. "It's enough to make anyone go sour when they have to live with a low-down circus girl like you!" she said, her tone so full of hate that the girls glanced at her in astonishment. Carlotta laughed.

"I'd like to see *you* in a circus!" she said cheerfully. "The tigers would like you for their dinner. And I don't believe anyone would miss you."

"Be careful, Carlotta," said Prudence. "I know all about you. All – about – you!"

"How interesting!" said Carlotta, though her eyes began to gleam dangerously.

"Yes – very interesting," said Prudence. "The girls would soon despise you if they knew what I know. You wouldn't have any friends then. No one would want to know a common little circus girl!"

"Shut up, Prudence," said Bobby, afraid that Carlotta might lose her temper. "Don't tell silly lies."

"It's not silly lies," said Prudence. "It's the truth, the whole truth. There's a circus camp over near Trenton, and I talked to a man there – and he told me Carlotta was a circus girl, and knew how to handle horses, and was nothing but a common little girl from a circus belonging to his brother. And *we* have to put up with living with a girl like her!"

There was a complete silence when Prudence had finished. Carlotta looked all round the girls with flashing eyes. They stared at her. Then Pat spoke.

"Carlotta – did you *really* live in a circus?"

Prudence watched everyone, pleased with her bombshell. Now Carlotta would see what decent, well-brought up girls would say to her. She, Prudence, would have a fine revenge. She waited impatiently for the downfall of the fiery little Carlotta.

At Pat's question Carlotta looked towards the twins. She nodded her head. "Yes," she said. "I *was* a circus girl. And I loved it."

The girls looked in amazement and delight at Carlotta. Her eyes were glowing and her cheeks were red. They could all imagine her quite well riding in a circus ring. They pressed round her eagerly.

"Carlotta! How marvellous!"

"I say, Carlotta! How simply wonderful!"

"Carlotta, you simply *must* tell us all about it!"

"I always knew there was something unusual about you."

"Oh, Carlotta, to think you never told us! Why didn't you, you wretch?"

"Well – I promised Miss Theobald I wouldn't," said Carlotta. "You see – it's a funny story really – my father married a circus girl – and she ran away from him, taking me with her, when I was a baby She died soon after, and I was brought up by the circus folk. They were grand to me."

She stopped, remembering many things "Go on," said Kathleen, impatiently. "Do go on!"

"Well – I loved horses, just as my mother did," said Carlotta, "so I naturally rode in the ring. Well, not long ago, my father, who'd been trying to find me and my mother for years, suddenly discovered that mother was dead and I was in a circus. Father is a rich man – and he made me leave the circus, and when he found how little education I'd had he thought he would send me to school to learn."

"Oh, Carlotta – how awfully romantic!" said Alison. "Just like a book. I always thought you looked unusual, Carlotta. But why are you so foreign?"

"My mother was Spanish," said Carlotta, "and some of the folk in the circus were Spanish too, though many of them came from other parts of Europe! They were grand people. I wish I could go back to them. I don't fit in here. I don't belong. I don't think like you do. Our ideas are all different – and I'll never never learn."

She looked so woe-begone that the girls wanted to comfort her.

"Don't you worry, Carlotta! You'll soon fit in – better than ever now we know all about you. Why didn't Miss Theobald want us to know you'd been a circus girl?"

"Well, I suppose she thought maybe you might look down on me a bit?" said Carlotta. The girls snorted.

"Look down on you! We're thrilled! Carlotta, show us some of the things you can do!"

"I promised Miss Theobald I wouldn't do any of my tricks," said Carlotta, "in case I gave the show away. I broke my promise the other day in the gym – but somehow I simply couldn't help it. I'd been thinking and dreaming of all the old circus days – and of my darling beautiful horse, Terry – and I just went mad and did all those things in the gym. I can do much more than I showed you then!"

"Carlotta! Walk on your hands upside down!" begged Bobby. "Golly! What fun you're going to be! You're a fierce creature with your fly-away tempers and ready tongue – but you're natural and kind and we shall all like you even better now we understand the kind of life you've lived before. It's a wonder you've fitted in as well as you did. What a mercy you were honest about it – we wouldn't have admired you nearly so much if you'd been afraid to own up."

"Afraid to own up – why, I'm proud of it!" said Carlotta with sparkling eyes. "Why should I be ashamed of knowing how to handle horses? Why should I be ashamed of living with simple people who have the kindest hearts in the world?"

The girl threw herself lightly over and stood on her hands. Her skirt fell over her shoulders as she began to walk solemnly round the room on her strong, supple little hands. The girls crowded round her, laughing and admiring.

"My word – the second form will be jealous when they hear about Carlotta!" said Bobby.

"They certainly will!" said Sadie, who was just as full of astonishment and admiration as anyone else. It all seemed most surprising and unreal.

Everyone was pleased and thrilled – save for one girl. That girl, of course, was Prudence. She could not understand the attitude of the girls. It was completely opposite to what she had expected. It was hard to believe.

Prudence stood in silence, listening to the squeals of delight and admiration. Her heart was very bitter within her. The bombshell she had thrown had certainly exploded – but the only person it had harmed had been the thrower! Instead of making the girls despise Carlotta and avoid her, she had only succeeded in making them admire her and crowd round her in delight. Now Carlotta would show off even more – she would get more friends than ever. How *could* everyone like a nasty common little girl like that?

No one took any notice of Prudence. For one thing they were so excited about Carlotta – and for another thing they despised her for her mean attempt to injure another girl for something she couldn't help. Bobby elbowed her a little roughly, and Prudence almost burst into tears of rage and defeat.

She slipped out of the room. It was more than she could bear to see Carlotta walking on her hands, cheered on by the rest of the first formers. The last words she heard were, "Let's get the second formers in! Where are they? In the gym? Do let's go and tell them to come and see Carlotta! She's marvellous!"

"I meant my news to hurt her – and it's only brought her good luck and friendship," thought Prudence bitterly. "Whatever shall I do about it?"

THE SECOND FORM AT ST CLARE'S

AN EXTRACT

≈ ILLUSTRATED BY ≈

W. Lindsay Cable

*Gladys, a very quiet newcomer to the second form, is at first known as
"the misery-girl" because she doesn't want to make friends with anyone.
However, another new girl, Mirabel, realises that Gladys's reserve springs partly from
her worries about her mother, who is extremely ill. Mirabel's concern leads to friendship,
which gives Gladys the confidence to overcome her shyness and to develop her skill
at lacrosse — also her flair for dramatics. This causes an upset for the twins' cousin
Alison, who has a "crush" on the drama teacher, Miss Quentin . . .*

CHAPTER XIX
ALISON AND MISS QUENTIN

The term hurried on its way. The girls began to talk about Christmas holidays and what they were going to do – pantomimes, parties and theatres were discussed. Gladys looked a little bleak when the girls began to talk excitedly about the coming holidays.

"Will your mother be well enough to leave the hospital and have you home with her?" asked Mirabel.

"No. I'm staying at school for the hols," said Gladys. "Matron will still be here, you know, and two girls from the third and fourth form, whose parents are in India. But I shall be very lonely without you, Mirabel."

"Poor Gladys!" said Mirabel in dismay. "I should hate to stay at school for the hols I must say. After all, most of the fun of being at boarding school is being with crowds of others, day and night – it won't be any fun for you being with one or two! Won't your mother really be better?"

"She's going to have a serious operation soon," said Gladys. "So I know quite well she won't be able to leave the hospital, Mirabel. But the operation may make her well again, so I'm just hoping for the best – and I'm quite willing to stay on at school for the hols if only I hear that Mother is getting better after the operation."

Mrs Unwin had written to Mirabel about Gladys's mother. She had told Mirabel not to show the letter to Gladys.

"I feel rather worried about Gladys's mother," she wrote. "She is to have the operation soon – and I can't help wondering if she really will get over it, because she is very weak. If there is bad news, you must comfort Gladys all you can. She will be very glad to have a friend if sadness comes to her. I will let her know at once if the news is good."

Mirabel said nothing to her friend about the letter – but she was extra warm and friendly towards Gladys. It was unusual for the rather selfish, thick-skinned Mirabel to think of someone else unselfishly and tenderly. It softened her domineering nature and made her a much nicer girl.

Gladys was pleased to be able to tell her mother about the match. She wished she had shot a winning goal – but it was something to shoot the goal that made a draw!

"*I* shall write and tell your mother too," said Mirabel, who could not do enough for her friend just then.

"Oh Mirabel – you are good!" said Gladys, delighted. "You wrote to Mother after the concert, and I guess she was pleased to hear all you said. My word – what a silly I was at the beginning of the term, all mopey and miserable, couldn't take an interest in anything. I should think you hated me."

"Well, I didn't like you very much," said Mirabel, honestly. "But I guess you didn't like *me* much, either!"

Gladys was not only shining at lacrosse but in the drama class as well! Miss Quentin, who had been really amazed at Gladys's performance on the night of the concert, was making a great fuss of her and her talent. Alison didn't like it at all. She was jealous, and there were some days when she could hardly speak to Gladys.

The play was to be performed at the end of the term. Miss Quentin had tried out Alison, Doris, Carlotta, and now Gladys in the principal feminine part. There was no doubt that Alison looked the prettiest and the most graceful, and that she was quite word-perfect and had rehearsed continually. But Gladys was by far the best actress.

Miss Quentin had given Alison to understand that she would have the chief part. She had not actually said so in so many words, but the class as a whole took it for granted that Alison would take the part. They found it quite natural too, for they knew how hard the girl had worked at learning the words, a task always difficult for her.

Alison was really silly about Miss Quentin. She waited round corners for her, hoping for a smile. She hung on every word the teacher said. She was worse than she had been with Sadie Greene the term before – for one thing Sadie had had a little common sense and often laughed at Alison, but Miss Quentin had no common sense at all! So Alison became worse instead of better, and the second formers became quite exasperated with her.

Then Alison heard some news that gave her a great blow – Miss Quentin was not coming back the next term!

"Are you sure?" asked Alison, looking with wide eyes at Hilary, who had come in with the news.

"Well, I heard Mam'zelle say to Miss Quentin, "Well, well – so you will be on the stage next term, whilst we are all struggling with our tiresome girls!" Apparently Miss Quentin had only just heard the news herself – she had a letter in her hand. I think she must only have been engaged for a term – it's the first time we've had a proper drama class. Perhaps Miss Theobald was trying out the idea." Hilary looked at Alison, who had tears in her eyes. "Cheer up, Alison – the world won't come to an end because your beloved Miss Quentin isn't here next term! You'll find someone else to moon round, don't fret!"

It was a great shock to Alison. She had dreamt of term after term in Miss Quentin's drama classes, with herself taking all the chief parts in every play, hearing honeyed words of praise dropping daily from the teacher's lips. She went away by herself and cried very bitterly. The silly girl gave her heart far too easily to anyone who attracted her, or made a fuss of her.

"What's come over Alison?" asked Pat, in surprise, when her cousin appeared with swollen eyes. "Been in a row, Alison?"

"She's only sorrowing because her beloved Miss Quentin won't be here next term to pat her on her back and tell her she is very very good!" said Janet.

"Alison, don't be an idiot!" said Isabel. "You know perfectly well Miss Quentin won't be much loss. We all think she's too soft for words! And think how mean she was in taking the credit for Gladys's performance at the concert."

"I have never believed that," said Alison, tears coming into her eyes again. "You don't know Miss Quentin as I do – she's the truest, honestest, most loyal person! I've never met anyone like her."

"Nor have I!" said Pat. "And thank goodness I haven't. Alison, why must you go and choose the wrong people to moon round? Sadie Greene was amusing but she hadn't anything in her at all – and neither has Miss Quentin. Now, take Miss Jenks for instance . . ."

"Miss Jenks!" said Alison, with an angry sniff. "Who would want to moon round Miss Jenks, with her snappy tongue and cold eyes?"

"Well, I think she's pretty decent," said Pat. "Not that I should want to moon round her or anyone, for that matter. I'm only just saying you will keep on choosing the wrong people to lavish your affections on! Sadie has never even written to you – and I bet Miss Quentin won't, either!"

"She will! She's very fond of me," said Alison.

The others gave it up. Alison would never learn sense! "It's a pity she can't find out how silly her Miss Quentin really is – how undependable," said Hilary. "Your feather-headed cousin, Pat, wants to learn common sense – it's a pity she can't find out that all her ideas about Miss Quentin are only dreams – the real Miss Quentin isn't a bit as Alison pictures her!"

"Well, we can't teach her," said Pat. "She'll make herself miserable for the rest of the term now, and for all the hols too, I expect!"

Alison was really unhappy to hear that her favourite teacher was leaving. She thought she would hang about near the common-room of the junior mistresses, and watch for Miss Quentin to come out. Then she would tell her how upset she was.

So she went to a little lobby near the common-room, and pretended to be hunting for something there. She could hear Miss Quentin's voice talking to Mam'zelle, behind the closed door of the common-room, but she could not hear anything that was said.

Then someone opened the door and came out. It was Miss Lewis, the history teacher. "Leave the door open!" cried Mam'zelle. "It is stuffy in here!"

So Miss Lewis left the door open, and went off towards the school library. Alison stood in the little lobby, her heart beating fast, waiting for Miss Quentin to come out. Surely she would come soon!

The mistresses went on talking. Some of them had clear, distinct voices, and some spoke too low for Alison to hear anything. She did not mean to listen, she was only waiting for Miss Quentin – but suddenly she heard her own name, spoken by Miss Quentin herself. Alison stiffened, and her heart thumped. Was Miss Quentin going to praise her to the others? It would be just like her to say something nice!

"Alison O'Sullivan is going to get a shock," said Miss Quentin, in the low, clear voice that Alison thought so beautiful. "The silly girl thinks she's good enough to play the lead in the second form play! She's been wearing herself out rehearsing – it will do her good to find she's not going to have the part!"

"Who's going to have it, then?" asked Miss Jenks.

"Gladys Hillman," answered Miss Quentin, promptly "I've had my eye on that child ever since the beginning of the term. She's three times as good as anyone else. She will be marvellous as the Countess Jeannette."

"I wish Alison worked as hard in my classes as she does in yours," remarked Mam'zelle, in her rather harsh, loud voice. "Ah, her French exercises! But I think, Miss Quentin, she really does work at drama."

"Oh well, she simply adores me," said Miss Quentin, easily. "I can always make her type work. She'll do anything for a smile or a kind word from me – like a dear little pet dog. But give me somebody like that wild Carlotta – somebody with something in them! Alison bores me to tears with her breathless 'Yes, Miss Quentin! No, Miss Quentin! Oh, *can* I, Miss Quentin!' It will be good for her to have a shock and find she has to take back place to Gladys Hillman."

"I'm not so sure," said Miss Jenks, in her cool voice. "Shocks are not always good for rather weak characters, Miss Quentin. I hope you will break your news kindly to poor Alison – otherwise she will weep all day, and as exams are coming on tomorrow, I don't want bad work from her because of you!"

"Oh don't worry! I'll just pat her curly head and say a few kind words," said Miss Quentin. 'She'll eat out of my hand. She always does."

Miss Lewis came back and shut the door. Not a word more could be heard. Alison sat on a bench in the lobby, sick at heart, shocked and hurt beyond measure. Her mind was in a whirl. She had not been able to help hearing – and once she had grasped that her idol, Miss Quentin, was poking fun at her, she had not even been able to get up and go. She had had to sit there, hearing every cruel word.

She was not to have the leading part in the play. Miss Quentin wasn't fond of her – only amused with her, thinking her a little pet dog, someone to pat and laugh at! Miss Quentin had told a lie – she had not noticed Gladys Hillman at all until the night of the concert! Miss Quentin was bored with her!

Alison was too shocked even to cry. She sat in the lobby quietly, looking straight in front of her. What was it that Miss Jenks had said? "Shocks are not always good for weak characters!" Was she, Alison, such a weak character then? The girl rubbed her hand across her forehead, which was wet and clammy.

"I have to think all this out," said Alison to herself. "I can't tell anyone. I'm too ashamed. But I must think things out. Oh, Miss Quentin, how could you say all that?"

Poor Alison! This was the greatest shock she had ever had in her easy-going life! All her admiration and love for Miss Quentin vanished at once – passed like a dream in the night. There was nothing of it left, except an ache. She saw the drama teacher as the others saw her – someone pleasant and amiable, but undependable, disloyal, shallow.

Alison was a silly girl, as changeable as a weather-vane, swinging now this way and now that, easily upset and easily pleased. As the others often said, "she hadn't much in her!" But in this hour of horror – for it *was* horror to her – she found something in herself that she hardly knew she possessed. And that something was a sense of dignity!

She wasn't going to go under because of someone like Miss Quentin! She wasn't going to be a pet dog, eating out of her hand! She had too much dignity for that. She would show Miss Quentin that she was wrong. Hurt and shocked though she was, Alison had a glimmering of common sense all at once, and she held up her head, blinked away the tears, and made up her mind what she was going to do.

So it came about that when Miss Quentin broke the news to the drama class that Gladys was to have the leading part, and not Alison, the girl gave no sign at all of being disappointed. Her face was pale, for she had slept badly that night, but it had a calmness and dignity that astonished the watching girls.

"So Gladys is to have the part, you see," finished Miss Quentin. She lightly touched Alison's curly head. "I'm afraid my Alison will be disappointed!"

"Of course not, Miss Quentin," said Alison, moving away from the teacher's hand. "I think Gladys *should* have the part! She is the best of us all – and I am very glad."

The girls stared at Alison in the greatest amazement. They had expected tears – even sulks – but not this cool acceptance of an unpleasant fact.

"Who would have thought Alison would take it like that?" said Janet. "Well – good for her! All the same, I think it's a shame. Miss Quentin made us all think Alison would have the part."

Alison would not meet Miss Quentin's eye. She played the part she was given very well, but seemed quite unmoved when Miss Quentin praised her. Miss Quentin was puzzled and a little hurt.

"Girls, I have something to tell you," she said at the end of the lesson. "I shall not be here next term. I shall miss you all very much – especially one or two of you who have worked extremely hard!"

She looked hard at Alison, expecting to see tears, and to hear cries of "Oh, Miss Quentin! We *shall* miss you!"

But Alison did not look at the teacher She gazed out of the window as if she had not heard. Hilary cleared her throat and spoke politely. "I am sure we are all sorry to hear that, Miss Quentin. We hope you will be happy wherever you go."

Miss Quentin was hurt and disappointed. She spoke directly to Alison.

"Alison, I know you worked specially hard for me," she said.

"I worked hard because I like drama," said Alison, in a cool voice, looking Miss Quentin in the eyes for the first time. This was a direct snub and the girls gasped in surprise. Whatever made Alison behave like that? They gazed at her in admiration. So Alison had seen through her beloved Miss Quentin at last — and instead of moaning and wailing, had put on a cloak of dignity and coolness. One up to Alison!

Miss Quentin retired gracefully to her next class, very much puzzled. The girls crowded round Alison.

"Alison! What's happened? Has your beloved Miss Quentin offended you?"

"Shut up," said Alison, pushing her way between the girls. "I can't tell you anything. I don't want to discuss it. Let me alone."

They let her go, puzzled, but respecting her request.

"Something's happened," said Hilary, watching the white-faced girl going out of the room. "But whatever it is, is for the best. Alison seems suddenly more grown-up."

"Time she was," said Pat. "Anyway, if she stops mooning round somebody different each term — or at any rate chooses somebody worthwhile — it will be a blessing!"

Nobody ever knew what had made Alison "grow up" suddenly. Only Alison herself knew, and out of her hurt came something worthwhile, that was to help her in many years to come.

CLAUDINE AT ST CLARE'S
AN EXTRACT

≈ ILLUSTRATED BY ≈

W. Lindsay Cable and Jenny Chapple

Among the new girls in the fourth form are the Honourable Angela Favorleigh,
a pretty but spoilt girl who is always boasting about her rich, elegant and
aristocratic family, and Claudine, the unconventional and wayward niece
of Mam'zelle, the school's French teacher . . .

CHAPTER IX
PREPARING FOR HALF-TERM

Half-term came along very shortly, and the girls were excited because their parents were coming to see them. There were to be tennis matches and swimming for the parents to watch. Hilary, Bobby, the twins and one or two others were excited about these, because they hoped to be in the teams.

"I'd like my mother to see me swim under water for the whole length of the pool," said Bobby. "She was a very good swimmer herself when she was young. Hope I'm chosen for the swimming competitions."

The twins hoped to be in one of the tennis matches. They were both good at tennis, and it would be lovely for their mother to see them play together and win a match. Both girls were intensely proud of St Clare's, and badly wanted to show off their school, and their own prowess, to the best advantage.

Hilary was to play in a singles match with one of the fifth formers. She had been chosen for her very graceful style, and it was to be an exhibition match more than a battle. Both girls had a beautiful natural style and the games mistress was proud of them.

Mirabel was hoping to win the one-length race in the swimming. She was very fast and very strong. Her smaller friend, the mouse-like Gladys, was also in the swimming competitions for, although she was small, she was a beautiful little swimmer. She was longing for her mother to see her. She had no father and no brother or sister, so her mother was everything to her.

"Half-term will be fun," said Hilary. "Is your mother coming, Angela?"

"Of course," said Angela. "And Daddy too. I'm longing to see their new car. It's a Rolls Royce, black with a green line, and . . ."

"I bet you're looking forward to seeing the new car more than to seeing your people!" said Bobby, with a chuckle. "You never talk of your parents except in terms of the wealth they own, Angela. Did you know that?"

Angela looked sulky. "I don't know what you mean," she said. "I guess you'd talk about cars and things if your parents had the same as mine. And you just see my mother when she comes! She will stand out above everyone else. She's absolutely beautiful – golden hair like mine – and the bluest eyes – and she wears the most marvellous clothes . . ."

"And even the safety-pins she uses are made of pure gold set with diamonds," finished Pat.

"That's not funny," said Angela, as the others shouted with laughter. "I tell you, you just wait and see my mother! She's the most beautiful person you'll ever see."

"*What* a pity you don't take after her, Angela!" said Bobby, sorrowfully. "Isn't your mother sorry to have a daughter like you? You must be a terrible disappointment."

Angela flushed with anger. She could never bear this kind of teasing. "All right," she said, in a bitter voice. "All right. But just wait till you see my mother – and then tell me if she isn't the most wonderful person you ever saw in your lives. I hope she wears her double-string of pearls. They are worth five thousand pounds."

"Well," said the soft voice of Gladys, who rarely butted in on any conversation of this sort, "well, I don't care if *my* mother wears her very oldest clothes, I don't care if she's got a ladder in her stockings, I don't care if she hasn't even powdered her nose – so long as my mother comes to see me and I can be with her for a few hours, she can be the untidiest, ugliest, poorest-dressed there – but I shall still be proud of her, and think she's the best of all!"

This was a long speech for the timid Gladys to make. Everyone was silent when she stopped. Pat found that she suddenly had tears in her eyes. There was such love in Gladys's voice – and what she said was fine. That was the way to love someone – not to care how they looked or what they did – but just to welcome them all the same!

Even Angela was taken aback. She stared at Gladys in surprise. She was about to make a sneering remark but Bobby stopped her.

"Now you shut up," said Bobby, in a warning voice. "Gladys has said the last word about mothers, and she's right. Good for you, Gladys."

After that Angela said no more, but privately she rejoiced when she thought of her own beautifully-dressed mother, and how the girls would have to admire her and her clothes when she came.

Isabel giggled. "Well, I'm rather glad our mother is just ordinary," she said, "pretty and kind and sensible, just an ordinary nice mother!"

The girls all practised hard for half-term, swimming and playing tennis as much as they could, so that their parents might be proud of them. There was to be an exhibition of pictures too, done by the girls themselves, and a show of needlework. Here Claudine expected to shine. She had done a really beautiful cushion-cover, on which was embroidered a peacock spreading its lovely tail.

Mam'zelle was intensely proud of this. She bored everyone by talking about it. "It is exquisite!" she said. "Ah, the clever little Claudine! Miss Ellis, do you not think that Claudine has done the tail most perfectly?"

"I do," said Miss Ellis. "Much better than she does her maths or her history, or her geography or her literature, or her . . ."

"Come, come!" said Mam'zelle, hurt. "It is not given to us to have great gifts at everything. Now, the little Claudine, she . . ."

"I don't expect Claudine to have great gifts at anything but needlework," said Miss Ellis. "All I ask is a *little* attention in class, and a *little* thought in prep time! You spoil Claudine, Mam'zelle."

"I! I spoil Claudine!" cried Mam'zelle, her glasses falling off her nose in rage. "I have never spoilt any girl, never. Always I am strict, always I am fair, always I am . . ."

"All right, Mam'zelle," said Miss Ellis, hastily, seeing that Mam'zelle was going to make one of her long and impassioned speeches, "all right. I must go. You can tell it all to me when you see me next."

Mam'zelle sought out Claudine. She fell upon her and hugged her, much to Claudine's surprise. But it had suddenly occurred to Mam'zelle that "the poor little Claudine" would not have parents visiting her at half-term, for they were in France. So, immediately on thinking this, she had gone to comfort Claudine, who, however, was not in any need of comfort at all. She liked her parents, but as she was one of a very large family, and had only got a small share of their love and attention, she had not missed them very much.

"Ah, my little Claudine!" said Mam'zelle, flinging her arms round the astonished Claudine. "Do not be sad, do not be discouraged! Do not fret yourself – you shall not be alone at half-term."

Claudine wondered if her aunt had gone mad. "I am not sad, *ma tante*," she said. "What is the matter? Has anything happened?"

"No, no," said Mam'zelle, still full of tender thoughts for her little Claudine, "nothing has happened. It is only that I feel for you because your parents will not be with you at half-term. When everyone else has their handsome fathers and their so-beautiful mothers, you will have no one – no one but your loving Aunt Mathilde!"

"Well, that's OK," said Claudine in English. Mam'zelle wrinkled up her nose and her glasses fell off.

"Do not use these expressions!" she said. "They are vulgar. Ah, my little Claudine, you will not have any parents to admire your so-fine cushion-case with its magnificent peacock — but I will be there, my little one, I will stand by your cushion-cover all the time, not one minute will I go away, and I will say to everyone: 'See! See the beautiful cover made by the clever Claudine! Ah, it needs a French girl to do such work as this! Regard the tail, regard each feather so finely-done in silk, regard the priceless cushion-cover, the most beautiful thing in this school today!'"

"Oh, Aunt Mathilde, I wish you wouldn't think of saying anything like that," said Claudine in alarm. "The girls would laugh like anything. They would tease me terribly. Please don't. I shan't be lonely, I shan't mind not having anyone there."

"Ah, the brave little one!" sighed Mam'zelle, wiping away a tear from her eye. "I see your courage. You will not show others that you suffer."

"I *shan't* suffer," said Claudine, getting impatient. "I shan't really, Aunt Mathilde. Please don't make a fuss like this. It would be dreadful if you stood by my cushion-cover all the afternoon and made remarks like that."

The idea of Mam'zelle standing like a bull-dog on guard, telling surprised parents of her poor lonely little Claudine, and praising to the skies the little cushion-cover, filled Claudine with horror. She began to wish that half-term was safely over.

But it hadn't even come! Four days away — three days — two days — the night before. Ah, now it really *was* near! The girls went to bed very excited that night and talked in whispers long after lights were out. Susan Howes, the head girl of the form, pretended to be asleep She could not bear to be a spoil-sport on the night before half-term, strict as she was on all other nights.

Angela was thinking of the wonderful impression her mother would make, and how she would bask in her reflected glory. She hoped her mother would wear her famous pearls.

CHAPTER X
HALF-TERM AT LAST

Half-term Saturday was a perfectly beautiful day. The sun shone down from a blue sky that hadn't a single cloud in it. "Gorgeous, isn't it, Claudine?" said Doris happily to the little French girl. "Couldn't be better."

Claudine groaned. "To think we shall all have to be out-of-doors in this terrible sun!" she said. "I know I shall get a freckle. I wish it had rained."

"You spoil-sport!" said Bobby, grinning. "You would like to huddle indoors even on a day like this. Come on, cheer up and smile – it's really a heavenly day."

The art exhibition was all ready for the parents to admire. There were some really good pictures there. Miss Walker, the art mistress, was proud of them. She had a water-colour class which went out regularly to paint country scenes with her, and some of them were very good.

"Good enough to sell!" said Claudine. "Do we sell our work? How much would you get for this so-beautiful picture, Hilary?"

Hilary laughed. "You have got funny ideas, Claudine," she said. "Of course we don't sell our work. As if our proud parents would let us! No, they will take our pictures home, and our pottery, and place them in conspicuous places on the walls, or mantelpiece, so that all their friends can admire them, and say, 'How clever your daughter must be, Mrs So-and-So!'"

"I bet your mother will be pleased if you send her that lovely cushion-cover of yours for her birthday," said Pat. Claudine laughed.

"I have three sisters who do much more beautiful work than I do," she said. "My mother would look at my cover and say, 'Ah! The little Claudine is improving! This is not bad for a beginning.'"

"Mam'zelle thinks it's wonderful, anyhow," said Bobby, grinning. "There's one thing about you, Claudine – you're not in the least conceited. With all the fuss that everyone has made of your embroidery, you might quite well have begun to swank about it. But you don't."

"Ah, I know that it is good compared with the sewing of you English girls," said Claudine, seriously, "but, you see, I know that it would be quite ordinary in France. I have a different standard to compare that so-beautiful cover with, and I cannot think it is as wonderful as you do."

Claudine was a very funny mixture of honesty, sincerity and deceitfulness. Even her deceitfulness was odd, because she did not attempt to hide it. She often tried to deceive Miss Ellis, for instance, and if Miss Ellis saw through it, Claudine would at once admit to her attempted deceit without any shame. It was almost as if she were playing a game with the teachers, trying to get the better of them, but not trying to hide the fact. The girls could not quite make her out.

Pat and Isabel were playing together in a school match, and they were delighted. They looked out their white skirts and blouses, their red socks and white shoes, and took the clothes to Matron for the laundry staff to iron. Everyone had to look their best when parents came!

Mam'zelle had displayed Claudine's beautiful cushion-cover in a very prominent place. She still seemed inclined to fall on Claudine's neck, and tell her she must not feel lonely, and the little French girl kept out of her way as much as possible, slipping deftly round the corner whenever she saw her aunt approaching.

"Sort of hide-and-seek you're playing, Claudine!" said Bobby. "You'll have to have a word with Mam'zelle soon, or she'll burst. She's longing to show you how beautifully she has arranged your so-marvellous cushion-cover!"

Lunch was a very scrappy affair that day because the cooks were concerned with the strawberry tea that the parents were to have in the afternoon, and scores of pounds of strawberries were being prepared in big glass dishes. The cooks had made the most lovely cakes and biscuits, and there were sandwiches of every kind. The girls kept peeping into the big dining-room, where the dishes were all set out.

Claudine slipped in and sampled some of the strawberries. She was the only one who dared to do this.

"You'll get into a row if anyone catches you," said Bobby.

"You go and taste them," said Claudine, running her little pink tongue round her crimson lips. "They are so sweet and juicy!"

"No," said Bobby. "We've been put on our honour not to sample this afternoon's tea, and I wouldn't dream of breaking my honour."

"This honour of yours, it is a funny thing," said Claudine, "It is a most uncomfortable thing. It stops you from doing what you want to do. I have no honour to worry me. I will never have this honour of yours. I do not like it."

"You're awful, Claudine," said Angela, screwing up her nose. "You do exactly as you like. I'm glad I'm not as dishonourable as you are."

The tone was very unpleasant, but Claudine only laughed. She hardly ever took offence. "Ah, Angela!" she said, "you think it is worse to take a few strawberries than to tell untruths about another girl behind her back? Me, I think it is really dishonourable to speak lies against another girl as you do. To me you are dishonourable, a worth-nothing girl, not because of a few strawberries but because of your evil tongue!"

The listening girls laughed at this. It was said in a pleasant voice, but there was such truth in it, and the tables had been turned so cleverly on Angela that the girls couldn't help being amused. Only Angela was angry. But there was little time to quarrel on half-term day. There were so many jobs to do, and everyone had her own allotted task.

Some had to do the flowers all over the school, and this took a long time. The vases had to be washed, old flowers thrown away, new ones picked, and then arranged to the best advantage in all kinds of bowls, jars and vases. The twins were especially good at this, and were very busy all the morning.

After lunch everyone changed into either sports clothes or school uniform. The summer uniform was a brightly-coloured tunic. The girls could choose any colour they liked, so every girl was able to wear the one that suited her best. Dark girls, like Carlotta, chose reds and oranges, fair girls like Angela chose pale colours, blues and pinks. They looked like flowers, moving about against the green lawns of the school grounds, on that hot summer day.

"The parents are arriving!" squealed Alison, as she heard the sound of wheels coming up the drive. "The first lot are here. Who are they?"

The fourth formers looked out of their windows, but nobody knew the people in the car. "They must belong to some of the lower school," said Bobby. "Here come some more!"

"They're mine!" cried Janet. "Oh goody-goody! I hoped they'd come early. I say, doesn't my mother look nice and tanned. I'm going to greet them."

An enormous car rolled up the drive, with a smartly uniformed chauffeur in front. It was a beautiful new Rolls Royce, black with a small green line. It came to a stop and the chauffeur got out. Angela gave a loud squeal.

"That's our new car! Look, everyone, isn't it a beauty! And do you like the chauffeur's uniform, black with green piping to match the car? The cushions are black too, with green edges and green monograms."

"I should have thought you would have been so excited to see your parents that you wouldn't even have noticed the car!" said Janet's cool voice. But Angela took no notice. She was very pleased indeed that so many of the fourth formers were near when her grand new car drove up!

The chauffeur opened the car door. Angela's mother stepped out. Certainly she was a vision of beauty! She looked very young, was extraordinarily like Angela, and she was dressed in a most exquisite fashion.

The girls stared at her. She looked round with brilliant blue eyes, also very like Angela's. After her came her husband, a tall, military-looking man, with rather a serious face. Angela gave another squeal.

She ran to her parents and flung her arms round her mother as she had seen the others do, purposely exaggerating everything because she knew they were watching.

"Angela dear! Be careful of my dress!" said her mother. "Let me see how you are looking."

Her father gave Angela a good hug, and then pushed her a little way away so that he could have a good look at her.

"She looks very well indeed," said her father.

"But this awful school uniform spoils her," said her mother. "I do think it is most unbecoming. And I can't bear those terrible school shoes, with their flat heels."

"Well, all the girls wear the same," said Angela's father, reasonably. "I think Angela looks very nice.

"If only the school had a prettier uniform!" said Angela's mother, in a complaining voice. "That was one reason why I didn't want to send her here – the dress was *so* ugly!"

CHAPTER XI
ANGELA'S "WONDERFUL" MOTHER

The complaining voice of Angela's mother could be heard very often indeed that afternoon. Beautiful as she was, attractive and exquisite in her dress and looks, the lovely face was spoilt by an expression of discontent and boredom.

She complained of so many things, and her voice was unfortunately harsh and too loud! She complained of the hard bench that she had to sit on to watch the tennis matches. She found fault with the cup of tea that Angela brought her. "What terrible tea! They might at least provide China tea. You know I can't drink Indian tea, Angela."

She complained of the cake she took. "Awfully dry," she said. "I can hardly eat it."

"Leave it then," said Angela's father. And to Angela's horror her mother dropped the cake on the ground, where it could be trodden underfoot. The sharp eyes of the other girls noted all these things, and Angela began to feel rather uncomfortable.

"Isn't my mother lovely?" she whispered to Alison. "Don't you think those pearls are marvellous? Hasn't she got beautiful hair?"

Alison agreed. Privately she thought that Angela's mother acted like a spoilt child, complaining and grumbling all the time. She did not praise the pictures in the art exhibition, neither did she show any enthusiasm for the pottery work. She was forced to express a good opinion on Claudine's cushion-cover, because Mam'zelle stood there like a dragon, looking so fierce that everyone felt they must praise her niece's handiwork.

"Ah! So this is your mother, Angela?" said Mam'zelle, in a most amiable voice. "We will show her the work of the little Claudine! Is it not beautiful? See the exquisite stitches! Regard the fine tail, spreading so well over the cover!"

Angela's mother looked as if she was going to pass the cover by without saying anything, but Mam'zelle was certainly not going to let that happen. She took hold of the visitor's arm and almost forced her to bend over Claudine's cushion-cover "You have not seen it! It is a work of art! It is the finest thing in the exhibition!" said Mam'zelle, getting excited.

"Very nice," said Angela's mother, in a tone that seemed to say "Very nasty!" She took her arm away from Mam'zelle's hand, brushed her sleeve as if it had some dust left on it, and turned away impatiently.

"Who is that awful old woman?" she asked Angela in much too loud a voice. "Surely *she* doesn't teach you, my dear? Did you ever see anyone look so dowdy?"

The girls were very fond of Mam'zelle, and they were angry to hear this remark. Bobby felt certain that Mam'zelle herself had caught some of it. The Frenchwoman was standing looking after Angela and her parents with a puzzled and hurt expression in her eyes.

"Well – I always thought Angela was pretty beastly," said Bobby to Pat, in a low tone, "and now I see where she gets her cattiness from! How ashamed I'd be of *my* mother if she walked round like that, criticising things and people at the top of her voice. Poor old Mam'zelle! It's a shame to hurt her."

Claudine had overheard the remarks made by Angela's mother, and she too was hurt and angry. She was fond of her Aunt Mathilde, and though she was cross with her for standing by her cushion-cover and behaving in such an exaggerated way about it, she saw that it was the intense love and pride she had for Claudine herself that made her do it.

She looked at Angela's beautiful mother. She noted her discontented face, and the petulant droop of the mouth that at times quite spoilt its loveliness. She thought of all the hurts and insults that that beautiful mouth must have uttered through the years. And Claudine longed to punish Angela's mother in some dramatic way for the cruel words she had spoken about her Aunt Mathilde!

Angela took her parents to the swimming-pool. St Clare's was proud of this, for it was one of the finest and biggest swimming-pools owned by any school in the kingdom. The water lapped against the sides, a beautiful blue-green colour.

But even here Angela's mother had fault to find. "I suppose they change the water every day, Angela?" she said.

"No, Mother, twice a week, sometimes three times," said Angela. Her mother gave a little disgusted squeal.

"Good gracious! To think they can't even change the water every day! What a school! I really must make a complaint about it. Angela, you are not to bathe in the pool unless the water has just been changed. I forbid it."

"But, Mother," began Angela, uncomfortably, "I have to do what the others do – and really, the water *is* quite clean, even when it's two days old, or three."

"I shall complain," said Angela's mother. "I never did like the idea of sending you here. It's a second-rate school, I think. I wanted to send you to High Towers School. *Such* a nice school! I can't think why your father wanted to send you here. Perhaps now he has seen it he will think again."

"Pamela, don't talk so loudly," said Angela's father. "People here don't like to listen to what you are saying. You are in a minority – it is plain that all the other parents here think as *I* do – that St Clare's is splendid in every way!"

"Oh, *you*," said Angela's mother, as if what her husband thought was of simply no account at all. She shut up her scarlet lips, and looked just as sulky as Angela always did when anybody ticked her off.

No – Angela's mother was certainly not a success! Beautiful she might be, expensive she certainly was – but she had none of the graciousness of the twins' mother, or the common sense of Bobby's jolly-looking mother, or the affection of Gladys's plainly-dressed but sweet-faced mother.

"I'm jolly glad I haven't got a mother like Angela's!" said Janet to Alison. "Isn't she perfectly awful?"

Loyal though Alison wanted to be to Angela, she couldn't help nodding her head. She had overheard many of Angela's mother's rude remarks, and she had not liked them, because even feather-headed Alison felt a deep sense of loyalty to St Clare's and all it stood for. She was not at all eager to be introduced to Angela's mother now – but the time came when she had to be, for Angela sought her out and took her off.

"Mother, this is Alison, the friend I told you about in my letters," said Angela. Her mother looked at the pretty, dainty girl with approval. Alison was like Angela, and could wear the school uniform well.

"Oh, so this is Alison," said Angela's mother. "How do you do? I must say you look a little more attractive than some of the girls here. One or two that Angela has introduced me to have been perfect frights!"

Bobby had been introduced to Angela's mother and was presumably one of the "frights". Her frank freckled face was not at all attractive to anyone as exquisite as Angela's mother.

"Where is your mother?" asked Angela. "We must introduce her to mine. Mother wants to ask if you can spend some of the summer hols with me."

But, rather to Alison's relief, when the introduction had been made, and the two mothers had greeted one another, the invitation was quite firmly declined by Alison's own mother!

"Thank you," she said, "but I am afraid I have other plans for Alison."

She did not explain what these were. She did not say that she had watched Angela's mother, and had heard some of her insolent remarks and detested them. She did not say that Angela's mother was the sort of person she would hate Alison to spend even a day with! But Alison knew what her mother was thinking, and silly girl as she was, she knew that her mother was right.

Angela's mother sensed that the other mother was snubbing her, and she was surprised and annoyed. She was about to say something more, when a bell rang loudly.

"Oh! Must they ring bells like that!" said Angela's mother, putting her hands to her ears. "How crude!"

"But sensible, don't you think so?" said Alison's mother drily, and left her.

"That's the bell to tell us to go and watch the swimming," said Alison, slipping her hand into her mother's arm. "Come on, Mummy. You'll see Bobby swimming there – you know, the freckled girl you liked. And Mirabel too – she's awfully fast."

The hot sun blazed down as the company took its place round the swimming-pool. The parents sat at the edge of the baths, but the girls were in the big gallery above, watching eagerly. Many of them were not taking part in the swimming, but they were all keen to see the performers diving, somersaulting and swimming. It was fun to hear the continual splashes, and to see the rippling of the blue water.

"Isn't it a gorgeous afternoon!" said Janet, happily. "I *am* enjoying myself! I feel so glad that it's a fine day so that we can show off St Clare's at its very best."

"All our parents seem to think it's a great success," said Bobby. "Well – except *one* parent!"

She meant Angela's mother. Angela heard this remark and flushed. She had been so pleased to show off her beautiful mother – but somehow everything had been spoilt now. She couldn't help wishing that her mother had made nice remarks like the others had made. But then, Mother wasn't usually very pleased with things, no matter what they were.

Claudine, Alison, Angela and many others not in the swimming, got front places in the big gallery above the water. Claudine leant over rather far, not so much to look at the swimmers, in their navy-blue swim-suits, but to see the rows of parents.

"Look out, Claudine, you'll fall in!" said Alison, in alarm, trying to pull her back.

"I shall not fall," said Claudine. "I am just looking at that so-discontented person below, with the voice that makes loud and rude remarks!"

"Sh," said Alison. "Angela will hear you."

"I do not care," said Claudine. "Why should Angela expect us to praise a mother who is beautiful only appearance, and whose character is ugly?"

"Do be quiet," said Alison, afraid that Angela would hear. "I'm sorry Angela's mother said that about your aunt, Claudine. I heard it, and I'm sure poor Mam'zelle was hurt."

The swimming began. Angela's mother looked disgusted when a drop of water splashed on to her beautiful dress. She shook it daintily and tried to move backwards a little – but other people were behind her and she couldn't.

It was an exciting hour, for the swimmers were fast and good, and the divers graceful and plucky. But the most exciting bit of the whole afternoon was not the swimming or the diving, or the backward somersaulting done so cleverly by Bobby.

It was an unexpected and highly dramatic performance, quite unrehearsed, given by Claudine!

She was leaning well over

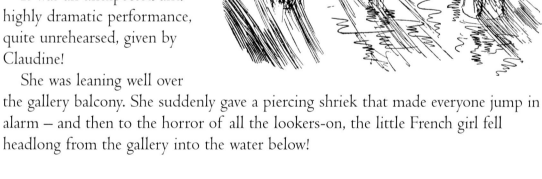

the gallery balcony. She suddenly gave a piercing shriek that made everyone jump in alarm – and then to the horror of all the lookers-on, the little French girl fell headlong from the gallery into the water below!

CHAPTER XII
A HAPPY TIME

She made a most terrific splash. The water rose up and fell all over Angela's mother, soaking her from head to foot! "Good gracious!" said Miss Theobald, the head mistress, startled out of her usual calm dignity. "Who has fallen into the water? Get her out, quickly!"

Claudine could not swim. She sank under the water, and then rose to the surface, gasping. Bobby and Mirabel who were in the water, too, at once swam over to her. They got hold of her and helped her to the steps.

"Claudine! Whatever happened?" said Bobby. "You *are* an idiot!"

Claudine was gasping and spluttering. She cast an eye towards Angela's mother, and saw, to her delight, that she was drenched. Miss Theobald was by her, apologising, and saying that she must come at once to the school, and allow her, Miss Theobald, to lend her some clothes whilst hers were drying.

Angrily Angela's mother followed the head mistress from the swimming-pool. She looked a dreadful sight, with her dress soaked and clinging tightly to her, and her beautiful hat dripping with water. Angela looked very distressed.

"You too, Claudine, you must go with Matron and get into dry clothes," said Miss Ellis to the soaking wet fourth former. "Get into another tunic, quickly, or you'll catch cold. Hurry, now."

Claudine, out of the tail of her eye, saw Mam'zelle bearing down upon her, alarm and anxiety written all over her. The little French girl at once fled off up to the school. She felt she could not bear to be enwrapped in Mam'zelle's overwhelming affection just then.

"Wait, wait, Claudine," called Matron, who was annoyed that Claudine had caused her to leave the company and go back to the school. But Claudine did not wait. Better to face Matron's annoyance rather than Mam'zelle's loud exclamations of dismay and sympathy!

"How exactly like Claudine to cause such a disturbance!" said Pat to Isabel. "Oh, Isabel – I can't help feeling delighted that the person who got soaked was Angela's tiresome mother!"

"I suppose Claudine couldn't possibly have done it on purpose, could she?" said Isabel, doubtfully. "You know, she doesn't care in the least what she does, if she wants to get a result she has set her heart on. I bet she wanted to punish Angela's mother for her rudeness to Mam'zelle!"

"But Claudine simply hates and detests the water!" said Pat. "Nothing will make her undress and have a swim. And to let herself fall from the gallery into the water would be a very brave thing to do, considering she can't swim."

Claudine soon returned, in dry clothes, looking demure and innocent. She could look just as innocent as Angela when she liked — and now that the girls knew her better, they were certain that the more innocent Claudine looked, the worse mischief she had done or was about to do!

Angela's mother also returned, after a while — dressed in Miss Theobald's clothes! Miss Theobald was about the same size as Angela's mother, but a little taller, and although she always looked nice, her clothes were very simple, plain and dignified.

They did not suit Angela's mother at all. In fact she looked very extraordinary in them and she knew it. She was angry and she showed it. It was bad enough to be drenched like that by some silly, careless girl, but much worse to be made to wear clothes too long for her, and so dowdy and frumpish after her own!

But somehow Angela's mother could not be rude to Miss Theobald. The head mistress was extremely kind and apologetic, but she was also calm and dignified, and she acted as if she expected Angela's mother to be calm and dignified also. And, much to her surprise, the spoilt woman found herself guarding her tongue and behaving quite well, whilst she changed into Miss Theobald's clothes.

CHAPTER XIII
JANET AND THE 'STINK BALLS'

After the excitements of half-term the girls felt flat and dull. There didn't seem anything to look forward to now. Lessons were boring. The weather was too hot. It seemed a long time till the summer holidays.

"Janet! Bobby! Can't you think up some trick or other?" said Pat, with a yawn. "I wish you would. I shall die of boredom this week if something doesn't happen."

Janet grinned. "I've got rather an awful trick from my brother," she said. "I don't really know if we ought to play it, now we're fourth formers."

"Oh, don't be an idiot!" said Doris. "Why can't we have a few jokes, even if we *are* fourth formers! What's the trick?"

"Well – it's a perfectly frightful smell," said Janet. "Wait a bit – I'll get the things."

She went up to her dormitory, rummaged about in one of her drawers and then came down again with a small box.

The others crowded round her. The box was full of what looked like tiny round glass balls, full of some sort of clear liquid.

"What are they?" said Pat, puzzled. "I've never seen them before."

"They are smell balls,"

said Janet. "Stink balls my brother calls them. When you break one and let out the liquid, it dries up at once – but leaves the most frightful smell behind."

"What sort of smell?" asked Doris, with great interest. "Like drains or something?"

"Well – like very bad eggs," said Janet. "My brother – he's simply awful, you know – he broke one of these balls at a very solemn meeting once, in our sitting-room at home – and in less than a minute the room was empty! You simply can't imagine what it was like!"

Bobby chuckled. "Let's break one in French class tomorrow," she said. "It's going to be terribly dull – translating pages and pages of that book Mam'zelle is so keen on – that French play. This trick is absolutely *sent* for things like that. Will you break one of these balls tomorrow, Janet, or shall I?"

"Well, you take one and I'll take one," said Janet. "Then if mine doesn't work – my brother says they are sometimes disappointing – you can use yours. See?"

The whole class were thrilled about the "stink balls". Everyone but Eileen knew about them. The girls were afraid of telling Eileen in case she sneaked to Matron, and the secret was found out. So Eileen was not told a word. She was astonished to find that so many of the girls hurriedly stopped talking when she came up, and then began chattering very loudly about quite silly things. She was sure they had been talking about her, and she felt hurt.

"If they're going to be beastly to me, I shall tell Mother and they'll all get dozens of stockings to mend!" thought Eileen, spitefully

Janet and Bobby went into the French class the next day with the little "stink balls" in their pockets. The lesson was just before break.

"We'd better not choose any lesson except one just before break," Janet had said, "because the smell goes on too long, it might still be there in Miss Ellis's class, and I bet she'd smell a rat."

"She'd smell much worse than a rat once she sniffs one of your 'stink balls'," said Bobby, with a grin.

"You see, we can open all the windows and doors and let the smell out well during break," said Pat. "There won't be anything of it left by the time maths lesson comes afterwards with Miss Ellis."

The class were standing politely and silently when Mam'zelle came in. She beamed at the girls.

"Sit! Now today we will go on with this play of ours. I will allot the parts. You, Janet, can take the part of the old servant; you, Alison . . ."

The girls opened their books, hiding their grins as best they could. A trick performed by Janet or Bobby was always fun, great fun! The girls remembered the many other tricks the two had played, and chuckled. This would liven up a dull French lesson very considerably.

"Janet, will you please begin?" said Mam'zelle, amiably. She liked this fourth form. They were good, hard-working girls – and her dear little Claudine was there too, her face buried in her book – the good, good little girl!

Janet began reading in French. Her hand stole to her pocket. The girls behind her saw it, and tried to choke back their giggles. That was the worst of playing a trick – you always wanted to begin giggling far too soon, and it was terribly difficult to stop real giggles. Doris gave one of her sudden snorts, and Mam'zelle looked up in surprise.

Doris turned it into a long cough, which set Mirabel off into giggles too. Mam'zelle glared at Mirabel.

"Is it so funny that the poor Doris has a bad cough?" she inquired.

This seemed funnier still to Mirabel and she went off into more helpless giggles which began to infect the others. Janet turned round and frowned. She didn't want Mam'zelle to suspect too soon that she was playing a trick. The others caught her warning look, and became as serious as they could again.

The lesson went on. Janet slid the little glass ball out of her pocket. Her hand was behind her, and the girls saw her press firmly on the tiny glass ball. The thin glass covering broke, and the liquid ran out, drying almost as soon as the air touched it. The liquid disappeared, and the tiny fragments of thin glass dropped unheeded to the floor.

After a few moments a curious smell drifted all round. Doris coughed. Alison sniffed loudly and said "Pooh!"

It was a horrid smell, there was no doubt about that. It smelt of bad eggs, drains, dead rats, old cats' meat . . . all that was horrid!

Mam'zelle did not smell the smell at first. She was astonished at the sudden outburst of sniffing and coughing. She looked up. She saw expressions of disgust on everyone's face, mixed with the desire to giggle.

"What is the matter?" demanded Mam'zelle, suspiciously. "Why do you pull these faces? Alison, stop saying 'Pooh!' Janet, why do you look so disgusted?"

"Oh, Mam'zelle – can't you smell it?" said Janet, an agonised expression on her face.

"Smell *what*?" said Mam'zelle, exasperated. The smell had not drifted her way as yet.

"Oh, Mam'zelle – the *smell*!" chorused half a dozen voices.

Mam'zelle looked puzzled and angry. She took a few enormous sniffs of the air, which made Doris explode into laughter.

"I smell no smell," said Mam'zelle. "This is a silly trick, yes. Stop sniffing, Janet. If you say 'Pooh' again, Alison, I will send you out of the room. Claudine, do not look like a duck that is dying."

"But, Aunt Mathilde, the smell, the smell! *C'est abominable!*" cried Claudine, who detested bad smells, and looked as if she was about to faint.

"Claudine! You too!" rapped out Mam'zelle, who, safely away at the end of the room, had not even got so much as a sniff of the evil smell yet. "Now listen, *mes enfants* – one more mention of a smell, and I fetch Miss Theobald herself here to smell it! It is all pretence. You are bad children."

This was a truly terrible threat! Miss Theobald would certainly be able to smell the smell as soon as she got into the room, and then there would be a big row. The girls looked at one another in dismay. They put their handkerchiefs to their noses and tried not to sniff up the ghastly odour.

Mam'zelle began to read out loud from the French play. After a few lines, she stopped. Strange! She felt as if she too now could smell something. She took a cautious sniff. Was it a smell, or was it not? Nonsense! Strange and horrible smells do not invade classrooms all of a sudden. Mam'zelle took another breath and went on reading.

The smell stole round her. Mam'zelle could smell it quite distinctly now. She stopped reading again and sniffed wildly. Yes, there was no doubt about it, a perfectly horrible smell was in the room! The poor, poor girls – they had smelt it first – and she had not believed them.

Mam'zelle gave a gulp and a choke as the smell really took hold of her. She fished about for her handkerchief. The girls, divided between disgust at the smell and an intense desire to giggle at Mam'zelle's horrified face, stuffed their hankies into their mouths, making all kinds of most peculiar noises.

"Girls," said Mam'zelle, in a choking kind of voice, "girls, you are right. There is a terrible smell in here. What can it be?"

"A dead rat under the floorboards?" said Doris, obligingly, removing her hanky from her mouth for a moment.

Mam'zelle gave a small shriek. Rats, dead or alive, gave her shivers all down her back.

"Perhaps a drain has burst outside the window," said Pat, speaking in a muffled voice. "I'll look."

She went to the open window and leant out, taking in deep breaths of the pure air there. One or two others joined her, thinking it was a very good idea.

"Perhaps it will go away," said Mam'zelle, hopefully. "Open the door, Janet, and maybe it will help to clear the room of this evil odour."

Janet thankfully opened the door. This was an amusing trick to play – but it had its drawbacks!

The draught of air took a good strong dose of the smell over to Mam'zelle's desk. She gave a loud exclamation "*Tiens!* This is terrible! We shall all be ill. Pick up your books quickly and we will finish our lesson in the garden. I will tell Miss Theobald and maybe she will have the boards up to seek for a rat that is quite dead."

All but Claudine were delighted to go out into the garden. Claudine did not know which was worse – the smell in the classroom, or the insects out-of-doors. She thought there was very little to choose between them!

Soon the girls were sitting in a nice shady part of the garden, giggling whenever they thought of the awful smell drifting round their classroom. The lesson was no longer boring or dull! The smell had made it a great success.

Mam'zelle kept her word and reported the smell to Miss Theobald. "Ah, Miss Theobald!" she said, "it is a smell truly unbelievable! Of dead rats and mice, of eggs that are bad, of drains that are broken! It came into our classroom whilst the girls were reciting their French lesson, and it spoilt the whole hour. We had to leave the room and go into the garden."

Miss Theobald was surprised to hear of such a very strong and disgusting smell. In all her experience of schools, she had never yet come across a smell that had driven a class from the room.

"I will go and smell it," she said to Mam'zelle. "If it is a dead rat, or bad drains, then, of course, we must have the smell seen to at once, this very afternoon. The smell will remain there, if those are the causes."

But, to Mam'zelle's great astonishment and to Miss Theobald's mild astonishment, not a trace of the smell remained. The two of them sniffed all round the room, but it smelt fresh and clean.

"Extraordinary," said Miss Theobald, gazing at Mam'zelle. "You are quite sure, Mam'zelle, that it *was* a strong smell, a really bad one?"

Mam'zelle was most indignant. What, the head mistress was doubting her word? Mam'zelle at once began to describe the smell all over again, this time making it a smell ten times worse than before. Miss Theobald smiled to herself She knew Mam'zelle's indignant exaggerations by this time.

"Well," she said, "I won't have the floorboards up, or the drains inspected today — maybe the smell will not return. If it does, Mam'zelle, kindly report it to me at once, please, so that I may smell it myself before it goes away."

"Yes, Miss Theobald," said Mam'zelle, and went to the mistresses' common-room, full of the smell and of its power in sending her class into the garden. Everyone listened in astonishment. It didn't occur to anyone but the first form mistress, Miss Roberts, that it might be a trick. But Miss Roberts had had much experience of Janet's jokes, and it did cross her mind to wonder if this could be one of them.

"Let me see, Mam'zelle," she said, thoughtfully, "Janet is in the fourth form, isn't she?"

"Yes," said Mam'zelle, "but what has that got to do with my smell?"

"Oh — nothing I expect," said Miss Roberts. "But — if I were you, Mam'zelle, if that smell appears again, you trot down to Miss Theobald at once. I think she may be able to find the cause of it without taking up any floorboards and examining any drains!"

"Of course I shall report to the head at once," said Mam'zelle, with dignity.

And the time came when she did!

CHAPTER XIV
MISS ELLIS PLAYS A TRICK TOO

The girls had been really delighted with the success of Janet's "stink ball". Whenever Eileen had not been in the room, they had chattered and laughed about Mam'zelle's disgust and astonishment.

"All the same, we'd better not do it again," said Janet. "I have a sort of feeling that once would be a success, but that twice would be a failure! You can pull Mam'zelle's leg beautifully once in a while, but not all the time."

"If you do the smell again, I shall be sick and go out of the room," said Claudine. "It is the worst smell I have ever sniffed."

"We won't do the smell again," promised Bobby "But I tell you what we will do. We'll pretend there is a smell, shall we — and get old Mam'zelle all hot and bothered expecting one — she'll sniff and snuff, and we shall die of laughing!"

"Oh yes — that's a good idea," said Janet. "Doris, you can start off about the smell again in tomorrow's French Grammar class."

Doris grinned. She could act that kind of thing very well. So the next day, when Mam'zelle was ensconced safely in her desk at the end of the room, Doris began her act.

There was a very nice smell in the room, for Alison, the girl doing the flowers for the classroom that week, had filled a big vase with white pinks, and they scented the room beautifully. The girls could smell them as they worked.

Doris began to sniff. At first she gave very little sniffs. Then she gave two or three bigger ones.

"Doris! Have you a cold?" said Mam'zelle, impatiently. "Are you a first former, come to class without a handkerchief?"

"I've got a hanky, thank you, Mam'zelle," said Doris, humbly, and took it out.

Then Janet began to sniff. She screwed up her nose, sniffed, and looked all round. Bobby gave a chuckle and turned it into a long cough. Mam'zelle frowned. She did not like behaviour of this sort! It made her angry.

Then Pat began to sniff, and pulled out her hanky too. Soon the whole class, all except Eileen, who was not in the joke, were sniffing as if they had bad colds.

Mam'zelle gazed at the sniffing girls, exasperated. "What is all this noise? Sniff-sniff-sniff! I cannot bear it."

Doris put on an expression of disgust. Mam'zelle saw it, and an alarming thought came into her head. Could it be that terrible smell again?

"Doris," she said, urgently, "what is the matter?"

"I can smell something," murmured Doris. "Distinctly. It's very strong just here. Can't you smell anything, Mam'zelle?"

Mam'zelle couldn't, which was not at all surprising. But she remembered that before she could not smell the smell until after the girls. She looked anxiously at the class. They all seemed to be smelling it.

"I will report it at once," said Mam'zelle, and she left the room in a hurry.

"Crumbs!" said Bobby. "I don't know that we wanted her to go to the head about it! I say – she shot off so quickly we couldn't stop her!"

Unluckily for Mam'zelle the head was out. Mam'zelle was annoyed and upset. Here was the smell again, and no Miss Theobald to smell it, and to know that she, Mam'zelle, had not exaggerated last time!

Mam'zelle popped her head in at the mistresses' common-room as she hurried back to the classroom. Miss Ellis was there, correcting exercise books belonging to the fourth form.

"Miss Ellis – I regret to say that that terrible smell is back again," said Mam'zelle. "It is *abominable*! I do not think you will be able to take the fourth form in your room next lesson."

She withdrew her head and hurried back to the fourth form. She went in, expecting to be greeted by a wave of the terrible smell. But there seemed to be no smell at all. Very strange!

"Miss Theobald is out," said Mam'zelle. "Alas, she cannot smell our smell. Neither do I smell it yet!"

It was good news that Miss Theobald was out! The girls felt cheerful about that. Doris spoke up at once.

"Don't worry, Mam'zelle. We know what the smell was this time – quite different from last time. It was only these pinks!"

Doris picked up the big bowl of pinks, walked jauntily to Mam'zelle and thrust them under her big nose. Mam'zelle took a sniff and the strong and delicious scent went up her nose.

"So!" she said to Doris. "It was the pinks you smelt. Well, it is a good thing Miss Theobald was not in. She would have come to smell for nothing!"

There were a few giggles – and then, as the door opened, the girls fell silent, and looked to see if it was Miss Theobald coming in after all.

But it wasn't. It was Miss Ellis, who, curious to smell this extraordinary smell that Mam'zelle seemed continually to get excited about, had come to smell it herself. She stood at the door, sniffing.

"I can't smell anything, Mam'zelle," she said, surprised. Mam'zelle hastened to explain.

"I smelt nothing, either, Miss Ellis. It was the pinks the girls smelt. Doris has just told me."

Miss Ellis was surprised and most disbelieving. "I don't see how the girls could mistake a smell of pinks for the kind of awful smell you described to me last time," she said. "I am not at all sure I believe in that smell at all."

She gave her form a glare, and went out.

Mam'zelle was indignant. Had she not smelt the smell herself last time? For the rest of the lesson the class had a very peaceful time, discussing smells, past and present, with their indignant French mistress.

After break came geography, taught by Miss Ellis. She came into the room looking rather stern.

"I just want to say," she said, "that I shall regard any mention of smells, bad or good, as a sign that you want a little extra work given to you."

The class knew what that meant. "A little extra work" from Miss Ellis meant a good two hours' extra prep. So everyone immediately made up their minds not to mention the word smell at all.

But a terrible thing happened in ten minutes' time. Bobby had quite forgotten that she still had her "stink ball" in her pocket, left over from the day before. And, in sitting down rather violently, after going with her book to Miss Ellis, she broke the thin glass surrounding the liquid. Then, in a trice, the perfectly awful smell came creeping round the classroom once more!

Doris smelt it. Janet smelt it. Bobby smelt it and put her hand at once into her pocket, desperately feeling about to see if she had accidentally broken the little "stink ball". When she found she had, she gazed round, winking and nodding at the others, to tell them of the awful accident. Miss Ellis's sharp eyes caught Bobby's signs. So she was not really very surprised when she smelt the smell coming towards her. What a terrible smell it was!

Miss Ellis thought things out quietly. Evidently yesterday's smell had been this same horrible one – and the one Mam'zelle had reported today, and which Doris had said was pinks after all, was nothing to do with the real smell – just a silly joke played on Mam'zelle.

"But this awful smell is the real thing again," thought Miss Ellis. "And, judging by Bobby's signs to the others, was a mistake. I don't think the girls would dare to play a trick like this on me. Well – I will just play a little trick on *them!*"

Quietly Miss Ellis wrote a few directions on the board. Then she turned and left the room, closing the door after her. The girls stared at the board.

"Page 72. Write down the answers.

"Page 73. Read the first two paragraphs and then rewrite them in your own words.

"Page 74. Copy the map there."

"I say!" exploded Doris. "She's gone – and we've got to stay here in this awful smell and do that work. Bobby, you absolute idiot, why did you break that stink ball?"

"It was an accident," said Bobby, most apologetically. "I sat on it. I quite forgot it was there. Isn't this frightful? Miss Ellis has smelt it, of course, guesses it's a trick, and for punishment we've got to sit through the smell and work at our geography – and we simply daren't complain!"

"I am not going to sit in the smell," announced Claudine, emphatically. She got up. "I feel sick. I go to be sick."

She went off, and she made such wonderful sick-noises as she passed Miss Ellis in the passage outside, that Miss Ellis said nothing, but let her go to the bathroom. Trust Claudine for doing what she wanted! Not one of the others dared to leave the room.

They sat there, choking into their handkerchiefs, moaning over their fate, but not daring to scamp their work. At the end of the hour, when the smell had somewhat lessened, Miss Ellis opened the door.

She left it open. "You may go for a short run round the garden and back," she said. "Bobby, remain behind, please."

With a wry face Bobby remained behind whilst the others fled out gladly into the fresh air.

"I was the one who caused that terrible smell this time," said Bobby, at once. It was never any good beating round the bush with Miss Ellis — not that Bobby was given to that, anyway. She was a straightforward and truthful girl. "But it was an accident, Miss Ellis, really it was. Please believe me."

"I do," said Miss Ellis. "But it is an accident that is on no account to happen again. You have all had your punishment, so I shall say no more about it. But I want you to warn the fourth formers that any future smells will result in quite a lot of punishment!"

FIFTH FORMERS OF ST CLARE'S

AN EXTRACT

≈ ILLUSTRATED BY ≈

Jenny Chapple

When Angela becomes a senior she proudly brags that she can make any of the juniors
'hero-worship' her and gladly do little jobs for her. Jane, one of her most devoted admirers,
is then persuaded by games-captain Mirabel to give away a lot of her free time
to practising lacrosse. Jane tells Angela that because of this she will not be able
to do much mending for her, and Angela is very angry.

CHAPTER VI
ANGELA AND THE YOUNGER GIRLS

Angela made such a fuss of Violet Hill, in order to punish poor Jane. She gave her one of her best hair-slides and a book, which sent the foolish Violet into transports of delight. Violet showed them to Jane and Sally.

"Look," she said, "isn't Angela a dear? She's so generous. I think she's wonderful. I do think you were silly to quarrel with her, Jane. I think Angela is worth three of Mirabel!"

Jane looked miserably at the book and the hair-slide. Angela had never given *her* a present. She wished she could dislike Angela, but she couldn't. Every time she saw the golden-haired girl, with her starry eyes set in her oval face, she thought how wonderful she was.

Sally was sorry for Jane. "Cheer up," she said. "Angela isn't worth worrying about. I believe she's only making up to Violet just to make you jealous. I think she's being beastly."

But Jane would not hear a word against Angela, however much she had been hurt by her. Violet too was cross at Sally's remarks.

"As if Angela would give me presents just to make Jane jealous!" she said, sharply. "If you ask *me*, I think she gave me them because I mended her blue jumper so neatly. It took two hours."

"Do you do her mending then?" said Jane, jealously.

"Of course," said Violet. "I don't care what Mirabel says to *me* – if I prefer to do things for Angela, I shall do them."

Violet told Angela how upset Jane was, and Angela was glad. She could be very spiteful when anything upset her. She was especially sweet to Violet and to the other first former who came when Violet could not come. The two of them thought she was the nicest girl in the whole school.

Antoinette, Claudine's little sister, also at times had to do jobs for the fifth and sixth formers. She did not like Angela, and always found excuses not to go to her study, even when an urgent message was sent.

"That young sister of yours is a perfect nuisance," Angela complained to Claudine. "Can't you knock some sense into her, Claudine? When I sent for her yesterday, she sent back to say that she was doing her practising – and now I hear that she doesn't even *learn* music!"

"She might have been practising something else," suggested Claudine, politely. "Maybe lacrosse."

Angela snorted. "Don't be silly! Antoinette gets out of games just like you do – the very idea of thinking she might put in a bit of practice is absurd. I believe you encourage her in these bad ways – slipping out of anything she doesn't like."

Claudine looked shocked. "Ah, but surely the little Antoinette loves everything at this so-English school?"

"Don't pretend to me," said Angela, exasperated. "I should have thought that in all the terms you have been here, Claudine, you would have got more English – you're just as French as ever you were!"

Claudine would not lose her temper at this ungracious speech. "It is good to be French," she said, in her light, amiable voice. "If I were English I might have been *you*, Angela – and that I could not have borne. Better a hundred times to be a French Claudine than an English Angela!"

Angela could not think of any really good retort to this, and by the time she had found her tongue Claudine had gone over to speak to Mam'zelle. Angela knew she had gone to Mam'zelle on purpose – no one would dare to attack Claudine with Mam'zelle standing by! Mam'zelle was intensely loyal to her two nieces.

"All right," thought Angela, spitefully. "I'll just get that slippery sister of hers and make her do all kinds of things for me! I'll speak to Hilary about it, and she'll tell Antoinette she's jolly well got to come when I or Alison send for her."

Hilary knew that Antoinette was being very naughty about coming when she was sent for – but she knew too that Angela used the younger girls far too much. She used her prettiness and charm to make them into little slaves. So she was not very helpful to Angela when the girl told her about Antoinette.

"I'll tell her she must obey the fifth and sixth formers," she said. "But Angela, don't go too far, please. Most of us know that you are using your power too much in that direction."

"What about Mirabel?" said Angela, at once. "Doesn't she throw *her* weight about too much? She's unbearable this term, just because she's sports captain!"

"There's no need to discuss Mirabel," said Hilary. "What we've all got to realise this term, the term before we go up into the sixth, is that this is the form where we first shoulder responsibilities, and first have a little power over others. You're not given power to play about with and get pleasure from, Angela, as *you* seem to think. You're given it to use in the right way."

"Don't be so preachy," said Angela. "Really, are we never going to have any fun or good times again at St Clare's? Everyone looks so serious and solemn nowadays. Bobby and Janet never play tricks in class. We never have a midnight feast. We never . . ."

"Remember that we are all working jolly hard," said Hilary, walking off. "You can't work hard and play the fool too. Wait till the exam is over and then maybe we can have a bit of fun."

Hilary spoke to Antoinette and the small, dark-eyed French girl listened with the utmost politeness.

"Yes, Hilary, I will go to Angela when she sends for me," said Antoinette. "But always she sends for me at so – busy a time!"

"Well, make your excuses to me, not to Angela," said Hilary, firmly. Antoinette looked at Hilary and sighed. She knew that Hilary would not believe in her excuses, and would insist, in that firm, polite way of hers, that Antoinette should do as she was told.

Angela saw Hilary speaking to Antoinette and was pleased. She decided to give Antoinette a bad time – she would teach her to "toe the mark" properly.

"Violet, I shan't want you for a few days," she told the adoring girl. "Send me Antoinette instead,"

"Oh, but Angela – don't I do your jobs well enough for you?" said Violet in dismay. "Antoinette is such a mutt – she can't do a thing! Really she can't. Let *me* do everything."

"Antoinette can sew and darn beautifully," said Angela, taking pleasure in hurting Violet, who had been very silly that week. "You made an awful darn in one of my tennis socks."

Violet's eyes filled with tears and she went out of the room. Alison looked up from her work.

"Angela, stop it," she said. "I think you're beastly – making the kids adore you and then being unkind to them. Anyway – you'll have a hard nut to crack in Antoinette! *She* won't adore you. She's got her head screwed on all right."

"She would adore me if I wanted her to," boasted Angela, who knew the power of her prettiness and smiles, and who could turn on charm like water out of a tap.

"She wouldn't," said Alison. "She's like Claudine – sees through everyone at once, and sizes them up and then goes her own way entirely, liking or disliking just as she pleases."

"I bet I'll make Antoinette like me as much as any of those silly kids," said Angela. "You watch and see. You'll be surprised, Alison."

"I'll watch – but I shan't be surprised," said Alison. "I know little Antoinette better than you do!"

CHAPTER VII
ANTOINETTE DEFEATS ANGELA

The next time she was sent for, Antoinette arrived promptly, all smiles. She was just as neat and chic as Claudine, quick-witted and most innocent looking. Miss Jenks, the second form mistress, had already learnt that Antoinette's innocent look was not to be trusted. The more innocent she looked, the more likely it was that she had misbehaved or was going to misbehave!

"You sent for me, Angela?" said Antoinette.

"Yes," said Angela, putting on one of her flashing smiles, "I did. Antoinette, will you clean those brown shoes over there, please? I'm sure you'll do it beautifully."

Antoinette stared at Angela's beaming smile and smiled back. Angela felt sure she could see intense admiration in her eyes.

"The polish, please?" said Antoinette, politely.

"You'll find it in the cupboard, top shelf," said Angela. "How chic and smart you always look, Antoinette – just like Claudine."

"Ah, Claudine, is she not wonderful?" said Antoinette. "Angela, I have five sisters, and I like them all, but Claudine is my favourite. Ah, Claudine – I could tell you things about Claudine that would make you marvel, that would make you wish that you too had such a sister, and . . ."

But Angela was not in the least interested to bear what a wonderful sister Claudine was, and she was certain she would never wish she had one like her. Angela preferred being a spoilt only child. You had to share things with sisters!

"Er – the polish is in the cupboard, top shelf," she said, her bright smile fading a little.

"The polish – ah yes," said Antoinette, taking a step towards the cupboard, but only a step. "Now, Claudine is not the only wonderful sister I have – there is Louise. Ah, I wish I could tell you what Louise is like. Louise can do every embroidery stitch there is, and when she was nine, she won . . ."

"Better get on with my shoes, Antoinette," said Angela, beginning to lose patience. A hurt look came into Antoinette's eyes, and Angela made haste to bestow her brilliant smile on her again. Antoinette at once cheered up and took another step towards the cupboard.

She opened her mouth, plainly to go on with her praise of Louise or some other sister, but Angela picked up a book and pretended to be absorbed in it.

"Don't talk for a bit," she said to Antoinette. "I've got to learn something."

Antoinette went to the cupboard. She took a chair and stood on it to get the polish. Then she stepped down with a small pot in her hand, and a little secret smile on her mouth – the kind of smile that Claudine sometimes wore. Angela did not see it.

Antoinette found a brush and duster and set herself to her task. She squeezed cream on to the shoes and smeared it on well. Then she brushed it in and then rubbed hard with the soft duster. She held the pair of shoes away from her and looked at them with pride.

"Done?" said Angela, still not looking up in case Antoinette began talking again.

"They are finished," said Antoinette. "Shall I clean yet another pair, Angela? It is a pleasure to work for you."

Angela was delighted to hear this. Aha – Alison would soon see that she could win the heart of Antoinette as easily as anyone else's.

"Yes, Antoinette – clean all the shoes you like," she said, smiling sweetly. "How beautiful that pair look!"

"Do they not?" said Antoinette. "Such beautiful shoes they are too! Ah, no girl in the school wears such fine clothes as you, Angela – so beautifully made, so carefully finished. You have more chic than any English girl – you might be a Parisian!"

"I've been to Paris and bought clothes there two or three times," said Angela, and was just about to describe all the clothes when Antoinette started off again.

"Ah, clothes – now you should see my sister Jeanne! Such marvellous clothes she has, like those in the shops at Paris – but all of them she makes herself with her clever fingers. Such style, such chic, such . . ."

"You seem to have got a whole lot of very clever sisters," said Angela, sarcastically, but Antoinette did not seem to realise that Angela was being cutting.

"It is true," she said. "I have not yet told you about Marie. Now Marie . . ."

"Antoinette, finish the shoes and let me get on with my work," said Angela, who felt that she could not bear to hear about another sister of Antoinette's. "There's a good girl!"

She used her most charming tone, and Antoinette beamed. "Yes, Angela, yes. I am too much of a chatter-tin, am I not?"

"Box, not tin," said Angela. "Now, do get on, Antoinette. It's lovely to hear your chatter, but I really have got work to do."

Antoinette said no more but busied herself with three more pairs of shoes. She stood them in the corner and put the empty pot of cream into the waste-paper basket. "I have finished, Angela," she said. "I go now. Tomorrow you will want me, is it not so?"

"Yes, come tomorrow at the same time," said Angela, switching on a charming smile again and shaking back her gleaming hair. "You've done my shoes beautifully. Thank you."

Antoinette slipped out of the room like a mouse. She met Claudine at the end of the passage and her sister raised her eyebrows. "Where have you been, Antoinette? You are not supposed to be in the fifth form studies unless you have been sent for."

"I have been cleaning all Angela's shoes," sat Antoinette, demurely. Then she glanced swiftly up and down the corridor to see that no one else was in sight, and shot out a few sentences in rapid French. Claudine laughed her infectious laugh, and pretended to box her sister's ears.

"*Tiens! Quelle méchante fille!* What will Angela say?"

Antoinette shrugged her shoulders, grinned and disappeared. Claudine went on her way, and paused outside Angela's study. She heard voices. Alison was there now too. Claudine opened the door.

"Hallo," said Alison. "Come for that book I promised you? Wait a minute – I've put it out for you somewhere."

She caught sight of all Angela's shoes standing gleaming in a corner. "I say! Did young Violet clean them like that for you? She doesn't usually get such a polish on!"

"No – Antoinette did them," said Angela. "She was telling me all about your sisters and hers, Claudine."

"Ah yes," said Claudine, "there is my sister Louise, and my sister Marie and my sister . . ."

"Oh, don't *you* start on them, for goodness' sake," said Angela. "What's the matter, Alison, what are staring at?"

"Have you used up all that lovely face-cream al*ready*?" said Alison, in a surprised voice, and she picked an empty pot out of the waste-paper basket. "Angela, how extravagant of you! Why, there was hardly any out of it yesterday – and now it's all gone. What *have* you done with it?"

"Nothing," said Angela, startled. "I hardly ever use that, it's so terribly expensive and difficult to get. I keep it for very special occasions. Whatever can have happened to it? It really is empty!"

The two girls stared at each other, puzzled. Claudine sat on the side of the table, swinging her foot, her face quite impassive. Then Angela slapped the table hard and exclaimed in anger.

"It's that fool of an Antoinette! She's cleaned my shoes with my best face-cream! Oh, the idiot! All that lovely cream gone – gone on my shoes too!"

"But your shoes, they look so beautiful!" remarked Claudine "Maybe the little Antoinette thought that ordinary shoe-polish was not good enough for such fine shoes."

"She's an idiot," said Angela. "I won't have her do any jobs again."

"Perhaps that's why she did this," said Alison, dryly. "It's the kind of thing our dear Claudine would do, for the same kind of reason, isn't it, Claudine?"

"Shall I tell Antoinette you will not need her again because you are very angry at her foolishness?" said Claudine. "Ah, she will be so sad, the poor child!"

Angela debated. She felt sure that Antoinette had made a real mistake. She was certain the girl liked her too much to play such a trick on her. How thrilled Antoinette had seemed when she had smiled at her! No – the girl had made a genuine mistake. Angela would give her another chance.

"I'll try her again," she said. "I'll forgive her this time. We all make mistakes sometimes."

"How true!" said Claudine. "Now, my sister Marie, hardly ever does she make a mistake, but once . . ."

"Oh, get out," said Angela, rudely. "It's bad enough to have you and Antoinette here without having to hear about your dozens of sisters!"

Claudine removed herself gracefully and went to find Antoinette to report the success of her trick. Antoinette grinned. "*C'est bien*," she said. "Very good! Another time I will again be foolish, oh so foolish!"

Angela sent for her again the next day. Antoinette entered with drooping head and downcast eyes.

"Oh, Angela," she said, in a low, meek voice, "my sister Claudine has told me what a terrible mistake I made yesterday. How could I have been so foolish? I pray you to forgive me."

"All right," said Angela. "Don't look so miserable, Antoinette. By the way, I think I'll call you Toni – it's so much friendlier than Antoinette, isn't it?"

Antoinette appeared to greet this idea with rapture. Angela beamed. How easy it was to get round these young ones! Well – she would get all the work she could out of this silly French girl, she would wind her round her little finger – and then she would send her packing and teach her a good sharp lesson!

"What would you have me do today?" Antoinette asked, in her meek voice. "More shoes?"

"No," said Angela. "No more shoes. Make me some anchovy toast, Toni."

"Please?" said Antoinette, not understanding.

"Oh, dear – don't you know what anchovy toast is?" sighed Angela. "Well, you make ordinary buttered toast – and for goodness' sake toast the bread before you put the butter on – then you spread it with anchovy paste. You'll find it in the cupboard. Make enough for three people. Anne-Marie is coming to tea, to read us her new poem."

"Ah, the wonderful Anne-Marie!" said Antoinette, getting out the bread. "Now one of my sisters, the one called Louise, once she wrote a poem and . . ."

"Toni, I've got to go and see someone," said Angela, getting up hurriedly. "Get on with the toast, and do it really carefully, to make up for your silly mistake yesterday."

"Angela, believe me, your little Toni will give you such toast as never you have had before!" said Antoinette with fervour. She held a piece of bread to the fire.

Angela went out, determined not to come back till Antoinette had made the toast and was safely out of the way. Talk about a chatterbox! She seemed to have a never-ending flow of conversation about her family. She might start on her brothers next – if she had any!

As soon as Angela had gone out of the room. Antoinette put aside her artless ways and concentrated on her job. She made six pieces of toast very rapidly and spread them with butter. Then she got a pot down from the cupboard shelf – but it was not anchovy. It was the pot of brown shoe polish that she should have used the day before!

It looked exactly like anchovy as she spread it on the toast. Carefully the little monkey spread the brown paste, piled the slices on a plate and set them beside the fire to keep warm. Then she slipped out of the room and made her way to the noisy common-room of her own form.

Soon Alison came in and sat down by the fire. Then Angela popped her head round the door and saw to her relief that Antoinette was gone.

"I simply couldn't stay in the room with that awful chatterbox, drivelling on about her sisters," said Angela. "Ah, she's made a nice lot of toast, hasn't she? Hallo – here's Anne-Marie."

Anne-Marie came in, her big eyes dark in her pale face. "You look tired," said Angela. "Been burning the midnight oil? I wish *I* could write poems like you, Anne-Marie."

"I worked on a poem till past twelve," said Anne-Marie, in her intense voice. "It's a good thing no one saw the light in my study. Ah – tea's ready, how lovely! Let's tuck in, and then I'll read my latest poem."

CHAPTER VIII
THREE DISGUSTED GIRLS

Angela lifted the toast on to the table. "I got Antoinette to make anchovy toast for us," she said. "It looks good, doesn't it? Take a slice, Anne-Marie." Anne-Marie took the top slice. It seemed to have rather a peculiar smell. She looked rather doubtfully at it.

"It's all right," said Alison, seeing her look. "Anchovy always smells a bit funny, I think."

She and Anne-Marie took a good bite out of their toast at the same second. The shoe-cream tasted abominable. Anne-Marie spat her mouthful out at once, all over the table. Alison, with better manners, spat hers into her handkerchief. Angela took a bite before she realised what the others were doing.

Then she too spat out at once, and clutched her mouth with her hands. "Oh! Oh! What is it? I'm poisoned!"

She rushed to the nearest bathroom and the others followed, their tongues hanging out. Anne-Marie was promptly sick when she reached the bathroom. Tears poured from her eyes and she had to sit down.

"Angela! What filthy paste! How *could* you buy such stuff?" she said.

"Horrible!" said Alison, rinsing her mouth out over and over again. "All that toast wasted too. It's wicked. Angela, whatever possessed you to get paste like that? I've never tasted anchovy like that before, and I hope I never shall again. Ugh!"

Angela was feeling ill and very angry. What in the world had that idiot Antoinette done? They went back to the study and Angela opened the door of the little cupboard. She took down the pot of anchovy. It was untouched. So Antoinette couldn't have used it. Then what *had* she used? There was only jam besides the paste.

Alison picked up the pot of brown shoe-cream and opened that. It was practically empty. "Look," said Alison, angrily. "She used the shoe-cream – plastered all the toast with it! She deserves a good scolding."

Angela was white with anger. She put her head out of the door and saw a first former passing. "Hey, Molly," she called, "go and find Antoinette and tell her to come here at once."

"Yes, Angela." said Molly, and went off. Very soon Antoinette appeared, her dark eyes wide with alarm, and her lips trembling as if with emotion.

"Antoinette! How *dare* you put shoe-cream on our toast?" almost screamed Angela. "You might have poisoned us all. Can't you tell the difference between anchovy paste and shoe-polish, you absolute idiot? You've made us all ill. Matron will probably hear about it. You ought to be reported to Miss Jenks, you ought to . . ."

"Ah, ah, do not scold your little Toni so," said Antoinette. "You have been so kind to me, Angela, you have smiled, you have called me Toni! Do not scold me so! I will give up my tea-time, I will make you more toast, and this time I will spread it with the anchovy, there shall be no mistake this time."

"If you think I'm ever going to trust you to do a single thing for me again, you're mistaken," said Angela, still tasting the awful taste of shoe-cream in her mouth. "I might have known a French girl would play the fool like this. I tell you, you've made us all ill. Anne-Marie was sick."

"I am desolated," wailed Antoinette. "Ah, Angela, I pray you to let me come again tomorrow. Tomorrow I will be good, so good. Tomorrow you will call me Toni and smile at me again, tomorrow . . ."

"Tomorrow I'll get Violet Hill," said Angela. "Clear out, Antoinette, you're a perfect menace."

Antoinette cleared out and there was peace. "Well," said Angela, "she'll wish she'd been more sensible tomorrow. Serves her right! I was nice to her, and she thought the world of me — but I can't put up with idiots. She'll be jolly sorry when she sees I don't mean to give her another chance!"

"I don't feel like any tea now," said Alison, looking at the remains of the toast with dislike. "Do you, Anne-Marie?"

"No," said Anne-Marie, and shuddered. "I still feel sick. I don't even know if I can read my poem. It doesn't go very well with shoe-polish."

"Oh, do read it, Anne-Marie," begged Angela, who really did admire her poems. "What's it about?"

"It's all about the sadness of spring," said Anne-Marie, reaching for her poem. "It's a very sad poem, really."

"All your poems are sad," said Alison. "Why are they, Anne-Marie? I like poems that make me feel happy."

"I am not a very happy person," said Anne-Marie, very solemnly, and looked intense. "Poets aren't, you know."

"But some must have been," objected Alison. "I know lots of very cheerful poems."

"Shut up, Alison," said Angela. "Read your poem, Anne-Marie."

Anne-Marie began her poem. It was very doleful, full of impressive words, and rather dull. Neither Alison nor Angela liked it very much, but they couldn't help feeling impressed. However could Anne-Marie write like that? She must indeed be a genius!

"It must be nice for you, sharing a study with Felicity, who thinks as much of music as you do of poetry," said Alison. "You ought to get Felicity to set some of your poems to music. That would be wonderful."

"I've asked her. She won't," said Anne-Marie, shortly. The truth was that Felicity would not admit that Anne-Marie's poems were worth tuppence. It was very humiliating to Anne-Marie.

"Write something real, and I'll put a tune to it," Felicity had said. "I'm not going to waste my music on second-rate stuff."

The door opened suddenly and Matron looked in. "I hear you poor girls have had a nasty dose of shoe-polish," she said. "I hope it wasn't anything very serious."

Angela thought she would take the chance of getting Antoinette into trouble, so she exaggerated at once.

"Oh, Matron, it was awful! We had our mouths absolutely full of the beastly stuff. Anne-Marie must have swallowed a lot, because she was sick. I shouldn't be surprised if we are ill, seriously ill, tonight." said Angela.

"I know I swallowed some," said Anne-Marie, looking solemn. "I expect we all did."

"Then you must come and have a dose at once," said Matron. "That shoe-cream contains a poisonous ingredient which may irritate your insides for a week or more, unless I give you a dose to get rid of it. Come along with me straight away."

The three girls stared at her in alarm. They simply could not bear Matron's medicines. They were really so very nasty! Angela wished fervently that she had not exaggerated so much.

She tried to take back what she had said. "Oh well, Matron," she said, with a little laugh, "it wasn't as bad as all that, you know. We spat out practically all of it – and we rinsed our mouths out at once. We're *perfectly* all right now."

"I dare say," said Matron. "But I'd rather be on the safe side. I don't want you in bed for a week with a tummy upset of some sort. Come along. I've got something that will stop any trouble immediately."

"But Matron," began Alison.

It was no good. Nobody could reason with Matron once she had really decided to give anyone a dose. The three girls had to get up and follow her. They looked very blue, and felt most humiliated. As a rule Matron left the fifth and sixth formers to look after themselves, and seldom came after them, suggesting medicine. They felt like first or second formers, trooping after her for a dose.

Matron took them to her room, and measured out the medicine into tablespoons, one for each of them. It tasted almost as nasty as the shoe-polish toast!

"Pooh!" said Alison, trying to get the taste out of her mouth. "Why don't you get some nice-tasting medicines, Matron? I've never tasted any so beastly as yours."

"Well, I've got a much worse one here," said Matron. "Would you just like to try it?"

"Of course not!" said Alison. Then a thought struck her. Matron – how did you know we'd had shoe-polish on our toast today? We hadn't told a soul. Who told you?"

"Why, the poor little Antoinette told me," said Matron, corking up the bottle. "Poor child, she came to me in a terrible state, saying she had poisoned you all by mistake, and what was she to do if you died in the night, and couldn't I do something about it?"

The three girls listened to this with mixed feelings. So it was Antoinette who not only provided them with shoe-polish toast, but also with medicine from Matron! The little horror!

"You've no idea how upset she was," went on Matron, briskly. "Poor little soul, I felt really sorry for her. An English girl might have been amused at the mistake she had made, but Antoinette was so upset I had to comfort her and give her some chocolate. It's wonderful what chocolate will do to soothe the nerves of a first or second former! Nothing but babies, really."

The thought of Antoinette eating Matron's chocolate was too much for Angela, Alison and Anne-Marie. They felt that they simply *must* get hold of Antoinette and tell her what they thought of her.

"Where is Antoinette, do you know, Matron?" asked Angela, wishing she could get the combined tastes of shoe-polish and medicine out of her mouth.

"I sent her to her aunt, Mam'zelle," said Matron. "I'm sure she would cheer her up and make her think she hadn't done such a dreadful thing after all! Fancy thinking she really had poisoned you!"

The three fifth formers went back to the study. It wouldn't be a bit of good going to fetch Antoinette now. She would probably be having a nice cosy tea with Mam'zelle, who would be fussing her up and telling her everything was all right, a mistake was a mistake, and not to worry, *pauvre petite* Antoinette!

"I'll send for her tomorrow and jolly well keep her nose to the grindstone," said Angela, angrily. "I told her she needn't do anything more for me — but I'll make her now. I'll make her sorry she ever played those tricks. Clever little beast — going off to Matron and play-acting like that. She's worse than Claudine!"

Alison was alarmed to hear that Angela was going to make Antoinette do some more jobs for them.

"For goodness' sake, don't be silly!" she said to Angela. "Antoinette is far too clever for us to get even with. She'll only do something even worse than she has already done. I told you she wouldn't be like the others, silly and worshipping. I told you she would size you up! I told you . . ."

"Shut up, Alison!" said Angela. "I hate people who say 'I told you, I told you!' I won't have Antoinette if you think she'll play worse tricks. She'd end in poisoning us, I should think. I wish I could pay her out, though."

"It's partly your own fault, all this," said Alison. "If only you'd treat the younger ones like the others do, sensibly and properly, we shouldn't have all these upsets."

Anne-Marie thought it was time to go. She always said that quarrels upset her poetic feelings. So she went, taking her mournful poem with her.

"We'd better not say a word about this to anyone," said Angela. "Else the whole school will be laughing at us. We won't let it go any further."

But alas for their plans — Antoinette told the story to everyone, and soon the whole school was enjoying the joke. It made Angela furious, for she hated being laughed at; it humiliated Alison too, for even Miss Willcox got to hear of it and teased her and Anne-Marie.

"What about a little essay on 'Anchovy Sauce'," she said. "Poor Alison, poor Anne-Marie, what a shame!"

Enid Blyton

≈ ACKNOWLEDGEMENTS ≈

We gratefully acknowledge permission to reproduce copyright
material from the following books:

The Naughtiest Girl in the School (for the illustrations by W. Lindsay Cable)
The Naughtiest Girl Again (for the illustrations by W. Lindsay Cable)
The Naughtiest Girl is a Monitor (for the illustrations by Kenneth Lovell)
She Hadn't Any Friends (illustrations)
Very Mysterious (illustrations)
First Term at Malory Towers (text and illustrations)
Second Form at Malory Towers (text and illustrations)
Third Year at Malory Towers (text and illustrations)
Upper Fourth at Malory Towers (text and illustrations)
In the Fifth at Malory Towers (text and illustrations)
The Twins at St Clare's (text and illustrations)
The O'Sullivan Twins (text and illustrations)
Summer Term at St Clare's (text and illustrations)
The Second Form at St Clare's (text and illustrations)
Claudine at St Clare's (text and illustrations)
Fifth Formers of St Clare's (text and illustrations)
reproduced by permission of Egmont Children's Books Limited

Thanks also to Gillian Baverstock for kindly providing
original photos, and to Joy Mutter for her text design

While every effort has been made to obtain permission, there may still
be cases in which we have failed to trace a copyright holder. The publisher
will be happy to correct any omission in future printings.